BILLIONAIRE'S SECOND CHANCE IN PARIS

REBECCA WINTERS

CINDERELLA'S SECRET FLING

MICHELLE DOUGLAS

MILLS & BOON

First published in Great Britain 2023
by Mills & Boon, an imprint of HarperCollins*Publishers* Ltd,
1 London Bridge Street, London, SE1 9GF

www.harpercollins.co.uk

HarperCollins*Publishers*, Macken House, 39/40 Mayor Street Upper, Dublin 1, D01 C9W8, Ireland

Billionaire's Second Chance in Paris © 2023 Rebecca Winters

Cinderella's Secret Fling © 2023 Michelle Douglas

ISBN: 978-0-263-30646-0

06/23

MIX
Paper | Supporting
responsible forestry
FSC™ C007454

This book is produced from independently certified FSC™ paper to ensure responsible forest management.
For more information visit: www.harpercollins.co.uk/green.

Printed and Bound in the UK using 100% Renewable Electricity at CPI Group (UK) Ltd, Croydon, CR0 4YY

BILLIONAIRE'S SECOND CHANCE IN PARIS

REBECCA WINTERS

MILLS & BOON

This book is dedicated to my darling sister Kathie, who loves a dose of danger in some of the romances she reads. She has always championed my writing.

PROLOGUE

Causcelle Estate, La Racineuse,
eastern France, ten years earlier

FOR ONCE, seventeen-year-old Fleurine Dumotte had the house to herself. Her out-of-control father would be working at the Causcelle dairy until late, thank goodness. Her sweet, wonderful mother had gone to town in La Racineuse with her two siblings to shop. She'd be gone a long time. Fleurine had volunteered to do the laundry for the five-member household in order to be alone.

Knowing there wasn't a moment to lose, she did her chores in record time. Then she got busy making bread, shaping pieces of it into five-inch boy figures. Normally she placed raisins down their tummies to look like buttons. But these were for Raoul Causcelle, so she baked the figures without adornment.

After they cooled, she put tiny dobs of frosting for buttons and added little *pépites de chocolat*. She'd made his favorite milk bread *mannele*. He loved the chocolate on top. It would be her going-away gift to him, but no one could ever know about it. Not even her mother. Her terrifying father forbade her from being with any boy, so her feelings for Raoul had always remained a secret from everyone.

He'd seen her in town helping with the marketing yesterday and had asked her to meet him at the west hay barn at the end of his work today. They could talk one last time while he did his chores, but her excitement was swallowed up in despair. The day after tomorrow he'd be leaving home with his brothers to go to college in Paris hundreds of miles away.

Fleurine had been born and raised on the Causcelle estate. All the kids in the area had gone to the same schools. She and Raoul were eleven months apart. Over the last two years he'd found dozens of ways to meet her accidentally at school and on her way home after the bell rang.

The knowledge that Raoul was leaving had become unbearable, and she'd wanted to do something for him. After wrapping the *mannele* in a bag, she cleaned up the kitchen so her father would never know what she'd done. Next, Fleurine hurried into the bedroom she shared with her thirteen-year-old sister, Emma. Their eleven-year-old brother, Marti, had his own room.

Fleurine had no choice but to put on one of her ugly white dresses that fell below the knee. It had long sleeves that looked like a nursing uniform from a hundred years ago. He'd never seen her in anything else. She wished she were allowed to go to mass like her friends and wear something pretty. How she hated her brown shoes that laced up to the ankles. So many wishes had never been fulfilled...

The women in their household weren't allowed to wear makeup or perfume or cut their hair. All she could do was brush hers that hung down her back. She'd been forbidden to use ribbons or barrettes. Modern styles of clothes were out of the question. She could still hear her father say, "Fleur and Emma Dumotte, you'll live in my house like proper daughters of the Jura-Souboz where your ancestors came from and obey my rules!"

His despotic eighteenth-century rules!

Not wanting to feel pain today, she raced out of the house with her gift and climbed on her bike. Raoul had always been a hard worker and obeyed his nice-looking widower father, who everyone knew had high expectations for him and his brothers. The country's renowned billionaire Louis Causcelle kept his children close. Fleurine had seen him on several occasions but had never met him. She was pained by her father's hatred for the patriarch of the Causcelle dynasty and his family, especially his triplet sons.

On her approach, she saw Raoul's bike outside the barn. She rode hers around the back. She didn't dare leave it where her father could see it from the road on his way home from the dairy.

"There you are, Fleurine," she heard Raoul say while she rested her bike against the barn. He'd walked in through the back to find her. "I hoped you'd be able to make it." His smile lit up her universe.

No one knew her as Fleurine. Only Raoul had started calling her that name last year. He'd said it was because her eyes reminded him of the violet flowers growing in the northern pasture. To her mind, her eyes were a boring gray with tinges of violet. But since he'd given her that name, she'd begun thinking of herself as Fleurine. He'd made it sound beautiful.

"Let's take your bike inside." They walked to the front with it and went in the barn where he shut the big door.

Raoul was fun and exciting. He was also so handsome it made her breath catch. His dancing black eyes and black hair thrilled her as much as his smile. Sometimes he resembled a dashing pirate. She'd always felt insipid around him by comparison.

No young men in school, let alone France, matched the looks of the tall, gorgeous and well-built Causcelle triplet sons. Her girlfriends had told her their pictures had been in all the newspapers and magazines and on TV, but her father didn't allow radio, TV or printed matter in their home.

"I had to do the laundry first, or I would have come sooner. Here." She handed him the bag. "I baked these for you."

His intense gaze made her feel warm all over. He opened it and pulled out one of her treats. "Let's find out if you're still the best cook in France."

Heat crept into her face. "Don't be ridiculous."

"I swear I'm telling the truth. I've eaten your treats before. You could run your own five-star cooking school." On that note he took a bite and ended up devouring the whole thing with those perfect white teeth. "Yup. You deserve the grand prize for these. Let me thank you properly and give you whatever you want."

Whatever she wanted? Would that Fleurine had the temerity to tell him she wanted the one thing he could never give her. Her father had forbidden her and her siblings to have anything to do with the Causcelle family. If they ever did, they would pay the ultimate price. He terrified them. What an absurd, foolish girl she'd been to have secret dreams about a life with Raoul.

Fleurine had been dreading the moment when he would leave the estate. The end of their childhood had come. To a degree, childhood had been the common denominator that made a more equal playing field for them to be together, but no longer. There wasn't a thing she could do about this parting of their worlds, and already she was dying inside. To face a day without Raoul meant no more adventure or wonder. No more feeling alive.

"Mind if I thank you in the way I've wanted to for a long time?"

Something in his tone sounded different. "What do you mean?"

"Have you ever been kissed by one of the guys around here, Fleurine? Really kissed? I've noticed Remy and Thomas. They never leave you alone."

"They're just friends." Her heart pounded in her throat.

"Do you put me in the same category as *just a friend*?"

She averted her eyes. "A good friend. Are you trying to embarrass me?"

"Anything but. I'd like to know if there's some guy

you're interested in on the estate you've kept secret from me."

"How can you ask me that?" Her voice shook. "You know my father."

"Forget your father for a minute. Is there someone you care about and have been alone with?"

She shivered. "That's private, Raoul."

"So there *is* a guy—" He sounded upset.

Her head flew back. "What if I asked you if there's a girl on the estate *you've* kissed?"

He shifted his weight. "Do you want to know the answer? Or aren't you interested enough to find out?"

Fleurine shook her head. "I wouldn't dare ask you. It's none of my business."

"Maybe it's because you're frightened of the answer. Yes, I've kissed a few."

"I think I'd better go."

She turned to leave, but he grasped her arm. "You *are* frightened."

"Please, Raoul. I don't know what you want from me."

He inhaled sharply. "The truth. Nothing more, nothing less. For once in our lives, we're truly alone. I know you're frightened of your father, but he's nowhere around to hear us."

"What truth?" she cried, not understanding him. Something was wrong.

"That you love me as much as I love you!" The interior of the barn resounded with his declaration. "Isn't love the reason you came at the risk of your father finding out? Isn't love why you brought me this gift?"

A gasp escaped her lips. She backed away from him. "E-even if the answer were yes," she said, "you couldn't possibly love me, Raoul Causcelle. Not *you,* who could have any girl, I mean *any* girl, in the world. Are you telling the Dumotte daughter, who's been told to go back to the dark ages where our family belongs, that you love *me*?"

"Don't talk about yourself that way, Fleurine."

"You haven't lived in my skin, Raoul. I'm the offspring of old man Dumotte who lights fires and would have been the first to set a torch to Jeanne d'Arc. Did you know *he* and the demented friends in their cult were the ones who set fire to the monastery when he was a young teenager?

"He helped murder all those monks to get rid of your father's brother-in-law Gregoire. My father was taught to hate every Catholic before his family moved here from Switzerland and started working for your family. He's forbidden our family from ever stepping inside a Catholic church."

"I've suspected it for a long time."

"He's insane, but most of all he hates your father for marrying your mother."

Raoul moved closer. His black eyes flashed. "What do you mean?"

"He wanted Delphine Ronfleur for himself, but she wanted your father and married him. My mother broke down one day and told me everything. She lives in fear of him. So do I. If she tries to leave or expose him, he has threatened to kill the whole family. Lately he's been watching me."

"I knew that was the reason why you've tried to be so careful around me," Raoul murmured.

"Then, you should know there's never been anyone else for me but you, and there never will be. But you're the son of the man my father despises. I'm afraid *you're* another object of his hatred now. Run to Paris while there's still time and stay safe! He mustn't ever see us alone together. I'm a nothing who's not worthy of you, Raoul."

"Don't you ever say things like that, Fleurine." He reached out and crushed her in his arms, holding her until her thrashing stopped, but her body kept heaving sobs. "I've always loved you and have sensed deep down you felt the same way. Let me kiss you so I can show you how I feel. We'll deal with everything else later."

Fleurine couldn't believe this was happening. Raoul honestly loved *her*?

"Right now, we need this time together before I have to leave. Once I'm gone, we know letters and phone calls will be impossible." He lowered his head. First, he planted soft kisses near her mouth then her lips. She kissed him back the same way. Slowly they melded.

Their kisses grew deeper and longer. She threw her arms around his neck and clung to him, exhilarated by new sensations of being kissed and held in his arms. If only this could go on forever.

"I love you, Fleurine. I can't remember a time when I didn't."

"I won't be able to live without you!" she cried, kissing him over and over again.

"All these years we've shared everything but this. I have plans for us. When I come home at Christmas, you'll have turned eighteen the day before. I'll make all the arrangements, and we'll run away immediately to get married at the church in Paris. Your father won't know what happened until it's too late."

"Oh, Raoul. *Your* father would never permit it."

He kissed every feature. "Don't worry. He married my mother in their teens and won't be able to raise an argument. We'll live in Paris in an apartment. You're the smartest girl at school and can start college. We'll go together, and I'll pay for it, and after graduation we'll buy our own home while I work for the family business. We'll be away from your father and live the rest of our lives the way I've always dreamed."

"If I thought that could happen…" She returned his kisses with shocking hunger.

Suddenly the barn door lifted. In the late-afternoon light she saw her father, a tall, powerfully built man with a ruddy complexion and beard. He held a hunting rifle aimed at Raoul.

"Get your hands off my daughter or I'll shoot you dead this instant."

Fleurine pulled out of Raoul's arms. How had her father known she was here? "We weren't doing anything wrong!" she cried in absolute horror. "I was just saying goodbye to him."

She heard him cock the rifle. "Get in the truck, Fleur."

"Don't hurt him!" she screamed.

"Do as I say. If I ever catch the two of you together

again, you'll both be dead. You've shamed me, daughter."

Knowing what he was capable of, she ran out of the barn to the truck. Before she got in, she threw up, terrified of what he'd do to Raoul. As she heaved her trembling body into the truck, her father got in on the other side. He put the rifle on the rack behind their heads.

When she looked back, she saw Raoul standing at the barn entrance.

Dieu merci he was still alive!

CHAPTER ONE

Paris, France,
late August, ten years later.

RAOUL CAUSCELLE ENTERED Causcelle headquarters. He climbed the marble staircase of the converted palace to the second floor and knocked on the private office door of the CEO.

The new head of the Causcelle empire looked up. "Raoul—"

"*Eh bien*, Pascal."

"I'm glad you got my message. Thanks for coming. Since I knew you were already in town on business, this is perfect timing. I need your input."

"I like dropping by my old stomping grounds. It gives me an excuse to see you." Raoul walked into the office. They hugged before he sat down on a chair near the desk. "How's Janelle and the family?"

"We couldn't be better."

"And Oncle Blaise?"

"Papa is still in heaven teaching at the university and writing more books. Tell me about my Oncle Louis."

"It's a miracle Papa is still hanging in there with his bad heart."

"That's amazing. Hey, I hear Jean-Louis was discharged from the military and came home to get married privately."

Raoul nodded. "Something like that. Now that he and Nic have wives, they walk around like grinning bears. Papa has rallied a little since Jean-Louis's return."

Pascal smiled. "I'm glad to hear it."

"Just so you know, Papa asked me to tell you you're doing a superb job of running the corporation. That's my opinion too. He couldn't be happier with you."

"I appreciate that, but it's early days yet. Taking over for you and Nic has been an enormous challenge. I couldn't do it without my co-CEO, George."

"I agree his legal help is invaluable. Papa always said George was his right-hand man. Please tell me you want to stay on as CEO." Raoul had always liked his cousin. Outside of his brothers, Pascal was the only other man he'd ever confided in.

"You guessed it a long time ago. I *love* what I do."

"It shows, and that's all I needed to hear. Now, tell me what it is you need."

"First, I want to hear how *you* are doing. You know what I mean. What's going on with you and Mademoiselle Mornay? I hear she's crazy about you."

He eyed Pascal. "The truth?"

"Uh-oh."

"I wish I felt the same way about her."

Last night Lisette Mornay had begged Raoul not

to leave Paris yet. The new marketing consultant for Causcelle's *parfumerie* wasn't satisfied with an occasional dinner with him when he came to Paris on estate business. She wanted more. Raoul found her interesting, but he wasn't emotionally involved. It was why he didn't let her know he'd decided to stay in Paris one more day to help Pascal.

Raoul had dated many women for years, but he never felt compelled to take the relationship to its ultimate level. He ached for marriage like his brothers. But no matter how many women he spent time with, the desire that would lead to marriage and commitment had never happened.

"After all these years, it's the same old problem, right?"

"I'm stuck, cousin." Raoul hadn't told anyone Dumotte had threatened him and Fleurine ten years ago, but Pascal and his brothers knew he'd loved her from an early age. They encouraged him to keep looking until the right woman came along.

"She's out there somewhere, Raoul. You're still young with a whole world of love ahead of you yet."

He'd thought he had a whole world of love ahead of him at eighteen when he'd been desperately in love. But it had ended in disaster. The only love of Raoul's life—the sweetest, most angelic girl on earth who neither asked nor expected anything from him—had been snatched away at gunpoint. He never saw her again, and he'd been forced to leave for Paris the next day with his brothers.

A month later word reached him about Fleurine

from his oncle Raimond, who ran the estate at La Racineuse. He learned she'd moved to Switzerland and
had married the son of her father's Swiss friend. The
news had gutted Raoul.

For the last ten years he'd been with dozens of
women like Lisette, but they were worldly and more
material-minded, the antithesis of the woman he'd
loved. Fleurine had possessed an untouched quality
he'd never found in another woman. As such, his love
life hadn't made sense since that horrific moment in
the hay barn years ago.

"I appreciate what you're saying, Pascal. I want to
believe it… But enough about me for the moment."

"No, no. Don't change the subject. Janelle and I
are not giving up on you. In fact, my wife has met
a woman she believes would be a perfect match for
you. So I'm inviting you for dinner tonight. She'll be
there, and we won't take no for an answer."

He eyed Pascal. "You're a good man." He couldn't
turn him down. "I'll be glad to come. Now, tell me
what's going on."

Pascal sat forward. "George and I are planning to
acquire Rayonner-Tech in the Eighth Arrondissement
for the Causcelle Corporation. But the recent death
of the principal software engineer has left a vacancy.
Since then, Rayonner-Tech has received a flood of
qualified applicants.

"The person with the most outstanding reviews so
far is an engineer still working at Aire-Tech under
their CEO, Philippe Charbon. She's been there five

years since receiving her master's degree at Paris-Saclay University. Her name is Laure Millet.

"Despite her excellent credentials, George and I feel she should have at least ten years' experience to be the *chief* software engineer. We thought if you sat in on the interview with the CEO, Jules Vaugier, at Rayonner-Tech, you'd get a feel if she could handle the position. You'll be our eyes and ears for this last interview. We can't buy the company until we have more information about the engineer who will fill this position. I value your intuition on this sort of thing."

"I'll be happy to do it."

"*Merveilleux!* The interview with the CEO will be held in their conference room at three o'clock on the main floor. After you've sat in and listened, give me a verdict at dinner." Pascal squinted at him. "Who knows? Maybe our guest will capture the attention of the only single Causcelle billionaire triplet left on the planet."

"*Tu dis n'importe quoi*," Raoul muttered.

"I'm *not* full of it, cousin. The press can't get enough of you. Nor can the women apparently. Every month in the news there's another photo of you with your latest gorgeous date. But Janelle swears you'll really like *this* one. All I'm allowed to say is that she's different. Only your Causcelle genes will let you know if we've helped you solve your quest for a lifetime companion. Her looks you'll have to determine for yourself."

His comment forced a laugh out of Raoul who'd heard enough. "You've actually managed to intrigue me. I'm going back to the *palais*. After I sit in on that interview, I'll see you at dinner. Thanks."

Pascal's eyes twinkled. "I have a feeling this evening might prove to change your life. See you later."

Raoul got to his feet. Though he had little hope of developing a meaningful relationship with a woman at this point, his mood had been lightened by being with Pascal. He left headquarters and headed on foot for the Causcelle family hotel a block away called the *palais,* another palace. He and his brothers had lived there while they'd gone to university.

It had now been converted into a hostel for military vets who could live there free while getting trained for jobs. Jean-Louis had turned it into his dream project. Two of the twelve suites were still reserved for family.

Both his brothers had moved on and found the kind of fulfilling happiness with their wives that had eluded Raoul. He was ecstatic for them. But deep down he envied them in every particle of his being.

While Fleurine Dumotte was working in her office at Aire-Tech, she checked her watch. A second job interview had been arranged for her at Rayonner-Tech at three. In an hour she'd be meeting again with the CEO, Jules Vaugier.

She'd been so happy at Aire-Tech until her boss had hired a new software engineer named Paul Loti. He was smart and attractive, and from day one he'd let her know he wanted to date her. She had gone out to dinner with him once, but the magic hadn't been there, and she'd turned him down for another date.

From then on things grew difficult because he didn't understand why she wouldn't go out with him again.

It alarmed her that he refused to leave her alone. When she told him she only wanted to be work friends, he insisted he'd fallen in love with her. If she'd only give him a chance. Paul had asked her if she was hung up on someone else. She'd told him there wasn't anyone. He didn't like it that she'd turned him down.

Fleurine came to the point that she couldn't bear to work with Paul every day knowing how he felt. He always waited for her before and after hours to talk. She couldn't concentrate on her job any longer but didn't want to get him in trouble by telling her boss.

In truth, the only man she'd ever loved had been driven off by her father ten years earlier with a death threat. After the ghastly confrontation in the estate barn, Fleurine never saw Raoul Causcelle again. That very night her father took her to his sister's home in Switzerland where the older woman kept a close watch on her. Four months later Fleurine turned eighteen and ran away before she was forced to marry the son of her father's friend.

Since that time, she'd studied and worked her heart out to become a success. She'd dated quite a few guys, but nothing serious had developed. After talking it over with her friend, Deline, she realized the only thing to do about Paul was resign and work for another company.

She'd seen several openings online at different software companies. The one at Rayonner-Tech for the position of principal software engineer drew her attention. They were renowned for being the best. It was an ambitious move on her part to apply for the position since she'd never been a chief software engineer and didn't have the years of experience required. Yet, because of her excellent work record, they'd allowed her to interview. This second interview gave her hope they were willing to give her a chance.

Rayonner-Tech had a reputation for being outstanding, and they paid an awesome salary. If they still decided they wanted a person with more experience, then she'd interview for a position somewhere else, even if it meant finding work in another city.

She left her office at two thirty and drove there. At five to three she entered the main building where the woman at the front desk she'd met before named Gabrielle greeted her.

"Mademoiselle Millet, you're right on time. Monsieur Vaugier will be down in a minute. Follow me to the conference room." She got up from her desk. "The other gentleman has already arrived."

Fleurine had legally changed her name to Laure Millet ten years ago. She'd done it to prevent her father from tracking her. She also knew that with the Causcelle headquarters based in Paris where Raoul would be in and out, she didn't dare use her birth name. "I didn't know this interview would include anyone else."

Gabrielle turned to her as they walked. "It's Raoul Causcelle, representing the Causcelle Corporation. They are considering buying Rayonner-Tech. Monsieur Vaugier asked him to sit in on this interview."

Raoul? Fleurine's Raoul?

He was in the conference room?

Just hearing his name came as such a shock, she tripped and fell.

"Oh, no!" the woman cried. "Are you all right?" She lent a hand to help her get up.

Fleurine couldn't think. "Forgive me, Gabrielle. I'm afraid I wasn't watching where I was going in these new high heels. I've hurt my bad knee," she lied, needing an excuse to get away quickly. "Please tell Monsieur Vaugier how sorry I am, but I can't be interviewed right now. I'll call him later. If you could just help me to the entrance, I'll drive to the hospital and have it looked at."

"Of course. Lean on me. I'm so sorry this happened, *mademoiselle.*"

"So am I." Fleurine faked a limp as the woman walked her all the way out to her car in the side parking lot. "This is so kind of you."

"Don't give it another thought."

"I can't thank you enough."

Once the receptionist was out of sight, Fleurine started the engine and drove back to her office. The knowledge that Raoul had been inside that conference room had frightened her to the core of her being.

He didn't know it, but after that horrific moment at the hay barn ten years ago—once her father had her under lock and key at his sister's house—he'd hired a man in the cult to watch Raoul wherever he went 24-7. Garber had vowed to kill Raoul if he ever caught him with Fleurine again.

Her mother had written all that information in a letter she'd hidden for Fleurine to find before she was kidnapped by her father to Switzerland. Her mother had told her everything and begged her to believe that her father would never stop if it took a lifetime. He'd been a madman since his teens and was living for the day he caught her and Raoul together so he could kill both of them.

Fleurine had lived with that dire warning for ten years and broke out in a cold sweat. Even after all this time, the man or men he'd hired could be outside Rayonner-Tech *right now*, watching and waiting for Raoul to be caught with her. After years of protecting Raoul from her father by staying away from him, how could this have happened?

Surely Raoul didn't know the true identity of Laure Millet. How could he, when Fleurine had disappeared from his life a decade ago after changing her name and appearance? Nothing made sense.

Once back in her private office, she phoned Monsieur Vaugier's office, and a secretary answered. Fleurine apologized for what had happened outside the conference room. She explained about hurting her knee and that it would require surgery. She thanked him for the chance to interview with him. Maybe another time.

On that note, she hung up and sat there with her head in her hands. She couldn't stop trembling. Had Raoul somehow discovered who Laure Millet really was? How was that even possible? In all these years there'd never been a slip.

A knock sounded on the door. "Laure?"

She jumped. Paul's voice. Of course. He just wouldn't leave her alone. "Yes?"

"I saw you come in. Do you have a minute?"

"Not right now. I'm sorry."

"It's almost closing time. I was hoping you'd let me to take you to dinner so we could really talk."

"Paul, we *have* talked, and you know I just want to be friends. Please don't ask me again."

"So you haven't changed your mind?"

"No, I'm sorry."

Go away. Please, go away. I'm dying inside.

There was something seriously wrong with him.

For the next little while she tried to get into a project she'd been working on, but her fears made it impossible to concentrate. After giving up, she reached for the phone to call Deline, an accountant at Samaritaine.

Fleurine had met her a year ago while solving a software problem at the department store. They were single and close in age. Before long they became good friends and attended mass together. It felt so good after being forbidden to go to church. Hopefully Deline could come over to Fleurine's apartment this evening. They would order Chinese and talk.

She'd just started to tap the digits on her phone when there was another knock on the door. "Laure?"

It was Paul again. Now she really was angry. "What is it?"

"As I was leaving, a tall, powerful-looking man came in. I told him it was after hours and he'd have to come again on Monday. He told me he had an appointment with you, but he found out you'd had an accident. He wanted to know if you were in the building.

"His aggressive attitude concerned me, and I realized you don't tell someone like him anything. After asking him to wait, I came back up here to warn you about him. If I don't go downstairs in a minute, he'll come up anyway."

Alarmed, she hung up and got to her feet. A tall, powerful, *aggressive* man? Was it possible her father had found her after all these years? How did he know she'd fallen? Had he been tracking Raoul? How had a connection been made?

"Did you ask his name?"

"No. I doubt he would have given it to me."

"Did he have a beard?"

"No."

Maybe he'd finally found her and had come to Paris himself. All he had to do was follow her to that interview where Raoul was waiting. No doubt he'd shaved in order to trick her. Fleurine gasped at the thought and felt sick to her stomach. If there was going to be another murder like the ones he and his friends had committed in their teens, then the police would know about it this time.

"Just a minute." She grabbed the phone and called 1-1-2. After reporting a life-threatening emergency at this address, she hung up. "Come inside quick and close the door, Paul!"

After he'd done her bidding, he stared at her. "You're as white as a sheet, Laure. What's going on?"

"I don't know. But if this is what I think it is, I need

you for a witness. I've called the police. Don't go downstairs. Stay here and flatten yourself against the wall behind the door. When he comes up and bursts in, I don't want you getting hurt." She would be her father's first target.

"You really mean it, don't you?"

Yes. Her father had his own arsenal of weapons on the estate and was an expert marksman. For all she knew, he'd already shot Raoul at Rayonner-Tech before coming for her.

Paul moved over to the wall. She stayed at her desk and prayed the police would get here in time.

CHAPTER TWO

RAOUL GOT TO his feet as Jules Vaugier entered the conference room at Rayonner-Tech. "Thanks so much for coming to this second interview, Monsieur Causcelle. I believe this engineer could be the right one even if she doesn't have as much experience. Since your corporation is considering buying Rayonner-Tech, I thought it appropriate that you sit in on this meeting."

"Our CEO asked if I would do this since I'm in Paris. I'm happy to follow through." Raoul knew Pascal was anxious to get this situation resolved before any negotiation took place.

They'd just started to talk when the receptionist came into the conference room looking anxious. "I'm afraid Mademoiselle Millet tripped and fell on her way in here and has driven herself to the hospital to see about her injured knee. She said she'd call you later, Monsieur Vaugier."

"I'm surprised she could drive," Raoul said to Jules. "Since I'm free, I'll check the nearest hospitals and InstaCare facilities to learn how she is. Then I'll get back to you."

"Thank you, Raoul. I truly appreciate that."

He left the building, knowing this was urgent. Pascal would want to hear what happened right away. After a half hour of inquiries, he discovered that a Laure Millet hadn't reported into any hospitals or care facilities in the area.

Curious about that, Raoul decided to drive to her office. Perhaps someone at Aire-Tech knew what was going on or could give Raoul her phone number. Pascal was depending on him.

"It's closing time," he was told by a thirtyish man when he walked into Aire-Tech. The man's hostile attitude surprised him.

"I'm here to find out if Mademoiselle Millet is in the building. She missed an appointment because of a fall. I'd like to know if she's all right. If you can't help me, I'll go up to her office." The building directory indicated Laure Millet had an office on the second floor.

The man shook his head. He seemed to have taken an odd dislike to Raoul. "Hold on. I'm one of the engineers here. I'll go up and find out," he muttered before taking the elevator.

Raoul waited a few minutes. When the man didn't materialize, he was convinced something was off. Deciding not to wait any longer, he had started for the elevator when a contingent of armed police burst in the entrance of the building. In a second, he was surrounded. The lead officer and two others went up in the elevator. The other two remained with Raoul.

One of them turned to him. "Who are you, and why are you here? It's after hours."

"I'm Raoul Causcelle from the Causcelle Corporation. I came to see one of the engineers. She had a fall before she could make it to a private job interview at Rayonner-Tech scheduled at three. I came here to find out if she was here and if she was all right.

"One of the engineers was just leaving the building. I told him I wanted to talk to Laure Millet if she were here. He went back up to see if he could find her, but he never came down. Frankly I'm glad you're here to investigate."

The officer nodded. "You'll have to stay here for now." He radioed someone while the night security guard came down a hall and locked the front door.

A few minutes later the other officers reappeared. The lead officer flashed Raoul a glance. "The situation has been resolved. You're free to go up, Monsieur Causcelle."

On that brief note the police left the building. Raoul passed the engineer coming out of the elevator. He looked upset. After sending Raoul an angry glare, he walked outside past the security guard.

Now it was Raoul's turn to do his own investigating. He went upstairs and headed down the hall to her office. The door had been left open, and he saw a woman seated at a desk in front of a computer. She had attractive dark blond hair highlighted by gold strands. The neck-length cut looked professionally tousled with loose waves that fell from a side part.

Raoul knocked to let her know he was standing

there. When she raised her head, the motion exposed her face and throat to his gaze. He hadn't known what to expect. For a moment the world stilled. There was no question he was staring at the most beautiful woman he'd ever laid eyes on in his life.

He walked in, aware of a sweet flowery fragrance coming from her. The open-collared white blouse worn beneath a stunning navy jacket framed her gorgeous oval face and high cheekbones. He noticed her creamy complexion and the pink lipstick on the enticing curvature of her lips.

Incredibly, their shape reminded him of someone else's lips and mouth. Someone from long ago who'd been a young beauty at seventeen... With his pulse hammering in his throat, he moved closer.

A pair of soft gray eyes between dark lashes stared back at him in what he could only describe as wonderment. The subtle lavender eye shadow brought out their violet flecks, taking him back ten years. A moan escaped. It couldn't be, but it was...

"Fleurine—"

"I—I can't believe it's you." Her voice faltered. She'd turned into a raving beauty.

He could hardly breathe. "You're so lovely, I can't believe my own eyes. After all these years... To think it was you, not Laure Millet, coming in for that interview. You've changed your name."

"Yes." In the twinkling of an eye, she'd paled. "A great deal has changed since the last time we saw each other, Raoul. What terrifies me is that even if you know that's not my birth name, you should *never* have come up here."

Her comment puzzled him. He moved closer. "The receptionist at Rayonner-Tech said you fell before you could keep your interview. The secretary you phoned explained that you'd need surgery on your knee. But it appears you didn't go to a hospital. I came here to inquire about you for Jules Vaugier. I didn't have a clue I'd find *you* sitting here."

"Thank heaven for that." She gripped the edge of her desk. "Please don't stay here any longer. You need to leave this instant! Run, Raoul!" She'd lost more color.

"Wait a minute." He rubbed the back of his neck trying to take this all in. "What's going on?"

"*My father!* He's after you and always has been. A little while ago Paul told me a man had come here to see me. I asked him to tell the man to call or come on Monday, but he explained this person didn't care it was closing time and seemed aggressive. That intimidated Paul who said you didn't tell a man like him anything."

"The man seemed to take an instant dislike to me."

"Paul can be difficult. I asked him if the man had a beard. He said no, but I could tell he didn't trust him. I started to get nervous and suddenly could imagine my father bursting into my office the way he'd done at the barn. He could have shaved off his beard. I almost died believing he'd finally found me. I asked Paul to stay with me, and I called the police, hoping they could prevent a murder from happening."

Raoul's blood froze in his veins. He leaned on her desk with his fists. "You're not making sense." None of it made sense. Not anything she'd told him or her new name. "What do you mean you thought he'd finally found you?"

She wiped the moisture from her cheeks. "I ran away from my father ten years ago, but that's a long story. The only thing you need to know is that before my father drove me to his sister's in Switzerland that ghastly night, my mother hid a letter with money and my birth certificate inside the lining of my winter coat. She told me he'd hired men to watch your every move whether on or off the estate. She said that no matter how many years it took—even a lifetime—he would never stop until he caught us together and killed both of us."

"He *what*?"

"Four months later, I escaped from my aunt's house. It was Christmas, and my mother had sent me another note in a gift. She said that over the years your father had paid mine an incredible salary for his work running the dairy. That's how he was able to hire certain henchmen to spy on you around the clock over all these years."

"I don't believe it." Raoul was incredulous.

"My mother would never have lied about this. Don't underestimate her on this. He's been playing a waiting game all this time, expecting me to make contact with you at some point. Now that I know it's *you* Paul spoke to downstairs, you'll never know my relief. As for the police, I told them I thought I was in danger from an older man in my past."

"I'm beginning to think you're in danger from this Paul."

"Of course not. The officer said the only man in the building was a man named Raoul Causcelle from the Causcelle Corporation to see me because he learned about the fall before the interview.

"When I heard that, I told the officer I'd made a terrible mistake. The man I feared was in his sixties and probably gray with a beard. After I apologized for the emergency call, they left. I'm so sorry you were caught up in any of this."

"Sorry?" Raoul was ready to explode over a situation that made no sense to him. He was so thrilled to have found her again he couldn't think about anything else.

"Yes! I'm now convinced my father hasn't found me yet, but *your* life is in constant jeopardy. You know what he's capable of. Never doubt it. That's the reason you need to leave the building right now. Go out the same way you came in, and never come near again so his spies don't suspect anything."

The terror in her eyes and voice was so real he had to believe her for now. She'd called the police out of fear. What more proof did he need? He pulled out his cell. "Tell me your phone number, quickly."

"No." She shook her head and put her hands out. "Let this be the end of it. We never met. You understand?"

"But we have!" he declared. "If you don't give it to me, I'm not going anywhere."

"Please, Raoul." Those exquisite violet eyes begged him. "You're still alive."

"And I plan to stay that way. I have sources who can get your cell-phone number, but I would rather you told me."

After a shaken sigh, she said, "All right," and gave it to him. "Now go!"

He sent her a text so she would have his number then put his phone back in his pocket. "If you decide not to answer when I call, those same sources will know your address."

"Enough threats, Raoul. Just leave for your own sake! My father will never have let go of his vendetta. He lives for the excuse to kill you if he finds us together."

Her concern for him tore him up inside. "How soon are you leaving?"

"In a minute, but I go out the rear entrance to my car."

"Is there a security guard?"

"Yes. I'll be fine."

A lot of good that would do if that madman Dumotte had hired thugs who would kidnap her on sight or, worse, because Raoul had been here. "Expect a call from me tonight."

Before he changed his mind, he rushed out of her office and down the hall, taking the stairs instead of the elevator. The night guard opened the front door for him. He hurried around the parking area to his car, keeping an eye open for those who might be following him. En route, he phoned the *palais* and was answered in record time.

"I'm glad it's you, Guy." The man was now running the vet hostel for Jean-Louis.

"*Salut*, Raoul! *Ça va?*"

"I'm not sure, but I believe someone is following me. I'm headed to the *palais* in the silver Lexus right now and should be there in five minutes."

"What can I do for you?"

"Will you talk to the security guys in front and around the side? As I drive in, ask them to check if I'm being followed or if there's someone parked there who could be watching for me. Tell them to get a picture and a license plate if they notice anything suspicious. I'll check the surveillance-camera footage tonight to see if they've picked up something."

Guy whistled. "Will do."

Raoul hung up, trying to comprehend that at the very lowest ebb of his life, a miracle had just happened. Like a glorious vision, Fleurine had suddenly appeared before him all grown-up. Yet she was still so sweet and breathtaking, it caused him soul-wrenching pain to think of these lost years.

She looked early twenties, not twenty-eight. The transformation from timid schoolgirl in the eighteenth-century white dress to the stylish female engineer at Aire-Tech blew his mind. For being a married woman with possible children, Fleurine looked untouched. He hadn't seen a wedding ring. When had she and her husband moved from Switzerland to Paris?

No gossip on the estate had reached him about that. Again, nothing added up.

He needed to phone Jules and let him know Mademoiselle Millet's knee would heal, but she wouldn't be going in for the interview now. With that call made, he phoned Pascal and told him that something of a personal nature had come up. He was sorry, but he wouldn't be able to make dinner after all. Raoul explained that the interview had never taken place and the reason. He sent his regrets to Janelle. They'd do this another time.

Once off the phone, Raoul's hands tightened on the steering wheel. He needed answers by tonight or he would go mad.

Ten minutes after Raoul left her office, Fleurine stole out of the building the back way to her green Peugeot. For once Paul didn't appear to be around, thank goodness. After seeing Raoul again, she shook so hard driving home she couldn't believe she'd made it into the garage without having an accident. Thank heaven for this secluded place.

Five years ago, a wealthy older couple living in a large home in the Sixth Arrondissement had advertised for a renter. Fleurine had just received her master's degree in computer science engineering. To her joy she'd been hired at Aire-Tech with a wonderful salary. All she'd needed was a respectable place to live.

A realtor she'd consulted knew of a possibility for her. She could live in a room in this couple's home or take the furnished two-bedroom apartment over their garage with its interior stairway. Fleurine chose the second option. She could be separate yet connected to the owners and feel safe from her father. So far so good, but she was terrified for Raoul.

He'd be calling her before she went to bed. There was no way of stopping him. Paul had been more than right. The fierce fire in Raoul's black eyes she'd looked into a little while ago would silence anyone. Combined with his tall, powerful physique dressed in the kind of expensive dark blue suit that proclaimed him one of *the* Causcelle sons, any man would be intimidated.

The handsome eighteen-year-old on the estate with the dashing pirate smile had grown into a breathtaking, just-turned twenty-nine-year-old man. Raoul had always had the most gorgeous wavy black hair imaginable. Along with his brothers, he blew all other men out of the water. There were no words to describe his charisma or masculine beauty.

Fleurine got out of her car and raced up the stairs to the apartment. She'd missed lunch. Maybe if she ate something, she'd stop shaking. After changing into a robe, she hurried into the kitchen barefooted. Soon she'd made coffee and toast. She'd only started to sip the hot liquid at the kitchen table when her phone rang.

One glance at the caller ID confirmed it was Raoul. She had to answer, but the experience of seeing him today had turned her inside out. To think how many thousands of times in the past she would have done anything just to hear his voice again.

She reached for her cell with an unsteady hand and clicked Accept. "Hello?"

"Fleurine?"

"Yes." It was still unbelievable to hear him on the other end.

"Thank you for answering," came Raoul's deep voice. "Where are you?"

Her heart was in her throat. "I'm home."

"Does your husband know what happened a little while ago?"

Fleurine almost dropped the phone. "What did you say?"

"You don't have to pretend with me. Everyone on the estate knows you got married ten years ago and have been living in Switzerland. What I don't understand is why I never heard any talk that you were in Paris now."

A groan of disbelief escaped her lips. "Raoul, I didn't get married. I'm still *single*! My mother told me my father invented that lie. He spread that story at the dairy in order to explain my absence from the estate."

"What?"

She gripped the phone tighter. "When he drove me away from you that nightmarish evening ten years ago, he took me home to pack my things before driving me to Switzerland.

"My mother helped me and packed my winter coat I would need later. She told me she'd sewn a lot of money she'd been secretly earning and saving into the lining along with my birth certificate and a letter I should read. Maman said she would send me a birthday present by Christmas with a hidden message so I could escape because I wasn't safe from my father."

"You have an amazing mother, Fleurine."

"I know. Later that very night he drove me to his older sister's house in Souboz, Switzerland, to that off-shoot cult neighborhood he'd come from. His plan was to force me to marry the son of one of his cult friends as soon as I turned eighteen. I had to stay his sister's prisoner for four months. As you know, I turned eighteen the day before Christmas and had the legal right to leave. The next day I ran away."

He made a sound like he'd been shot. "Fleurine—"

"Please hear me out. When a neighbor came over to talk to my aunt on Christmas night for a few minutes, I climbed out a second-story window and across the icy roof. I had to jump into a snow-filled wagon. All I had on was my coat over my dress. When no one was around, I started running in my brown shoes, praying I wouldn't get caught. If I did, I prayed to die."

"This sounds so incredible!"

"It *was*!" Her voice caught. "The birthday present Maman had sent me was an alpine hat with a message and some more money fastened inside the wide band. She told me to run away and never come back because my father would never stop looking for me or you.

"Maman said my father had you under constant surveillance no matter where you went or what you did. That terrified me, but I was thankful she'd given me my passport to freedom with that money and birth certificate."

Her mother had also given her advice about never

depending on a man for anything. Most women did that and came to grief like she had. Fleurine needed to depend on herself from now on. It was the only way to have a life. But that was thinking that she didn't share with Raoul.

"How did you manage?" The tremor in his voice shook her.

"I'd planned for my escape during those four months, procured a passport and caught a train leaving for Paris. Once there, I asked a traveler's-aid person at the station where I could find a cheap rooming house. She gave me directions. I took a taxi there and stayed under the new name I'd given myself. The next day I bought a blouse and skirt and normal shoes, then I looked for work."

"This is unbelievable."

"Looking back, it sounds that way to me too. I remembered what you'd said about my baking. I found a job at a bakery near the rooming house. When I told the owner I could make *mannele*, I was given a chance to prove it. He liked the chocolate bits on top, and I ended up getting the job."

She heard his sharp intake of breath. "You're absolutely amazing."

"No. Just desperate. I asked the shady guy working in the back where I could find someone to make me a new legal birth certificate."

"What did he want in return?" The savage tone in his voice made her shiver.

"I paid him my first month's wages so he wouldn't tell anyone."

"And he took it," Raoul bit out.

"Yes. I didn't care. I now had the legal name Laure Millet on that document. My father wouldn't be able to trace me. Pretty soon the owner was letting me prepare all the bread recipes I'd learned from my mother, and my salary increased substantially.

"I worked there full-time until fall. At that point I'd saved enough money to start my studies at the university to become a computer science engineer. I went to classes while working part-time. Five years ago I graduated, found a suitable apartment and got the job at Aire-Tech."

"You've left me speechless."

"I've done too much talking and hope you'll be able to forgi—"

"Look." He broke in on her. "I can't handle all this over the phone. We need to talk in person."

"We mustn't."

"Before you tell me no, I have an idea. I'm staying at the *palais* right now. I've told you about it before. These days it's being used to house vets and a lot of maintenance is going on. So here's what we're going to do."

"Wait—"

"Please let me finish, Fleurine. We've used the same painting firm for years and they're working on one of the suites right now. Tomorrow I'll have two of the female workers come to your apartment in a small van from *Adolphe Entreprise de Peinture*. Its logo is on the side.

"One of them will let you put on her uniform, and you'll leave with the driver, fully disguised. The other woman will wait ten minutes then go. I'll be in my suite when you reach the *palais*. Guy, the man at the entrance, will show you the elevator to my suite. Whoever is tailing me won't have a clue about you. What's your address?"

"Stop, Raoul. It's too dangerous."

"Then, I'll get your address another way. Be prepared to open your apartment door at eight in the morning. I'll be waiting for you at the *palais*."

"Wait—don't hang up!" she cried. "Since you're insisting, here's the address." She gave it to him. "I live in an apartment above a two-car garage next to the home of the owner. I'll leave the garage door open. When they drive in, I'll close it, and they can come up the interior stairs. No one will know what's going on."

"Perfect."

"Except for one thing." She took a steadying breath. "Don't underestimate my father. He's looking for me with a special vengeance. When I ran away from my aunt's, another sin had been committed in his eyes. He'd promised to make me the wife of his friend's son, the one I supposedly married. My escape deepened his rage. He never forgives or forgets."

"Neither do I, Fleurine. Neither do I…"

CHAPTER THREE

SATURDAY MORNING COULDN'T come soon enough for Raoul who'd tossed and turned all night. That monster Garber had played him and Fleurine with the master touch.

Spreading the lie on the estate that Fleurine had been married all this time had been the Dumotte coup de grâce. From the very beginning no one had questioned his colossal prevarication that prevented Raoul from trying to find Fleurine. The man's evil soul had no equal.

Showered and shaved, Raoul dressed in the same kind of jeans and T-shirt he'd worn on the estate in his teens. While he waited, he made coffee. Earlier he'd asked for fruit and ham and cheese croissants to be brought from the kitchen.

It was ten after nine. Too impatient to wait any longer, he walked through the suite to the foyer. He was about to take the elevator down to the main floor when the door opened. His heart slammed into his throat to see five-foot-seven Fleurine looking adorable in her disguise. Yet no cap or overalls could hide her dazzling violet eyes and beauty from his gaze.

"Thank you for coming, Fleurine. I know this has taken courage." His gaze fused with hers. "I'm still trying to grasp the fact that you've been in Paris all these years and were never married." His hands curled into fists. "If I'd had any idea…"

"It had to be that way. My father is a monster, Raoul, and his diabolical propaganda did exactly what he'd intended it to do. Your father stole the woman he loved away from him. In return he made certain I could never be with you. In his cruelty, he found the perfect way to keep us apart and hold my mother hostage.

"Among the other things she wrote to me, she admitted that if she told the truth to anyone else, he would kill her and my siblings." Fleurine's eyes reflected a world of pain.

"His threat succeeded," Raoul ground out. "But we have your mother to thank for keeping her silence. You and I are still breathing and together again. Let's celebrate that much, at least. Why don't you come into my lair and we'll get you out of that disguise, fetching as it is."

That sweet smile he'd loved broke the tension. She followed him into the salon, removing the cap that released her luscious hair. Next, she undid the overalls and stepped out of them, revealing her gorgeous figure.

Raoul picked up both items and put them on a chair. It was still incredible to see her in anything but a white dress. Today she'd worn stylish tan pleated pants and a short-sleeved crewneck aqua top. His gaze wandered over her. "I feel like we're in a time warp."

"Maybe we are." Her eyes had filmed over.

"All these years I've imagined you living in Switzerland with some deranged man your father picked out from their cult. Someone who treated you the way your father treats your mother as long as she behaves."

She shuddered. "Thank heaven for my mother who made it possible for me to escape before his cohorts trapped me for good."

"Amen," he said in a thick voice. "You look a little unsteady, Fleurine. Sit down on the couch, and I'll bring us coffee and food."

"I could use some." She sank down on the end of it.

"Du sucre? De la crème?"

"Both. Thank you."

He hurried into the kitchen and came back with their mugs and a plate of croissants and fruit. After he set everything on the coffee table, she reached for a mug and started sipping the hot liquid. "Oh, this tastes good."

Raoul sat in a chair across from her and began drinking his. "You'll like the croissants, but I'd rather devour..." He was about to say he wanted to devour her. "I'd give anything for some of your *mannele*. They were to die for."

Her mouth curved in remembrance of that moment in the hay barn when he'd devoured the one she'd made for him. She sat back and crossed her elegant legs, looking relaxed. "I've seen your picture in the paper and on TV. The news of your brothers' marriages made the front page of a dozen newspapers and tabloids across France. I've kept expecting to see your wedding announced at some point. Are you secretly married, and the intrusive reporters haven't found out about it yet? I promise I won't tell."

Her question threw him off guard. This teasing, more assertive side of Fleurine was so different from the vulnerable girl he'd loved he was incredulous. But he had to remember that seventeen-year-old Fleurine had never been allowed access to the media or newspapers.

Hers had been an isolated world until she'd run away from all that. Since then, she'd been living in the modern world and was a brilliant software engineer. The change in her shouldn't have surprised him, but it did. He'd been living in the past too long.

"I'm still single like you, Fleurine. But it's taking me time to comprehend that over all these years, *you've* been living in Paris and never were married. That engineer Paul I met last evening appeared so protective of you I couldn't help but wonder if he's someone special to you." If they were in a relationship, that might explain his strange behavior toward Raoul.

She shook her head. "He's a recent hire. Nothing more."

Her clipped answer relieved him, yet he could tell she was holding something back. The teenage Fleurine who'd opened her heart to him—the girl he'd known and adored—seemed to have disappeared. Her whole demeanor was different. "I want to know details of what happened to you after your father drove you away from the barn."

He heard her take a deep breath. "Because I was on the other side of the truck, you wouldn't have known

I got sick to my stomach. When I finally climbed inside, I felt more dead than alive."

"That describes me, not only then, but for many years after."

"I hear you, but I want to know about you." Again, their gazes caught. "Did you leave for Paris the next day?"

He nodded. "With my brothers. We flew here and settled in our suites. This one has always been mine. It became my study hall for four years until I graduated in business administration along with Nic. At that point Papa put us in charge of running some of the businesses for the company."

She reached for a croissant. "What about Jean-Louis?"

"He'd never wanted to leave the estate."

"I remember he was always working in the garage after school."

"That's my brother. He couldn't take Paris or the studying, so he dropped out of school after a few weeks. The next thing we knew he'd joined the army under an assumed name. He disappeared, and we didn't see him again until this last June after we hired a private detective to find him."

Her eyes widened. "He's been gone ten years too?"

"He wanted a different life. Losing him and you within a month did a lot of damage to me. It's a long story, but now he's home and married. So is Nic, as you have discovered in the news. They both oversee special projects and live on the estate as I do. Everything has changed because Papa had to retire."

"*Your* father retired? I didn't know that."

"He has heart disease, but we never allowed his retirement to be made public. My cousin Pascal and his co-CEO, George Delong, have been quietly running Causcelle since then. This is where you come in, Fleurine."

"What do you mean?"

"They're on the verge of buying Rayonner-Tech for the corporation. I was asked to sit in on the interview when their CEO, Jules Vaugier, talked to you. Pascal wanted my opinion of the software engineer Jules might hire before he and George acquired that company."

She stirred. "So *that's* how it happened. I know they questioned my lack of experience. Now it all makes sense why you were brought in. Little did you know I'd turn out to be Fleur Dumotte in disguise."

Fleurine, Fleurine. Where have you gone?

Though he found pure pleasure in just looking at her again, this new layer of sophistication and attitude she displayed troubled him because it didn't seem real. "I'd like to think fate decided it was time to bring us together."

"Our meeting should never have happened." Her flat statement minus any emotion startled him. "When the receptionist told me your name and said that you were in the conference room waiting for the interview to start, you can't imagine my terror."

"Obviously not."

"The second I heard your name, I tripped and fell. In that instant I had to make up a story to get out of the building before you saw me. I knew you were being watched, and I feared a catastrophe would occur the second we were caught together."

Raoul took a quick breath, trying to figure out this version of Fleurine. He understood the fear part, but not her pragmatic, detached aloofness so unlike the loving, sensitive girl who'd won his heart. "Both Jules and I were surprised when we heard what happened in the foyer."

"I had to do something so you wouldn't see me, but I hated taking up Monsieur Vaugier's valuable time."

If Raoul didn't know better, he could almost believe another woman inhabited Fleurine's body at this moment. She didn't sound like his childhood sweetheart. "You don't need to be concerned about that."

"But I am, of course," she asserted.

He finished his coffee. "I phoned him later to let him know you were all right."

"That was kind of you, Raoul. You always were the perfect gentleman. But after this experience, I've ruined my chances to interview with him."

Wait—it was *that* important to her? Nothing could have pained him more. "That's not true. I'm your advocate and will arrange another interview if that's what you wish. I'd do anything for you."

Fleurine shook her head, hurting him more. "You're sweet, but I wouldn't expect that, Raoul. In truth I've changed my mind about that job."

What?

"Tell me something. Is your Oncle Raimond still running the estate?"

Now she'd changed the subject.

Fleurine...what's going on with you?

"He died four months ago."

"Oh, I'm sorry. Then, who's running things now?"

He rubbed the back of his neck. "*I* am."

She put down her mug. "*You* are the head of every-thing there now and still do business in Paris?"

"When necessary. Papa put me in charge when he retired."

"Does that mean you know where my father is and what he's been doing? I know nothing."

Clearly her fear of her father was real, but where was her interest in the love they'd once shared? "I know a lot."

Fleurine jumped to her feet. "Did he force my mother and family to live in Souboz? Do you know how she is? Anything? Since I left for Paris, it's been the greatest pain of my life not being able to see or talk to her, never knowing anything."

But you haven't been in pain over me?

This was a nightmare. His stomach muscles clenched. "Relax. Your whole family is still living on the estate in the home where you were born."

"Thank heaven!" she cried.

"We don't talk, but I see them every once in a while. She and your siblings are fine."

"I'm so thankful for that, but where's my father?"

Raoul stood up, knowing in his gut she wouldn't like his answer. "He's living right there with your family and still runs the dairy."

"*No!*" Her pained cry reverberated in the room.

She spun around as tears gushed down her cheeks that had suddenly paled. The real Fleurine had broken through for a moment. "I don't believe it! Why did you never tell your father what my father did to us so he could at least be thrown off the estate?"

He understood that anguish. "I could ask you a similar question. When you fled to Paris, why didn't you tell the police what happened on that horrific evening?"

"Because my mother had sworn me to secrecy and had a plan for my escape. I didn't want to go against her for fear of her life."

His insides twisted. "That's my answer too. I didn't dare reveal what he'd done for fear of retaliation that could end in bloodshed. We knew your father hated mine. If he had brought a criminal lawsuit against Garber for threatening us at the point of a rifle, all hell would have broken loose, and you know it."

She moaned. "But with you in charge, I still don't understand how you can stand to allow my father to remain on the property after what happened."

"Think about it, Fleurine. His crimes were against the Church as well as humanity. The knowledge of what he and his cohorts did to those monks could cause a conflict of national proportions, let alone to your family."

A shudder ran through her. "You're right. My father is a vile criminal, and he has hired men to spy on you all these years. This simply has to end for all our sakes!" she cried.

"Understand one thing, Fleurine. I may be the head of the estate, but it's still my father's decision. Your father has always done his job well and knows how to run the dairy. If I were to fire him, Papa would have to know the reason. Once he heard the whole truth—including your father's part in the monks' deaths—his heart would give out on the spot. I couldn't bear to be the one to bring on a fatal attack."

She hugged her waist. "Naturally you couldn't let that happen." Her voice trembled. "But don't forget my father would kill us right now if he saw us together."

"Let's view this a different way. Nothing bad has happened yet. Furthermore, your mother has never gone to the authorities with proof of what she knows. It would take her coming forward for him to be imprisoned, but she never has. Instead, she has stayed with him and made the best of a ghastly situation to protect and take care of your siblings. She helped you get away because she knew he hated me for loving you."

Fleurine looked devastated. "That's true, and she won me my freedom, thus preventing *your* murder so far. What you're saying is that she's a saint, and she is, but it's so horribly wrong! I can't stand that she still lives with that monster. My poor brother and sister. They're terrified of him. It isn't right they have to live under his edicts for the rest of their lives. It isn't fair what he's done to you and your family, Raoul!"

He could tell she was at the breaking point and pulled her sobbing body into his arms, aching to comfort her. For the next few minutes, he rocked her, kissing her wet face until she started to quiet down.

"Then, it's time we ended his tyranny for good. Now that we both know the whole truth, we can change everything. Here's what is going to happen."

"No, Raoul! *We're* not going to do anything."

In a decisive move that stunned him, Fleurine broke free of his arms and put distance between them. "I ran away from my father. That part was my fault and put your life in danger. You're a Causcelle who would fight to the death against cruelty. But this is one fight that will result in the loss of both our lives. I refuse to allow that to happen."

He watched her pull the overalls over her lovely body and sweep her hair up under the cap. "You can't leave yet. We haven't begun to talk about *us*." He was dying to kiss her and never let her go.

Her eyes flashed. "There's no *us*, Raoul! Don't you get it? Now that we both know exactly where he is and what he's been doing, the knowledge makes our lives worse than ever. Nothing has changed in ten years. You and I could still be seventeen and eighteen, my father's pawns. But by some miracle we're both still walking and functioning. Let's keep it that way."

"Fleurine—"

"We have nothing to talk about. We never did because we were children. Go back to your life I've seen on the news. Most men would give their souls to lead the life of Raoul Causcelle. *Femmes d'Aujourd'hui* voted you the most desirable man in Europe. Wow!

"While you enjoy that life, I'm going back to mine as a software engineer. I love it, and right now I'm headed downstairs to find the other painter. She'll drive me back to my apartment, and this will be the end of it."

She pivoted and hurried to the elevator in the foyer.

Raoul didn't try to detain her. Fleurine wasn't herself. He'd decided she was in shock. So was he. How did you process ten years' worth of unknown information in one fell swoop?

He reeled with exultation. She wasn't married, and knowing the full truth had set them both free at last. Her father could no longer stop them from finding their way back to each other now. He would see to it.

By the time the elevator door closed, Raoul was already working on a plan in his mind to take care of her father so they could be together. Within a few weeks he'd be able to put it into action. Best of all, Fleurine wouldn't be going anywhere. He knew exactly where to find her.

Three weeks later on a Monday morning, Fleurine knocked on her CEO's open door. "*Bonjour*, Philippe."

"Oh, good, Laure. You're here. Come in."

Fleurine walked into his office, fearing he knew about her visit to Rayonner-Tech three weeks ago. No doubt he'd called her in for an explanation. Paul had been in her office when the police had talked to her. She imagined that because she'd hurt him, he would tell their boss everything he'd overheard. Philippe would probably let her go.

All Fleurine could depend on was herself and her education. If she lost this job at Aire-Tech, she would find another one. She was sorry about it, because Philippe had been such a wonderful employer. Never would she have considered a move if it hadn't been for Paul.

Fleurine sat down in front of his desk. "Bruno saw me as I came in from the parking lot and said you were looking for me. I witnessed a car accident on my way here and had to give the police a statement. That's why I'm late."

"Was anyone hurt?"

"No, thank heaven."

"That's good. It's an odd coincidence that you would mention police."

Oh, no—he *did* know what had happened three weeks ago.

Philippe smiled. "Over the weekend I had a conference call with the chief of police in Nice on the Côte d'Azur. He'd been talking to the chief of police here in Paris. The man told him about the terrific job *you* did solving a serious problem with their department's computer system last year. Your fame has been spreading."

What? "I don't understand."

"He wanted to know if you were available to sort out some problems for them since their move to another part of Nice. He estimates it could take a week."

Wait—had she just heard him correctly? Philippe *wasn't* terminating her? That meant Paul hadn't said anything yet. He was probably still holding out hope to get together with her. *Never.*

"You mean you want to send me to Nice on a job?"

He nodded. "Not if you don't want to or can't. They need an expert. I told him they wouldn't find anyone better than you. Would that be a problem for you?"

"Of course not. I'm just…surprised." Shocked.

Dumbfounded. For seventeen years she'd never been anywhere but on the estate. After a brief four months in the Jura mountains of Souboz, Switzerland, she'd spent the rest of her life in Paris. She'd never traveled anywhere, let alone been on a jet.

"It's a compliment to you and our company, my dear. There's a big bonus involved. What's your schedule like?"

She needed to get hold of herself. "I'll be finishing up at the Guerlain Institute by tomorrow."

"Then, can I tell him you'll fly down on Wednesday? They'll pay for your flight and hotel accommodations while you're there."

"Yes! I'm thrilled for the opportunity and would like to go." Since walking out of Raoul's suite three weeks ago, Fleurine had made up her mind to move on with her life. He belonged in the distant past, and his world could never be hers. Her mother had been right about that.

"My secretary will supply you with the details at the end of your workday tomorrow."

"Thank you for everything, Philippe."

Fleurine got up from the chair and left his office slightly dazed by this unexpected turn of events. This job opportunity couldn't have come at a more propitious moment.

A week away from Paul would be a blessing she hadn't expected. It would also give her time to look into job opportunities elsewhere if Paul continued to harass her after she returned.

Raoul was another matter. She'd been forced to

live with the pain of losing him years ago. It had been clear from the start that their relationship had been doomed. Nothing had changed since then. Her father was still front and center. Garber Dumotte, the monster, would always be on the hunt for the two of them and a danger to her mom and siblings.

Thankfully Raoul had gotten the message to leave it alone and hadn't called her since she'd left his suite at the *palais*. That was because they'd both grown up and changed. In truth, they weren't in love. Not anymore. For a decade their lives had been on different paths. He had one destiny. She had another. Except that wasn't completely true. She'd never stopped loving him and never would. He would always be her heart's desire, which made it imperative she push him away to keep them both safe.

Raoul might not be married, but he was an important man in the business world. The news featured him with many beautiful women. It crushed her every time she saw his picture or an article about him.

As for Fleurine, she had a wonderful career and friends and looked forward to all the new opportunities ahead of her. Maybe there'd be a special man one day, but she couldn't imagine it.

This trip to the South of France would give her a change of scenery. She needed a diversion before she had to face Paul again. One more difficult confrontation with him and she would leave Aire-Tech without hesitation.

CHAPTER FOUR

ON TUESDAY EVENING after work, Fleurine had to call Deline and cancel their plans to go to a film. She'd needed time to get packed. She would call her when she returned from the job she had to do in Nice for Aire-Tech. They chatted for a few more minutes. Deline had sounded excited for her after learning it would be her first flight. Fleurine wasn't so sure about it before they said goodbye.

Philippe's secretary had laid out the plans for her. She was ready Wednesday morning wearing a three-piece apricot suit when a taxi came to take her to Charles de Gaulle Airport. After a flight to Nice first class, a police escort would pick her up and drive her to her hotel.

Fleurine hadn't known what to expect, but her nervousness subsided once the jet gained altitude in a sea of blue September sky. To think her mother and family would never have an experience like this...

She felt an acute loneliness as she noticed the number of couples on the flight. Fleurine had a feeling that one of them seated in front of her was on their *lune de miel*. She could only wonder what it would be like to honeymoon with her own husband. With Raoul. No one else.

Only once years ago in the hay barn with Raoul had she experienced moments of pure joy and the fleeting promise of marriage in their nonexistent future. Perhaps another good man might come into her life one day. She couldn't imagine it. There was only one Raoul. If it didn't happen, she'd take her mother's wisdom to heart. Millions of happy women were fulfilled without a man.

Later, during the descent, the view of the coastal city with its elegant bay and palm trees at the foot of the Alps amazed her. Once they'd landed on the runway, the jet eventually taxied to a stop. Fleurine filed out with the other passengers. Two police officers approached her, staring at her with decidedly masculine interest.

"Mademoiselle Laure Millet from Aire-Tech?" She nodded. "We're Officers Bernard and Tremblay, asked to meet you and take you to Cagnes-sur-Mer."

"I was told I'd be met by the police, but I thought I'd be working in Nice."

"You're needed in Cagnes-sur-Mer first. It's a town close to Nice."

"Oh, well, thank you very much."

"If you'll follow us to that helicopter over there."

She saw it in the distance and clutched her purse in reaction. "Can't we just drive there?"

"The helicopter is faster and avoids traffic, unless that makes you uncomfortable."

Instead of a woman of the world, Fleurine felt like

a fool. "I'm sure it will be fine. It's just that I've never been on one before." A helicopter was so different from a huge jet.

"You'll like it a lot."

"What about my suitcase?"

"Lieutenant Bernard will bring it to the helicopter."

"Thank you. It's a jade-colored spinner with my name on the tag."

"He'll find it. If you'll come with me."

While one officer went in search of her luggage, Fleurine followed this one across the tarmac to a gleaming white-and-blue helicopter. A man inside opened the door for her to board.

"Mademoiselle Millet?" the officer said. "I'll leave you in the hands of your pilot, Yves Cervaine. This will be her first time, Yves."

What? She turned to her escort in surprise. "You're not coming?"

"If you're comfortable taking the helicopter, Officer Bernard and I will answer another call that just came in, but he'll be here with your bag momentarily. Be assured you'll be greeted when you arrive in Cagnes-sur-Mer."

"Of course. Thank you for meeting me."

"It's been our pleasure."

As he walked away, she climbed on board. The pilot told her to sit behind him and fasten her seat belt. "I'll be gentle. It's only a short flight, and I'm sure you'll enjoy it." He put on his headgear.

"I'm sure I will." Again, she was irritated at herself for being so nervous and tried to act nonchalant. Thousands of people did this every day.

She looked around the elegant white interior, noticing it had three seats on each side and picture windows. This had to be the height of luxury, something she'd never experienced. From her window she took in a partial view of Nice. The city seemed larger than she'd imagined with its hilly landscape and beaches lapped by the Mediterranean.

While Fleurine watched another jet land, she heard men's voices. The officer must have come with her suitcase. She was still staring out the window when the door closed. To her surprise he came in and sat down opposite her. She turned to him, wondering why the officer hadn't joined his partner.

"Raoul!" Her cry rang out. She felt as if she were going to faint.

"Relax, Fleurine. Please hear me out. Before we go anywhere, this is a chance for us to reconnect. I won't force you to go against your will, but I would like very much if you accepted. Surely after ten years you didn't think our meeting at the *palais* would be the end of everything." His deep voice curled to her insides. "The truth is, there is no job."

Her breath caught. Another lie, but Raoul had been the author of this one.

"Your boss doesn't know that," he enlightened her. "The beauty of it is that you've been given a whole week off. Nic and Jean-Louis are taking over for me on the estate so I can have a week's vacation too."

With those revelations, realization dawned. She wasn't sitting across from just any man in this helicopter. This was a breathtaking, black-haired Adonis with unfathomable money, connections and the means to do anything he wanted, anytime. He still didn't understand the danger he was in, but she knew there'd be a horrible price to pay for this.

"You know you're being followed? And have you forgotten my mother and siblings are at risk?"

"They're the reason I haven't been able to come to you before now. Since we've been apart, I've arranged to keep them safe. I swear it. Don't be afraid, Fleurine. Nothing's going to happen to anyone. Believe me when I tell you I've provided all of us protection."

Fleurine would always believe him, but she was terrified and struggled to swallow.

"Will you at least give us the time to talk things over in favorable surroundings? It's up to you. If you want to fly back to Paris right now on the Causcelle jet, you can. Or you can come with me so we can discuss the situation in more depth before we part company for good. After ten years apart, we need this time. What's your answer?"

Her answer would be to fling herself into his arms. Barring that, she would agree to go with him because she loved and trusted him. "I'll come if we're not gone long."

"Thank you, Fleurine." He told Yves to start up the helicopter.

Between the shock of seeing him and the sound of the rotors whining, any more words caught in her throat. Again, she felt like she was going to faint.

While he fastened his seat belt, she took in the gorgeous sight of him dressed in casual white trousers and an open-necked hunter-green sport shirt. Those black orbs studied every inch of her, igniting flares of awareness she couldn't prevent from exploding throughout her body. She loved him so desperately. She clutched the armrests as the helicopter rose in the air.

While they passed over the landscape below, her sanity started to return and, with it, her fear. Her emotions were spilling all over the place, but she fought to maintain her composure in front of him.

Raoul studied her profile. "We're headed for the island of Ischia. It's one of my favorite seaside resorts in Italy that isn't yet overrun with every tourist on the planet. We'll be staying at a friend's villa and will be there soon. I'd planned to take you there on our honeymoon, but we know what interfered with those dreams. Today I can promise you nothing will interrupt our pleasure on this trip."

Right now, Fleurine was too upset to talk. He eyed the woman he loved, pained because she'd lived her whole life in fear. Growing up with a father like Garber shouldn't happen to any child. Raoul had talked to Father Didier at the church in La Racineuse about his love for Fleurine and the pain she and her family were still forced to endure.

The priest had had to remind him that Garber had once been a good little boy who'd grown up in a dysfunctional family belonging to a cult.

What Raoul needed to do was be a loving support to Fleurine and earn her trust before he did anything else.

That's what Raoul hoped to accomplish this trip. While they were together, he'd tell her about the steps he'd taken to ensure everyone's safety. In time there'd be more information forthcoming to set her at ease because this was only the beginning, and he'd never let her go.

By three o'clock, the pilot set them down on the pad at the rear of a private villa made of stone tucked in greenery and flowers. After Raoul helped her out of the helicopter with her suitcase, he walked her around where a handsome older couple came out to greet them, first in Italian, then French.

Raoul hugged both of them, then turned to her. "Fleurine Dumotte, I want you to meet Genevra and Alonzo Romano, my parents' best friends from years ago. They're my favorite people too."

Raoul had been planning all this while Fleurine had assumed she'd seen the very last of him. She was still trying to comprehend everything going on before she looked up at him. "They knew your mother?"

His vibrant black eyes searched hers. "It's why I've liked to vacation here over the years when I've been able. I love hearing about her. Genevra tells me things that make Maman live for me. I love her and Alonzo."

"I can see why." She turned to their hosts, unable to prevent her eyes from misting over. "This is the most beautiful place I've ever seen in my life. All the flowers and that dazzling blue Mediterranean. I've never lived near water. Thank you for letting me be a guest here."

Genevra took her arm. "While Raoul talks to Alonzo, let me show you to your room where you can freshen up. We haven't seen him for at least six months."

Try ten years.

Fleurine followed her through the charming villa to a bedroom with its en suite bathroom and a terrace. Someone on their staff had already brought in her suitcase and put it on a bench at the end of the double bed.

"We want you and Raoul to relax and do whatever you like. I miss all of Delphine and Louis's children, but this one has been sad for many years. Today some of that sadness is gone. I think I know why." Her brown eyes twinkled before she kissed Fleurine's cheek.

The older woman's words touched her deeply. If Raoul had been sad all these years, had he been thinking about Fleurine, longing for her as she had for him? But maybe that was foolish to believe when he was constantly photographed with beautiful women on his arm. For all she knew he'd gotten close to one special woman after all this time.

"Do you know the boys look the most like their mother? She was a dark-haired beauty who bewitched men everywhere. But the only man she ever could see was her handsome Louis, who was a wonder in his own right."

Fleurine knew all about that from her own mother. Delphine Ronfleur had bewitched Louis Causcelle and had unconsciously cast a spell on Fleurine's father, but she didn't want to think about that right now.

"Those triplet sons turned out to be the most beautiful boys imaginable. For my best friend to have died giving birth to them will always be my greatest sorrow. Now they're too handsome for their own good, as you have found out."

"I and all the girls." Fleurine nodded. "I grew up on the Causcelle estate and have known Raoul and his brothers since we were little children. As he got older, he reminded me of a dashing pirate."

Genevra laughed softly. "He's that, all right, and you—like his mother—had to be the most beautiful girl on the estate. It's the reason why Raoul has brought you here and never took his eyes off you out there." The other woman saw what she wanted to see because she didn't know what was really going on.

"How did your two families meet?"

"Alonzo and I got to know them right after they were married and vacationing here in Ischia. We'd just been married too, and all four of us were still in our late teens. While Alonzo and I were out fishing, we met Louis and Delphine at the same spot and started talking. My husband ran his father's business, as did Louis. Both men had a lot in common and struck up a lasting friendship.

"Delphine and I were so much alike we became friends overnight. We became pregnant around the same times with our first three. I had two girls and a boy. She had three girls. Then came three boys she would never see." Her eyes filled with tears. "Before they were born, she had dreams for her triplets to help their father in business and support him after all his hard work."

Fleurine's eyes smarted. "What a tragedy she died."

"It was, and so very hard on Louis. But he rose to the occasion in a most magnificent way. Six children to raise on his own with all his tremendous responsibilities. Thousands of people throughout France have relied on his leadership and generosity for years. He's a saint. We've been to see him recently. It's a miracle he's still alive considering his bad heart."

Until three weeks ago, Fleurine hadn't known anything about Louis Causcelle. Hearing Genevra's loving defense of him made her ashamed of her outburst on that last day with Raoul at the *palais*. The reason why Louis had never known what Fleurine's father had done to her and Raoul was because Raoul had wanted to protect his father from too much pain.

Fleurine was also ashamed for having nursed a resentment against Raoul's father for making him and his brothers go to college in Paris. She'd felt at the time he'd been too strict with his boys. His father had taken Raoul away from her. This woman's revelations helped her see things clearly, including Fleurine's selfishness and immaturity at seventeen.

She understood Raoul's reasoning now and his wisdom. She also understood something else. Raoul had believed Fleurine had been married all those years. In order to keep her and her family safe, he'd never done anything to find her. Raoul was made of the true stuff of heroes. She would always revere him, but that time had passed for both of them and couldn't be recovered.

Fleurine put a hand on Genevra's arm. "You won't understand this, but I'm grateful to you for everything you've told me. It has answered some questions for me, and I can't thank you enough for confiding in me. It's no wonder you and the Causcelles gravitated to each other years ago. Raoul told me he feels closer to his mother when he's here. You're an angel yourself."

As she leaned over to kiss the older woman's cheek, Raoul walked in the bedroom. "Is everything all right, you two?"

A smile broke out on Genevra's face. "Everything is perfect when *you* come for a visit, *mon fils*. Your bedroom is ready for you downstairs."

The woman had a special spot in her heart for Raoul to call him her son. "Now, I'm going to find my husband, and I'll see that your dinner will be served whenever you're ready." She kissed his cheek and left.

Suddenly Fleurine realized they were alone and in a bedroom. How many times in the past had she dreamed of a situation like this where they could give in to their desire? But this was no fantasy trip, and it was ten years later. They were strangers now, never destined to be one.

As her mother had written on that message long ago:

You and Raoul were born into separate worlds. You were never meant to step out of them to be together. Remember that a woman can be fulfilled and successful without a man.

Even if danger from her father weren't a factor, Fleurine's hopes for them had died in the past.

Fleurine was a twenty-eight-year-old career woman at this point, no longer a starry-eyed teenager. Looking at life honestly, she could never hope to be with a man like Raoul. They weren't from the same class of people. That old cliché that water and oil don't mix rang true in their case. Raoul would never marry a software engineer, of all people. The thought was ridiculous.

"Genevra is wonderful, Raoul. She loves you."

"It's mutual, and from my vantage point, she's taken with you."

"She's made me very comfortable, but this isn't my reality. I flew down here thinking I had a job to do, but all this—"

"Is just too much?" he finished for her.

She stared at him. "In all honesty, I'm thrilled to see you again in person and know that you are well. But I need to get back to the work I love."

Something flickered in the recesses of his eyes. "Why don't you change into something comfortable, Fleurine? When you're ready, join me on your terrace where we can talk as long as we want. Take your time."

"I'll be right out." She moved past him and went inside to the bathroom where she could freshen up. Raoul believed he could triumph over Garber Dumotte. Unfortunately, her mentally ill father would continue to be relentless in tracking him.

As Genevra had said, the triplets had inherited their

mother's looks. Every time her father saw Raoul, he imagined the woman he'd never had a chance to love, all because of Louis Causcelle. Fleurine had always known what she had to do to prevent a disaster. It had meant never being with Raoul again.

If only she hadn't applied for that position at Ray-onner-Tech…

Fleurine had unwittingly set wheels in motion that had brought Raoul back into her world. Only he with his Causcelle connections could have planned a secret rendezvous to get them back together. But rather than be upset about it, she realized this trip to Ischia *was* giving them a chance to say a real goodbye.

With her mind made up, she refreshed her lipstick. He would always be the most desirable man alive, but she couldn't give in to momentary pleasure. She'd meant it when she'd told him she wanted to go her own way. Fleurine needed to be in charge of her life while her father was still alive and free to commit mayhem. Raoul had also been leading his own full life for years. From everything she'd read about him in the newspapers and seen on TV, he'd been enjoying his bachelor status since his university days.

Forget the belated honeymoon he'd imagined here in Ischia. It would never happen because she and Raoul weren't meant to be together.

One day Raoul would get used to seeing Fleurine in a modern-day wardrobe. But when she first walked out on the terrace in a luscious pink top and tan capri pants a few minutes later, he had to purposely erase his earlier vision of her in eighteenth-century garb.

She smiled. "Why are you staring?"

"You're a stunning woman."

"But?"

"I don't want to say something that will bring back bad memories for you."

"You mean of always seeing the pathetic girl in white?" Fleurine could read his mind. She sat down on a chair opposite him at the patio table. "After I escaped, it took me a year to accept the fact that I could resemble a twentieth-century French girl. I used to look in the rooming-house mirror at the new clothes I was wearing and think it was some kind of trick."

He cocked his dark head. "I'm going to let you in on a secret. The face and long flowing hair above the dress enchanted me from day one. Those white dresses couldn't hide your gorgeous figure. In fact, they made you more alluring, even with those brown ankle shoes your father forced you to wear. You always stood out, like the violets in the pasture that reminded me of your exquisite eyes."

"I had no idea."

"Forgive me if I've embarrassed you, Fleurine, but you have to know how attractive you always were and are. Why do you think Thomas and Remy followed you around with their tongues hanging out?"

"If they did, I didn't notice."

"They weren't the only ones. Every guy at the school wanted a chance with you, but they were too terrified of your father."

"That didn't stop you."

"No, because I had help. Oncle Raimond ran the estate. He knew how I felt about you, and he told me to waylay you at the north pasture after school on your way home. It was the one time of day when he arranged for your father to visit the other farms."

"He actually did that?" The news shocked and delighted her.

"Even if our meetings had to be out in the open, we got lucky for a long time."

"Until—"

"Let's not go there. We're here now. It's time for you to know what I've done to keep all of us safe."

She leaned forward. "As long as my father is alive, we can never be seen together."

"That's where you're wrong. I have the best minds in the country working on our problem."

"It won't work, Raoul."

"The day I left your office, I had the security guards at the *palais* watch to see if I was being followed. We went through the surveillance-camera footage that covered the last three months and discovered one man who shouldn't have been driving in and out at all hours. The police traced the plate to a man who lives and works in Paris."

Fleurine gasped quietly. "I knew it."

"This is only the beginning. After you left my suite wearing your disguise, I set up a meeting with two men to devise a plan. George Delong is the co-CEO with my cousin Pascal, but he's also a brilliant attorney who helped my father rise to power. He knows the ins and outs of the law.

"The other man, Claude Giraud, is the former secret-service agent who worked for the last president of France. He's the one who found Jean-Louis for our family. The two men have contacts and inside connections with police and judges that reach everywhere. Between their findings, we've already taken steps to tie your father's hands."

She shook her head. "I don't see how."

"With that license plate lead, they got a warrant to tap the man's phone and that of your father."

After a long silence she said, "That's incredible."

"At that point they discovered that your father is in constant contact with him. He's the one being paid to follow me. When I'm in the city, he tails me and reports back to your father. That man is called Franz Brust. Does that name ring any bells?"

"Yes. *He* was one of those teenage guys from Switzerland my father ran around with. He works with my father in the dairy on the estate. Maman couldn't stand him."

"Well, it appears your father moved him to Paris, and he works at the Causcelle cheese outlet watching my every move when I'm there."

"Maman spoke the truth, didn't she?"

"There's more. Do you remember a local farmer, Ernst Keller?"

He saw her shudder. "Keller was also part of that teenage gang from Souboz. It's his son my father had planned for me to marry."

Raoul nodded. "Keller spies on me when I'm in residence on the estate. We now have proof your father's well-paid cronies *have* been watching me all these years, just as your mother told you. Her testimony means everything."

She turned away to look out at the water. "What you've learned proves that my actions in going to that interview unknowingly put you in danger."

"Not any longer."

"How can you say that?"

"The police have put both men under surveillance around the clock. I made it easy for Franz to follow me to Nice. Instead of flying, I drove the company Lexus from Paris. I made certain he saw me drive to the airport and talk to the two police officers."

"You mean he followed you?"

"In his car. One of the officers went to get your luggage. Brust followed me to the waiting helicopter. He saw me take the bag from the officer and climb aboard. The second I closed the helicopter door, both officers arrested him on the spot for stalking and took away his phone."

Fleurine wheeled around, her expression one of total disbelief. "I'm having trouble comprehending any of this."

He longed to crush her in his arms, but he couldn't. Not yet. She wasn't ready. "I know how you feel. While we were on board the helicopter, the officers texted me that Brust is in jail in Nice awaiting arraignment before the judge. This means your father won't have further contact with him. You and I are safe for the time being."

Fear darkened her violet eyes. "But Franz would have phoned him to report that you were last seen at the airport in Nice and could be anywhere. When my father can't get hold of him, I'm afraid he'll take his fury out on my family."

"No, Fleurine. First of all, he won't know what happened to Franz for a long time. More importantly, I promise that your family is being protected day and night."

"I believe you, but Raoul—when he doesn't hear from Franz, he'll call one of the cult in Switzerland to help track you down."

"We're hoping he does. Your father is the key that will give the police more names. They want to arrest all the men who murdered those monks and get confessions. Just remember, the police are surveilling him around the clock. So are my brothers who are making sure no harm comes to your mom and siblings. Everyone is on the alert."

"I'm sure you're right, but I can't stop worrying." She got up from the table and walked to the end of the terrace to look out over the sea.

He followed and put his hands on her upper arms from behind. "I realize you've been terrified for years," he murmured into her hair. "Can't you trust me for a little while longer? Your father is going to be arrested."

A tremor that he could feel shook her body. "I've always trusted you. It's my father I can't trust. He's capable of anything. There are many things about his cruelty I learned when I had to stay with his sister. After ten years, his rage is stronger than ever."

He pulled her back against his chest. It had been so long since he'd held her in his arms. "So is my determination to stop him, Fleurine. I swear I won't let him hurt you or your family ever again. Can you let go of your fear for this next week and allow us to enjoy some time together we've never had before?"

She pulled away and turned to him. "I appreciate more than you know what you're trying to do to solve this, but we're not in school anymore, Raoul. We can't pick up where we left off. What we felt years ago has been lost. Too much of life has happened to both of us.

"I'd like to leave in the morning, and you need to get as far away from this part of the country as possible. When I get back to work, I'll think up a reason to tell my boss why I didn't stay in Nice."

Pick your battles, Raoul.

He sucked in his breath. "We'll fly to Naples in the morning and take the company jet back to Paris. I'll phone your boss and explain that the new facility for the police department didn't work out. We'll pay you and Aire-Tech for your time and a lot more."

"Thank you," she whispered, sounding shaken.

"Tell me something, Fleurine. Why were you prompted to apply for the position at Rayonner-Tech in the first place?"

"It has a sterling reputation and offers a fantastic salary."

"I see, but there's more."

"It's true I took a chance on getting the position when I knew they wanted a person with more experience. I was hoping to be hired on probation, but fate stepped in before the interview could take place."

He frowned. "That's because I'd been called in and the receptionist told you my name. It ruined your plans. If you need money, I'll give you whatever you need, Fleurine. In fact, I have a solution so you never have to worry about that again."

"That's incredibly generous of you, but I'm able to take care of myself. Let's just be thankful no damage has been done to Rayonner-Tech or your family's corporation. I'll go back to my job and you to yours."

Her refusal to have a heart-to-heart talk with him not only frustrated him, it crushed him. "After everything we meant to each other, is that all you have to say to me?" He didn't understand her.

"It's been so long, Raoul. Our lives have undergone tremendous changes."

"But not our memories."

"True. We'll always be able to remember wonderful times from our childhood. But we're not the same people now."

His body stiffened. Since when? "We weren't children when we kissed and talked about marriage."

"That was a teenage dream I'll always treasure. Everyone has those, but life has taken us different places. I haven't begun to achieve what I want to do."

"Like what, for example?"

"We don't have time for this, Raoul. We need to go downstairs." She started to walk out of the room.

"Genevra said she and Alonzo have prepared your favorite dinner for us. I wouldn't dream of disappointing them when they love you so much and have been so kind."

Mystified and wounded by the change in her, Raoul followed her womanly figure down the stairs. "We'll do their meal justice, but while we enjoy it, I want to know what aspirations Fleurine Dumotte has been entertaining. I used to love talking everything over with the loveliest girl on the estate. I've been waiting ten years for the privilege."

She remained curiously silent as they walked out on the lower patio overlooking the water. He helped her to the table and chairs shaded from the sun by a colorful umbrella.

Trust Genevra and Alonzo to remain invisible while the kitchen staff feted them with Neapolitan *risotto alla pescatora* and *sfogliatelle*.

Fleurine commented on everything. "I've got to get this dessert recipe from Genevra. The shape is like leaves and so unusual."

Raoul smiled at her. "They make it to resemble a monk's cowl. It came from the Santa Rosa Monastery on the Amalfi Coast in the seventeenth century. I can never get enough of the ricotta filling."

"The *boulangerie* where I worked could have made a fortune off these. Maman was a great cook and would die over the taste of it as well as the entire meal. I've never eaten such fabulous food, and this red wine is perfect."

"*Aglianico* is made here in Campania," Raoul informed her.

She sipped more of it. "No wonder you love to vacation here."

One black brow lifted. "Is it possible you're looking to open your own *boulangerie* one day?"

"Maybe after I become CEO of my own software corporation."

"I take it Paris has won your heart."

"As you know better than anyone, the proverbial City of Lights is a great place to do business and network. The cost of real estate isn't bad either."

He put down his wineglass, attempting to deal with this ambitious side of Fleurine he didn't recognize. "I'm going to ask you again. What's the real reason you applied for the position at Rayonner-Tech?"

She sat back in her chair with a sigh. "The fact that the Causcelle Corporation wants to buy it should answer your question."

With that admission he had his answer for what had been driving her. She wanted to be on top. But her shrewd response didn't sound like the Fleurine of his past. "Still, you knew they were looking for someone with more experience."

"True. I hoped they'd want me enough to give me a trial run in order to prove myself. I would have liked to be its chief engineer. But that didn't turn out when I missed my second interview. However, since flying here on the helicopter with you, I've been inspired to create my own software company even sooner than

I'd planned. That form of transportation surpasses everything else, but it takes assets to afford one."

He couldn't credit that this was *his* Fleurine talking. "I don't doubt that you'll do it, but don't you have other aspirations too?"

"Like what?"

His emotions raw, Raoul pushed himself away from the table. "Like the fact that it's not too late for us to get married and have children. Remember what we talked about in the barn? I want you to be my wife so I can take care of you and love you. I promise you'll never have to worry about anything again."

She eyed him for a moment. "What you want isn't real, only a dream from long ago, Raoul. Admit we're not in love. In truth, we're strangers at this point, and you know it. I realize you see me as poor Cinderella, the Dumotte girl who was forced to wear outdated clothes and needs a prince to rescue me. But I'm not that girl, Raoul. I never was, and I would rather be in charge of my own life."

"I would never try to be in charge of your life, Fleurine."

"I'm sure you believe that, but it's a male instinct. My mother didn't find out until after her marriage." Fleurine had to keep telling him that lie. The truth was, she'd love him forever, but he deserved a woman who was his equal. She was just the Dumotte girl from the estate.

Raoul groaned inwardly. The damage Garber had done to their family had gone soul deep, robbing Fleurine of her dreams.

Had she truly grown into someone so different? This wasn't the woman he'd loved. If she were speaking honestly from her heart, then he could see that a future for the two of them would never happen. But there remained a problem. He needed her cooperation to get Dumotte arrested.

Be careful, Causcelle.

"Do you still consider me a friend, Fleurine?"

She gave him an impish smile. "As long as you promise never to waylay me again, even with the best of intentions. Still, how can I sit here and complain in these glorious surroundings?"

"They're even more glorious from the water." Raoul got up and walked over to the railing. "Alonzo's cruiser is calling to me from here. Would you take a ride with me before dark? Don't worry. I've heard what you've said, and I won't bring up marriage or our past relationship again. However, we do have to talk about your father. He's been a pall on the estate since he first arrived years ago and must pay for what he's done."

"It should have happened years ago."

"It can happen now, Fleurine. Let's go."

He went around to help her with her chair, and they headed down the side steps to the private cove below. The sun had just fallen below the horizon. Alonzo's cruiser was tied to the dock. The set up made it easy for them to step onboard. Raoul reached for a life jacket for her to wear and handed it to her, knowing she wouldn't want help putting it on.

"Thank you. I've never been on a boat like this."

She didn't look at him. "Today has been a succession of firsts."

Raoul couldn't begin to describe what had happened to him today. This was an unknown Fleurine. "If you'll sit right here, I'll untie the ropes and we'll take a short spin."

He led her to a seat next to the captain's chair. In another minute he'd untied both ropes and climbed behind the wheel to start the engine. Slowly he eased them out toward a buoy. "Twilight is the perfect time to see the charm of Ischia."

After a long silence she said, "The lights from the villas and boats make me feel like I'm in fairyland. If you had to go to such lengths to get me away from Paris for this talk, you certainly couldn't have brought me to a more magical place."

His hands tightened on the wheel before he took them on a roundabout tour. When he imagined she'd seen enough, he turned off the engine so they could drift.

"I'll get right to the point," he said, turning to her. "Over the last three weeks I've been working with a criminal attorney and other authorities to build a case against your father. To make it work, they need the testimony of three witnesses that include you, me and—"

"My mother," she supplied. "I haven't seen or talked to her since the night my father drove me to Switzerland. She doesn't know if I'm dead or alive. Even if she were willing to come forward, a spouse can't testify against her husband."

"There are exceptions," he interrupted her. "One is

when the spouse has threatened a crime against the other spouse's child. Your father threatened to kill both of us at gunpoint. The other exception involves communication about a crime that took place long before the marriage of the two spouses."

She shook her head. "I don't know if she'd be willing to volunteer what she overheard, even after everything he's done. Her fear might be too great."

Raoul breathed deeply. "Once she finds out you're alive, I believe she'll do whatever it takes to free all of us and your siblings from his tyranny. I can arrange for the two of you to be together in a safe place. She'll be overjoyed to know she was able to keep you alive and safe all these years. You're the only one who can convince her that all the problems with your father will be over once she goes to the police with what she knows. They'll guarantee her safety."

He watched her clutch her hands together. "I don't see how you can guarantee anything where my father's concerned."

"You told me you trust me. Do you honestly think I would put you and your mother in jeopardy if I couldn't promise you the right outcome?"

Her head lowered. "No." He could hear her mind working. "What's your plan?"

Dieu merci. She wasn't fighting him on this. Her question filled him with unmitigated relief. "It has all been worked out with the chief detective on the case. Since you already packed for a week's vacation, we'll fly from Naples to La Racineuse in the morning."

She turned away from him.

"After we land, I'll be the only one leaving the Causcelle jet so that Keller will follow me to my work. Later, you'll leave the jet with an undercover detective who will check you in to the Petite Bergère hotel. Other undercover officers will be stationed there 24-7 to keep you safe. Another one will bring your mother to the hotel for this reunion. Your two siblings will both be working in the *fromagerie*."

Her head came up. "That's where they are now?"

"They've been working there since high school graduation. Your father keeps them close."

"But he'll—"

"His phones are monitored around the clock, and he'll be at the dairy under the strictest surveillance. Since I will have returned to the estate, he won't have a reason to call in another cult guy yet. He'll be waiting to hear from Brust, who was arrested in Nice. This will be the perfect time to get your mother's testimony. Your father won't have any idea what's going on."

Realizing Fleurine had a lot to process, he started the engine and headed back to the Romanos' private dock in the small cove. The return didn't take long. He tied up the boat and helped her off, and together they walked along the path leading to the stone steps. When they reached the upper level of the villa, he paused outside her room before going downstairs to his.

"Think about everything tonight, and give me your answer in the morning. I'll see you on the lower patio at eight. If the answer is no, we'll fly from Naples to Paris." The next few words were necessary, but it took all the strength he had to say them. "You have my word I'll never ask you to marry me again. *Bonne nuit,* Fleurine."

Raoul had spoken the truth about leaving her alone: Fleurine had felt it. She ran through the room to the terrace where she clung to the railing. She'd really done it now, but it had torn out her heart.

A light breeze ruffled her hair. She had no doubt Raoul would try to make it all work where her father was concerned. But it would take her being as brave as she'd been in her office when she'd thought her father might come bursting through the door and shoot her. She'd made herself a target while Paul had been pasted against the wall.

Flying to the estate with Raoul meant she needed to find the courage to be her father's target again. Not just for herself and family but for Raoul. He'd had the burden of keeping quiet about her father. All these years he'd been forced to deal with him since he ran the dairy. Because of his terrorizing hatred against the Causcelles and Catholics, Raoul's brothers hadn't even dared marry in the cathedral.

She got ready for bed but slept poorly. Deep down she suffered for Raoul, who'd been held hostage by her father. It hadn't been fair to Raoul whose one sin in life was to have been born a Causcelle. In truth only she and her mother could deal with the man who'd ruined all their lives.

To see her mother again after all these years…

By the time morning came, she had determined

to do everything possible to help Raoul. Once her father was arrested, everyone could move on with their lives. As for her own, it meant loving Raoul in silence forever.

After dressing in the same apricot suit she'd worn from Paris, she joined Raoul on the patio with her suitcase. He stood there dressed in a light gray suit and white shirt, the essence of masculine perfection.

There was no man in the world like him. His fiery black eyes played over her as she walked toward him. "*Bonjour*, Fleurine."

"*Bonjour*, Raoul. I thought the Romanos would be out here. I wanted to thank them for everything."

He shook his dark head. "I told them we were leaving early and explained we'd eat breakfast on the plane. The question is, in what direction will we head?"

The Raoul of those teenage years had vanished. Pain seared her to realize she'd done the damage that had changed their relationship. But the irony of that thought lay in the fact that they hadn't been in a relationship as adults and were virtual strangers at this point. She wasn't even going to be allowed to say goodbye to Genevra who'd told her private things about Raoul and his parents which she'd always cherish.

She lifted her head. "For everyone's sake I want my father's reign of terror to end, so I'm anxious to go along with your plan."

"*Merci*," he muttered in his deep voice. "You won't regret it. The helicopter is waiting to take us to Naples International Airport. We'll fly to La Racineuse from there." He reached for her suitcase. They walked up the side steps and around the back of the villa where the helicopter awaited them.

He opened the door and helped her inside. The pilot smiled at her. "We meet again, Mademoiselle Millet."

"*Bonjour*, Yves."

She took a seat and strapped herself in. Raoul talked to Yves for a moment then found a seat across from her. Within seconds the rotors started, then came liftoff.

Fleurine looked out the window where she saw the Romano couple waving to them from the terrace. Tears filled her eyes as she waved back. Soon she'd find a way to thank them for being so wonderful to her.

The landscape became a blur during the short flight to the airport. Raoul didn't speak until they landed near the Causcelle jet waiting on the tarmac. "As I told you, there'll be an undercover detective on board. His name is Dennis Landrie. He'll arrange everything. I know both you and your *maman* will like him. He's following orders from the head detective in Paris. You'll be in good hands with him. Shall we go?"

She did his bidding as he helped her out of the helicopter. While they walked, he carried her suitcase. The steward welcomed her onboard the jet. When they reached the lounge compartment, a fortyish, attractive man with light brown hair stood there waiting. He wore jeans and a shirt.

"You have to be Mademoiselle Dumotte. I know Raoul has told you I'll be assisting you and your mother. I'm Dennis. It's a pleasure to meet you."

His smile made her less nervous. "You're a brave man to do this, Dennis."

"Between my boss and Raoul, we've been working out a strategy I'm confident will succeed. After we reach cruising speed, I'll discuss the plan with you."

Raoul took her arm. "Sit over here, Fleurine."

Once all three were ensconced, the seat-belt light flashed on. After she fastened hers, they taxied out to the runway. Soon they were winging their way to eastern France.

Home.

She had a hard time believing this was even happening.

The steward served them breakfast. She only ate a roll and drank some coffee. After their trays were cleared away, Dennis turned to her. "Mademoiselle Dumotte?"

"Please call me Fleur."

"*Très bien*, Fleur. When we land at Chalon Champforgeuil, we'll stay on the jet until Raoul leaves. Then you and I will drive in a taxi the fifteen miles to the Petite Bergère hotel in La Racineuse. We'll get you settled in the room for your meeting. I understand you haven't seen your mother in ten years. That will be quite a reunion."

"It's been too long since I've seen her."

"Understood. Another undercover officer will bring your mother to the hotel."

Raoul leaned forward. "After you and Simone have talked, I'll join you, and we'll go from there. This is going to work, Fleurine."

She sucked in her breath. "I can only pray that it does. Your courage is awesome."

While he and Dennis talked, she looked out the

window, getting more and more excited at the thought of seeing her dear mother again. But she'd hardly slept the night before and drifted off until it was time to land at the airport. She fastened her seat belt, but as the ground came up to meet them, she got that knot of fear in her stomach.

No matter what Raoul had said, her father would be wondering why he hadn't heard from Brust and would find some way to learn what had gone wrong in Nice.

The second the jet came to a stop, Raoul got to his feet. His dark eyes found hers. "I'll see you later at the hotel. Don't worry. We have this all covered."

She watched him leave the lounge and felt an ache in her heart for all he'd had to endure because of her father. This plan had to work!

Ten minutes later she followed Dennis out of the jet to a waiting taxi. He put her suitcase on the back seat, and they drove to the town Fleurine hadn't seen since she'd been taken away. There were a few changes, but nothing of significance. This was still home. Paris seemed as far away to her as another universe.

At ten after one they pulled up in front of the hotel. Dennis helped her out. Carrying her suitcase, he accompanied her past the front desk to a room on the second floor down the hall from the elevator. Using a key, he let them in. There were two double beds and an en suite bathroom. A basket of fruit sat on a table near a small fridge.

"Make yourself at home, Fleur. It's for you and your mother to use for as long as necessary. Officer

Thibault is bringing her now. Consider it your room until you go back to Paris."

Go back to Paris...

Fleurine freshened up in the bathroom. Her heart pounded so hard she thought she'd be sick. When she emerged, he said, "They're on their way."

"How much does my mother know?"

"Only that you've been found and that she's meeting you under the safest of circumstances to solve the problem with your father."

She couldn't sit and instead looked out the window, but it faced the rear of the hotel. "I'm frightened."

"Raoul explained to me that you've been living in fear for ten years. Let's hope today marks the beginning of a life of freedom for all of you."

Fleurine couldn't imagine a life where her father didn't dominate every facet of it. Suddenly there was a knock on the door. She jumped and whirled around in time to see Dennis open it. Her eyes caught sight of her lovely mother who was an inch shorter than Fleurine. She'd grown older, but nothing else had changed. Her light brown hair still hung down her back, and she still wore a dated white dress with long sleeves.

"Maman—" Fleurine's cry reverberated in the room before they flew into each other's arms, clinging for dear life. She could smell the wonderful scent of lavender from the soap her mother had always used.

"Ma belle fille." Tears gushed from their eyes while they rocked back and forth, never letting go. "Thank heaven you're still safe after all this time—and so beautiful!"

"So are you. How are Marti and Emma?"

"They're fine."

"Do they know anything?"

"Nothing."

"Not even about Raoul and my feelings for him years ago?"

"I knew how you felt about him, but his name has never passed my lips in all these years. It had to remain a secret to keep us all safe." Her mom's gray eyes kept staring at her. "I can't believe we're together again. It's a miracle."

"That's because of you, Maman. You saved my life when you gave me the money and birth certificate so I could escape. There's so much we need to catch up on… I don't know where to begin."

Her mother nodded. "I understand we have Raoul to thank for this reunion."

"Yes. It's a long story, and one day I'll tell you everything. What's important is that we owe you and him our lives for staying quiet about Father's criminal activities over a lifetime. Right now, let me introduce you to Detective Dennis Landrie. He's working with the head detective in Paris on this case."

He shook her mother's hand. "Madame Dumotte, you're a remarkably brave woman to come here under these circumstances. Monsieur Causcelle will be here any second while I take your testimony. I'm aware you want to be home when your son and daughter return from the *fromagerie*, so we'll get started now. I'll be recording our conversation."

Fleurine wrapped her arm around her mother's

shoulders, and they walked over to the couch to sit. The detective sat on a chair opposite them and began speaking into the recorder.

"I'm taking the testimony of Simone Binoche Dumotte, fifty-nine, of La Racineuse, France. Born in said town, married at age twenty-seven to Garber Dumotte in said town. Her home is on the Causcelle estate. She's the mother of two daughters, Fleur, twenty-eight, Emma, twenty-four, and one son Marti, twenty-two, all born in said town."

While he gave background information on her mother, a knock sounded, and Raoul walked in. Nothing ever prepared her for the sight of his handsome, virile presence and dark coloring. The sight of the most attractive man on the planet caused her to gasp quietly. The man she'd pushed away.

Dennis got to his feet. "Come and join us, Raoul. We're ready to hear Madame Dumotte's story."

Raoul smiled at Fleurine's mother. "We've never been able to talk before. I've been waiting for this day for a long time, Simone. I swear you are safe here, and so are Marti and Emma."

"Thank you, Monsieur Causcelle."

"The name is Raoul. It has taken ten years for us to be our real selves."

Her eyes filled with tears. "Yes, Raoul. God bless you for what you're doing."

One black brow lifted. "Even if it means your husband will be going to prison?"

"Now that I have my Fleur back, it's a relief to tell my story at last."

Raoul had predicted her mother would cooperate once they were united. He sat down on another chair. His glance flitted to Fleurine, then he concentrated on her mother. "Please go ahead."

For the next half hour Fleurine listened to the ghastly story of the fire. As a sixteen-year-old, her mother had been in the hen house gathering eggs early in the morning when Garber and his friends suddenly came in. She had been behind a stack of empty crates and overheard everything they'd done at the church during the night. Her horror over the fire with the monks inside caused her to moan.

Garber picked up on the sound. He caught her and vowed to kill her and her family if she ever breathed a word. She'd been his hostage from that morning on. Years later he forced her to marry him under threat of death. During her testimony to Dennis, she gave him the names of the teens involved.

He praised her for her courage, then it was Fleurine's turn to give her account of what had happened in the hay barn. She and Raoul had been confronted by her father, who'd aimed his rifle at them, threatening death. After Raoul corroborated her testimony, the detective made a phone call, then stood up with a satisfied expression.

"Thanks to all of you, I now have the evidence we've needed to bring this case to a close. As we speak, Garber Dumotte is being arrested at the dairy along with Ernst Keller and the other men involved for their heinous crime committed years ago."

"But what about the men in Switzerland?" Simone

had voiced the question paramount in Fleurine's mind too. She couldn't bear the thought of any of them still running loose.

Dennis smiled. "They're being arrested at this very moment. Thank you for your courage in coming forward, Madame Dumotte. A huge wrong against you and your children, against Raoul and his family, against humanity and against the Catholic Church has been righted at last."

Fleurine gripped her mother's hand as the detective walked out of the room. She lifted her eyes to Raoul. "So we're really free?" she cried.

"Like you've never been before," he answered in his deep, vibrant voice. "All it took was for the three of us to give testimony. The law is doing the rest. It's only the beginning, of course. In time your father and his friends will be tried before a jury and convicted. But what matters is that your lives are no longer held hostage by him or his henchmen. You can go anywhere, anytime, without fear."

"This is like a dream I never thought could happen," her mother murmured.

"Believe me, I know the feeling." He got to his full height. "If you're ready, I'll drive you to your house. Another officer has already taken Marti and Emma home from the *fromagerie*. They're waiting for you. I have no doubt it will be a reunion the four of you have anticipated for years."

Her mother walked over to him. "After what you've done for us, I owe you a debt of gratitude I can never repay, Raoul Causcelle."

"If you're talking gratitude, it works both ways, Simone. The Causcelle family intends to help make up for your years of suffering. I'll tell you about it when we get you home. My car is out in front." He reached for Fleurine's suitcase and headed for the hall.

Fleurine was in a daze as she caught hold of her mother's arm. They followed him out of the hotel to a waiting black Mercedes. He helped them get in and drove them to the estate.

She stared at the back of Raoul's head with its black, luxuriant hair. He'd risked everything for this day to happen. The moment felt surreal. There was no more fear from her father. Fleurine had never known this kind of freedom before.

Yet relief from the paralyzing dread of his evil didn't mask her churning emotions where Raoul was concerned. But there was no time to examine what was going on inside her because they'd pulled up to the one-story farmhouse where she'd been born and raised. All looked familiar except for the police car out in front.

Raoul helped them from his car and carried her suitcase to the front porch. Before they reached the door, Emma flew out of the house and ran to embrace Fleurine with cries of joy. Over the years Marti had grown as tall as Raoul. They hugged long and hard.

CHAPTER FIVE

THE UNDERCOVER OFFICER who'd brought them home walked out to talk to Raoul. "My job here is finished. I'll leave them in your hands."

"Thank you for everything you've done. This is a day to go down in history."

"You can say that again. My folks had a relative who died in that fire years ago."

"Like so many others, our family had one too. Now it's over."

The two men shook hands before he walked to the police car. By now the family had gone inside. Raoul waited until Simone signaled him from the doorway to join them.

He'd never stepped on Dumotte property, let alone stepped over the threshold. Once inside, the austerity of the interior twisted his gut. But that would change now that Simone had free rein of everything, including their bank account and possessions. Raoul would make sure of it.

"Raoul? Come in the living room and explain to everyone how you managed for all of this to happen."

Fleurine sat on the couch between her siblings.

Raoul sat in one of the wooden chairs opposite them next to Simone.

"After ten years, your sister and I met by accident in Paris a little over three weeks ago. She'll tell you the details in her own time. But what you need to know is that with her and Simone's help, I learned your father had hired his friends to keep me and my brothers under surveillance all these years. He hated my father and our family. If he had caught me or my family talking with anyone in your family, he would have had everyone killed."

Emma gasped. So did Fleurine who realized Raoul was still keeping quiet about his relationship with her.

"However, the accidental meeting in Paris with your sister has changed the course of all our lives. I called in the police, and they devised a plan to arrest your father for a crime against the Church. He's now in custody for that crime in La Racineuse, along with his cohorts. They'll be flown to Paris tomorrow to face trial, conviction and imprisonment."

Marti sat forward with a solemn expression. "Are you talking about the fire that burned those monks alive?"

Raoul cleared the blockage in his throat. "Yes."

"So our father *was* responsible."

"He and his friends. I realize this can't be easy for you to hear. But as Father Didier at the cathedral told me weeks ago, Garber was once an innocent child. Through being abused, he learned to hate, and God will deal with him. What's important is that he and Simone produced three wonderful children, and you have your whole lives ahead of you. That's what I want to talk to you about.

"Your father did run the dairy faithfully for years. Despite her constant fear of all of you being killed because of his threats, your mother supported him while raising you to keep you safe. Out of respect for your mom and you, our family held a meeting and want to do something for you in return.

"Emma and Marti, you can go on working at the *fromagerie* or whatever you'd like to do on the estate. But maybe you'd like to look for work elsewhere or go to college here in France. That decision is up to you. Just know the family will be funding those expenses and give you each a car of your choice. It's the least we can do."

Marti jumped to his feet. His gray-blue eyes lit up. "You really mean that?"

Simone nodded. "He means it, *mon fils*. His word is his bond."

Raoul smiled at her. "Your *maman* is a saint, Marti. The reward money offered years ago by the community for finding the person causing the fire is hers. As for the Causcelle family, we will always look after your family's needs. That includes a new car for her too. It and your truck will be out in front in the morning, Simone."

He noticed Emma sobbing against Fleurine's shoulder.

"You need to know your *maman* kept secrets all your lives, and they kept you safe. In truth, she helped your sister escape to Paris where she's been living and working all these years."

"You've been in Paris?" Emma cried. Both she and Marti stared at Simone and Fleurine in wonder.

Raoul smiled. "Did you know your mother made bakery items that she secretly sold on the estate? She's a saint. That money helped your sister when the time came to run away from your aunt in Switzerland. Your sister is a heroine too. She worked in a bakery in Paris using your mother's delicious recipes. That's how she paid for college and is now the head software engineer at Aire-Tech."

Marti looked stunned. "You're a software engineer?"

Raoul nodded. "She's a whiz. Top of her class. All of you Dumottes are exemplary people who've had to endure pain no one else can comprehend. Please keep in mind that if you don't want any help at the moment, money will be put in your individual accounts at the bank of your choice to be used however you please.

"I have one more thing to say before I have to leave. You've been given time off from the *fromagerie* to enjoy this reunion. Since the company jet will be flying your sister back to her job in Paris within five days, you're all welcome to fly with her. If you decide to come, I'll accompany you and install you in the guest suite at the *palais* where I live when I'm in Paris. It can sleep four.

"You're welcome to stay there as long as you want and enjoy the sights. Whatever your plans, the jet will be available to take you. Now I'll say good-night."

Simone followed him out to the porch. "Please, won't you stay for dinner?"

"That's very kind, but I have to get over to the dairy."

She nodded. "Words can't express my feelings, Raoul."

"I think we both have the same problem. With your willingness to have revealed the truth, our lives are forever changed. We can all relax and enjoy the future, wherever it leads."

"I'll always be in your debt for making this happen."

"It took Fleurine's courage too," he said before he realized he'd revealed the nickname for the woman he'd loved and lost.

Pushing thoughts of her from his mind, Raoul raced out to the car. He drove straight to the dairy where six police cars, two paddy wagons and an ambulance had assembled. After he got out of the car, Dennis walked over to him. "The suspects are loaded, Raoul."

"How did it go?"

"Like clockwork. Dumotte never saw it coming."

A deep sigh escaped Raoul's lips. "The Ministry of the Interior will be giving you the Medaille d'Honneur de la Police Nationale for this, Dennis. It's a privilege to have worked with you."

"This crime might never have been solved without your help."

"Simone Dumotte is the one we have to thank, Dennis. She's one saintly woman." Her sacrifice so Fleurine could escape her father's tyranny had to be her crowning glory. This arrest went a long way to help Raoul get rid of some of his guilt. He was a Causcelle and that fact had put her in danger in the first place.

"I couldn't agree more."

He eyed the ambulance. "Was someone hurt?"

"No. We brought it as a precaution."

"What's next, Dennis?"

"We'll take Dumotte, Keller, Hartzel and Richter to the jail in La Racineuse. Tomorrow they'll be transported to the airport and flown to Paris for their arraignment. The four in Switzerland will also be flown to Paris. We have it all sewn up now."

"Dieu merci." Raoul took a deep breath, trying to comprehend that the nightmare was over. "What else can I do to help?"

"Nothing for the time being. I'll stay in touch with you."

"Then, I'll go into the dairy to explain everything to the workers. A new head has to be named tonight."

"Life goes on, doesn't it?"

"Amen." Raoul patted the man's shoulder and had just started walking toward the entrance when his brothers came rushing toward him. All three of them teared up as they hugged.

What would Raoul have done without them guarding the Dumotte family? They'd helped him with everything.

"This marks the beginning of a new era," Nic spoke in a broken voice.

Jean-Louis let out a long sigh. "Thank heaven Dumotte is gone with all his evil cronies."

"We'll tell Papa the truth tonight," Raoul announced. "He loved Gregoire, and this news will make a new man of him. First, however, we need to go in and announce that Gaston will be the new head of the dairy. He should have been put in charge years ago."

The second they entered the building, all the workers stood in the aisle shouting *Bravo!* and clapping hard. Each one came up to shake their hands and thank them for getting rid of Garber, whom they'd secretly named the *menace de Saône.*

Dumotte's crime had not only put the Saône department in eastern France on the map, everyone had suffered because of it.

And no one more than Simone and her children.

Raoul didn't dare dwell on the reunion going on in their home. The thrilling period of his teenage life with Fleurine had come to an official end.

He no longer recognized the girl he'd loved. A beautiful, determined and talented woman had taken her place. Someone, it seemed, who could not love him. He had no choice but to let her go.

After sending Dumotte to prison at last, he realized a miracle had happened. Maybe one more lay in store for him. The next time Raoul met with Pascal in Paris, he'd go to his cousin's home for dinner and meet the woman who might be the perfect match for him.

Another thunderous cry of approval broke out when Raoul announced that Gaston Farouche had been named the new head of the Causcelle dairy. While everyone celebrated the welcome news, Raoul and his brothers left to drive to the chateau.

They found their *papa* in the family room, putting a puzzle together with Françoise's great aunt after dinner. Françoise sat nearby reading a book. Jean-Louis gave his wife a kiss and asked her to wheel Nadine to her room. He and his brothers needed time alone with their father.

Louis looked up. "Well, well. You're back, Raoul. What's going on with the triumvirate tonight?"

They took a seat. "We have vital news."

His chin lifted. "That sounds serious."

"It *is*, Papa," Jean-Louis murmured, "but in a way that should bring peace to your soul as well as to the estate and the Church."

"My soul has been at peace for years."

"Except for one thing," Nic interjected.

Their father looked away. "*Eh bien, mes fils.* Don't keep me in suspense."

Raoul leaned forward. "The men responsible for the monastery fire that killed Gregoire and the monks have been arrested. Soon they will face imprisonment."

Louis's bald head turned toward Raoul in amazement. "Who did it?"

"Brace yourself, Papa. Garber Dumotte, Keller, Hartzel and Richter, along with four others rounded up in Switzerland."

Their father shook his head. "Garber?" he whispered.

"His wife Simone gave testimony to the police. She knew what he did and held her peace under threat of death all these years. She also helped Fleur escape after he threatened her and me. It turns out Garber wanted to marry Maman. Maybe you knew that."

"I suspected."

"When she chose you, he couldn't handle it and wanted to hurt both of you in a way to make you suffer."

His father moaned. "He accomplished his purpose and hurt you too."

"But that's old history now, and Gaston Farouche has been named the new head of the dairy."

"Excellent choice." After a long pause he said, "All this happened today?"

"That's right, and the world is a better place for it."

Tears dripped down his cheeks. "Poor Simone and her children."

"They're going to be fine."

He stared at the three of them. "*Mes fils*, we need to help that family."

No one had a bigger heart than their father. "It's being done," Raoul assured him. "More importantly, we hope this news will help you sleep better from now on."

Fleurine loved it that their mother was in charge for the first time. They'd just finished dinner. The last few days with the family had been a healing time for all of them. They'd strengthened their bonds and found joy being together.

"Emma? Marti? Have you two decided what you'd like to do? Raoul has texted that he'll come by here at eight in the morning to take Fleur to the airport."

There'd been no text to Fleurine, no greeting, no conversation or questions. He'd kept his promise and hadn't come near since leaving her and her mother at the door of their house four days ago. It shouldn't have surprised her. He'd always been a man of his word, but it brought her indescribable pain.

Marti eyed their mother. "We've never been anywhere, so I'd like to go to Paris and stay in that *palais* for a few days. I don't know about work or school yet."

Emma nodded. "I'd like to do the same thing. What about you, Maman? Will you come with us?"

Nothing had been settled where her siblings' future plans were concerned. The thought of leaving her mother for long periods of time tormented Fleurine.

"I don't think so. While you're gone, I'd like to do some shopping and visit my friends."

Marti grinned. "In your new Renault."

"No one deserves free time more than you, *chère* Maman," Fleurine commented. She looked at her siblings. "I'm thrilled you guys are coming with me. After my work we'll go out for dinner to some famous places, and I'll show you around. We'll shop for new clothes, get new hairdos. The works!"

"I can't wait!" Emma cried.

"Then, I think we'd better do the dishes and get our packing done. Eight comes early. We'll eat breakfast on the jet."

Marti let out a whoop of excitement before helping to clear the table.

Later that night as Fleurine was on her way to bed, her mother stopped her in the hallway. "I've loved our time together." She hugged her.

"I'll visit whenever I can and phone you every day,

Maman. If you want to move to Paris, you can live with me. Just say the word."

"No. My home is here, but I'll visit." She smiled at her. "Before I go to bed, come in my room and talk to me for a minute." They went inside. "I'm curious about something. When did Raoul start calling you Fleurine?"

Her heart thudded. *What?*

"We were on the porch when he accidentally called you that on the day he dropped you off here at the house."

Fleurine swallowed hard. "He nicknamed me that after I turned seventeen."

Her mother smiled. "It's beautiful and suits you perfectly. You never said a word to me, but it's obvious you captured this young man's heart before your father tore you from our family." Her eyes misted over. "I'm so sorry. Garber said he caught you in the barn with Raoul."

"Yes. I went there to say goodbye to him, but that was a long time ago."

"And now you're living a full life in Paris?"

"I am, and I love it."

"Is there a man you're interested in?"

"I've dated from time to time, but no one special."

"Please tell me how you actually happened to meet up with Raoul again."

"There are so many things to tell you. You have to know the beginning first. Within a month of arriving in Paris I had my name legally changed to Laure Millet so I couldn't be traced."

"You smart girl."

"Now leap ahead to a few months ago where I was working as a software engineer at Aire-Tech. Another engineer working there named Paul began pursuing me. We had one date, and that was it. I wasn't interested, but he became impossible, so I decided to try for employment elsewhere. I decided to go for an interview with Rayonner-Tech, the best software company in Paris. That turned out to be a move that has changed my life.

"As the receptionist led me to the conference room for my second interview, she mentioned that Raoul Causcelle was in there with the CEO."

"Oh, *ma chère Fleur*. What a shock!"

"You have no idea. It frightened me so badly I tripped and hurried out of the building. Later, Raoul came to my office at Aire-Tech to find out what had happened to Mademoiselle Millet. He'd been called to sit in on the interview. Causcelle planned to buy Rayonner-Tech but needed to approve the person who'd be hired for the chief engineer position."

"Meaning *you*. That's incredible. I bet you had no trouble recognizing him."

She hugged her arms to her waist. "No. He's a breed apart from other men."

"Your transformation must have shocked him."

"You mean no more Cinderella-in-white."

Her mother studied her for a moment. "Then what happened?"

"We met again at the *palais* where he stays when in Paris. I told him I'd never married."

A slow smile broke out on her mother's dear face.

"When he learned you were still single, it's obvious he wasted no time arranging for your father's arrest. What else haven't you told me?"

Fleurine knew what her mother was getting at. "He arranged a bogus interview for me three weeks later in Nice where he showed up. We flew to Ischia, Italy, and stayed with friends of his family overnight. He wanted us to pick up where we'd left off, but I took your advice because you've never led me wrong."

"What are you talking about?"

"You sent me a note with that money ten years ago. It said, *You and Raoul were born into separate worlds. You were never meant to step out of them to be together. Remember that a woman can be fulfilled and successful without a man.*"

"I said that because you were only seventeen."

"Even so, being with him again made me realize you'd spoken the truth. We come from separate worlds. He's a bachelor with a lifestyle most men would give anything to have. I've taken your advice to heart and am determined to own my own software company someday. I haven't looked back, and it's because of you. You're a saint, Maman, and I adore you. Now we both need to get to bed."

She kissed her cheek and rushed out in the hall to the bedroom she was sharing with Emma.

"I'm so excited, Fleur. I've never been on any kind of plane before."

Fleurine laughed. "I know how you feel. You'll love it."

"Do you have to go to work tomorrow?"

"Of course not. I'll call my boss and ask for a few more days off. He'll understand when he learns you and Marti have come with me for a short visit."

They talked until they turned out the lights. Emma kept her distracted from the conversation she'd had with her mother until her sister fell asleep. Unfortunately, she tossed and turned for the rest of the night. She kept remembering the worried look in her mother's eyes after she'd hurried out of the bedroom. What had caused it?

Worse, her dreams were filled with Raoul and that moment in Ischia when he'd asked her again to marry him. She'd turned him down and wanted to die.

Long before it was time to get up, Fleurine showered and dressed once more in her apricot suit she liked for travel. She put out one of her skirts and print blouses she'd brought so Emma could wear them. Her sister was the same height, so she also let her borrow a pair of her flats.

"Oh, Fleur—these clothes look like my friends' outfits! I can't believe it." She ran around the house showing Marti and their mother. "I need to get my hair cut. So do you, Marti. Yours is too long."

"That's one of the first things I'm going to do."

"What's the other?"

"Buy some cargo pants and sandals."

Fleurine smiled as she watched the two of them step out of the eighteenth century into life. The giant hand of their father no longer crushed them in his grasp. She had Raoul to thank for their liberation. But knowing he would be coming by for them in a few minutes had made her restless.

Her mother came out to the porch where Fleurine waited with her suitcase. "I'll get rid of their clothes while they're with you in Paris," Simone whispered. "Make sure Emma gets a haircut like yours. It will suit her too."

Fleurine turned to her. "You're so wonderful, Maman. It's hard to leave you, but I promise I'll be back soon."

"I have no doubt of it. Don't tell the others, but I'm following your example. Later today I'm interviewing for the position of head pastry chef at the Beauchamps *boulangerie* in La Racineuse."

With a cry, Fleurine threw her arms around her. When she let her go, Raoul had pulled up in the Mercedes.

Her heart leaped as she watched the man she used to think of as a dark-haired pirate get out and walk towards them. Today he wore a tan suit with white shirt and striped tie. In the news or otherwise, he and his brothers always looked like they'd just stepped off the front page of *GQ*.

"Bonjour, tout le monde!" he called out.

"Bonjour, Monsieur Causcelle!" Emma and Marti had come out on the porch with their overnight bags and hurried toward the car like young children on holiday. The scene tugged at Fleurine's heart.

He came closer. His black eyes blazed. "*Eh bien*, Simone. It looks like everyone is ready for a trip to

Paris. Are you prepared to be an empty nester for a few days?"

"I'll manage somehow," she answered with a broad smile. Fleurine knew her mother was excited to get going on a career for herself.

"You have my phone number, and I have yours. Be assured I'll return your children safely to you."

"I know you will. Bless you, Raoul."

After another hug, Fleurine hurried down the steps to the car carrying her suitcase before Raoul could take it from her.

He loaded their cases into the trunk and opened the rear door. The three of them got in the back. After he took his place behind the wheel, he honked and waved to their mother before pulling away. They drove through the estate past the chateau in the distance and reached the highway leading to the airport in Chalon Champforgeuil.

She experienced another surreal moment riding in Raoul's car with her excited siblings on either side of her. They talked about what they wanted to do on their trip, while Raoul made several calls on his phone. During his last one, he caught her staring at him through the rearview mirror.

Feeling uneasy, she turned her head to look out the window. Fleurine had let him know there could be nothing between them. Her father had been arrested. That action ended any more association with Raoul. But it was difficult not to look at him while they were together in the car.

After her dreams of last night, she knew she'd

thrown away the possibility of something wonderful by turning him down. She'd have to be careful and stay occupied with her siblings after they boarded the jet. Once in Paris, she and Raoul would go their separate ways for good.

"Wow," Marti blurted when they reached the airfield and parked near the Causcelle jet. Several airport workers came running and helped with their luggage.

"*Eh bien*, you two." Raoul smiled at her siblings. "Let's get onboard. Once we're seated, we'll buckle up and be off. It's a perfect fall day, so I know you'll enjoy your first flight."

They followed him up the steps and into the lounge compartment. Fleurine knew how overwhelmed they were feeling. The Causcelle lifestyle couldn't be compared to anything they'd known before now. Raoul introduced them to the pilot and steward who promised to serve them breakfast once they were in the air. Raoul had a way...

Fleurine found her own seat while he answered their questions. He soon had them laughing and feeling totally comfortable. This was the Raoul who'd charmed her from the first second she'd met him as a young girl on the estate.

The seat-belt sign flashed on, and they all buckled up. Fleurine stared out the window so she wouldn't be caught a second time gazing at his incredibly handsome features and dark hair.

Once they'd reached cruising speed, breakfast with all the trimmings turned out to be one happy event. After the steward cleared their trays, Raoul asked them what they would like most to do after they arrived in Paris.

Marti spoke first. It came as a surprise since he'd always been quiet and rarely assertive. "You mentioned we could stay at the *palais* where you live when you come to Paris. Is it a real *palais*?"

"It used to be and looks like one from the outside. My sister's suite on the main floor is vacant with two bedrooms. You and your sister are welcome to stay in it for as long as you want." He turned to Emma. "What sounds good to you?"

"I—I'd like to stay there too," she stammered. "Is that all right with you, Fleur?"

"I would have been surprised if you'd said you wanted to stay with me." Who would choose her apartment after being offered the world?

Raoul nodded. "Then, it's settled. The *palais* has laundry service. There's also a kitchen staff that provides meals day and night. Just call on the phone. We keep an Audi in the parking lot if you want to drive around. Guy, the man in the foyer, will give you key. I'll be on the second floor in my own suite in case you need to phone me for anything."

They plied him with questions for what felt like ages. Then to her surprise he got to his feet. In the next breath he pulled two envelopes from his pocket and handed them to her siblings. "This money set up in your own accounts is for you to go on a shopping spree. Fleur will help you navigate around Paris and find what you're looking for.

"After we arrive, we'll drive to the *palais* to get

you situated. I have work today, but tonight it will be my pleasure to take all of you to dinner on top of the *Tour Eiffel*. It's a wonderful place to drink in the atmosphere of Paris on your first visit."

Emma squealed for joy. As for Marti, Fleurine thought he looked like he'd died and gone to heaven.

Following Raoul's unexpected dinner invitation, and his display of unimagined kindness and generosity, the seat-belt warning flashed. He sat down once more, and they buckled up for the descent. She needed another belt fastened around her chest to quiet her palpitating heart. The sooner she didn't ever have to see him again, the better.

CHAPTER SIX

RAOUL DROVE THEM into Paris from the airport. He alerted Guy to make sure his sister Corinne's suite would be ready for the Dumotte family. If ever three people deserved to be showered with a few gifts after a lifetime of emotional abuse, they did.

Once upon a dream he'd planned to marry Fleurine and spoil her with everything her heart could desire. But those days were over. Though he would always be in love with his memory of her, she'd changed beyond recognition. They could never have a relationship now.

Still, he found it cathartic to do something of value for Simone's younger children who deserved a fresh start. After he pulled up in front of the *palais*, he walked inside the foyer and introduced them to Guy. The man had a friendly, warm nature they would enjoy.

"Have a great day, guys," Raoul said a few minutes later. "I'll meet you out in front at seven thirty, and we'll enjoy a night out." Avoiding Fleurine's eyes, he returned to his car and took off for headquarters a block away.

"Hey, Raoul," his cousin cried out when he walked

in the office. "I'm so glad to see you. My wife and I were just talking about you so we could set up a dinner engagement for tonight with you-know-who."

"Tonight I'm busy, but how about tomorrow night? A river cruise on the Seine?" He needed his cousin to divert his attention while he entertained Fleurine and her siblings one more night. Then he could walk away forever.

Pascal's head flew back. "Are you serious?"

"I'm playing host to the Dumotte family while they're in Paris."

"You *what*?"

"I know what you're thinking, but no. Fleurine and I will never be together, but Jean-Louis and I are doing this for their family. I'll tell you the reason later. Do you think you and Janelle could join us and bring this new woman with you? I'll be going back to La Racineuse the day after tomorrow, so that might be the only time for a while."

"I'll phone my wife. If it can work, I'll let you know."

"*Bien*. We'll board the cruise from the Pont de Bir-Hakeim at eight o'clock."

He left his cousin and walked down the hall to George's inner sanctum. His first priority was to call Philippe Charbon, the CEO at Aire-Tech. After he was put through, he explained he was phoning for the chief of police in Nice. The chief was a friend of his father's and was willing to help.

"The real-estate arrangement fell through so we couldn't use Mademoiselle Millet after all. She flew back to Paris this morning. We've reimbursed her and your company for your willingness to loan her to us. If we can find another property, we'll be calling both of you again. *Merci bien, Monsieur* Charbon."

With that lie taken care of, he called Marcel, the maître d'hôtel at the *Tour Eiffel* restaurant.

"Ah, Raoul!" he exclaimed excitedly. "What can I do for you?"

"Tonight I'm bringing guests for dinner, two women and a man. We'll be there by eight o'clock. They'll order whatever they want, but I'd like the best champagne served. Will you seat us at a window where they can see everything? This is their first trip to Paris."

"I understand and will find the perfect spot, Raoul. What about flowers?"

"Perhaps a red rose in a vase for both women at their places."

"A delightful touch. *Merci,* Raoul. *À bientôt.*"

Raoul hung up and made a third call to Simone. She'd left her voice mail on. He let her know they'd arrived. "All is well with your *enfants.*"

For his last call, he phoned Jules Vaugier at Rayonner-Tech. "Jules? Have you filled the position of chief software engineer yet?"

"No. We have to get the best person, and I'm not convinced we've found one yet. It was a shame that Laure Millet had that accident. The reports on her were outstanding, even if she hadn't worked in the business ten years."

"I agree, and I have good news. She had a slight ankle sprain but is now back to normal. I'm impressed with the reviews on her from all the Aire-Tech clients. My instincts tell me she'd be a good candidate for the position if you decide to hire her on probation. Who knows? The CEO at the Causcelle Corporation might still be willing to talk business with you."

"You think?"

"You never know."

"That's true. I'll get Gabrielle to contact her about another interview. I'm curious to find out what your gut is telling you."

"Best of luck, Jules."

Raoul clicked off, wanting this to be his farewell gift to Fleurine. She'd hoped to work for Rayonner-Tech. Heaven knew she deserved it with her outstanding credentials and all she'd been through.

He got up from the desk and walked back to Pascal's office. "Tell me, cousin. What is the latest decision on Rayonner-Tech?"

"We're still waiting to find out who they hired for the chief software engineer. Janelle is working on that date for tomorrow night. I'll call you when I know anything."

"Perfect. Now I've got to run."

Out in the car, he phoned Guy and learned that their guests had left in the Audi to shop. With that good news, he returned to the *palais* where he could relax in his own suite and make a ton of calls.

The first one to his father made Raoul happy. He could tell his *papa* had definitely found peace after learning of Garber's arrest. The police had informed Father Didier about it. He paid a visit to the chateau to thank Louis and the family on behalf of the Church. Their gratitude caused his father to weep over the phone.

After ordering a sandwich from the kitchen, Raoul was able to get hold of Jean-Louis.

"What's going on, *frérot*?"

"The Dumotte family is now installed at the *palais* in Corinne's old suite."

"Does that mean Fleurine and her mother too?" Jean-Louis and Nic had always known about his love for her. But he'd let them know there was no possibility of a future for them now.

"It turns out Simone wanted to stay home. As you know, Fleurine has her own apartment and will probably go back and forth while her siblings are in Paris. It's just Emma and Marti I'm concerned about. Guy's being a great help to them."

"There's no one better."

"The reason I'm calling is that I could really use your expertise. All the work you've done for the vets is phenomenal, and I'm hoping you can help them."

"What Garber did to those poor kids was criminal. I'll do whatever I can."

"Have I told you lately how glad I am you're back from the army?"

Jean-Louis laughed. "No one is happier than I am."

Raoul knew his brother's life had turned around since his return. Françoise had become his great joy. "If your wife doesn't mind, would you be able to fly to Paris in the morning and meet with them in their suite? I'll have the jet waiting at the Chalon Champforgeuil Airport for you. They need guidance about their future education. You're the one to do it, and you know all the important contacts."

"Will do. I should be there by ten thirty."

They hung up, and he called Damond, his assistant at the estate office. They discussed business and a few problems before it was time to shower and shave for the night out.

Dressed in a navy suit and tie, Raoul left the *palais* at twenty after seven and went out to the parking area for his car. He pulled up in front of the entrance and waited.

Between becoming new hairstyles that brought out their blond hair and attractive features, he hardly recognized his guests. Emma wore a valentine-red cocktail dress. Marti looked like the elegant young man about town in a charcoal suit and paisley tie. Their shopping spree had produced stylish results. Raoul took a picture of them with his phone to send to Simone.

He'd already been stunned by Fleurine's transformation weeks ago, but he couldn't take his eyes off her in a breathtaking black sheath with long sleeves. They climbed in the back and couldn't stop talking about their adventures all the way to the Champs de Mars.

Fleurine didn't say anything. Her siblings talked nonstop, making it difficult to get a word in. Raoul couldn't remember the last time he'd been so entertained. The oohs and aahs continued when they got up close to the *Tour Eiffel*. They might be in their early twenties, but their reactions were childlike, and Raoul couldn't stop smiling.

Like his brothers, he'd always felt guilty about the Causcelle billions, but not tonight. It brought him joy to spread some happiness to Garber's innocent children. The fact that Fleurine didn't fight him and his family on doing what they could for her mother and siblings made this what his father called a *sacred experience.*

After he parked the car, they wove their way through the ever-present crowds and rode the elevator to the restaurant. Marcel came hurrying up to them.

"Soyez la bienvenue, Raoul!" He clapped his hands.

"*Merci*, Marcel. Meet my guests Emma, Marti and Fleur Dumotte from eastern France."

"*Enchanté*. Let me show you to your table. It's ready for you."

They followed him through the room to a table next to the window that looked out over Paris.

"Please be seated, and we'll take care of you."

Raoul purposely helped Emma, leaving Marti to assist Fleurine. Soon a waiter came with menus, and orders were taken. Next came the *sommelier*, who poured the champagne.

After he walked away, Raoul raised his glass. "You guys look terrific! I want to welcome you to Paris and propose a toast. May this be the beginning of new hopes and dreams."

They all clinked glasses and sipped his favorite vintage.

Emma beamed at him. "I feel like I'm in a dream

right now. Thank you, thank you for everything you've done for us, Raoul."

Marti nodded. "All this is fantastic."

"You've done too much," Fleurine murmured, avoiding his gaze.

He expected that from her. "Not at all. There's more to come. I'll tell you about it while we eat."

They chose fish since they rarely ate it at home. Raoul loved it too. At the end of their meal, he tapped his glass with a spoon. "My father is grateful for Marti and Emma's work at the dairy and for everything your mother has done to bring your father to justice. Now he'd like to do something for you in return. Maybe you want to stay on the estate and work. Maybe not. But he's hoping you'll consider going to college here in Paris the way my brothers and I did.

"I have business tomorrow morning, but my brother will be meeting with you at the *palais*. He'll arrive around ten thirty to talk about your plans for the future. He's been helping returning veterans go to school to earn degrees or to learn a trade. Jean-Louis has many connections and can answer a lot of questions you might have. If or when you decide to fly home, I'll make sure the jet is available."

"You're unbelievable," Marti blurted with tears in his eyes.

Raoul shook his head. "My entire family admires you. It's a pleasure to bring you and your mother a little happiness. Now it's late. If you're ready to go, I'll get you back to the *palais* for a good night's sleep."

Emma gazed at him. "Would it be all right if I took this rose? I'd like to keep it to remember."

"By all means."

Fleurine said nothing before he got to his feet and walked them to the restaurant entrance. Marcel shook their hands before they went down the elevator.

In the car Emma exclaimed, "I'll never forget this night for as long as I live."

"You can say that again," Marti agreed.

Raoul started the engine, and they took off. "I, too, enjoyed it more than I can say."

Again there was no comment from Fleurine. He knew she couldn't wait to say good-night, and this caused him unimaginable pain, but she had made her feelings clear. All he could do now was see that her family were happy. Fleurine was lost to him...

Before long they reached the *palais,* and the three of them got out of the back, but Emma held back.

"I'll be thanking you over and over again for all you've done for us and are still doing." Her eyes shone as she looked up at Raoul. "It's so strange to think we could live on the estate all these years and never have known each other. Yet now, I feel so close to you and your family. I wish I could do something personal and important for you."

He smiled at her. She had that same sweetness and vibrancy he'd seen in Fleurine during those growing-up years. It touched his heart. Her lovely gray eyes didn't have violet flecks, but in some respects she resembled her elder sister, especially with her new hairdo.

"There *is* one thing you can do for me, Emma. Don't let anything stop you from finding your happiness. *That's* what's important."

"I think I already have."

Fleurine overheard them talking. She thanked Raoul before hurrying inside to their suite for the night in order to get a grip on her emotions. Tomorrow night she'd go back to her apartment. Though she'd said goodbye to him in Ischia, minutes ago the sight of a lovesick Emma gazing up at Raoul as if he were her whole world had turned Fleurine inside out. It never occurred to her that something like this could happen.

All Raoul had to do was be kind to Emma and flash her his heart-stopping smile. Like every smitten woman within his orbit, the very last thing on earth her vulnerable sister would want was to escape. Emma was a twenty-four-year-old woman, no longer a child. She'd never met a man to compare to Raoul.

She never would...

Fleurine thought back to her conversation with Emma at the house. Her sister had admitted to having a slight crush on one of the guys working in the estate hothouse. But any chance of dating him had been impossible since their father had arranged for her dreaded marriage to a man in Switzerland at the end of the year.

Now Raoul's intervention had changed everything for Emma who couldn't stop talking about Raoul and how wonderful he was. Fleurine groaned. Emma knew nothing of Fleurine's history with Raoul. There was no question her sister had fallen for him. This called for an intervention of her own making.

Before it was too late, she would have to tell her everything. The mere thought of them being together brought such exquisite pain she could hardly breathe.

While she agonized, Marti came in. He was over the moon about everything, especially Raoul who'd won her brother's heart from the beginning.

"C'est un etalon!"

That was Marti's French slang for the American word *stud*. High praise indeed. Fleurine looked past him. "Where's Emma?"

"She's still talking to Raoul about living here at the *palais* if she decides to stay in Paris."

How well Fleurine understood what drove her sister! Tomorrow she'd have a serious talk with her. Right now, it was time for bed.

Fleurine experienced another bad night with little sleep. Nothing had been settled where her siblings were concerned. Raoul had orchestrated everything which meant she couldn't avoid him altogether. At least not yet.

Jean-Louis arrived at the appointed time the next morning. Like Raoul, he was gorgeous and also had a way that charmed her siblings. He asked the right questions and showed an interest that made them feel incredibly comfortable.

When they'd finished eating, he looked around. "I did some snooping and discovered that the two of you graduated from high school with excellent grades. That means I can get you enrolled at a university here. After listening to you, I would advise that you attend the Sorbonne here in Paris and take the normal general classes to get started. There will be housing available. How does that sound?"

"Fantastic!" her siblings blurted in unison.

When he smiled his slow smile, it reminded Fleurine of Raoul, something she didn't need right now.

"*Très bien*. Then, let's leave now and get you two registered. Classes started two weeks ago, but I have no doubt you can catch up. Later in the day Raoul will meet us at one of our car dealerships and you can each pick out a new car you would like."

At the mention of Raoul, Fleurine's heart turned over. She got to her feet. "Before any more plans are made, we need to tell our mother what's going on and get her approval. Right?" She stared at them.

Marti pulled out his phone. "I'll call her now and put her on speaker phone." Fleurine would never forget the look of elation on her brother's face. There was no stopping him.

Their mother answered and an animated conversation ensued. Jean-Louis took over and explained what had been discussed. "It's up to you, Simone."

"You're giving my children a priceless gift. It sounds like they've made up their minds."

"We have!" Emma affirmed. "Are you okay with it?"

"What mother in her right mind wouldn't be?" She laughed.

"Guess what? We get to pick out new cars today!" This from Marti.

"I know I love my new car, *mes enfants*. Have fun. I'll see you on your first break home. Thank you, Monsieur Causcelle, from the bottom of my heart."

Another burst of excitement came out of both of them. "We'll call you tonight," Emma assured her. "Love you, Maman."

Two hours later, after leaving the student office at the Sorbonne, Jean-Louis drove them to the main Causcelle car dealership in Paris. After he'd parked, Raoul and another man walked toward them while Fleurine got out of the back seat. No matter how hard she tried, she couldn't prevent her pulse from racing when she saw him.

But it was impulsive Emma who dashed toward Raoul. "Marti and I are now enrolled at the Sorbonne because of you and your family. We're overwhelmed with gratitude." In the next instant she raised up to kiss his hard jaw with a familiarity that shocked Fleurine.

Always the gentleman, Raoul patted her shoulder and moved toward the rest of them. "Since you're now matriculated, I'd like you to meet Pierre Amant, the manager, who will help you. He's going to walk around with you, answer any questions and let you do a test drive. When you see something you like, come back over here and we'll talk."

"Let's get started," Fleurine urged them, not wanting to monopolize Raoul or his brother. "We can't afford to waste Monsieur Amant's time."

For the next hour they followed the manager around to inspect the new cars. In the end Marti chose an Alpine and talked Emma into buying one too. She loved the blue. He picked silver.

The manager took them inside the dealership to finish up business and congratulated them for their excellent choices. He told them to come back in the morning. The cars would be serviced, washed and ready to go.

They walked back out to Jean-Louis's car where the two brothers were still talking.

Raoul turned to them. "Tell you what. We'll go back to the *palais* and get ready for a dinner cruise on the Seine."

"You're kidding!" Emma cried.

"You'll love it," Jean-Louis interjected. "I'll call ahead for a reservation on *Le Capitaine Fracasse*. The food and wine are spectacular."

Raoul nodded. "Everyone should take the cruise once because the monuments are illuminated. It's a history lesson that takes you past seventeen sites including La Cathédrale Notre-Dame, my favorite."

"At night *La Tour Eiffel* is also amazing," Jean-Louis added.

Marti nudged Emma. "Are we lucky or what?" But his sister's eyes were focused on Raoul. Emma appeared oblivious to anything else going on around her, sending an unmistakable message to Fleurine.

Her chest tightened, and she hurried to get back in the car before...

Before *what*, Fleurine? She couldn't answer that question. After returning to the *palais*, she rushed inside their suite. Marti followed.

She turned to him. "Where's Emma?"

"Still talking to Raoul about living here instead of a dorm near the university. I'm going to shower and get ready."

By the time Emma came in, Fleurine had showered and put on her dress for the evening. She would have to wait another night to go back to her apartment. "I've been waiting for you."

"It won't take me long to get dressed."

"Marti told me you were talking to Raoul about living here at the *palais* while you attend college."

"Yes. He said it was fine with him."

Fleurine drew in a quick breath. "That may be, but it's really up to Jean-Louis, who runs the *palais*. In any event, I want you and Marti to live with me at my furnished apartment if you end up staying in Paris. My place has a guest bedroom and a sofa that is a pullout bed. You and Marti can live with me for as long as you want."

"But he already loves it here at the *palai*s, and Raoul lives here. He said he'll always be willing to help us."

"Emma, there's something you don't understand. Raoul only stays here when he comes to Paris on occasion. He lives in the chateau on the estate and runs it."

A frown broke out on her face. "Why are you being negative about this?"

Whoa...

She leaned forward. "I guess you didn't understand what I told you at the house. This *palais* has been turned into a hostel for returning vets. It's Jean-Louis

Causcelle's humanitarian project to help returning vets. No women live here."

"But—"

"No *but*s, Emma. Raoul and his brother are doing this favor for our family, but it's only through tomorrow. Once you pick up your cars, it's over. Look at all they have provided. We can't take any more advantage of them. Their family arranged to buy both of you a car. They opened bank accounts for you and are giving us an evening out to remember forever. Tonight has to be the end of it."

Her sister sat down on the end of one of the beds, not happy with their conversation. "Raoul is the most fabulous man I've ever met or known, Fleur. I can't begin to explain how he makes me feel. He's bigger than life and so handsome I can't think when I look at him."

Stifling another moan, Fleurine got up from the chair. "The Causcelle triplets have a reputation for making women feel that way. Just remember they come from a family of remarkable people like their father. Louis Causcelle gave our father the head dairy job all those years ago. They are decent, honorable people. As Maman says, they're in a league all their own. We need to show respect."

Emma walked over to the closet to get her dress. "Maman said Raoul is the only one not married yet."

She struggled not to say anything. "That's right. When he does come to Paris, his evenings out with glamorous women are on the news. It's clear he's a confirmed bachelor."

One eyebrow lifted. "Maybe not for much longer."

Non, non, non.

Fleurine's stomach muscles clenched in response. "Please tell me I didn't hear you say that."

"What's wrong with you, Fleur? You're not my mother."

True. That's what she sounded like to her twenty-four-year-old sister. Fleurine headed for the door. "It's time to go. Marti is waiting for us in the living room."

CHAPTER SEVEN

"Raoul?"

Pascal's voice could be heard through the crowd of diners seated in the big dining room restaurant aboard the Capitaine Fracasse. Raoul stood up and motioned him over to their table. Janelle accompanied him along with an attractive, redheaded woman.

After he hugged his cousin and Janelle, Pascal said, "Raoul, I'd like you to meet one of my father's new assistants at the Sorbonne, Dr. Sylvie Moreau. She's an historian who's an expert in Egyptology."

"My oncle Blaise is a fortunate man," Raoul commented and shook her hand. "May I introduce you to the Dumotte family from La Racineuse. Fleur is the top software engineer at Aire-Tech. Emma and Marti will be attending the Sorbonne starting tomorrow. It will be their first college experience."

"I know what that's like," Sylvie said and smiled with a genuine warmth Raoul could feel. "If you need anything, come to the office of Dr. Causcelle in the history department, and I'll be happy to assist you in any way I can. I know you're going to love it there."

"Thank you," they murmured.

Raoul sat down at the rectangular table next to Dr. Moreau. Pascal and his wife sat on his other side. They faced Jean-Louis and the Dumotte family, and dinner was served.

While his amiable cousin and wife talked to Fleurine and her siblings, Raoul made a monumental effort to drag his attention from the woman who had captured his heart and focus it on the woman they'd thought might be perfect.

She came as a pleasant surprise. Throughout dinner they discussed her teaching schedule and the latest history books his oncle Blaise had written. Raoul found she'd led a fascinating life during her work in Egypt. When the cruise ended, he told her he would get in touch with her the next time he was in Paris.

Two limos were waiting for them when they went ashore. "You've done me a favor, cousin. I'll be calling you soon."

"What do you know." A smiling Pascal gave him a hug. Jean-Louis left with the three of them.

Raoul followed Marti into the limo with the others. They raved about the salmon fillets with spinach mousse and asparagus. When they arrived at the *palais*, Raoul helped them out and went into the foyer with them.

"I'll say good-night to all of you here."

"Won't you come in for a little while?" Emma pleaded with him. "We want to thank you for everything."

"You already have a dozen times. Unfortunately I have to leave for the airport at six in the morning.

But Jean-Louis will be by at seven to drive you to pick up your cars."

"I wish you didn't have to go." She sounded upset. "When will you be back in Paris?"

"Because of my workload, I can't answer that question, Emma. But you and Marti will be in perfect hands with my brother and Guy."

For the first time all evening he turned to Fleurine. She stood there wearing the same black dress she'd worn last evening. He thought she looked a little pale.

"Dennis will keep you and your mother well-informed about your father."

"Thank you for everything you've done for us, Raoul. We'll never forget your kindness." Her tone sounded genuine, but he heard no softness in her.

"This has been something our whole family has wanted to do for you and your family for a long time. Now I'll say good-night and a final *adieu*."

Just leave, Causcelle, and never look back. Don't gaze into my eyes that once upon a time revealed that my heart, body and soul were yours.

He strode down the hall to the elevator and went up to his suite. After getting ready for bed, he made a call to his pilot. The other call to his assistant on the estate kept him busy for another half hour while they discussed some problems needing solving. It helped him from turning inside out over Fleurine.

Knowing he'd sent Simone the picture he'd taken of her children the night before, he climbed under the covers to sleep. Then his cell rang. It was Jean-Louis checking in with him. He tapped to accept the call. "Don't you ever go to bed?"

His brother laughed. "Pascal seems to think you hit it off with his father's assistant tonight. With that red hair, she's one attractive woman, *frérot*."

"She is, but I lied to him so he wouldn't be disappointed until I told him the truth later."

His brother let out a groan. "I knew it! What kind of chemistry is it going to take? You need to move to the other side of the planet and start over."

"Never. With Dumotte headed for prison, home is where I'm staying for good. Think about it. Our father has been alone twenty-nine years. He could never replace our mother. I've been alone ten years and have decided I take after him. Like father, like son. Have a good night. You're the best. I'll call you tomorrow evening."

He hung up and buried his face in the pillow, praying for sleep.

His prayer wasn't answered. He relived that time on the estate when Fleurine had been the love of his life. His body thrashed around as he thought of old man Demotte, the monster who'd created the situation in which Raoul found himself at this very moment. Fleurine had undergone a seismic change, and there wasn't a damn thing he could do about it. What haunted him now was this darkness closing in on him, choking the very life out of him.

During the night, Fleurine was in so much agony over Raoul she couldn't sleep. His final words of goodbye played through her mind and body over and over again. When he'd used the word *adieu*, it felt as if a javelin had sliced her heart into a million pieces. Historically, the word *adieu* meant goodbye forever.

She hadn't used that word when she'd rejected him, but he'd internalized her goodbye that way. Tonight he'd used the word and he'd meant it because it had come from the depth of his being.

Unable to bear the pain of what she'd done and the hurt she'd caused him, she put on a robe and went in the other room not knowing where to turn. By tomorrow night she'd be sleeping at her apartment. That's when she heard quiet sobbing coming from the couch. "Emma?"

Her sister sat up. "Sorry. I didn't mean to waken you."

"You didn't. I couldn't sleep either. Why are you crying?"

"It doesn't matter."

"Of course it does." She sat down across from Emma. "Tell me what's wrong."

"I feel like a fool." Her voice trembled.

"Why?"

"You saw what happened earlier tonight. That woman came on the cruise with Raoul's cousin and wife and sat next to him. I thought I'd have time to really talk to him during dinner. I'd hoped to make some plans with him, but she took over and left me no chance. You heard what he said when he drove us here. He's leaving for La Racineuse in a few hours, and I don't know when I'm going to see him again. I can't stand it."

Neither can I.

"He runs the entire estate, Emma, yet has taken time out to look after our family after our father's arrest. Now he has to get back."

"I know. So I've been thinking about not going to the Sorbonne. I'd rather go home and keep working at the *fromagerie*. That way I'll be able to see him a lot and try to get him interested in me."

With those words, Fleurine got up from the chair, unable to sit still. "You could do that, but do you really want to give up the opportunity of a lifetime?"

"You don't understand, Fleur. I've fallen in love with Raoul. It happened the second I met him. That may sound crazy to you, but I know it's real."

Fleurine's eyes closed tightly as she hugged her arms to her waist. "I believe you. In fact, I once had the exact same experience." The time had come to tell her sister the truth.

"Who was it?" Emma asked. "Why didn't you tell me about your old boyfriend when we were back at the house?"

"Because I wasn't ready to share. My love for this man began when we were in grade school on the estate. He was a year older than I. During recess we'd play together. Every school day I waited for recess like it was Christmas Day."

"How cute."

"He was the cutest boy at school. I dreamed about him every night."

"That sounds serious. I never felt like that about a guy until I was a senior and met Vince while I was walking past the hothouse on my way home from school. He was really cute too. We met there a few times, but someone told our father they'd seen us to-gether talking. He forbade me from being anywhere around Vince since I'd be married soon to a man he'd chosen for me."

Fleurine shivered. "As horrible as that sounds, it's nothing compared to what happened to me."

"Tell me everything."

"My life centered on him. When he wasn't there, my day was ruined. I longed for middle school so we could begin having some classes together. My whole world turned to heaven the day we had a history class. We couldn't sit by each other, but he'd pass me notes. You'll never know how happy it made me.

"Pretty soon he'd be waiting for me on my way home from school. We'd talk by the fence until I had to go."

"Did you ever sneak off with him someplace?"

"Never. I was too afraid of our father. But the worst news came in secondary school when he told me that he had to leave the estate and go to college. I almost died hearing that news. He asked me to meet him at the hay barn where he worked so we could say good-bye."

"How awful he had to go away."

"You'll never know my pain. Anyway, I made him some *mannele* for a farewell gift and rode my bike to the barn. He took me and my bike inside and shut the barn door. It was the first time we'd ever been alone where no one could see us."

Emma sat up straighter. "What happened?"

"He started kissing me, then he proposed."

"He *what*?"

"His plan was to come back to the estate at Christmas. I would have just turned eighteen, and we could run away and get married. He promised to love me forever and take care of me. I'd never known such joy in this life, but it was short-lived."

"Why?"

Fleurine trembled. "Papa found out I was in there and opened the barn door. Worse, he held a rifle and aimed it straight at us."

"Oh, Fleur—"

"He said, 'Get your hands off my daughter or I'll shoot you dead this instant.'"

At that point Emma jumped off the couch and ran over to embrace her. "I can't even imagine how terrifying that must have been for you. I knew our father was crazy, but to threaten you!"

"It was truly horrifying, Emma. He ordered me to get in his truck outside. I started throwing up before he drove me home. I never knew what happened to the guy who'd proposed to me until later because Papa drove me to his sister's house in Switzerland that night. He spread the lie that I'd gotten married. Nothing could have been further from the truth."

"I remember Maman saying you'd gone away to get married. I didn't understand."

"How could you? I was kept prisoner there until Maman's money helped me escape on Christmas Day. She'd sent me a present and a note that said the boy

I'd loved was fine. I was so thankful and took a train to Paris to start a new life where I changed my name legally. That way our father couldn't find me."

Emma stepped away from her. "That was ten years ago. Who was the guy, Fleur? You can't leave me hanging, not after everything you've told me."

Now came the difficult part. "Raoul."

In the dim light, Fleurine watched her sister's face crumble. Emma paced the floor for a minute, then whirled around. "The Raoul Causcelle we were with tonight?" Her cry resounded in the living room. "*He* asked you to marry him? Why in heaven's name didn't you tell me the second I told you how I felt about him?"

She took a deep breath. "Because it was past history. We hadn't seen each other in ten years, and our lives have gone in different directions. We're strangers to each other at this point."

Emma shook her head and stared at her. "I don't believe a love like that just disappears. It's probably the reason why he has never married *and* the reason he has been so good to our family. I couldn't understand why such an extraordinary, out-of-this-world man would do what he's done for us. Now it's making sense."

"Emma—"

"He's still in love with you, isn't he? Come on. Be honest."

Fleurine looked away. "After we accidentally met here in Paris and he found out I'd never married, he wanted to get back together. I told him it wasn't possible because we weren't the same people anymore. He had his life, and I had mine."

Her sister shook her head. "You mean you'd rather be in Paris working as a software engineer than be married to him? Are you insane?" Her voice rang out again. "I'd give anything on earth to meet such a fantastic man. I just wish I'd known about the two of you before I threw myself at him. I've made a fool of myself."

"No, you haven't, Emma. Don't ever think that. It's my fault." Fleurine knew she was hurting. "I should have said something back at the house before we flew here with him. But Maman told me to say nothing until the situation with our father had been resolved. My hands were tied."

"Well, there are no secrets now. I want to know how you saw him again here in Paris."

"Let's sit down, and I'll tell you everything."

For the next half hour, she explained the circumstances. When she'd finished, Marti suddenly appeared out of the woodwork.

He smiled. "At last I understand what's been going on since that detective drove us home from the *fromagerie*. Everyone working there has speculated about Raoul's single status. To think *you're* the woman Raoul loves! That's the coolest thing I ever heard. He's the best!"

"I found that out the day I met him years ago."

"No wonder he's remained single all these years, because you're the best too. So, what's stopping you? All that malarkey about being strangers is a crock.

You fell in love as kids. That kind of love *never* goes away."

"Oh, Marti!" She hugged him hard. "My cruel rejection hurt him. He'll never forgive me."

"Want to bet? He didn't give us those cars and pay for four years of university for nothing!"

Fleurine moaned. "Our father was a monster, and Raoul and his family are the kindest people I've ever known to want to help us. But I don't want him to feel he owes us anything more."

Marti frowned. "Haven't you been listening? This isn't about us. He's head over heels in love with *you*. But if you're too stubborn to see it, then you don't deserve him."

"You don't know everything. Maman was right when she told me that Raoul and I come from two different worlds."

"That's a ridiculous cliché, and you know it. If it's true, how come he proposed to you at eighteen? He wasn't blind to our world back then and knew exactly what he wanted when he pursued you."

"He's right," Emma chimed in. "Listen to our brother."

Marti moved closer. "The man asked you to meet him in secret while our father was still terrorizing everyone. Now it's a decade later. He's going to prison because of Raoul, who still wants you and lives on the estate. Why are you holding back on this?"

She got up from the couch. "I'm afraid I've hurt him too deeply."

"Then, there's only one way to find out. Go to him."

"Let's not talk about Raoul. Right now, I'm concerned about you guys. What do you say we go to bed for a few more hours? Tomorrow I'll take a taxi to my apartment and come back for you in my car by seven.

"We'll drive to the dealership so you can pick up your new cars. Then you can follow me to my apartment and have a look for yourself before you go to class. If you like it, then I'd love you to stay with me. Otherwise, I presume you'll decide on student housing, because you can't stay here. Try to get a little sleep now. I love you both so much. Emma, I hope you know I never meant to hurt you by withholding information."

"I get it, and I'll get over it because I love you too. Don't worry. It's not too late where Raoul is concerned, but don't wait too long."

"Emma's right," her brother said before going to his bedroom.

Sleep eluded Fleurine completely. The conversation had forced her to confront her feelings for Raoul. Were her brother and sister right? Did she still have a chance with Raoul? Or was her mother's advice true, and Fleur was right to keep Raoul at arm's length because it could never be? Those questions tortured her.

Early in the morning, she packed and called for a taxi. At six fifteen she went out in front. There was no sign of Raoul or his car, intensifying her pain. She left for her apartment. After grabbing a cola from the fridge, she got in her car and headed back to the *palais* to pick up her siblings and their belongings.

Within another hour they'd gone by the dealership

to get their new cars and followed her to the apartment. They made the decision to stay with her for the time being, then they left for the university.

After they drove off, Fleurine lay down on the bed and phoned her mother.

"Maman, did you get the job at the *boulangerie*?"

"I did, and I'm working as we speak."

"That's the greatest news I could have. I'm so proud of you."

"It's a miracle. Do you know Raoul sent me a picture of all of you going to the Tour Eiffel for dinner? Talk about a happy family. He's one incredible man."

"He's the reason I'm calling you. Maman, something has happened you need to know about before you hear it from the kids. Can you talk?"

"I'm alone right now. Go ahead."

"They've gone to the university in their cars, but they'll be back at my apartment later. They're planning to stay with me for a while anyway."

"Wonderful! Now, tell me what is worrying you?"

In the next breath Fleurine told her about the situation with Emma and her crush on Raoul. When she'd finished, her mother chuckled.

"That poor thing, but she's only been under his influence two days. She still has time to get over it because she loves you. As for Raoul, he has that effect on every woman living. But you and he imprinted on each other in childhood. It's the reason he's never found another woman he could love."

Fleurine trembled. "That's the thing, Maman. I ended it with him in Ischia after he asked me to marry him again. I told him I couldn't because I loved my life as a software engineer and planned to go to the top. By telling him that, I hurt him so terribly he'll never be able to forgive me or let me in his life again."

After a long pause Simone said, "You told him that because of what I wrote to you in my letter ten years ago. I knew you were hurting, and I didn't want you to die of love for him. So I told you to make a success of your life and not depend on a man.

"Surely you know why I said what I did. But that man adores you to the point he's turned himself inside out for you and our family. If you'll go to him and explain the real reason you turned him down, he'll fall for you all over again."

Fleurine couldn't hold back to her tears. "Marti told me the same thing last night."

"I raised a brilliant son."

"I'm afraid it's too late."

"Nonsense. Not everyone in this life gets a second chance. If I could give you a mother's wisdom one more time, I'd tell you to come home to La Racineuse and make your life here where your love ignited. Like his brothers, Raoul's heart is here on the estate. He's never going to leave. If he sees you back and settled, he'll know you can't live without him either. That'll be the proof he needs to know you love him more than life itself."

With pounding heart, she sat up on the bed. "If I thought that were true… I'd have to resign from Aire-Tech."

"Then, what are you waiting for, *ma fille*?"

She was way ahead of her mother. "I'm so glad you could talk to me. Thank you for everything. Your advice saved me once. I have faith it will save me again if my love for Raoul is meant to be. Have I told you how thrilled I am about your new career? I'll call you later when I know my plans. I hope you don't mind my moving back in with you."

"It's your home too and always will be."

After getting off the phone, she freshened up and left in her car for Aire-Tech. No doubt her boss wondered what was going on with her. When she entered the building, she went straight to Philippe's office and peeked inside.

He smiled. "Laure! At last!"

"I know I've been gone longer than you'd anticipated, but so much has happened I hardly know where to start."

"Sit down, and let's talk."

She sat opposite him. "I have to tell you that no one has ever had a better, kinder, more understanding employer than you. I'll never be able to thank you enough for hiring me and giving me all the opportunities I've enjoyed over these past five years."

His smiled faded. "Why do I get the feeling you're about to quit on me?"

"I have to! In order to be with the man I love heart and soul, I have to move back east where I was born. It's where he was born too and works and lives. If I want to spend the rest of my life with him, I can't stay in Paris. But please know I won't leave until you've found someone else."

"It will be difficult, if not impossible, to replace you."

"You know that's not true, but I love hearing you say it. I'm back right now and am ready to go to work until you've found the right person."

He sat forward. "From the beginning I've wondered why you weren't snapped up long ago. Now that I can feel your urgency and excitement, far be it from me to stand in the way of your happiness. If you want to clear out your office, you're welcome to leave as soon as tomorrow or the next day. I can tell you're in a hurry. He's a very lucky man."

Her eyes smarted. "Thank you, Philippe. You're the best, and I'll never forget you." She wrote out her address on the estate and handed it to him.

Fleurine left and went upstairs to her office to phone her landlords. She explained she had to leave Paris. However, her brother and sister were both attending the Sorbonne and would like to stay in her apartment. Fleurine offered to pay more rent for the two of them.

Her landlords sounded disappointed she was leaving, but they were delighted to know her family would like to rent from them. With that decided, she gathered up her things and left the building. Thank goodness Paul had been working outside the office and hadn't seen her.

Relieved, she drove back to her apartment and started to pack. After so many years, she was finally going home where she'd always yearned to be. Her heart leaped when she thought of seeing Raoul again in such familiar surroundings. She clung to her mother's last comment.

If he sees you back and settled, he'll know you can't live without him either.

CHAPTER EIGHT

RAOUL HAD BEEN back on the estate more than two weeks, knee-deep in work. But no amount of business prevented thoughts of Fleurine from torturing him. How long would he remain in this hell which was becoming more unendurable by the second? While he'd been analyzing figures from the livestock report, Damond came into his office late one afternoon and put a small white bakery box on the desk.

He eyed his assistant. "What's this?"

"Before l left town, I decided to pick up a treat for us." He opened it and pulled out a *mannele* with chocolate bits on top and ate one. "Have you ever had one of these? They've just started making them, and I could eat a dozen of them in one go."

The sight of his favorite bread brought so much pain Raoul squeezed his eyes together for a moment. He pushed himself away from the desk and stood up so he could breathe. "Where did you buy them?"

"At Beauchamps. It's the only *boulangerie* in La Racineuse I like."

Raoul wheeled around. "Who waited on you?"

"Maureen, the owner. Who else? What's wrong? You look like you've seen a ghost."

Maybe he *was* losing his mind. "I've got to go, but I'll be back soon to eat the one you brought me. Thanks, Damond."

He raced out of his office to his truck and headed for town at top speed. Raoul had bought pastry from Beauchamps for years, but he'd never known them to make *mannele* bread, let alone with chocolate bits. Only one person in the world had ever produced one like that.

When he rolled up in front a few minutes later and got out, he saw the Closed sign in the window. Muttering a few choice epithets, he walked back to the truck and climbed in. After rubbing his eyes, he turned on the engine and started for the estate.

Before he went home for dinner, he returned to his office, deciding to eat the treat Damond had bought him. He reasoned it couldn't possibly taste like Fleurine's and he'd be able to put this earthshaking incident to rest.

His assistant had gone home, leaving Raoul alone. He walked over to his desk and opened the box.

Here goes.

He reached inside.

One taste, and he was instantly transported back in time to the hay barn when he'd devoured Fleurine's parting gift. He swallowed it in two bites, wanting more. There could be no mistake. It meant that somehow the bakery had acquired a recipe like Simone's, the one Fleurine had learned from her mother.

Before he left for home, Raoul phoned Simone. He needed answers but reached her voice mail. He left a message that he needed to talk to her and asked her to call him back.

Once at the chateau he realized he had no appetite and went straight up to his suite. Raoul kept waiting for his phone to ring. It rang half a dozen times, all right, but nothing came from Simone. He finally climbed into bed. To his chagrin, restlessness kept him from getting a good sleep, and he awakened early. He planned to drive to the *boulangerie* before he showed up at his office.

"Raoul Causcelle!" a voice called to him as he entered twenty minutes later. "I haven't seen you in here for quite a while. What brings you around?"

He smiled at the owner. "*Bonjour*, Maureen. Last evening my assistant brought me some of your goodies. They were so delicious I've come back for more."

"That's good to hear. What would you like?"

"Your *mannele*. It has to be a new product you've introduced, and that bread happens to be one of my favorites."

"After all the years you've come in the bakery, I didn't realize you had a preference for it. You should have said something long before now. You'll be happy to hear my new pastry chef includes them in her repertoire."

"Anyone I know?"

"Simone Dumotte."

Simone? So he hadn't imagined it.

"When did you hire her?"

"About two weeks ago. It was after her husband's arrest. She's an outstanding pastry maker, and I was lucky to get her before she found work somewhere else. You remember Horace. He had to retire."

Raoul nodded. "Do you have any more *mannele* right now?"

"Sorry. They sold out so fast it was amazing. You're not the only one with a taste for it. Come by before we close this evening, and I'll have some boxed for you. How many do you want?"

"Save me a dozen." He pulled a bill out of his wallet and put it on the counter. "Thank you."

"*Bien sûr.* I'm glad you came by. It's nice to see you again. Have a great day."

"You too."

Raoul left and headed off for work. He couldn't get over Simone. That woman was something else. Already she'd become pastry chef of the best *boulangerie* in La Racineuse. She possessed a drive, the same drive she'd passed on to her daughter. After escaping to France from Switzerland, Fleurine had earned her living making bread and pastry so she could go to college. After doing a lot of research on what kind of career she wanted, she'd aspired to become a talented software engineer.

Untethered from Dumotte's leash, both she and her mother had been ready to conquer new worlds. Naturally he was thrilled Simone had refused to be a victim, but this new job had happened so fast! Evidently she'd wanted to be a pastry chef for years. All it took was getting rid of Garber to realize her dream.

Raoul had never seen that side in either of them. Except when he really thought about it, that wasn't true. Simone had helped Fleurine escape from her desperate situation years ago. In truth she'd methodically thought things out months before Christmas so Fleurine could get away, be safe and excel in a career she treasured more than anything else.

More than being with me.

Raoul's gut twisted. The Dumotte women were unstoppable. His head had been in the clouds where Fleurine was concerned.

At quarter after four that afternoon he left work for the *boulangerie* wanting to pick up the pastry his mouth watered for. But before driving away with it, he got in his truck and drove around the back. With the Renault still there, he waited in the cab for Simone to emerge from the rear exit.

As soon as she appeared, he got out and walked toward her. "Simone?"

"Oh, Raoul—*bonsoir!* I was planning to call you tonight. Last evening, I was out playing dominoes with my friends, and we all agreed to turn off our phones. Forgive me for not getting back to you sooner."

Simone already had a *coterie* of friends to enjoy. The knowledge warmed his heart.

"Don't think about that. I'm just glad I caught up to you. Maureen told me you'd been hired. Fleur always claimed you were the greatest cook on earth. Now you're the head pastry chef at Beauchamps. I'm proud of you."

"Thank you. I'm very happy. How are things for you?"

The woman had no idea the agony he was in. "I'm doing fine. What's new from Emma and Marti?"

"Lots of moans and groans while they catch up on several weeks of missed work. It's music to my ears, of course. Thanks to you and your family's incredible generosity, they're finally able to get the kind of education I've always wanted them to have. I swear I'll never be able to repay you, but I'm going to try."

He shook his head. "We've been all through this before, Simone. It's your goodness and sacrifice that kept everyone safe all these years. Our family can never repay you enough. No amount of money could equal your courage. You have maintained a loving, stable home that kept Garber doing his job at the dairy until he was caught.

"Speaking of Garber, I just learned today that his sentencing will be next week. The attorneys working with me have urged the judge to bring it forward as soon as possible and get it over with. You won't be required to attend unless you want to."

"I couldn't, Raoul. I never want to see that man again."

"I understand completely."

A shudder racked her body. "He came close to murdering me when I was sixteen. Knowing this is about to end is the best news possible."

Raoul reached out and drew her into his arms. "Your nightmare is over." He could wish that his own would end. "Everyone on the estate is feeling the relief. Remember that if you need or want anything, all you have to do is call me. I'll always be here for you."

She kissed his cheek. "Bless you, Raoul."

After he helped her into her car, he started for home. At least the air was cooler now that October had come. He could be grateful for that much respite, even if he wondered how much longer he could endure this life. It angered him that thoughts of Fleurine still held him captive. What in the devil was wrong with him?

A week ago, Fleurine had driven to La Racineuse from Paris and had settled in with her mom. She felt good about leaving Emma and Marti. They'd met the landlord couple and seemed perfectly happy living in Fleurine's apartment while they went to the university.

One uncomfortable moment happened when Fleurine went back to Aire-Tech to get the last few personal items from her office. Paul had learned she was leaving and wanted to know why. She told him she missed home but thanked him for his friendship and wished him well. He didn't like her response and followed her out to her Peugeot in back. Poor Paul. He needed help. Hopefully the new female software engineer Philippe hired would fall for him.

"Fleur?"

Her mom had come home.

"I'm in the kitchen fixing dinner."

"Something smells good."

She smiled. "I hope you like chicken stir-fry. It's Deline's recipe. I used to make it a lot in Paris." She would miss her friend.

Her mother walked in. "I'm sure I'll love it, but first I've got fantastic news for you. Maureen said she'd be happy to hire you as a favor to me in order to help me. The job starts tomorrow."

Fleurine ran over and hugged her. "She must think the world of you."

"Since I was hired, my specialty breads have been selling out. That's what did the trick."

"I'm not the least bit surprised."

"Guess what's the best seller?"

"The cinnamon *stollen*?"

"You're close. It's the *mannele*."

"Raoul's favorite," she whispered.

"That's right. And I found out his assistant on the estate bought some yesterday."

Fleurine pressed her hands to her heart. "If Raoul happens to notice, he might co—"

"He already did, *ma fille*. Earlier this evening I discovered Raoul out in back of the *boulangerie* waiting for me in his truck."

A gasp escaped Fleurine's lips.

"He said he wanted to know why I hadn't returned his phone call because he had news about Garber. I lied and said I'd been out playing dominoes with my friends and turned off my phone."

"Uh-oh."

"Don't worry. He didn't mind, and he gave me the best news I could have heard. Your father will be facing the judge next week instead of months from now. That's all because of Raoul and his family's influence. It won't be long before he begins his prison sentence."

"That's a miracle."

"It is." Her mother wiped her eyes. "But another one is about to happen too."

"What do you mean?"

"He recognized my recipe for *mannele*. The next time he comes to get more because he can't resist, he'll find out you're working there too. Anything can happen after that."

Fleurine took a shaky breath. "Still, you don't know the damage I've done to him."

"I think I do. He asked about Marti and Emma but didn't mention you while we talked. That was the surest sign he's still fighting to get over you. I know it's not too late. You came home in time to fix this situation."

"I don't have your faith, Maman."

She put her hands on her hips. "The fact that you're home, working in the *boulangerie*, of all places, instead of solving software problems in Paris will once again upend his universe. This time with the right results. Mark my words."

"I'm going to pray for that."

"We both will. Now, I'm hungry. Let's eat."

Mid-October brought Raoul and his brothers to the courtroom of the Ministry of Justice for criminal proceedings in Paris. The day they'd all been waiting years for had arrived. Fleurine's father would be sentenced for crimes committed against the monks of the Church, the property, his family and Raoul.

The judge read each charge. After he'd finished, he ordered the defendant to stand. "It's the finding of this court that Garber Dumotte will receive consecutive life sentences and be remanded to La Santé Prison in Paris, without the possibility of parole."

At that pronouncement, the three brothers hugged each other before they embraced Claude Giraud and George Delong, the two men who'd helped put Garber away.

Raoul watched old man Dumotte being led out of the courtroom in ankle chains and handcuffs. As wretched a creature as he was, he had to remember that Garber happened to be Fleurine's father.

When the side door closed behind Garber, Raoul felt it as if a sonic boom had pronounced the end of an era. Now a new one was beginning, but he didn't know what that looked like. Today they would fly home and let their father know the outcome. Beyond that, all Raoul could do was take it one day at a time.

They took a limo to the airport and left for home. By evening their father and the whole family had gathered around the dining room table to hear what had gone on in court. After Raoul had given an account, he turned the conversation over to his father, who had the last word before dinner was served.

"I'm grateful this day has come, and I only have one thing to say. We reap what we sow. Let us all try to sow the best of ourselves."

"Amen," everyone murmured, and they started eating.

Corinne eyed Raoul. "Nic said that none of the Dumotte family were in court for the sentencing today, not even Fleur who'd helped give earlier testimony against her father."

Raoul had to clear his throat. "That's right. Simone told me last week that it would be too painful for all of them."

"I can't even imagine it," Yvette interjected. "Come to think of it, my friend Marie said she saw Fleur at the Beauchamps *boulangerie* in La Racineuse yesterday. I thought she lived and worked in Paris."

Raoul almost dropped his cup of coffee. He wished to heaven his sisters would get off the subject of Fleurine, but it was impossible. "She does. Marie had to be mistaken."

"No," she argued. "Marie said she heard someone call her name, but after ten years she hardly recognized her because she's absolutely gorgeous."

Anne, another Causcelle sister, nodded. "Fleur and her sister are lovely girls."

His brothers flashed Raoul private messages of commiseration. The news that Fleurine was on the estate had taken the three of them by surprise, and they knew he was in pain. Certainly, he hadn't had any idea she'd come home.

No doubt she'd wanted to keep her mother company during the sentencing. It made sense that she'd visit her at work. Raoul reasoned that in a day or two Fleurine would be back in Paris. Once she'd left, he'd check on Simone.

No longer able to tolerate sitting there with Fleurine the subject of conversation, he got up from the table. "If you'll all excuse me, I'm afraid I have a backlog of work to deal with before bed."

Once outside the chateau, he got in his car and

found himself headed for the office. But halfway there, he made a left turn toward the Dumotte house. Fleurine had probably flown here or taken the train. He was crazy to go by there when he wouldn't be able to see her.

Nor did he want to.

Her rejection would haunt him to the grave. Soon he came to the road in question and slowed down.

What in the hell was he doing?

Had he gone out of his mind?

In the next breath he started to turn his car around. That's when he spotted a green Peugeot parked behind Simone's Renault. He slammed on his brakes.

Fleurine had driven here?

Why would she do that?

With his torment off the charts, he took off for his office. It was the only place where he could have a meltdown in private and attempt to catch up on a ton of work. He'd put everything on hold because of Fleurine, but he couldn't allow himself to flounder any longer.

While on the jet flying home, he and Nic had volunteered to help on the construction of the house Jean-Louis and Françoise were building on the property. Between that project and his estate work, it would keep him busy and save his life for a while longer. Beyond that he didn't dare speculate.

A week later Raoul had to go to town on an errand and decided to drop by the *boulangerie* to see Simone. to his frustration, Maureen wasn't there, and a salesclerk he didn't recognize told him it was Simone's day off. Not about to be put off, he would run by her house on the way home.

"May I help you?"

"Please. I'd like a dozen *mannele*."

"They disappear as fast as they're made. I'll see if there are any more in back."

While he checked his phone messages, the woman returned to the counter. He lifted his head and found himself staring into a pair of violet eyes he could never get enough of. His heart thundered. "*Fleurine!* What are you still doing in town? Why are you wearing that apron?"

Her expression fell, as if she were upset by what he'd said. "You *knew* I've been here?"

"Yes." He fought a losing battle with his emotions. "At dinner last week my sister told me her friend saw you in here. How's your mother?"

She bit her lower lip, drawing his attention to her exquisite features and that mouth he craved waking or sleeping. "Doing better than I could have imagined."

He shifted his weight. "Are you all right now that your father has gone to prison?"

"Like Maman, I've never been happier, knowing he can never hurt any of us again."

This was agony. "Our family will be glad to know how you feel."

"But not *you*?" She sounded devastated, and her unexpected question felt like a stab.

"What do you mean?"

A look of sadness crossed over her face. "You've known I've been here for over a week, but you never came in."

He couldn't figure her out. "What's going on with you, Fleurine? We said our goodbyes in Ischia. I made a promise. Why would I come near you at this point?"

She avoided his gaze. "You wouldn't, and of course you'd have every reason not to. But I'll admit I've been praying every day that you'd walk in here. You see, I've been hired as Maman's assistant pastry chef."

Her admission came at him like a bolt of lightning. "You mean she asked you to help her?"

"No. I resigned from Aire-Tech and have moved home for good."

He ran trembling hands through his hair, trying to assimilate what she'd just said. "That means you've come because your mother is ill."

"No, Raoul," she countered. "This is a permanent move on my part for my own reasons."

Beyond bewildered, he stared hard at her. "Then, it's *you* who is ill. Otherwise you wouldn't be here. Do you have cancer or something else life-threatening and need her to care for you? All you have to do is let our family know and we'll cover the cost."

Tears filled those glorious eyes. "Only you would say that, because you're the most generous man in existence. I don't have cancer. It's something much more serious. Worse, there's just one treatment to cure what's wrong."

His body grew cold. "What are you saying?" He was ready to explode in pain.

"Look… I'm still working and can't talk about it right now. In fact, I shouldn't have said anything at all. I'm so sorry I did." She started to turn away.

"Oh, no, you don't, Fleurine!"

She stopped in her tracks and looked back at him.

"You can't drop a bomb like that and leave me to disintegrate."

Tears filled her eyes. "That's the last thing I meant to do."

There it was…that old sweetness. But he refused to be taken in again.

"I want an explanation, Fleurine. I'll go around the back of the *boulangerie* so you can let me in."

"Don't do that, please," she begged. Wringing her hands she said, "Since the *mannele* won't be ready until later today, I promise to bring it to you when I'm off work. Tell me where, and I'll be there."

His hands formed fists. "How do I know you'll keep your promise?"

"I—I guess you don't," she said uncertainly. "But if you knew the truth, you'd understand that my whole life depends on talking to you about what's wrong."

"*Now* what are you saying?" He couldn't take any more.

"Shh! People can hear us. You have to leave," she whispered. "I swear I'll meet you wherever you say."

He didn't have to think. "Come to my office at seven. We'll be alone." His office had turned into his cave.

"I'll be there. Honestly, I will." She kept swallowing hard. "Thank you."

Fleurine hurried back to the kitchen, so excited she felt sick because she'd be seeing Raoul at the end of the day. But on the heels of her euphoria came fear because she'd done such a thorough job of pushing him away. How would he ever be willing to listen to her and understand why she'd said those cruel things to him?

She'd treated Raoul like a child who'd played with a favorite toy until she didn't want it anymore and carelessly threw it away. Fleurine was mortified by what she'd done. The only reason he'd agreed to meet with her after work was because he believed she was on the verge of dying.

Fleurine worked hard for the rest of the day, struggling not to break down. Tonight would be her one and only chance to lay her heart at his feet. But the question remained. Could she truly expect him to want her after the way she'd thrown his proposal back in his face? Her father hadn't been the only monster living in the Dumotte home.

When the time came for her to leave work, she flew out the back door with a box of *mannele* and drove straight home.

"Maman?"

"I'm in the bedroom!"

With tears gushing, she rushed in and flew into her mother's arms. "Raoul came in to the *boulangerie* and found out I worked there. I'd hoped he would realize why I'd come home and be convinced I'd given up everything for love of him." She shook her head. "Nothing could have been further from the truth."

"Why do you say that?"

"When he learned I gave up my job and had been here over a week without telling him, he jumped to the conclusion I'd come home because *you* were terminally ill."

"What?"

"Of course I told him no. That's when he assumed that *I'm* the one battling an incurable disease and came home so you could take care of me! But here's the amazing part." More tears flowed. "Even though I know he'll never take me back, he still offered to pay the medical costs."

"That Raoul is a saint, but what he said still doesn't sound like a man who has lost all hope."

"His innate goodness has nothing to do with love. He came to earth that way."

"I agree."

"Maman, I was dying to tell him everything right then, but I couldn't talk with customers around. He assumed I'd been talking about an illness, and he wouldn't leave. I could tell he didn't believe me, and I begged him to go. I promised to meet him later and explain. When he still hesitated, I told him that my whole life literally depended on being able to talk to him about my condition, but it had to be in private."

"That poor man must be twisted in knots."

"No, Maman. I'm the one in that state. He finally told me to come to his office at seven, but I can't imagine him wanting to start over with me again after what I've done."

Her mother patted her arm. "In that case there's only one thing to do. Since you started this by coming home from Paris in the first place, you have to be the one to end it. No matter your fear of the outcome,

I suggest you honor your promise to him this evening and bare your soul. You owe him that much."

"I owe him everything," she said, her voice shaking.

"He needs to hear that. It's the only way either of you is going to get on with your lives." Her mother glanced at her watch. "You'd better hurry if you're supposed to be there by seven."

Fleurine dashed into the bathroom to shower and wash her hair. Later, as she stood in front of the mirror to style it, she remembered that afternoon years ago when she'd gone to the barn to meet Raoul. She'd wanted to look beautiful for him but had been forced to wear one of those awful dresses and leave her hair long. No makeup, no perfume.

This evening she would pull out all the stops, hoping to erase his Cinderella image of her. At five to seven she was ready to leave wearing a new knee-length sky-blue dress ruched at the waist with three-quarter sleeves. Her heart raced so hard she felt sick.

She found her mother in the kitchen and gave her a kiss. "Pray for me, Maman."

"I've never stopped. Neither should you."

CHAPTER NINE

SEVEN MINUTES AFTER SEVEN. Fleurine wasn't coming.

Unable to take anymore, Raoul shot up from his desk. Who knew what was wrong with her. He couldn't handle it right now. The only thing to do was leave La Racineuse and move to the other side of the planet as Jean-Louis had suggested.

He flew out the main door and headed for his truck parked in front. But he'd only made it halfway when a blue Renault pulled up behind it. He came to a stop.

Simone? Something serious must have happened. His heart almost failed him.

As the driver's door opened, a shapely female vision in soft blue emerged. In the twilight he realized it was Fleurine! *Grâce à Dieu.* She hurried toward him, and he caught the flowery fragrance of her perfume in the night breeze.

"Thank you for still being here. I know I'm late. Please don't leave." Her heavenly eyes implored him. "I was afraid you'd think I wasn't coming." She looked in perfect, amazing health but sounded out of breath. "My car wouldn't start so I had to bring my mother's, the one you gave her."

He rubbed the back of his neck. "It's growing cooler, and you're not wearing a coat."

"I didn't want one because I was in too big a hurry to talk to you."

Raoul made an instant decision. "I'd rather not go back in the office in case Damond decides to do some work. Let's drive to the chateau where we'll both be more comfortable."

A look of alarm broke out on her gorgeous face. "The chateau?"

"Yes. My suite is like an apartment. Since you have something extremely serious to confide in me, we won't be disturbed there by anyone. We'll enter through a side entrance so no member of the family will be aware."

"I appreciate that."

"Follow me." He walked to his truck and started the engine while she got back in her mother's car. Through the rearview mirror he watched as they headed for his home. For years he'd longed for the day when she'd step inside the place where he'd always lived. He never imagined it would happen at a time when she would tell him the one thing that was worse than her rejection of him. Never had he needed strength of the kind necessary to get through this next hour.

He drove around the side and parked by the side door. This entrance gave him easy access to his suite. He walked over and opened it as Fleurine pulled up next to him. After getting out, she followed him inside and up the stairs to the second floor.

Raoul walked down the hall and opened his suite

door. "After you, Fleurine." She entered the foyer but seemed hesitant to go farther. "Why don't you go on through and sit on the couch."

"Thank you."

Her behavior confused him. She seemed wary rather than assertive, more like the old Fleurine. Her illness must be changing her in ways he was still trying to understand.

"Can I get you a drink?" he asked as she sat on one end of the sofa. "Do you need anything?"

She shook her head and looked at him with pleading eyes. "I don't need anything except the chance for a final talk with you."

Final. He groaned. At this point he sank down on a chair across from her and leaned forward with his hands on his knees. "After what you told me at the *boulangerie*, I haven't thought about anything else. Why don't you just say it and get it over with. How much longer do you have to live?"

She jumped up and walked around for a moment before standing in front of him. "Raoul—" she spread her arms as if in exasperation "—I'm not dying! I tried to explain earlier at the *boulangerie*, but there were too many people around."

"But you said—"

"I said that my only cure would be to talk to you, but it didn't mean it had anything to do with the physical."

Raoul's hands slid to his face before he lifted his head to stare at her. "So you're saying that you're *not* dying?"

"Yes, I am, but it's because… I'm dying of love for *you*!"

Shocked and confused, he got to his feet, convinced he was having an hallucination like before. "Fleurine—"

"Let me finish. I gave up my job and have moved back here for good because I've loved you from childhood, and that has never changed. It's true, my darling. I love you more than life itself, but I know I've killed every ounce of feeling you've ever had for me because of my cruelty. Everything I said to you in Paris and Ischia was a complete lie!"

Reeling, he took several breaths. "But why?"

"My reason stems from the words my mother wrote to me in that letter inside my winter coat ten years ago. Maman put the fear of my father into me to keep us both safe. She knew he'd threatened to kill us, and she didn't want me to go back to you and endanger us.

"Being the wonderful mother she was, she understood I might die over losing you, so she urged me to escape and become successful through work. She counseled me to live a happy, fulfilled life without a man. That meant you. I determined to follow her counsel and tried not to look back. But then you and I met accidentally at Aire-Tech, and from that moment on, my life has been pure torture."

"*Torture* is the word, all right," he ground out.

"You'll never know how much I've hated myself for pushing you away, convinced I was doing the right thing. But then everything got worse when I realized Emma was falling in love with you."

He frowned. "Emma?"

"I couldn't let that go on another second and sat her down to tell her you were and are the great and only love of my life. She never knew about us, and when I watched her fall for you the moment she met you, I couldn't handle it. You were so wonderful to her, my jealousy turned me inside out."

"But you *couldn't* have been jealous. She's your sister!"

"You can't comprehend how much I've suffered since seeing you again. I've been halfway out of mind and not thinking clearly. That day when you came in my office and we saw each other for the first time in ten years, I wanted to fly into your arms and hold onto you for dear life. I wanted to tell you I'd marry you that very instant. I still want to be your wife and love you until the day I die and beyond, Raoul. I want children with you. Everything! That's what I came here to tell you."

No one had ever told Raoul you could die of a heart attack from too much joy.

"I know you despise me for everything I've said and done, Raoul, so I'll leave. You have my promise that I'll stay out of your way now that I'm living here and planning to find computer work. Just so you know, I'm not really working at Beauchamps. Maman arranged for that so you would eventually find out I was working there. I prayed the *mannele* would lure you there. I needed to talk to you but was afraid to approach you."

Raoul shook his head again. "I don't believe what I'm hearing."

"I'm sure you don't, and if you tell me you want me to leave La Racineuse and never come back, I'll be on the next plane out. But you deserved to hear the truth from me first. Thank you for giving me this much time."

His adorable Fleurine was back and so damn sweet he was melting on the spot. She started to head for the foyer, but Raoul raced in front of her and put his hands on her upper arms. "You're not going anywhere."

Her head flew back, revealing the stunned expression in those violet eyes that looked at him with pure love.

"We have wedding plans to make, *mon amour.*"

The love and desire licking through those impossibly black eyes consumed her so completely, Fleurine had no words. She slid her arms around his neck, bringing their bodies together. He lowered his dark head and his compelling mouth found hers. This was no experimental kiss like the one in the barn. So great was their need to express their love, they came close to engulfing each other.

She lost track of time as they tried to become one, imprinting on each other, heart, body and soul. No dreams would ever match the reality of being in his strong arms again. "Darling," she moaned in ecstasy, "I love you. I love you so terribly it frightens me."

"You don't begin to know the meaning of fright. When you walked out of my suite at the *palais* declaring there was no us, I died inside."

"So did I, but that will never happen again." Ravenous for him after being deprived all these years, she covered his mouth with her own.

Once again he swept her away with overpowering passion. "How have I existed this long without you?" he cried much later, finally giving her a chance to breathe.

"It's a miracle we're still alive at all," she whispered against his lips.

"That's why we need to be married. I'm calling Father Didier right now. It's not too late." He picked her up like a bride and carried her back to the couch, kissing her with a hunger that matched her own. After sitting down with her ensconced in his lap, he eventually relinquished her mouth long enough to pull out his phone and call the church.

She buried her face in his neck. "How do you have his number?"

"I've talked to him many times about you and your father."

Fleurine nestled closer, kissing his jaw. "I had a long talk with my priest in Paris before I flew here. He knows of my deep heartache over you." She half lay in his arms in a euphoric trance while he made the call. Her heart thrilled to the pure happiness in his voice as he asked the priest to marry him and Fleur Dumotte right away. More jubilant conversation ensued before he hung up and pulled her closer.

"Father Didier said it was long overdue that at least one of the Causcelle triplets took his vows in the cathedral. We will have a ceremonial blessing after a civil marriage. He'll officiate any time we want because our marriage takes priority over everything."

His mouth captured hers and they clung in the kind of rapture she could never have imagined before this moment. Their wedding really was going to happen. He'd be the husband she would love and cherish forever.

"*Mon trésor*," he murmured, covering her face with kisses, "the only thing I want to do is take you in the bedroom and make love to you forever. But I want you to be my wife before I hide you away from the world and keep you to myself. What do you say we go downstairs so Papa can meet you in person? We'll tell him our news, then go to your house and inform your mother she's getting a new son-in-law. If it were up to me, we'd get married first thing in the morning."

"I'd give anything if we could." On fire for him, she kissed him hungrily, never wanting to leave his arms. A few minutes later they let go of each other long enough to stand up.

He kissed her again. "Wait here one second."

She stood there in a daze until he returned and grasped her left hand. "This ring has been sitting on top of my dresser since Ischia."

A cry escaped her throat as he slid a gold ring with a two-karat violet stone onto her ring finger. "Oh, Raoul, it's the most incredible diamond I've ever seen."

"I finally found the one I wanted to give you that comes close to the color of your eyes. It comes from the Argyle Diamond Mine in Australia, which is one of the only sources of violet diamonds in the world."

"I didn't know one like this existed!" She launched

herself in his arms again, unable to contain her love for him.

He cupped her face and kissed her. "We're finally engaged. I will never be separated from you again, my darling, but if you want to pursue your career in tech or be the finest baker in all of France, then you have my support. As long as you are by my side while you do it."

"Oh, darling! I want more than anything else to be your wife and the mother of your children. Beyond that maybe I could find a software-engineer position in La Racineuse or work at the *boulangerie*. All I know is I never want to be separated from you again."

"That's all I needed to know. Now I'm going to phone Luca, my father's health-care nurse. If Papa's still awake, I want him to hear our news."

While she repaired her hair and lipstick, he pulled out his cell phone. Seconds later, he hung up and said, "Let's go." Putting his arm around her shoulders, they left his suite. He walked her down the hallway in the other direction leading to the main staircase. Her eyes took in the magnificent chateau interior. Soon they walked down another hall and entered another suite.

Fleurine saw Luca standing next to Raoul's father in a wheelchair. The older man had dressed in pajamas and a robe. His lively brown eyes darted to the two of them in surprise.

"Papa? Forgive us for coming this late, but my news can't wait."

As they drew closer, he broke out in a broad smile. "Well, well, well. Little Fleur Dumotte, all grown-up.

You were the cutest little girl. It's no wonder my Raoul started following you around."

His words touched her heart. "Monsieur Causcelle, it's a privilege to finally meet you. I'll never be able to thank you enough for all you've done for me and my family."

"*Ma chère fille*, I had no idea what you and your family had been through until recently. I'm thankful all of you have survived and done so well."

Tears filled her eyes. "Everyone is more than fine, all due to your incredible generosity and goodness."

Raoul kept his arm around her shoulders. "Papa, tonight my Fleurine agreed to be my wife. You're the first to know."

His father's eyes watered. "Now my every prayer has been answered. Come here, Fleurine. Let me welcome you to the family." He held out his arms, and they embraced. "Finally my son is going to be happy again."

"We want to be married as soon as we can, Papa."

"Then don't let anything stop you."

"Father Didier will marry us in the cathedral."

"At last, we can all meet there together. Please let me offer the chateau for your wedding reception. The ballroom is large enough to hold all our families and friends."

Raoul hugged him. "That's my wish, *mon père*." He turned to Fleurine and kissed her cheek. "Would you like that, *chérie*?"

"I can't think of another place to hold it. This is your home and legacy. My mother will be overjoyed."

His father clapped his hands. "Joy has finally come back to the estate. I can die a happy man."

"Oh, please—don't say that!" Fleurine cried.

"We expect you around for many years, Papa. Now, if you'll excuse us, we're going to drive to Simone's house."

He eyed Fleurine. "Give her my very best and tell her to call me."

"I will, and thank you again. You've raised the most wonderful son on earth."

Raoul led her out and down another hall to the side door of the chateau. After another kiss to die for, they parted long enough to drive the short distance to her home. Fleurine was so happy she felt like they were floating on clouds.

"Maman?" she called to her when they entered the house.

"I'm coming!" She rushed in the living room from the kitchen. "Oh, Raoul—"

"Simone!" He let go of Fleurine and hugged her mother. "You don't know how long I've wanted to tell you how much I love your daughter. Tonight she agreed to be my wife. We want your blessing."

Tears ran down her cheeks. "You've always had it and should have been married years ago."

He shook his head. "None of that matters now. We're going to enjoy the rest of our lives now as man and wife. And you and Marti and Emma are going to be my family too."

Fleurine couldn't contain all the happiness building inside her. She ran to the two of them and threw her arms around both of them.

Her mother whispered, "He found out you couldn't live without him…"

La cathédrale in La Racineuse,
one week later

At twelve noon, Raoul waited impatiently outside the entrance of the *cathédrale* with his brothers. They were surrounded by the whole Causcelle family while they waited for the limo that would bring Fleurine and her family. Their wedding day was being celebrated not only as a marriage but a day of liberation and healing. A huge crowd of estate workers had assembled outside.

"Settle down, cousin. The limo has rounded the corner."

Grâce à Dieu.

"What would I have done without you all these years, Pascal? No man ever had a better friend."

"Ditto."

Another few seconds and Raoul hurried toward the place where the limo rolled to a stop. A chorus of *aah*s resounded when he opened the rear door and Fleurine stepped out on the cobblestones. In her flowing white wedding gown and long lace veil, she looked like a vision from heaven.

"My love," he whispered and grasped her hand as they made their way to the cathedral entrance. She carried her bridal bouquet of white roses in her other hand. He could hear the music inside as the doors opened. Father Didier, dressed in his ceremonial vestments, greeted them with a beautiful smile. He bade them follow him, and the processional began.

Everyone filed behind to fill the nave for the matrimonial mass. Raoul squeezed Fleurine's hand. She squeezed back harder, delighting him. They'd had a lot to do to prepare for this day. He'd purposely kept busy so he wouldn't kidnap her ahead of time and love her into oblivion. He had trouble believing that this day had finally arrived.

The priest turned and faced them. Emma stepped forward to relieve Fleurine of her bouquet, then he put up his hands. "In the name of the father, son, and holy spirit, grace to all of you and peace from God our father and the Lord Jesus Christ.

"Dearly beloved, you have come together into the house of the church so that your intention to enter into marriage may be strengthened by the Lord with a sacred seal.

"Christ abundantly blesses the love that binds you. Through a special sacrament, he enriches and strengthens those he has already consecrated by holy baptism, that you may be enriched with his blessing. And so, in the presence of the church, I ask you to state your intentions.

"Raoul Causcelle, have you come here to enter into marriage freely and wholeheartedly?"

"I have."

"Fleur Dumotte, have you come here to enter into marriage freely and wholeheartedly?"

"I have." Her voice sounded strong and clear.

"Since it is your intention to enter the covenant of holy matrimony, join your right hands and declare your consent before God and his church."

Raoul reached for hers with eagerness.

The priest sprinkled holy water on their rings before handing them over. "Raoul, repeat after me. Fleur Dumotte, receive this ring as a sign of my love and fidelity. In the name of the father, son, and holy spirit. Then put the ring on her finger."

Never had he wanted to do anything more than claim Fleurine for his own.

"Now Fleur, repeat after me. Raoul Causcelle, receive this ring as a sign of my love and fidelity. In the name of the father, son, and holy spirit."

Fleurine's fingers trembled as she slid home the gold ring she'd bought for him.

The priest smiled. "Now repeat after me. I, Raoul Ronfleur Causcelle, take you Fleur Binoche Dumotte, to be my wife. I promise to be faithful to you in good times and in bad, in sickness and in health, to love you and to honor you all the days of my life."

Turning to her, he repeated the vow that came from his soul.

The priest eyed Fleurine. "Now repeat after me. I, Fleur Binoche Dumotte, take you, Raoul Ronfleur Causcelle, to be my husband. I promise to be faithful to you, in good times and in bad, in sickness and in health, to love you and to honor you all the days of my life."

Fleurine's response thrilled him to the depths of his being.

"May the Lord in his kindness strengthen the consent you have declared before the church. What God has joined, let no one put asunder. May the God of Abraham, Isaac, Jacob, and the God who joined together our first parents in paradise strengthen and bless in Christ the consent you have declared before the church, so that what God joins together, no one may put asunder.

"In the sight of God and these witnesses, I now pronounce you husband and wife! You may now kiss."

Those violet eyes that had ensnared him as a young man gazed at him with so much love he trembled before lowering his mouth. No bride could ever have been more beautiful than Fleurine was to him. His brothers had warned him to be careful in front of a full audience of people. Somehow he managed not to devour her until the mass was over and they'd left the church to walk outside past the cheers of the crowd.

The bells rang out, proclaiming their joy as Raoul helped Fleurine into the rear of the waiting limo. Once they started moving, he pulled her into his arms. "Madame Causcelle… How long I've waited to be able to call you that."

"Not as long as I've waited to hear it, my darling Monsieur Causcelle." Their mouths fused in passion, and she received the husband's kiss she'd been dying for. They didn't come up for air until they reached the chateau fifteen miles away.

The limo parked in front of the entrance. "Beloved," he murmured against her lips, "all we have to do is get through the toasts. Once the helicopter arrives on the grounds, we'll escape to Ischia and blot out the world."

Her heart leaped in response. "You're taking us there?"

"Where else?" Giving her another kiss, he opened the door to help her out of the back seat and escorted her inside with her bouquet.

"Oh, Raoul," she gasped when they reached the ballroom, clinging to him. "Your sisters and mine have transformed this gorgeous room into a fairyland. Look at all the trees and tiny white lights!"

Her gaze took in the many round tables covered with fine écru-colored linen, baskets of white roses and candelabras. The rectangular head table on one side of the room featured two wedding cakes on either end. They were stunning replicas of the Château Causcelle. Her mother had truly outdone herself. She'd put small bride and groom figurines on top of both.

"Look, Raoul! Maman managed to affix a picture of our faces over the faces of the dolls. Can you believe it?"

His smile made her legs go weak. "My mother-in-law is not only an *artiste* she's one incredible woman who gave birth to the most amazing woman on earth. We'll have to save them for our children."

Their children...

He caught Fleurine to him and kissed her unabashedly in front of their guests who had filled the room and were taking their places.

She heard the sound of someone tapping the side of a goblet to get everyone's attention. The room quieted down as Raoul swept her along to the center of the head table. Once they were seated, Pascal stood up looking fabulous.

All the men in the wedding party including Marti, Raoul's father, brothers and brothers-in-law wore black tuxedos with flowers in the lapels. She looked around, but no one could match her new husband who always appeared drop-dead gorgeous no matter what he wore.

"Dear family and friends, my Oncle Louis asked me to greet all of you. We're honored to have Father Didier seated at the table with us on this red-letter day for Raoul and Fleur. He's been a comfort and friend to the Causcelle family and everyone on the estate.

"All of you who want to say a kind word to Fleur or embarrass Raoul will be given the chance later." A roar of laughter went up. "First let me say that Raoul and I became good friends when we were little and our fathers worked together. I never had so much fun in my life as I had with him.

"I never saw a man more in love than he was during his teens. Then he and Fleur became separated. Raoul and I have seen each other through thick and thin. It got pretty thin for him over the last ten years. Then he accidentally saw Fleur again, and a miracle happened that spread light over the whole estate. Fleur returned, and my cousin hasn't stopped grinning ever since." More smiles came from the crowd. "Enjoy this remarkable moment in time. *Bon appétit.*"

The food turned out to be a divine feast, but since

they'd taken their vows Fleurine couldn't have told any-one what she'd eaten. She kept glancing at Raoul in dis-belief that they were actually married. In the midst of her reverie about him, Pascal got to his feet once more.

"Before the cutting of the wedding cakes, Louis would like to make a toast." He handed the micro-phone to Raoul's father who remained in his wheel-chair.

"My wife and I were young like Fleur and Raoul when we fell in love. Fortunately for us, we were able to marry in our late teens and were blessed with six beautiful children. On the night before our triplet boys were born, we talked about the great responsibility and joy ahead of us.

"So much has happened since that moment. Today I'm surrounded by all my children and their spouses and my grandchildren. Of course I'm expecting more." Raoul winked at her. "Can you believe I'm still alive? My cup runneth over. Raoul and Fleur's marriage ful-fills the culmination of every dream.

"I only have one more dream, and that is for all of us one day to be united with my beloved wife, Del-phine…their mother and grandmother. Thank you all for making this the perfect day."

He raised his wineglass. "I propose a toast to Raoul and Fleur. May you cherish every moment of your lives from here on out."

The breeze off the Mediterranean filtered from the up-stairs patio into the bedroom toward morning. Raoul had taken his father's last wish to heart. In the last twelve hours he and Fleurine had become the lovers of Raoul's dreams. But the reality of making love to his adorable wife went beyond any expectations his mind could have conceived. They would never be able to get enough of each other. There was no end to her giving. He couldn't bear the thought of ever being alone again. He needed her like he needed air to breathe.

Ten years of hunger couldn't be satisfied in one divine wedding night. He thanked heaven they had the rest of their lives to show each other what it meant to lie entangled in each other's arms day and night and pour out their love. Her beauty enchanted him inside and out. They'd brought each other intense pleasure over and over again.

He particularly loved the curve of her luscious mouth that drove him crazy whether waking or sleeping as she was now. He kissed her cheeks and hair, the curve of her brows and the tender spot in her throat where a nerve throbbed. She moved closer to him, brushing her hand over his upper arm without realizing it. Her touch, her innate sweetness, overwhelmed him. Unable to hold back, he began kissing her mouth awake.

"Darling," she murmured and started to respond. He pulled her over so she half lay on top of him. Within seconds the whole wonderful ritual began again. The next time he became aware of their surroundings, the sun had come streaming in from the patio.

"Good morning, *mon épouse*."

She opened her violet eyes and gazed at him with

love. "Do you have any idea what you've done to me? How you've changed my whole life? I'm not the same person."

"Yes, you are. You're my precious Fleurine who enslaved me the first time I ever looked at you and heard your gentle laugh. I've never been the same since. You're all I've ever wanted. I'm so in love with you. Help me."

She smiled. "What do you mean?"

"I don't know exactly. I can't explain what I'm feeling."

Fleurine kissed his mouth. "I feel just like you. It's as if my love for you is exploding inside me. The solution is to hold onto each other for dear life."

"You don't have to worry about that," he cried.

They clung to each other. "We had the perfect wedding, Raoul."

"Amen. Even if we missed the first ten years, we're going to have the perfect life forever. We vowed to deal with the good and the bad times because our love will see us through anything."

"It already has. Look where we are now. I'm in your arms where I've always wanted to be. I'm the luckiest woman on the face of the earth. I love you, Raoul Causcelle."

"I love you, Fleurine Causcelle. I'm the happiest man on the planet. Come here to me and never, ever, let me go."

* * * * *

CINDERELLA'S SECRET FLING

MICHELLE DOUGLAS

MILLS & BOON

To Trisha Pender for her enthusiasm, support,
and a shared love of the romance genre.

PROLOGUE

My darling Audrey,
I know this is going to come as a great shock to you,
and I'm hoping you do not blame me too much for not
revealing this to you sooner, but I know how much fam-
ily means to you. And this is not a secret I can take to
the grave. The decision for how to proceed is yours, my
dearest girl—not mine, not your father's and certainly
not your mother's.

My mother? I can almost hear you ask. Yes. She is not
who she claimed to be and I have discovered her true
identity. I'm sorry to tell you she passed away many
years ago, and it was a brief news item reporting her
death that prompted my suspicions and subsequent in-
vestigations.

Rather than being a poor orphan, as she always
claimed, she came from a very old, very powerful and
very wealthy Italian family. And apparently, you have an
Italian grandmother and a plethora of cousins.

Your aunt Beatrice is now in possession of all the as-
sociated documentation, and she has been in contact
with your maternal grandmother's lawyers. Your grand-
mother's name is Marguerite Funaro, and she wishes to
meet you. If you wish to meet her, you can now do so.
The choice is yours.

*Wishing you all joy and every happiness and a life
filled with love and family.*
Your ever-loving Nonna

AUDREY STARED AT the letter in her hand and then up at her
aunt Beatrice. *Aunt* was an honorary title, but Nonna's best
friend had always felt like family. For the past month she'd
been in Lake Como staying with Aunt Beatrice, and yet all this
time she'd had a family she'd never known about? 'This says...'

'Yes.' Beatrice nodded.

'I have...?'

'A family? *Si*, Audrey, it would appear so. Your grandmother wanted me to make contact with them first as she
did not want you getting your hopes up if they did not wish
to recognise you. On the contrary, though, they very much
want to meet you.'

A champagne fizz of excitement bubbled in her chest. And
something deeper. Something that made her catch her breath.

If she was being brutally honest—and she was always brutally honest, at least with herself—she'd not fully regained her
balance since Johanna had died. Losing a twin... It felt as if
she'd lost a part of herself.

She'd been finding her feet again, though, slowly, every step
hard-won. Then her father had made the shocking announcement that he was marrying and relocating to America. She
hadn't even known he'd been seeing someone!

Then Nonna had died. Her throat thickened. She doubted
anything could fill the gap that now yawned through her. It
took a superhuman effort to swallow the lump stretching her
throat into a painful ache. Her family, never large, had suddenly dwindled to her, her cousin Frankie and her aunt Deidre.

But to now discover her mother's family... *A grandmother
and a plethora of cousins.* She'd been searching for something
to anchor her, a safe harbour. Could this be it?

'Would you like to meet them?'

It felt as if the sun had come from behind a cloud and bathed her in light. A big extended family? She clasped her hands in her lap. She wanted that more than she'd ever wanted anything. 'Yes, please. How soon can it be arranged?'

CHAPTER ONE

'YOU ARE READY, AUDREY?'

The words sounded more like a command than a question. Audrey glanced at her grandmother and found she couldn't push a single word from a throat that had grown too tight. She'd met Marguerite Funaro a week ago, and Marguerite was as unlike Nonna as it was possible to be.

'Appearances can be deceptive.'

She held that thought close; the voice—Nonna's—made the tight knot in her stomach loosen a fraction. Nonna had taught her the importance of family. Audrey had no intention of forgetting those lessons and abandoning all of Nonna's wisdom now, just because she was nervous and things felt a bit awkward.

Marguerite might not be touchy-feely and demonstrative, but Audrey had felt a bond with the older woman the moment they'd met. Marguerite hadn't felt like a stranger, although the world she inhabited did.

In her letter, Nonna had said Audrey's mother's family was wealthy and powerful. Audrey just hadn't realised how wealthy and powerful. Apparently, the Funaro name was synonymous with all the great aristocratic names of Italy.

She pinched herself. It was hard to believe that *she* was a member of such an old, powerful Italian family. Or that she was now a resident at their impossibly luxurious estate on the shores of Lake Como with its splendid Funaro Villa, extravagant gardens and extraordinary views.

She glanced at her grandmother again and her stomach churned. She didn't want to let Marguerite down. Didn't want to let any of the family down, but what did she know about this world? How would she ever fit in?

Just because Marguerite is regal and proud, it doesn't mean she has no heart or kindness or love.

The thought made her straighten. Marguerite had welcomed her into the Funaro fold without hesitation…and with her own brand of warmth. Lifting her chin, she nodded. 'I'm looking forward to meeting the rest of the family, Grandmother.'

Grandmother was what Marguerite had requested Audrey call her. She had no idea why she wanted her to use the English title rather than the Italian one. Maybe it was so she could tell her apart from the other members of the family.

Because, apparently, there were quite a few of them.

The wriggle of delight was cut short as Marguerite's gaze roved over Audrey's attire. Her lips didn't tighten and her nostrils didn't flare and nothing about her face gave anything away, but Audrey couldn't help but feel she'd been found wanting.

She glanced down at herself. 'Would you like me to change?' Not that she had anything else to change into. Not really. 'I only brought a limited wardrobe with me on this trip.' She only had a limited wardrobe period, but she had no intention of admitting that out loud. 'I've not had a chance to do any real shopping yet and—'

'Audrey!'

She snapped to attention. 'Yes, Grandmother?'

'You are a granddaughter of the Funaro family. You have royal blood flowing in your veins.'

She choked down an entirely inappropriate laugh. Royal blood? *Her?*

'Your attire does not define you.'

Easy to say when you happened to be wearing a delightfully chic Chanel suit in pink-and-white tweed.

'You will walk out there as if you own the room.'

Oh, just like that, huh? Easy-peasy. She had an insane urge to call her cousin Frankie and demand a pep talk.

'You will keep your back straight, your chin high and a pleasant expression on your face.'

She adjusted her stance to meet her grandmother's exacting requirements.

'Ours is a large family and, as with most families, some members get along better than others. You will not allow anyone to ruffle your peace or to allow you to feel inferior.'

Okay, now she really wanted to run back to Aunt Beatrice's and hide under the bed that had been hers for the past few weeks.

'Repeat that, please,' the older woman ordered.

'I won't allow anyone to make me feel inferior,' she obediently repeated. These people were her family; things were bound to be a bit awkward initially. But it wasn't money and position that made a person worthwhile. Just because her dress wasn't the latest fashion, it didn't make her a bad person.

Her heart beat hard. She had family. And she *would* fit in. It might take some time, but she *would* make them love her. There was strength in family, not to mention security. And a place to belong. Ever since Nonna's death, she'd felt cast adrift. But here was a place where she could find safe harbour and acceptance—where she could love and be loved.

'Remember, you have your grandmother's seal of approval.'

Marguerite might not be all touchy-feely maternal warmth, but her unerring support warmed Audrey from the inside out. 'I'm ready to meet everyone, Grandmother. I'm looking forward to it.'

Once this initial meeting was over, she could work at getting to know everyone on a more leisurely and less formal basis. She imagined lunches, dinners, outings. Hopefully by Christmas it'd feel as if they'd all known each other forever. She crossed her fingers.

'Remember, spine straight, shoulders back…and smile.'

Audrey followed the instructions to the letter, and then waited outside a set of gilded double doors while a butler or footman or...well, a member of staff who wore the most extraordinary uniform, flung the doors open. She half expected him to announce them.

He didn't, of course. This wasn't the set of a historical drama. She wasn't some Jane Austen heroine. This was the real world.

Except Audrey's real world wasn't Lake Como, glittering chandeliers, eighty-room villas and *a new family.*

Marguerite took Audrey's arm, as if for the support—as if she was an old lady who needed to lean on someone. Which was a joke, because *frailty, thy name is woman* wasn't Marguerite. She doubted she'd be able to best the older woman in an arm wrestle.

The thought, though, made her smile.

Then they stepped inside the room and her breath caught. There had to be at least forty people in here. It took all her strength not to clasp her hands beneath her chin and beam at them. How *wonderful*! She'd always wanted to be part of a big, loving family.

Nobody said a word as she and Marguerite split a path through the crowd towards a throne—

Not a throne. A chair. But it was all gold gilt and pink velvet and clearly Marguerite's. The silence raised all the fine hairs on her arms. She concentrated on keeping her spine straight, her chin lifted and her expression pleasant. This odd formality must be the way they did things here in her new world.

Still, she'd never hated her height more. It always made her stand out, gave her nowhere to hide and— Except...she wasn't the only tall person in the room! This stature must be a Funaro trait. Her smile widened. Surely, that meant she was fitting in already.

Marguerite removed her arm from Audrey's and sat. Audrey immediately felt cast adrift.

Don't be a baby.

It'd be easier if she knew what she was supposed to do. Should she sit? Except there was no chair beside her grandmother's.

You're not supposed to sit. You're supposed to mix and mingle and get to know everyone.

Not until she'd been introduced, though, surely? She felt as if she ought to have a sign around her neck saying Exhibit A.

The vision had her lips twitching. Once everyone got to know her, she wouldn't be such a curiosity. She'd be just another member of the family.

And still, the silence stretched. Though, she couldn't help feeling an awful lot of silent communication was happening among various family members. She hid a wince. Awkward much?

Finally, with an impatient huff, a child broke from the ranks and came hurtling out from behind the crowd to rush up to Audrey, hopping from one foot to the other in front of her. '*Ciao!* Hello!'

The pretty little thing couldn't be older than three or four. Something inside her melted. She hadn't thought, but of course, there'd be children. She knelt down to be eye to eye with her and held out her hand. 'I'm Audrey. And who might you be? A princess, maybe?'

'I'm not a princess. I'm Liliana.' She placed her hand in Audrey's and shook it earnestly. 'And you're my aunty.'

She stared at the little girl and her throat thickened; her eyes burned. She had a niece? She had to swallow before she could trust her voice to work. 'My niece? I have a niece?'

Little Liliana nodded eagerly.

The delight that flooded her couldn't be hidden, contained or otherwise tempered. She clapped her hands, grinning madly. She might've even shimmied. 'That is the best news I've ever heard!'

She had a niece!

Liliana grinned back like she couldn't help it, either.

And then they hugged each other like they meant it.

She had at least one friend here, then. And she had every intention of treasuring her.

Gabriel took one look at the tableau unfolding before him and wanted to swear long and hard.

One thing the world *didn't* need was another Funaro.

One thing that world *really* didn't need was a Funaro his daughter found irresistible.

Not that he blamed Lili for falling for the statuesque woman who'd folded down to her height with the ease and grace of a ballet dancer. Or who smiled at her as if her very heart's delight had just been handed to her on a diamond-encrusted platinum platter at Lili's announcement.

Even *his* heart had thrilled as he'd watched the scene unfold, and he was a hardened cynic who didn't trust in appearances or believe that anyone in the room had his or Lili's best interests at heart. He watched the stranger rise; watched the way Lili slipped her hand inside her new friend's; noted the way this Audrey's fingers curled around Lili's as if...

He rubbed a hand across his chest.

As if she welcomed that hand. As if she'd keep that little hand safe from all harm. As if...

He swallowed an indigestible lump. It is the way Fina should've held Lili's hand. But even if his wife hadn't died and was still in their midst, that wasn't the kind of woman Fina had been. None of the women in this room were. None of them would hold Lili's hand in that fashion.

He studied the quietly beautiful woman's face with its dark eyes. If one wasn't looking for it, they wouldn't immediately see the beauty there. But he had an artist's eye and recognised it immediately. This wasn't a woman who made the most of her assets by painting her face, by drawing her hair up into a complicated style that took myriad pins and a team of hairdressers to maintain. If her dress and shoes were anything to go by, she wasn't a woman who, before now, had the means to buy designer labels.

Several women in the room exchanged raised eyebrows. As if to say 'Look what the cat has dragged in.'

Mind you, all too soon this Audrey would have access to the funds to rectify every single problem the assorted horde would find with her appearance. And then they'd be jealous of her as she outshone them all.

For a brief moment, at least. Like a star shining its brightest before exploding. Or should that be imploding? Whatever one wanted to call it, it'd be spectacular. And then it'd be spectacularly disastrous.

Marguerite finally made a general introduction to the room at large, saying that she was pleased to welcome her granddaughter Audrey into the family fold. A chair was placed for Audrey beside Marguerite's, and he gave a silent, humourless laugh. Audrey didn't yet understand the honour being done to her with the placement of that chair. But she'd learn. And if she didn't want to be eaten alive by the piranhas in the room, she'd better learn *presto*.

The temperature in the room rose as resentment and *devilry* heated the air. What would most of the people here give to be seated in such close proximity to Marguerite, to have the opportunity to whisper sweet nothings and bitter calumnies in her ear for ten minutes? How many of them would like the opportunity to make a fresh impression on their stately elder?

And because they couldn't, because they'd messed up—in some instances again and again—the feuding family members in the room seemed to momentarily join forces against the newcomer. As if they couldn't wait until she, too, fell from grace.

A bitter sigh welled inside him. He didn't doubt that Audrey would indeed fall from grace. She *was* a Funaro, after all. Falling from grace was what the Funaros did. They knew of no other way of being.

As various family members were called forward to be introduced and pay their respects, he remained in the shadows—where he belonged. He wasn't a member of the family, thank God. He was tolerated as Lili's father, nothing more. Lili might be a Funaro, but she was also a Dimarco. His hands clenched. He would *not* allow her to go the way of her mother. He would *not* allow this family's excesses, their hedonism and extravagances, to destroy his daughter. He would do everything in his power to prevent that from happening.

He kept a close eye on Lili now and it took all his willpower not to call her back to his side. It would bring attention to the both of them, and that was something he'd avoid if he could.

The arrangement—one legally signed off by a team of lawyers—stated that during the summer Lili would spend uninterrupted time with her mother's family. He had no desire to engage in a protracted legal battle with Marguerite if she should happen to take exception to some interference of his, or imagined some slight or infringement to her rights.

Where he could, he'd keep things amicable. To her credit, on this one issue Marguerite had been in surprising agreement. When he'd demanded to be allowed to accompany Lili for her summers at Lake Como, Marguerite had acquiesced. They both knew his being there would keep Lili content and secure. In his turn, he ensured Marguerite could spend time with Lili throughout the rest of the year. They maintained an uneasy peace he would prefer not to shatter.

He glanced again at the newcomer's face and his chest clenched. Her height, the line of her nose and the aristocratic cheekbones pronounced her heritage. He saw Fina there, and her mother, Danae, too.

He would never again fall for a Funaro heiress, never again indulge a fascination for one, or even speak to one longer than necessary. Once had been enough. He would not live that nightmare a second time.

It didn't mean he relished the notion of witnessing another

heiress's fall from grace, though. Watching the newcomer suc-
cumb to the wealth and sophistication, the petty flatteries and
scheming seductions, the endless parties. Breath hissed from
his lungs. The drugs.

He loathed the thought of all the potential encased in that
elegant frame being brought low; watching as the fire in those
eyes dimmed and eventually went out.

'Gabriel!'

His name, an imperial command from the matriarch herself, snapped him back to himself.

'Come! I have a request to make of you.'

He kept his face a study of polite lines. What was the
scheming Funaro elder up to now? Whatever it was, he suspected he wouldn't like it.

Lili's wide smile and hopping excitement had him moving
towards the trio in the middle of the room, rather than heading for the door like his instincts told him to.

'This is Papa.' Lili leaned against Audrey's legs, smiling up
at her with the naive openness and utter assurance of a much-
loved four-year-old, clearly believing Audrey adored her every
bit as much as Lili did her. It made him want to snatch his
daughter up and bolt from the house and lock her in a tower
where none of these people could ever hurt her.

'I'm looking forward to meeting your papa,' Audrey said
with a wide smile that had a different part of his anatomy jerk-
ing to attention. He wrestled with the curse that rose to his lips.

'Good grief, Audrey,' said Marguerite, 'you don't need to
stand every time I introduce you to someone new.'

'It only seems polite,' Audrey returned mildly, apparently
unfazed by her grandmother's imperial tone.

'Audrey, this is my grandson-in-law. He was married to my
granddaughter Serafina.'

'My *mamma*,' Lili whispered. Though four-year-olds apparently couldn't manage a quiet whisper; they only thought
they did.

Audrey squeezed Lili's hand. 'And my sister.'

'Half sister,' Marguerite snapped with her customary autocratic tyranny.

Audrey winked at Lili. 'I bet your mamma and I would've been the best of friends.'

A titter went around the room. Quickly quelled by Marguerite's glare. But he silently agreed with everyone else. He doubted Audrey could've made Fina a friend, but he appreciated the kindness to his daughter.

'Gabriel,' he said, extending his hand as Marguerite had failed to mention that key piece of information.

She promptly placed her hand in his and something arced between them. Something that had her eyes widening and him frowning. They reclaimed their hands at exactly the same moment.

'Audrey apparently has some artistic talent,' Marguerite said peremptorily.

Uh-huh. A dabbler. He lowered his gaze to hide the derision in his eyes, the cynical twist of his mouth.

'She's been studying under Madame De Luca for the last month.'

His head shot up, and the way Audrey's lips twitched made him suspect he'd not hidden his shock very well. If she'd been studying under Madame De Luca, though, she must have a degree of talent.

Audrey registered Gabriel's surprise at the fact she'd been studying under someone so well regarded, and it made her smile.

But that didn't stop her hand from continuing to burn at the brief pressure of his, or help ease the constriction in her chest. This odd awareness didn't make sense. Gabriel wasn't classically handsome. He wasn't smooth or clean-cut or smilingly polished like the other men in the room. What he was, though, was thoroughly masculine. Dark haired, olive skinned and sporting several days' growth of beard, he seemed to *bristle*. Something primitive beat beneath the contained demeanour and it thrilled something primitive deep inside her.

She had no idea what that meant—he probably had that effect on every woman he met. Whatever it was, it was far from comfortable. And she had every intention of ignoring it.

She had enough to negotiate this summer. She wasn't adding men and romance to the mix. She wasn't thinking about any of that until she'd worked out her place in the family; had learned to negotiate this new world of hers.

Grey eyes continued to survey her, their colour taking her off guard. They should be dark like his hair. And yet…

Stop it!

'What medium is your speciality?'

The question had her swallowing. 'While Grandmother is correct, and I have been studying under Madame De Luca, it has been as a favour to a mutual friend of ours. Your first impression was the correct one—I am a rank amateur.'

Expressive brows rose as if he'd noted her evasion. It was just…when she told others her artform of choice, they usually laughed. And she didn't want anyone laughing. Not today. There were already enough undercurrents threading through the room that she didn't understand.

'I'd hate for Grandmother's words to mislead you.'

He stared at her for a long moment, flicked a glance at the rest of the room and nodded. She let out a breath, the tension in her shoulders easing. 'Are you an artist, Gabriel?'

Another titter sounded through the room, and she fought back a frown. What had she said now?

The Funaros might not be as warm as she'd hoped, but it was early days. She hitched up her chin. She'd make them love her yet. Resisting the urge to glance to Marguerite for an explanation, she held Gabriel's gaze and awaited his answer.

'I am a sculptor.' He pushed his hands into his trouser pockets. 'I work with recycled materials.'

'Like?'

'Like steel, wood, wire and such.'

Hold on...

Her heart started to thump. 'Do you work on large installations?'

He nodded.

His first name was Gabriel...

She swallowed. 'You wouldn't happen to be Gabriel Dimarco by any chance, would you?'

'*Si*, that is me.'

Her jaw dropped. She couldn't help it.

'Audrey, please,' Marguerite half sighed, half ordered.

'But—' She stared at her grandmother. 'His work is amazing.' She swung back to him. '*Your* work is amazing.'

Her hands fluttered in the air as if searching for all the things she wanted to say; all the things his work made her feel. She could no more control them than she could the sun—or the rest of the room's opinion of her. But the knowledge she was standing in front of such an artist drove all such concerns momentarily from her mind. Gabriel's installations stood in both public spaces and enviable private collections. He could demand whatever price he wanted. He was a *huge* name in the art world.

'I saw your installation titled *Maybe* in Como. It was the most amazing piece. I sat there for an hour watching how it changed as the sun passed overhead.' It sat in a pretty town square, and the sculpture was an Impressionist piece—half human, half butterfly...or, at least, if not a butterfly, something winged. 'It made me feel hopeful but sad. I couldn't work out if the figure wanted to take flight or return to its cocoon.'

Powerful arms folded across an impressive chest. Considering the tools he must use, he'd need every one of those impressive muscles. 'What was your conclusion?'

She pondered the question anew. 'I spent a lot of time trying to work it out.' She'd gone back the next day, earlier in the morning when the sun would hit it at different angles, to see if that would help her solve the conundrum. 'In the end, I decided it depicted the battle between security and adventure, and that the piece was deliberately ambiguous. I don't think the figure knew yet which it was going to choose.'

Grey eyes widened and nostrils flared. 'You—'

He snapped back whatever he'd been about to say with a shake of his head. 'I am glad you enjoyed the piece.'

She wanted to press him for what he'd been going to say, but it wouldn't be polite. And she suspected her grandmother would find it indecorous. Twice already this afternoon Marguerite had heaved a sigh and murmured, 'Dear Lord, Audrey, we're really going to have to take you in hand.'

She had no idea what that meant. She hoped it wasn't as ominous as it sounded. She liked Marguerite, and an additional point in the older woman's favour was the fact she clearly loved her great-granddaughter. She and Lili seemed to have a perfect understanding.

She was far from sure about the rest of the room, however. She'd seen the raised eyebrows, the speaking glances. She suspected she'd been meant to. Why didn't they want to embrace her the way she wanted to embrace them?

Was it about the money?

Surely not. The Funaro family had so much wealth that one more person sharing a portion of it wouldn't make any difference. Not that she wanted a portion of it. She just wanted the family. And she was determined to find a way to bring them around.

'What I would like for you to do, Gabriel,' Marguerite said now, 'is take Audrey's art education in hand. Determine where she's at and what she needs—' that imperious hand waved through the air '—and then use your connections to engage whatever teachers, tutors or experts you deem necessary.'

Audrey blinked. 'Grandmother, that's something you ought to consult with me about first.'

The room froze. Very slowly, Marguerite turned her head to meet Audrey's gaze, and the expression in her eyes had her gulping. 'It's just…' It took a superhuman effort to not wince, grimace, or backtrack. 'It'll be expensive to hire experts like that, and I've already told you I'm not here for your money. The money might not mean a lot to you, but…' It meant a lot to her and she didn't want anyone here thinking she was only out for what she could get.

Her grandmother gestured for Audrey to bend down. Hiding a wince, she did as she bid and prayed the older woman wasn't going to yell at high volume in her ear.

'Please…'

The word was nothing more than a whisper, but she heard the vulnerability threaded through it and it had tears prickling the backs of her eyes. Straightening, she swallowed and eventually nodded, turning back to Gabriel. 'I would be very grateful for any advice you'd be able to offer. If you have the time.'

When she was sure nobody was looking, she reached down and squeezed her grandmother's hand. 'Thank you.'

'Papa, can Audrey come with us to your studio tomorrow?'

'I think that's a remarkably fine idea, Lili.' A gleam lit Marguerite's eyes. 'Do you have any objections, Gabriel?'

The pulse in his jaw ticked. 'None whatsoever,' he eventually ground out.

Audrey's heart plummeted. Oh, God. He didn't want her invading his studio space. How on earth could she get out of this gracefully and save face for everyone?

'Be ready to leave at nine o'clock.'

'She'll be ready,' Marguerite said.

Before she could think of a way to extricate herself, Gabriel was already striding away. She glanced down at her grandmother, recalled her *please* and swallowed her protests, made herself smile. 'What a treat! Thank you.'

CHAPTER TWO

THE FOLLOWING MORNING Audrey made sure to be sitting on one of the hard-backed chairs in the foyer ten minutes before the assigned time. She had no intention of being late or putting anyone out more than they already had been.

Recalling again the less than thrilled expression on Gabriel's face, she grimaced. She didn't blame him for his lack of enthusiasm. He was an important artist. He was probably working on something amazing. He didn't need the likes of her underfoot.

Biting at a hangnail on her thumb, she made a resolution to do her best to remain in the background and not get in the way.

After pulling the thumb from her mouth, she clasped both hands in her lap. Apparently, Funaros didn't fidget. Apparently, they were always careful to appear composed and at ease, regardless of how they felt inside. The thing was she also happened to be a Martinelli, and they *did* fidget, and they had a habit of wearing their hearts on their sleeves.

She glanced up when the front door swung open to see Lili come skipping through it, her father following close behind. *Not* skipping. She shot to her feet and the little girl threw her arms around Audrey's legs, the little face smiling up at her with big shining eyes. Audrey swept her up in her arms and hugged her back. She had a niece! It made her want to dance.

Before any of them could speak, a door off to the left opened and Marguerite strode out. At seventy-four she was still as erect as she must've been as a much younger woman. Audrey envied her poise. She doubted she'd ever acquire that level of grace and command, no matter how hard she practised.

'Good morning, Audrey and Liliana. Gabriel.'

Clearly, Marguerite wasn't the kind of person to enjoy a morning lie-in.

Audrey set Lili back on her feet. 'Good morning, Grandmother.'

'Marguerite.' Gabriel nodded in the older woman's direction. 'Gently!' he ordered Lili as she raced across to hug her great-grandmother in the same way she had Audrey.

'Leave the child be, Gabriel. I'm not as frail as you and the rest of the family make me out to be.'

Marguerite clearly adored Lili, and while she might try to hide it beneath a crusty exterior, Audrey doubted she was fooling anyone. Least of all, Lili's father. She turned to Gabriel with a grin, expecting him to be amused, too, but he didn't so much as smile. The flat expression in his eyes as he stared back at her had the smile sliding off her lips. Pressing her hands to her waist, she reminded them to neither twist nor fidget.

'Now, Lili, I have a proposition for you. Tomaso informs me it's time to decide which puppy we're to keep from Tippy's litter.'

Lili's eyes grew wide. 'Can we play with them yet?'

'We can.'

The little girl hopped from one foot to the other. 'When?'

'This morning, and as it's the only morning I have free this week, I'm afraid you'll need to decide if you want to accompany your father and Audrey to the studio, or if you'd like to come to the stables and play with the puppies and help me choose which one to keep.'

Lili swung to her father. 'Can I stay with Nonna, Papa? *Please?* I want to play with the puppies.'

His jaw tightened fractionally and Audrey wondered if Marguerite noticed it, too. 'Do you mean to abandon your new friend so quickly, Lili?'

That little face fell and Audrey found herself crouching down in front of her. 'I totally understand, Lili. I mean...puppies, right?'

The little girl's relief was palpable and then her entire face lit up. 'We could *all* stay and play with the puppies!'

'*No.*'

The single word shot from Gabriel's mouth like a bullet and they all jumped.

'I mean,' he moderated his voice, no doubt for his daughter's benefit, 'that I shall be going to the studio today as planned. Audrey will have to make the decision whether to stay and play with the puppies or come to the studio for herself.'

Puppies would win in the ordinary course of events. And the 'No Trespassing' signals radiating from Gabriel in waves would normally seal the deal. But her grandmother drew herself up to her full height and sent her a look that told Audrey in no uncertain terms what was expected of her. Yet, it was that vulnerable *please* from last night that played through her mind.

'I've no desire to change our plans. I'm looking forward to seeing your studio.'

His lips twisted and his jaw clenched as if he was biting back something curt and succinct. His nose didn't exactly curl, but it felt like it did and she could feel herself shrivelling inside.

A Funaro always appears composed.

She planted as pleasant a smile as she could to her face and kept her chin high. She'd get this done—go and tour his studio, have a brief conversation about her artistic endeavours—to please Marguerite. She'd get the names of several suitable teachers whom she could contact, and then she and Gabriel need never have anything to do with each other again.

'Liliana, pop through the kitchen to Maria. I believe she has something special for you.'

With a wave, Lili raced off in the direction of the kitchen.

'A word if you don't mind, Gabriel. We won't be a minute, Audrey.'

Another flaring of those rather savage nostrils had Audrey internally quailing, but when Marguerite turned on her very elegant heel and strode back the way she'd come, he fell into step behind her.

Audrey took a seat and waited. It was no hardship. The villa was utterly extraordinary, and the foyer was all classic white marble with a vaulted ceiling housing a stunning chandelier whose crystals glittered in the light pouring in at the arched windows set high above. And complementing it all was the sweeping curve of a grand staircase.

'I am Cinderella.' She pinched herself. Rather than a fairy godmother, she had a grandmother.

And a niece!

She didn't have long to luxuriate in all the splendour, though. Less than five minutes later Gabriel appeared—turbulent, dark and crackling with barely restrained…um, energy. Without a glance in her direction, he strode out the door.

Was she supposed to follow him? For one brief moment she considered chickening out.

Please.

Marguerite's simple request with its underlying vulnerability pierced through her cowardice. Swearing under her breath, she leapt up and scrambled after him, catching him up before he reached the car.

He didn't utter a word, just slid inside the dark sedan. She moved to the passenger side but when she tried the door handle, it was locked. She had to tap on the window to get him to open it. For one awfully fraught moment she thought he wouldn't; thought he'd drive away and leave her there.

For heaven's sake! There was reasonable annoyance, but then there was also unreasonable rudeness.

He unlocked the door. She slid into her seat, pulled her seatbelt on and folded her hands in her lap.

Don't make waves. Don't rock the boat. Wait until you know how everything here fits together.

It took a superhuman effort, but she bit her tongue and kept her thoughts to herself. She didn't like confrontation. Nobody did, she supposed, but something about this man and his behaviour had her itching to take him to task.

She risked a glance at his profile as he set the car in motion and had to stifle a laugh. Take him to task? He looked like granite—hard and inflexible. She doubted anything she said or did would have the slightest effect on him.

He didn't speak, so she kept her gaze trained directly out to the front.

Comfortable? No. But luckily, the trip took less than ten minutes.

She blinked when he pulled the car to a halt in the carpark of a small marina. If she turned her head, she could see the Funaro Villa back along the lake, its grand arched balconies shining white in the morning sun.

He pushed out of the car so she did, too. Clearing her throat, she prayed her voice would sound normal. 'Where's the studio?'

He pointed at the water, before striding down to the dock towards a speedboat.

Her jaw dropped. An island? His studio was on an island?

And then she couldn't help it; she started to laugh.

'What's so funny?' he said with an irritable twist of his lips, though he did have the civility to help her step into the boat.

Where was she supposed to sit? He didn't give her any hints, so she chose the padded seat beside the driver's seat. It might not be large, but the boat looked built for speed, and this seat had handrails to the front and side for her to hold on to. Did he have any lifejackets?

'Under the seat,' he said, as if reading her mind.

She put it on. To her surprise he put one on, too.

'Can you swim?'

She nodded. 'Can you?'

He nodded back. *That* was the extent of their conversation

before he fired up the engine, undid the moorings and turned the boat's nose towards the middle of the lake.

They'd been travelling for five minutes, maybe a bit longer, when he cut the engine and she turned from admiring the view. Lake Como, the lakeside villas dotted here and there, the forests and mountains... Dear God, it was *breathtaking*.

'You didn't tell me why you laughed back there on shore.'

'I didn't,' she agreed, determined to keep a pleasant expression on her face. It would be good practise. If she could maintain her equilibrium around this man, she suspected the rest of mankind would be a walk in the park.

'You do not wish to tell me?'

Be pleasant.

'It's just...the way you people live. It's extraordinary, and so far removed from my usual world it boggles my mind.'

Dark eyebrows rose. '*You* people?'

'The Funaros and—'

'I am *not* a Funaro!'

Wow, okay. 'But you're clearly from the same world and—'

'I did not grow up with the kind of wealth and privilege that the members of the Funaro family were fortunate enough to enjoy.' Stern lips became positively grim. 'I am not of the same social standing or—'

He broke off, breathing hard. She'd clearly struck a nerve.

Keep your equilibrium, Cinders.

'Well, let's stick to the facts, then,' she said *pleasantly*. She held up one finger. 'You're ridiculously successful and wealthy.' She held up another. 'You have an art studio on an island in the middle of Lake Como.' She held up a third finger. 'And you're famous. This is not the usual state of affairs for the majority of people.'

Hooded eyes surveyed her for a moment. 'The studio is not on an island. It's simply located farther around the lake.'

'Oh, well, then that makes everything *ordinary*, then.'

Her eyeroll and the loud breath that shot from her lungs ruined the pleasant thing she'd had going. She comforted herself with the thought that she was a work in progress and that the poise would come with time.

'Signor Dimarco—'

'Gabriel!' he growled, a scowl darkening his face.

In that moment she decided pleasantness was highly over-rated. With a superhuman effort, she didn't growl back. She folded her hands in her lap and met his gaze. 'Do you have friends?'

He blinked as if the question was the last thing he'd expected. 'Of course, I do. I have many in Milan where I live. Not so many here around Lake Como, that is true. Why?'

'Are they nice, good, decent people?'

Grey eyes narrowed. 'I think so. Why?'

'It's just that I'm interested in how you manage to keep them if this is the way you treat people.'

His hands clenched so hard he started to shake. Reaching down, she trailed her finger through the water. 'At least the water temperature is pleasant.'

'For what?'

'For if you really do plan to throw me overboard.'

The thunderous expression that raced across his face had her eyes widening, and no amount of coaching herself to re-main composed could prevent it. But a moment later she was released from the fierce glare when he ran a hand over his face.

With a soft curse he eventually met her gaze once more, his expression milder. Or at least what she suspected he hoped would appear milder. It was debatable if *mild* was something this man could achieve. 'This is something you fear from me?'

Not really, but... 'I don't know you. I've been thrust upon you in a way that you obviously resent, and yet for some rea-son you didn't refuse when Marguerite made her request yes-terday. You don't want me here. You've made that very clear. You've barely been civil. One could even say you've been ac-tively rude.'

He blinked. 'I—'

'I'm sorry I couldn't find an excuse to get out of the studio visit in a way that would've seemed polite to my grandmother. But you have my assurance that I will do my best to stay out of your way when we reach your studio, and to take up as little of your time as possible.'

Grey eyes throbbed into hers.

She swallowed when he didn't say anything. 'And then, when we return to the villa, we need barely see each other again.'

'That will be impossible.'

She stared down at her hands and huffed out a laugh. 'Oh, I'm sure you'll find a way.'

'Lili.' He said his daughter's name as if it explained all. 'Unless I'm very much mistaken, you are as taken with my daughter as she is with you.'

Damn.

'She will wish to spend time with you.'

She wanted to spend time with Lili, too. She studied his face, blew out a breath. 'And you don't allow your daughter to spend time with people you don't know.'

'I do not,' he agreed.

She couldn't blame him for that.

'I owe you an apology, Audrey. I did not mean to take my bad temper out on you. You are right. I have treated you abominably and I humbly ask your forgiveness.'

It was her turn to blink. She, um…wow, okay. 'Consider it forgotten,' she mumbled.

They stared at each other. She couldn't read the expression in his eyes at all. 'What does your grandmother have on you?' he finally asked.

She wasn't sure she'd heard him correctly. 'I beg your pardon?'

'Why do you feel compelled to do Marguerite's bidding? What does she blackmail you with?'

'She's not blackmailing me!'

She leaned towards him, but it brought her in too close. His scent hit her and it was like a shock of cold water to her senses. She shot back, her heart pounding.

Stop being ridiculous.

And yet a strange new energy filled her, and it took all her strength to not lean forward and breathe him in a second time. Something about him invigorated her like a cold alpine breeze and sea spray, but it carried the heat of chilli peppers. That heat stole into her veins now.

She did what she could to shake the sensation off. 'Marguerite has unreservedly welcomed me into her family and her home. She's been kind and generous and everything that is benevolent. In asking you to assist me with my art, she's hoping to provide me with something that will make me happy. It would be ungrateful, not to mention ungracious, for me to refuse her that.'

He remained unmoved.

She started to lean towards him again, but caught herself in time. 'We're family, Gabriel. Family should pull together and look after one another. I know it's only early days, but that's what I would like to work towards with Marguerite.' It's what she'd like to work towards with all of the family.

'Then you are a fool.'

She turned and stared at the water, doing her best to rein in her temper. When she was pretty certain she'd managed it, she turned back. 'I thought you weren't going to be rude anymore.'

'I did not mean to be rude. I am simply telling you the truth. If you think Marguerite has your best interests at heart, then you are sadly mistaken.'

He loathed the Funaro family. Folding her arms, she swallowed. 'What's your reading of the situation, then?'

'Marguerite's only concern is to maintain the prestige of the Funaro name, nothing more.'

She recalled that *please*, the expression in her grandmother's eyes when they rested on Lili. 'I think you're mistaken.'

'And what if I were to tell you she is already regretting the rather spontaneous request she made of me?'

Her mouth went strangely dry. 'For what reason?'

'Because it belatedly occurred to her that I might taint another of her precious granddaughters.'

Her heart pounded against the walls of her ribs. 'That's what her *quick word* was about?'

Stern lips cracked open in a humourless smile. 'It was indeed.'

Her grandmother had *warned him off*? She didn't know whether to be offended or absurdly touched.

'Succeed in resisting my masculine charms, Audrey, and the plaudits will be yours.'

He stretched out his arms as if he were a prize or a trophy. She swallowed and shifted on her seat. The thing was she couldn't deny that he had a lot of masculine charm. Not that it meant anything. She wasn't going to pursue him or anything.

'Fail and allow yourself to be seduced by me, and you'll be considered a bitter disappointment and relegated to the ranks and ignored like everyone else.'

He didn't want to seduce her, that much was clear, and yet his words and their accompanying smile sent a chill racing down her spine. Along with a traitorous and wholly unwelcome thrill.

CHAPTER THREE

UNABLE TO STARE AT the incredulous expression on Audrey's far too expressive face a moment longer, Gabriel kicked the boat's engine back over with a curse and turned in the direction of his studio. He was careful, though, to keep the action of the boat as smooth as he could as an unfamiliar shame washed through him.

All of the anger and resentment he'd wanted to fling at Marguerite, all of the bitterness he felt towards Fina and the Funaro name, he'd just taken out on Audrey. Marguerite had disturbed old ghosts, but Audrey didn't deserve to bear his anger for that.

It took all his willpower not to lower his head to the steering wheel and give in to the exhaustion that crashed down on him. He and Lili had been at the Funaro estate for two weeks, and already he felt stretched to his limit. He had another ten weeks of this *imprisonment* to go. How would he bear it?

Gritting his teeth, he shoved his shoulders back. He would bear whatever was necessary for Lili's sake. He understood Marguerite's game—she hoped that if she made him uncomfortable enough, he would leave Lili with her for the duration of the summer and return to Milan.

His hands tightened on the wheel. *That* wasn't going to happen.

Blowing out a breath, he glanced at the woman beside him. Dismissing her as just another Funaro was far from fair. The stunned expression on her face just now… He shook his head.

This woman was completely unaware of her position as a pawn on the Funaro chessboard.

She was still an innocent. One who believed in the sanctity of family. One who took what people told her at face value. One who clearly believed the best of people rather than the worst.

His lips twisted. Over the course of the summer, as she discovered the *delights* of the Funaro lifestyle, he had no doubts that she, too, would change and adopt their ways, become lost to the glamour, the partying… The jockeying for position and Marguerite's favour. She'd become hard and sophisticated, devious and disingenuous, shrewd and conniving. Unscrupulous.

Maybe not, a tiny voice whispered. Maybe she'd walk away when she discovered what they were.

Family should pull together and look after one another.

Or they would break her and she would flee back home.

Which he suddenly realised he had no knowledge of, beyond the fact it was Australia.

Very gently, he brought the boat in beside the studio's tiny dock, slipped a rope over the mooring post and secured it fast. After leaping out, he held a hand out towards Audrey, but she remained seated. 'Can I say something before we do this?' She nodded at the path that led to the studio.

'Of course.'

That pointed chin lifted. 'I make my own decisions about who I date and when I date.'

Dark eyes flashed, and although he stood on firm ground, he had to widen his stance to keep his balance.

'Let me make this very clear. I'm not currently in the market for either a boyfriend or a lover.'

The way her lips shaped the word *lover* had heat licking along his veins. He had to ignore it. He had no intention—*none whatsoever*—of dallying with this woman.

'And you can act as cynical and mocking as you like, but I'm fully aware that a man like you wouldn't be interested in someone like me.'

What on earth…?

'So if you *are* plotting to seduce me with a view to aggravating Marguerite, you can forget about it.'

He wasn't planning any such thing!

'I'm not going to fall for it. And you can rest assured I won't be instigating any kind of flirtation with you either, so you can stop already with the exaggerated sighs and black looks.'

With the *what*?

'I'm fully aware that I'm neither polished nor beautiful, but nor am I an idiot and—'

'Your beauty is undeniable.' Maybe he shouldn't have said it, but he couldn't allow it to go unchallenged.

She blinked.

'It's true you're not polished, but look at the land behind me.' He gestured at the unmanicured woodland that surrounded his studio and cut it off from the rest of civilisation. 'It is not polished either, but one cannot deny its beauty. One can acquire polish if they wish to.'

She stared at him as if she didn't know what to say.

'In fact, Marguerite will require it of you.'

Something in her eyes dimmed, but a moment later she shook herself, and her expression became resolute once again. 'I just wanted us on the same page about…all of that. So you've no need to be so…'

He crouched down so that they were eye to eye, and her scent rose up around him. It was wholesome and restful…familiar. It took him a moment to place it. *Lavender.* She smelled of lavender. It made him want to smile. 'No need to be so…?'

'Guarded, I suppose. Suspicious. Disapproving. You don't know me and yet I feel you've already condemned me.'

He bit back a sigh. 'If I have been sighing and glaring, it's not because of you.'

One eyebrow rose. 'I'm not sure I believe you.'

Her words were like knives and he didn't know why they should sting him so. 'I am not a dishonest man. I do not lie.'

Eyes the colour of cloves scanned his face now, but he couldn't tell if she believed him or not. 'Then what has the sighing and glaring been about?'

'Marguerite.'

Both brows shot up. 'You're still brooding about that?'

'She is manipulative and imperious. I do not like to be manipulated.' His lips twisted. 'Or given orders.'

He rose and held out his hand. 'Will you now disembark?'

She took his hand, her fingers tightening in his as the boat rocked. But she didn't panic, merely looked for him to tell her where to put her feet, and before he was ready, she was standing in front of him, swamping him in the comforting scent of lavender.

He went to release her, but her hand tightened in his. 'Please tell me you believe I've no designs on you.'

'Of course, I believe you.' And he did. 'I have been rude and boorish and you have felt threatened by me—for which I again apologise. I cannot imagine you would wish to lumber yourself with such a bad-tempered lover. No sensible woman would. And I believe that you are very sensible.'

Her lips twitched. It told him she no longer felt threatened by him, and he gave thanks for it. The thought of frightening any woman, let alone one as alone as Audrey, made him sick to his stomach.

'Also, you spoke of beauty earlier as if it were a precursor to embarking upon an affair,' he continued, 'and I cannot be accused of being a beautiful man.'

'No,' she agreed, finally releasing him. 'But there is something compelling about you.'

A pulse inside him burst to life. He ignored it. Refused to allow himself to consider her words too closely.

She cocked her head to one side. 'Beauty and attraction don't necessarily go hand in hand.'

Dio! Was she saying—?

She stiffened as if suddenly realising how her words could

be interpreted. Coughing, she hastened back into speech. 'Besides, a person is so much more than what they look like. There's a woman I work with back home.'

Did she not now consider *this* her home?

'When you first meet her, you might think her plain, but when you get to know her, you realise she's one of the most beautiful people you'll ever meet.'

Affection brightened her eyes, and her lips curved in a way that had him catching his breath. When Audrey let her guard down, she—

She nothing!

He gestured for her to precede him on the path. 'Where do you work?'

'At a nursing home in Melbourne—an aged care facility.'

'You are a nurse?'

'More a nurse's aide, really. I didn't study nursing at university or anything.'

'Why not?'

She was quiet for a moment, before sending him a swift smile. 'I was busy with other things.'

He sensed she didn't wish to discuss it, and let the matter drop. After having been so ill-tempered, he needed to prove he could be a pleasant host now. Climbing the short rise in the path and then rounding the curve, his studio came into view and Audrey came to a dead halt. He only just managed to avoid walking into her.

Clasping her hands together, she stared at it with wide eyes. 'Oh, Gabriel, I think you are the luckiest man alive.'

'This is my summer sanctuary. Here I can retreat from the pressures of the Funaro family and lose myself in my art.'

At least, that had been the plan—it is what had happened in previous summers—but his art wasn't providing him with the respite, comfort or distraction it usually did. Instead, in failing him, it had become another source of tension.

He pushed that thought away. 'It is where Lili and I can

come for some quiet time—to picnic and swim if we so desire.' And to sleep, too, on occasion. There were sleeping quarters here. The Funaros didn't own this land. It was his and his alone. Here Marguerite had no sovereignty, and he was determined to keep it that way.

She swung around, her face falling. 'And I'm intruding. *That's* why you've been in such a bad mood.'

He wrinkled his nose. 'I…'

'You told me you don't lie.' Her hands went to her hips. 'Don't disappoint me now.'

He stared at his studio, letting out a long breath. 'I have never invited any member of the family to my studio before. I do not wish for their dramas and demands to sully this place.'

'And you haven't invited me now, either.' With a wistful glance in the studio's direction, she turned back to him and squared her shoulders. 'Marguerite has been unreasonable, Gabriel. Come,' she said, gesturing for him to turn around. 'Return me to the villa. I'm sorry you've been put to so much trouble. I'll explain to Marguerite that she had no right to ask this of you. You can keep your sanctuary safe and—'

'I would be honoured to share it with you.'

He wasn't sure who was more surprised by his offer, him or Audrey.

'You are an artist, are you not?' he demanded, not allowing himself to dwell on why he was willing to share this special place with her.

She huffed out a laugh. 'That's debatable.'

'When you get the opportunity, do you lose yourself in your work for as long as you can? When you are working on something, do you think about it all the time? When you cannot make the vision in your head a reality and everything you do fails, and the frustration builds and builds until you think you will burst, do you keep persisting because you cannot let it go? And when you have a breakthrough, can see a way forward, does it feel like you are flying?'

Her jaw dropped. Nodding, she dragged it back into place. Satisfaction rippled through him. An artist created, and Audrey clearly created. It didn't matter if others saw value in her work or not. It didn't matter if *he* saw value in her work or not. In that moment, though, he burned with a strange curiosity to see what it was that she made.

'Would you continue with your art whether people said it was good, bad or indifferent?'

'Yes.' The word was quietly uttered, but strong for all that.

'Then, Audrey, you are an artist. It is what you do.' He gestured towards his studio. 'Would you like to see inside?'

'Very much.'

'Then come.'

Without another word, he led her to the studio door and unlocked it. 'Ready?'

'For what?' she asked, entering behind.

He flicked a switch on the wall and her eyes widened as the steel shutters on the wall of glass directly in front of them slid up to reveal the remarkable view outside. Her mouth formed a perfect O and he couldn't help but smile. She swung to him, stared at him, then turned back to the view. 'Did I mention earlier that you are the luckiest man alive?'

He laughed. Here in this space it was easy to laugh, to relax, to be himself. 'I believe you did.'

'You get to work here whenever you want.'

'Not quite. I have a warehouse studio in Milan, which is where I work on my larger pieces. It would not be practical to work on them here. But yes, this is where I work in the summer—on smaller pieces, on sketches and ideas for bigger projects.'

'Oh, Gabriel, it's absolutely amazing. Show me around.'

He gave her a tour, showing her where he kept his materials and the tools of his trade, along with the various projects he was working on. His lips twisted—*trying* to work on, he amended silently.

In her turn, she asked intelligent questions—where did he source his materials? What did he do with the scrap? How long did he spend sketching before starting a sculpture? She gazed at it all, and behind the warm, spice-brown of her eyes he sensed her mind racing.

'It's absolutely amazing—all of it. The light and the view… the tranquillity.'

The quality of the light was why he'd bought the land. Ensuring he made the most of that light had driven the specifications for the building. He'd paid a fortune for it all, but as far as he was concerned it was worth every penny. The tranquillity, though, had sealed the deal. This view looked southward. From here, one couldn't see the Funaro Villa. Nothing here rang a false note or had painful memories clamouring to the surface. All was simple and breathtaking beauty.

She pointed. 'You have a mezzanine level?'

'There are sleeping quarters up there.' He had no intention of giving her a tour of those.

She smiled. 'For when you get too caught up in your work and can't bear to leave.'

For when he needed a break from the Funaros.

'It's all very impressive. Mostly, though, I'm in awe of your work.' She gestured to the nearby bench and the finished work he'd brought with him from Milan that he'd been hoping would inspire him—an Impressionist sculpture of an oak tree in the autumn when its leaves had started to fall. 'I could look at this all day. It's a bit dishevelled and shabby but so strong, so… timeless.' She turned to him. 'You have an amazing talent.'

'Thank you.'

He had been given this compliment before, but her simple sincerity touched him in a way few previous compliments had. 'Now it is your turn to share something of your work with me.'

Her throat bobbed convulsively, and she gripped her hands so hard the knuckles turned white. 'But…' She swallowed again. 'I didn't bring any of it with me.'

He gestured to the small backpack she carried. 'You must have pictures on your phone.' He understood an artist's reluctance to share their work, their concern that it would not be understood… The fear of criticism. It was also important for an artist to overcome such fears. One could learn much from constructive criticism.

'You do not trust me with your art?' The thought pierced him.

'You're an important artist. I am a nobody.'

His brows rose. She was a *Funaro*.

'Very few people consider what I do as art.'

'This was also the fate of Vincent Van Gogh—he was considered unsuccessful and a failure. You are in good company.'

Her nose wrinkled. 'I don't have those kinds of pretensions.'

He was silent for a long moment and then gestured around. 'I have shared all of this with you willingly. Will you not share a little of your art with me?'

'You make me sound churlish.'

She nibbled on her bottom lip and he tried not to notice the way it deepened the colour; the way that lip grew plump and inviting.

Her shoulders suddenly slumped. 'You promise you won't laugh?'

Who had laughed at her art? 'I promise.'

After pulling her phone from her bag, she opened a photo folder. Clutching it to her chest she met his gaze, grimaced. 'While you look at these, would it be okay if I were to go and explore out there?' She pointed beyond the window.

'Of course.' She didn't want to watch his face as he assessed her work. He had a good poker face, but this woman was proving surprisingly perceptive. 'The door is in the side wall there.'

Without a word, she disappeared through it.

He opened the folder on her phone.

CHAPTER FOUR

AUDREY DIDN'T PACE the path outside that extraordinary wall of glass. She ached to give vent to the nerves stabbing through her, but Gabriel would see. And she didn't want to betray herself like that.

She couldn't work him out. He'd been so rude earlier, and then shocked when she'd called him out on it. As if he'd been so deep inside his own tangled thoughts, he hadn't realised how he'd come across.

Since then, though, he'd been the perfect host.

To stop from turning and staring at him through the wall of glass, and possibly surprising him in the act of curling his lip as he flicked through her so-called *artworks*, she made her way down to the waterfront and a pretty, protected curve of bay. This must be where he and Lili sometimes swam. Kicking off her shoes, she welcomed the cool of the water against her toes.

The water was clear—unruffled and satin soft, the pebbles and sand at her feet easy to negotiate—and the forest around the lake shaded a deep healthy green, while the ridges that rose up all around were harmoniously majestic. Across the lake the buildings of a town glowed cream, yellow and warm ochre in the late-morning sun. Tiny waves splashed against the shore, and the scent of gardenias drifted on the air.

But none of it soothed the agitation rolling through her. The elevated heart rate, the alternate hot and cold flushes. She glanced at her watch and wrung her hands. He'd been looking at the photos on her phone for fifteen minutes! *Oh, God.* She hid her face in her hands. She couldn't believe the celebrated Gabriel Dimarco was currently assessing *her* work.

I don't lie.

Well, maybe he could make an exception this one time, and tell her he thought the pieces pretty and decorative and recommend a teacher or two. Then they could change the subject and never speak of it again.

'What are you afraid you're going to hear?'

She spun to find Gabriel standing on the path above her. Her heart practically hammered its way out of her chest.

'What do you think I'm going to say?'

I don't lie.

Well then, she wouldn't, either. 'That you think the work is trivial and of no consequence.' She kept her chin high. 'Saying that, though, makes it sound as if I have delusions of grandeur when I don't.'

In two steps he was at her side though she couldn't work out how he'd moved so quickly. 'Others have belittled your work?'

'You've seen my medium.' For God's sake, what she did was glorified embroidery—*needlework*. She didn't create post-Impressionist watercolours or grand oil paintings or extraordinary sculptures. She *sewed*. 'I mean, anyone with half a brain can learn to sew, right?'

'Just as anyone with half a brain can slap paint on a canvas or make something from clay. But just because they can, doesn't mean they're good at it.'

His vehemence made her blink.

'But these—' he held up her phone '—are extraordinary, Audrey.'

Had he just said…? Folding her arms to hide the way her hands suddenly shook, she drew herself up to her full height. At five foot ten inches in her bare feet, her full height was pretty impressive, but she still had to throw her head back to meet Gabriel's gaze. 'Don't lie to me. Not about this.'

'I don't lie. This I have already told you.' He waved an impatient hand through the air. 'It is true that when Marguerite asked me to look over your work, I didn't have high hopes. At best I thought you would be a competent amateur. Until she mentioned Madame De Luca.'

'Like I said, that was just a favour for a friend.'

'She does not do such things. Her standards are too high.' Those grey eyes surveyed her with an unblinking certainty that had her pulse easing. 'She might have told you that, let you believe it for whatever reason…probably to keep you humble, but where art is concerned, Madame De Luca does not lower her standards.'

Had Aunt Beatrice deliberately let her believe it was an arrangement between friends? But why…? Oh, Lord! Had Beatrice paid the outrageous fees Madame charged and didn't want Audrey finding out, so had concocted the fiction? Oh! But—

Gabriel shook the phone in front of her face, recapturing her attention. 'I'm telling you that you have a rare talent. Your work is powerful. And while it is also true that it is sometimes raw, none of it is insipid. It is infused with life and…'

She leaned towards him, hanging on his every word. His scent once again an electrifying jolt to her senses, but this time she welcomed the oddly enlivening sting of it.

'Emotion.'

Her throat went oddly tight and she had to press a hand to her breastbone to stop her heart from falling at her feet.

'Which comes first—the subject or the emotion?'

She'd never pondered that before. 'Sometimes it's the emotion, but more often it's the subject,' she said slowly. 'But when I'm working, even if I don't want it to, the emotion takes over and directs everything.'

He nodded.

She held herself on such a tight leash in her everyday life, always had—had needed to—and art had become her outlet.

'Did not Madame De Luca tell you of your talent?'

'She told me I had an excellent technique and that my work showed promise. But I thought she was just being kind.'

He raised his eyes heavenward, exclaiming, *'Dio!'* before grey eyes skewered her to the spot once again. 'Did your family, your Australian family, belittle your work? Is that why you have feared my assessment? If I'd known how concerned you were I wouldn't have left you hanging so long.'

'No! I mean, I don't think they really understood it, none of them are artistic, but Nonna and my cousin Frankie have always been ridiculously amazed and encouraging.' So had Johanna.

'Rightly amazed,' he corrected. 'Your father?'

She shrugged, her chest clenching at the mention of her father. 'He's more the mad scientist type. If it's not part of the imperial table of elements or has a formula an arm long, he doesn't recognise it.'

'I cannot believe you have gone undiscovered for so long.'

It was no surprise to her. 'I've never attended an art class or studied art at university. I just…dabble in my spare time. There's absolutely no reason why I should've been discovered.' She frowned. 'And you might change your mind once you see my pieces in the flesh.'

She wished she hadn't used the phrase *in the flesh*. Uttering those words at Gabriel seemed altogether too suggestive.

Something in his eyes flared, but it was quickly extinguished. 'I do not think so.'

She couldn't get her head around this conversation at all. He truly thought she had talent?

'I know of several teachers who would help you hone your craft.'

He did?

'Alas, they are all in Rome and Florence, though I think that I, too, could help.'

She moistened suddenly dry lips. 'You would consider taking me on as a student?' He was famously reclusive when it came to discussing his work. Rumour had it that many young artists had petitioned him for a mentorship, but all had been refused. Would he seriously make an exception for her?

'Our mediums are different, but many of our goals are the same.' Firm lips twisted. 'And as we're both stuck here for the summer… Think it over and—'

'I don't need to think about it. I would love to learn all I could from you, Gabriel. I'm fully aware of the compliment you pay me.'

'Good.' He nodded. 'I request, however, that you do not speak to the newspapers about this. I value my privacy.'

'You have my word.'

He stared at her for a long moment, and the air between them crackled. 'You have something else to say?' he demanded.

She chewed on the inside of her lip. 'Are you sure about this?'

His chin tilted at an unconsciously arrogant angle. 'I am not in the habit of making offers that I am not sure about. Why?'

She swallowed. 'Marguerite hasn't asked this of you, has she?' The thought of being foisted on him had everything inside her protesting.

'No. If she had I would not have made the offer.' A humourless smile touched his lips. 'In fact, she will probably be vexed by the arrangement.'

Which, as far as he was concerned, was a point in its favour, she realised.

Those grey eyes turned mocking. 'Do you dare risk her displeasure, Audrey? Which comes first—family or art?'

'Family.' She didn't even have to think about it.

He blinked.

'But I expect Marguerite will be fully cognizant of the honour you do me in offering to mentor me.' She nodded slowly, recalling the vulnerability in her grandmother's eyes. *Please.* 'I suspect she would consider me a fool if I were to refuse it.'

She *would* be a fool. This was a once-in-a-lifetime opportunity. Knowing her own weaknesses, though, knowing how much she yearned for family, if she wasn't careful the Funaro family would consume her completely. And that would defeat the purpose of being here. Accepting Gabriel's offer could help her prevent that from happening.

She wanted to be considered a legitimate member of the Funaro family, but she didn't want to lose her own identity. Or turn her back on her past. A chill chased down her spine. Accepting Gabriel's offer, having a chance to focus on her art, would give her something that was just her own, and might help her find a way to bridge past and present.

'Before we embark any further on this discussion, I need to make one thing very clear to you, Audrey.' His voice had gone chillingly serious and she met his gaze once more. 'I will not shackle myself to the Funaro family a second time.'

For a moment she didn't know what he was talking about. Then she stiffened. 'Didn't we just talk about this?'

'Is that clear?' he repeated, his brows drawing low over his eyes.

'Perfectly.' She didn't ask him why; didn't ask what made him hate the Funaro family so much. It was none of her business. 'Like I said, I'm not currently in the market for romance. For heaven's sake, look at my life!' She spread her arms wide. 'I think it's complicated enough without adding a romance to the mix, don't you?'

His lips twitched and it gave her hope that a sense of humour rested beneath that sober exterior. 'Perhaps,' he agreed.

She suddenly grinned. 'I'm a Funaro, and you're bad-tempered—it would be a most inauspicious match, don't you think? It will be much better to be colleagues, yes?'

He chuckled. '*Si*, this is true. Colleagues then. Come, let's shake on it.'

She placed her hand in his and they shook on it. Who knew? Maybe they'd even eventually become friends.

* * *

Audrey turned first one way and then the other in front of the mirror. Heavens! She eased back and twirled, only to discover her grandmother surveying her from the doorway.

She couldn't help but grin at the older woman.

'I did knock,' Marguerite said, 'but you obviously didn't hear me above that awful racket.' She pointed to Audrey's sound system.

Audrey immediately lowered the volume, but didn't turn it off. 'One day this summer, Grandmama, you and I are going to sip shandies out there on the terrace while I introduce you to the joy that is the music of Taylor Swift.'

'I will look forward to it,' Marguerite said with her customary poise, but Audrey could've sworn the older woman's eyes danced. 'In the meantime, you seem pleased with your new dress.'

She didn't just have a new dress. She had a whole new wardrobe! She'd never owned such beautiful clothes. Tonight she was to make her first appearance in public as a member of the family—at a lavish charity ball—and in its honour, Marguerite had commissioned this dress. Its folds of cream silk and pink lace made her look *beautiful*.

Or maybe that was the new hairstyle.

Or all of the makeup. She'd spent hours with a makeup artist being tutored in how to contour, shape and define each of her features. As if she were a painting or an embroidery—or a work of art.

'I feel like Cinderella,' she confided. Or Audrey Hepburn's character from *My Fair Lady*. On impulse she kissed the older woman's cheek. 'Does my appearance meet with your approval?'

'Yes.'

She'd discovered that her grandmother never gushed, but she also never lied about something as important to her as one's appearance. The hard knot at the centre of her that had been diminishing slowly over the past week eased further now. She wanted to do Marguerite proud, and tonight she meant to do exactly that. She'd be poised, polite and… Well, *polished* wasn't exactly the right word. Marguerite's level of polish came from having grown up in this world, and Audrey doubted she'd ever fully master it. But she'd be warm and kind, and she meant to enjoy every minute of the evening's festivities.

'Several other family members will be attending tonight.' She named two of Audrey's cousins and an uncle and his wife. 'And Gabriel, obviously.'

'Why *obviously*?' She hid a frown—rather well, she thought. She'd get the hang of this poise thing yet. 'He doesn't strike me as…'

Marguerite raised an eyebrow.

'The social type.'

Gabriel had decreed they'd start her lessons next week, and other than her visit to his studio, she'd only seen him one other time this week when she and Lili had spent a happy couple of hours exploring the grounds, Lili showing Audrey all of her favourite spots on the estate. That was when she'd discovered Gabriel and Lili didn't have a suite in the villa, but stayed in a cottage on the grounds instead. He'd not spoken much; had spent more time trailing behind them than taking part in the conversation.

Maybe he'd been thinking about a project he was working on.

Or just ensuring she didn't get the wrong idea and start making big moon eyes at him.

'Gabriel is a patron of this particular charity. It's one that is close to his heart.'

Shame hit her then in a hot rush. She'd been so focused on her new dress and how she looked that she'd not given a second thought to what the charity might be. What charity were they supporting tonight? She was too embarrassed to ask Marguerite.

Swallowing, she made herself smile. 'Shall we all arrive together?'

'Good heavens, no, child.'

Child? She wanted to laugh. She was twenty-six!

'You and I shall take the car together, but we're going to arrive fashionably late.'

So they could make a splash? Her stomach started to churn.

'The others have made their own arrangements. Now remember, this evening all eyes will be upon you. You will keep your shoulders back and your chin high. You are a Funaro.'

She nodded.

'And you will meet me in the foyer no later than eight o'clock.'

'I won't be late.'

With a nod, the older woman left.

Turning back to the mirror, she stared at the unfamiliar reflection gazing back at her. She pointed at it. 'You can do this.' She'd do whatever necessary to make her grandmother, and the rest of the family, proud of her.

She was in the foyer at ten to eight. She suspected Marguerite wouldn't tolerate tardiness, and she'd rather be the one kept waiting. Besides, waiting was something she was used to.

A footstep on the stair above had her turning away from surveying her face in one of the many mirrors that dotted the wall. 'Gabriel.'

He stopped dead. His eyes widened and lips thinned.

Heat rose up her neck and across her cheeks. She gestured to the mirror. 'I'm not usually so vain. I just can't believe what I look like.'

He didn't speak, but those grey eyes appraised her with a throbbing thoroughness that had her stomach clenching.

With an effort, she swallowed. 'I keep having to pinch myself to believe this is real.' She held out her inner arm to show him a red mark there. 'Which I better stop doing or I'll end up with a bruise.' And she doubted that'd meet with Marguerite's approval, either.

* * *

Gabriel stared at Audrey and couldn't utter a single damn word. At the back of his mind an ugly voice sounded: *And so it begins...* But his better self protested against the cynicism. Fina's fate didn't have to be Audrey's. It wasn't a foregone conclusion.

He was trying to protect himself. *Again.* Trying to avoid the soul-crushing disappointment of seeing another life wasted.

A hard knot squeezed his chest tight. If he'd tried harder with Fina—tried harder to break down her barriers, tried harder to make her see how self-destructive her behaviour had been—then maybe she'd be alive today and Lili would still have her mother.

He hadn't tried harder, though. He'd retreated to save himself from the pain of watching her drink herself into a stupor time and time again; retreated from her rants and rages, and from the line of lovers she'd taken such pleasure in parading in front of him. He should've realised it had been a cry for help. Instead, he'd taken righteous refuge in hurt feelings, hurt pride and his sense of betrayal.

Did he mean to bury his head in the sand again now? Did he really mean to stand by and watch another woman be ruined by the Funaro fortune and do nothing?

Rolling his shoulders, he did what he could to shake off the thought.

'Stop looking at me like that.' Audrey pressed her hands to her stomach. 'You're making me nervous. At least tell me I'm going to pass muster.'

'You look very beautiful, but then I think you already know that.'

He did what he could to keep his voice measured. She *was* beautiful. But with her hair piled up on top of her head in a sophisticated updo that showed off the elegant line of her throat, and a dress that clung to curves that had his mouth drying, the skirt floating around her legs like a dream, a deep, hard lust fired to life inside him.

It had him wanting to throw his head back and howl. He'd desired women since Fina's death, had even slept with a few, but he'd not wanted anyone with the fire that pierced him now.

It was just clothes. His hands clenched. And makeup. And a fancy hairstyle. It should make no difference. But together, all of it brought to the fore her beauty, forcing him to acknowledge it…and feel the burn of need in his very bones. It meant he could no longer hide from it.

It was her simple delight, however, her astonishment at her appearance, that eventually burned away some of the hormonal mist. Her enjoyment was oddly touching, and he did not wish to dim it.

'And here I was hoping you'd be more eloquent.' She laughed, part amusement and part shamefaced embarrassment. 'Serves me right for being so frivolous.'

He forced himself down the last few steps. 'I meant what I said. You do look very beautiful.' To his relief, his voice emerged smooth and sincere. Her gaze moved over him like a gentle touch, and his skin tightened.

'You look very debonair yourself.'

The way she suddenly glanced away to fidget with an earring betrayed the fact that she, too, was aware of him. Her frown told him she was no more pleased about it than he was.

He stared at his feet. They were adults. They could ignore this.

She sent him a tight smile. 'But we both know beauty is as beauty does. Tonight's purpose isn't about me looking beautiful.'

It wasn't?

'But supporting a good cause, like breast cancer.'

His head came up. Did she care about such things?

'Marguerite gave me to understand it's an important one to you.'

'My mother died of breast cancer.'

'Oh, Gabriel, I didn't know. I'm sorry.'

He shrugged. 'It was a long time ago now.'

Nodding, she glanced up the stairs and then back at him, a question in her eyes.

'I wanted to see Lili settled in the nursery before I left. I had planned to leave before now, but she talked me into reading her a second bedtime story.'

That made her laugh, and a whole new awareness rippled over the surface of his skin. 'I didn't think, but of course she'd be staying here tonight.'

He didn't want to dwell on that. He knew Lili would come to no harm under Marguerite's roof. It's just he wanted, *needed*, to ensure that the Funaro influence didn't dominate Lili's life. He wanted his daughter to grow up to be whatever she wanted to be, not moulded into a cookie-cutter socialite with no anchor to keep her grounded. That lack of an anchor had destroyed Fina. He was determined Lili would find one in him, in the values he meant to instil in her, and in helping her find her purpose in life. He would do everything he could to protect her, to prevent her from feeling cast adrift, worthless and filled with despair.

'I understand we're travelling separately.'

Her frown had him chuckling. 'I suspect Marguerite will want to make a splash tonight as she introduces you to…'

She raised one marvellous eyebrow. 'Her friends?'

'High society.' He shoved his hands into the pockets of his trousers. 'And I prefer to drive myself. That way I can come and go as I please.'

An uncomfortable silence opened up then. 'You know everyone is going to want the inside story tonight. So…what's the party line?'

He'd be questioned, too, but he had the skills to deflect and the bad manners to tell people to mind their own business. Marguerite's high society only tolerated him because of his fame. He clenched his jaw so hard it started to ache. If he didn't find a way to unblock himself soon, though, he'd not have even that.

Beneath whatever perfume she wore, he still detected a note of lavender when she leaned towards him. 'The what?'

'How are you explaining the discovery that you're a Funaro heiress?'

Her lips turned down a fraction. 'Well, we're saying that my parents had an intense whirlwind affair. That resulted in... me. My father never knew my mother's true identity. She went off to see more of the world, with promises to come back, but never returned. As a result, I never knew I was a Funaro until my nonna's death when I received the letter she'd left for me.'

He wondered what the real story was. The one throbbing beneath the sanitised version. The shadows in her eyes told him there was one.

She leaned across and suddenly gripped his hand. 'I'm glad you're going to be there tonight, Gabriel. It'll help to have a friendly face in the crowd.'

Damn. Damn and blast!

He wasn't any kind of knight. Fina had proven that.

She smiled and it was as if the shadows had never been. 'I also plan to have fun this evening. In all my life, I've never been to a party like this one.'

He couldn't help feeling she was going to be sadly disappointed. And—

And nothing! She had her art. It would help when all of this tumbled down around her ears. It would be something she could fall back on. And that at least was something he could help her with.

CHAPTER FIVE

GABRIEL GLANCED AT his watch. It was nearing midnight and his gaze once more drifted across the dance floor to where Alessio Russo expertly spun Audrey around before pulling her flush against his body.

His grip tightened on his champagne flute. It was the second time Alessio had danced with Audrey this evening, and not the first time he'd pulled her in far too close. Nor was it the first time his hand had drifted lower than it ought to. Audrey again lifted the errant hand back to her waist.

Gabriel had kept a surreptitious eye on her all night. He'd told himself it was the least that he could do. She was a lamb in a room full of wolves, and what kind of person would he be if he simply abandoned her?

He glanced at Marguerite on the other side of the room. It'd make him no better than her or any of the other people here.

In contrast to them all, Audrey glowed like a soft candle at midnight, bathing all around her in warmth and welcome. It made things inside him ache. He wanted to march her off the dance floor and order her to keep her guard up around these people. He wanted—

Alessio's hand lowered to Audrey's backside once more. Gabriel knocked back the rest of his drink in a single gulp, set his glass to the nearest table and strode onto the dance floor. 'I believe I'm going to cut in.'

'But the song hasn't finished yet,' Alessio protested, 'and—'

Gabriel bared his teeth and Alessio hastily unhanded her. 'By all means.'

Audrey gurgled back a laugh as he fled and Gabriel took her in his arms. 'You've frightened the poor man half to death.'

As her hand curved in his and the other came to a rest on his shoulder, things that had been jarring all night suddenly eased. Audrey was warm and alive and those dancing eyes had a smile reluctantly tugging at his lips. 'Alessio is a sleaze. He deserves to be frightened half to death.'

'Ah, but apparently his family is of impeccable stock.'

No doubt that had come from Marguerite. A union between the Funaros and the Russos would be undeniably beneficial to Funaro business interests. He'd bet Marguerite hadn't mentioned that Alessio was also a gambler who was in debt up to his ears. *That* would be beside the point.

She waggled her eyebrows. 'Apparently, that's very important.'

'Tut-tut. Don't let Marguerite hear you speak so irreverently of bloodlines,' he scolded with mock sternness. But the vision of Alessio's hands on Audrey's hips, pulling her closer, rose through him once more and it was all he could do to not bare his teeth again. 'The Russos are an old and connected family, but you would think that, as such, they'd have taken the trouble to teach their children better manners. I know you were dealing with him as efficiently as you could in the circumstance, and I suspect you didn't want to make a scene by walking off the dance floor, but it hardly seemed fair you suffer those wandering hands a moment longer.'

'I appreciate the intervention. I think he'd had a little too much to drink.'

Dio. Must this woman always make excuses for bad behaviour?

'And it's nice to dance with you, Gabriel. For once, I don't have to make small talk, sidestep impertinent questions and pretend to be...' She trailed off, but he knew what she meant.

'So Cinderella isn't enjoying the ball as much as she thought she would?'

'Oh, no, I am! I'm having the most exciting time.'

She was?

'The dinner was a revelation—I mean, *caviar*. Before tonight I'd never had French champagne, either.'

'And did you like them both?'

She nodded, those warm walnut eyes dancing. 'As my father would say, I've champagne tastes on a beer budget.'

An uncharacteristic snort shot from him, making several people glance around at him in surprise.

'What does your father think about all of this?'

When her face fell, he wished he'd not asked.

'Well, I only told him this week. Once I realised it was going to make the papers. He was a bit…shocked.'

He could imagine. Had the man really been in ignorance of Danae's true identity as a Funaro?

'But he's recently remarried and has started a new job in the States, and it's keeping him very busy, so he won't have much time to worry.'

'Speaking of marriage… Did he and Danae marry?'

'My dear Gabriel, you're definitely going off script with that question.'

He didn't know if her chiding was serious or not.

'Apparently, the right response is *my parents had a fiery affair.*'

Marguerite's hand again, no doubt.

She bit her lip. 'I always thought they had, but maybe I was wrong.'

Or maybe…

'But if they were, it clearly wasn't legal.'

Because Danae had never divorced from her first husband.

'Nobody talks of her, you know?'

Of Danae? Of course, they didn't. And he had no intention of talking out of school, either.

Before he realised it, they'd danced another dance, and he grew aware of the speculation growing rife in the eyes of those who surreptitiously but greedily watched. *Damn.* He didn't want to be the subject of that kind of gossip or—

Though... He glanced down at the woman in his arms. Perhaps it wouldn't hurt for people to think he was interested. It'd help keep the worst of the fortune hunters and those who wanted to use her for other kinds of gains—for family and business alliances, but who wouldn't care about her as a living, breathing person—at bay.

'More champagne?'

She gave a funny little shimmy as the dance came to an end. 'Yes, please. Who knew dancing could build such a thirst?'

After seizing two champagnes from a passing waiter, he led her to one of the chairs arranged at intervals around the dance floor.

She patted the chair beside her. 'Don't loom, Gabriel. Sit.'

He was used to the women at these events who wanted to cultivate his company by raising flirtatious eyebrows and sending him long, lingering glances. Or, alternately, giving a prim thank-you as their eyes scanned the crowd for someone more biddable and civilised.

Audrey did neither of those things and as her smile informed him she was enjoying his company, he sat, then watched as an expression of bliss crossed her face when she sipped her champagne. He sipped his, too, taking the time to focus on the spark and fizz. She was right. The wine was excellent.

When had it all become old hat to him? When had he started to take it for granted? When had he started hating it?

The answer came swiftly and surely: *Since Fina died.*

'Excuse me, sir, but Ms Marguerite Funaro asked me to give you a message.'

He glanced at the uniformed waiter who appeared at his elbow. 'Yes?'

'She had a headache and has retired early. She requested you see Ms Martinelli safely home.'

'Thank you.' He did what he could not to betray his surprise.

When the man moved away, Audrey frowned. 'Are you sure Marguerite warned you off? Are you sure she's not trying her hand at some kind of surreptitious matchmaking?'

He couldn't help it. He laughed. 'I'm certain.'

She blew out a breath. 'Good.'

He rolled his shoulders, tried to dislodge an odd itch. 'Why?'

'Because you told me you hate to be manipulated. And while the motives might be benevolent, I suspect you would hate someone trying to set you up.'

Benevolent? Dear God, this woman! 'I am certain your grandmother is not trying to set us up.'

'In that case…' She took her phone from her clutch and composed a text message. No doubt telling her grandmother that she hoped she was feeling better soon. When she was done, she turned back to him. 'Is it my imagination, or does the room sit up and take notice whenever I dance more than one dance with a partner?'

'It's not your imagination.'

'So the fact we just danced two and a half dances have set tongues wagging?'

'*Si.*'

Her pleated brow told him what she thought of that.

'Were you being honest with me when you said you were not currently interested in finding yourself a husband or having a romance?'

Those walnut eyes flashed. 'Of course I was.'

He liked her all the more for the fire. 'In that case, I apologise.'

'Eventually, I'd like to fall in love, marry…have children.' She shrugged. 'But it's the farthest thing from my mind at the moment. There's just too much to learn and come to grips with.' She bit her lip. 'I don't…'

He raised his brows.

She leaned a little closer. 'I don't wish to make the same mistakes my mother clearly did.'

Her words chilled him to the bone. He didn't want that for her, either. He *could* help. A little. 'In that case, what harm will it do if people do link us romantically?'

Her eyes grew comically wide.

The more he thought about it, the more the notion recommended itself to him. If everyone thought he and Audrey were dating, it would give her time to find her feet and work out who she could trust and who to keep her distance from.

'Are you suggesting we *lie*?'

'Absolutely not. *We* don't lie, remember? But very few people will ask the question outright. If they do, you can deny it.' They wouldn't believe her, but he kept that piece of information to himself. 'In the meantime, it will buy you time, and give you an excuse to refuse all the invitations single eligible men are going to start sending your way.'

'You think men are going to start asking me on dates?'

'I don't think, I know.'

She sipped her champagne. 'I don't want to go on dates.'

'See? My plan is pure brilliance.'

That made her laugh. 'Won't it cramp your style?'

'I am not currently interested in dating, either.'

'Why not?'

Things inside him clenched. 'I need to focus on my art and my daughter. I do not have room for other things.'

She looked as if she wanted to say something, but eventually shrugged. 'Okay.'

Her easy acceptance made him want to laugh.

'If you're going to be my lift home tonight, I want you to know I'm happy to leave the party whenever you are. Please don't change your plans to suit me. But if I don't at least sample that chocolate mousse before we leave, I'm going to regret it for the rest of my life.'

He stared at her. 'You are very easy to be with. Do you know that?'

She blinked.

'You are not—what do they say?—high-maintenance.' All the women he knew were high-maintenance.

'Low-maintenance, that's me.' She grinned. 'Apparently, I'm obliging to a fault.'

'Then I will oblige you in my turn and get you one of those chocolate mousses.'

'And then will you tell me how one goes about setting up a foundation like the one you have for your mother?'

He stared at her for a long moment, but those cinnamon-spice eyes stared back at him unfazed. What on earth was she up to? 'If you wish.'

'Thank you.'

'Which do you like better? The pink or white marshmallows?' Lili asked.

'I like the white ones best.' Audrey reached into the bowl, took a white marshmallow and popped it into her mouth.

Gabriel pretended to be immersed in his sketch—which was a joke in itself, but not one that was funny. He glared at the rose he was supposed to be sketching. It didn't speak to him at all. Maybe one of the Madonna lilies would be more suitable. He stared at the nearest one, but although it was perfection, not a ripple of enthusiasm lifted through him. Instead, his attention remained on his daughter and her aunt. They were currently stretched out on the blanket on the lawn in this sheltered corner of the garden. It was a corner few people came to, which is why he'd chosen it.

'But the pink marshmallows are *so* much prettier!'

'They are prettier, but I think the white ones taste nicer.'

He thought they tasted exactly the same. Clearly, Audrey held a contrary view on the matter.

Lili reached for a white marshmallow, then, just like Audrey had, and he bit back a smile.

'It's like clothes,' Audrey said, turning onto her back and pointing to a cloud. 'That one looks like a rabbit.'

For the briefest of moments, he imagined lying above her, staring down at her. Imagined the feel of her body; imagined the silken nakedness of her and—

Dio! He tried to banish the picture from his mind.

Lili, in perfect imitation of Audrey, lay on her back, too. 'What do you mean marshmallows are like clothes?'

'Well, Grandmama has insisted on buying me a lot of beautiful new clothes for all the balls and dinner parties and luncheons I'll be attending. And some of them are *so* beautiful. But you want to know what my favourite item of clothing is?'

Lili stared at her with wide eyes. 'What?'

'My really old jeans that I've had for a million years. I mean I know all the pretty clothes look nicer, but they're nowhere near as comfortable.' She sat up. 'Can you keep a secret?' Her eyes danced and he found himself as entranced as Lili. 'Grandmama told the maid to throw my old jeans away, but I sneaked out to the bin and retrieved them.'

Lili clapped her hands over her mouth, but girlish giggles still escaped.

'But you can't tell Grandmama! Promise?'

'I promise!'

And then Lili threw herself at Audrey, who caught her as if it was the most natural thing in the world, and who hugged her back with what looked like her entire being.

CHAPTER SIX

AUDREY'S ART LESSONS officially started the week following her society debut. Gabriel had insisted on three lessons a week—and by lessons he meant whole days spent at the studio working. It hadn't been a suggestion, more a command, but Audrey hadn't argued because, a) he was doing her a favour, and b) she wasn't used to having so much free time on her hands and she'd started to find herself searching for things to do.

Something beyond trying to work out the tangled tensions and strange undercurrents among the various Funaro family members.

They were nothing like her family back home in Melbourne. Surely, money and social standing shouldn't change family dynamics *that* much. She suddenly wished she'd taken her cousin Frankie up on her offer to come to Lake Como for moral support. Frankie was currently holidaying in Tuscany, and she had the ability to cut through nonsense and get to the heart of a matter.

Blowing out a breath, she told herself to stop being a baby. But that didn't stop the warning her grandmother had given her last night and the promise she'd extracted from weighing heavily on her shoulders.

Glancing across at Gabriel, who scowled with savage intensity at a half-finished sculpture, she had to suppress a shiver. He looked every bit as ferocious as Marguerite had claimed.

Does he, though?

Cocking her head to one side, she studied him more carefully. Maybe he was tired. Maybe he was wrestling with his muse and not happy with the way his work was going. Maybe he just had a headache.

A pulse pounded in her throat. Maybe Marguerite had misjudged him.

Chilly grey eyes lifted to hers with remarkable precision, as if aware she'd been surveying him. 'You've not managed a single stitch in the last thirty minutes.'

She shrugged and gestured at his sculpture. 'You haven't made any progress in the last thirty minutes, either.'

'I'm cogitating. What's your excuse?'

She was brooding. Not that she had any intention of telling him so. 'I'm just getting used to my new surroundings.'

'Did you have this same kind of trouble when you were working with Madame De Luca?'

No. But that was before her life had been turned upside down.

'I didn't think so.' Slamming hands to his hips, he let out an insultingly impatient breath. 'And you worked fine on Monday and Wednesday. Tell me what's bothering you.'

And just like that, without warning, anger flared. Anger she suspected she'd been tamping down for four long years. 'Stop ordering me about like some damn maidservant!'

He blinked.

She was so damn tired of being the good girl, the responsible one, the person who never rocked the boat; the one who always bent over backwards to make sure everyone else felt comfortable. Nobody here cared if she felt uncomfortable or out of her depth or *anything*. Why did she always feel as if she had to be the one to make up the shortfall?

A different expression took up residence in those grey eyes, but it wasn't one she could read. Swallowing, she waited for the customary guilt to hit her—to make her feel bad for stepping outside the lines she normally prescribed for herself. And kept right on waiting.

She let out a breath she hadn't realised she'd been holding. Maybe here in this extraordinary studio the normal rules didn't apply. It was a freeing thought.

Perfect lips pursed. 'I see we're not going to have the usual kind of teacher-student relationship.'

'I have a feeling sitting at your feet and staring adoringly up at you isn't the way to earn your respect.'

'And you want my respect?'

'Don't we all want to be respected?'

And liked?

She had a feeling, though, that Gabriel didn't care whether people liked him or not.

'It's more important to respect ourselves before we start worrying what other people think of us.' He folded his arms and widened his stance. 'I didn't mean to sound so abrupt before. I apologise if you felt I was ordering you about. I'm not used to having anyone else other than Lili in the studio.'

All of her righteous outrage dissolved at his words.

'However, I would honestly like to know what's bothering you.'

She glanced at his work in progress and then back up at him. 'I'd like to know what's bothering you, too.' She was tired of being the only one who felt clueless, the only one who felt vulnerable.

He pulled in a long breath that had already broad shoulders broadening and a deep chest deepening, and something inside her quickened. Swallowing, she forced her gaze back to his, refusing to notice anything else.

He stared at her for a long moment. 'What's said in the studio stays in the studio?'

She pondered that then nodded. 'Okay.'

He gestured at his sculpture. 'I'm blocked. I have been for months. Eight months to be precise.'

Her jaw dropped.

'It's not something I'd like made public. I have three commissions due by the end of the year and yet… I have nothing.' That dark scowl bloomed across his face again. 'It's beyond frustrating and makes me testy.'

She couldn't think of a single word to say.

'No platitudes to offer?'

His sarcasm, she finally saw, was a shield. It wasn't directed at her personally, but at himself. She lifted a hand and let it drop. 'I'm sorry, of course, but that's hardly helpful.'

He rolled his shoulders. 'Any advice to offer?'

'Me?'

'Yes, of course you.' That scowl became ferocious again. 'Why not you? You're an artist, aren't you?'

That was debatable. She stared at the screen in front of her, at her barely started embroidery, and forced her chin up. 'You said you've been blocked for eight months. Did something happen eight months ago?' Had he suffered a trauma or an accident? 'Have you been ill or anything?'

'No.' He was silent for a moment. 'You've never suffered from a creative block?'

'I've never had the opportunity. I've only ever worked on my embroideries in my free time and in stolen moments.'

Perfect lips twisted. 'So I'm wallowing in my malcontent and wasting the good fortune I've been given. Being self-indulgent.'

'That's not what I said!' But it's how he saw himself, she realised. 'I think you need to relax a bit and stop being so tense.' *And judgemental.* 'Coffee?'

She didn't wait for an answer, but strode across to the small kitchenette and the coffee machine, glancing up briefly at the mysterious mezzanine level that hadn't been part of her tour, before busying herself making coffee. 'When was the last time you made something just for fun? Just because you wanted to?'

'I…'

She looked at him. Could he not remember? 'I've fitted my embroideries in between work and other things. It has always been a form of relaxation and play.' That had to change once it became your day job.

'What other things?'

She glanced around at the unexpected question. For a moment she was tempted to tell him, but Marguerite would hate it if she did. Marguerite had requested Audrey not tell anyone.

Ice slid in between her ribs. Her sister Johanna wasn't anything to be ashamed of. She'd reluctantly agreed not to mention her twin in the near future, though. She wanted a chance for her and Marguerite to grow close, before putting forward the memorial she had in mind for her sister.

She busied herself with the coffee again. 'Oh, you know. Family and taking care of a house and chores and all the other things normal people do.'

He ambled across to lean on a kitchen bench. 'You do not consider the Funaros normal people?'

His lips had lifted in a smile, humour lurking in his eyes, making him look younger, and she shook her head, battling a strange sense of breathlessness. 'I do not. I doubt they'd know the first thing about keeping a house clean or how to do the grocery shopping or put on a load of laundry.'

His warm chuckle lifted the fine hairs on her arms.

'Do you?' The question blurted out of her unbidden, and he sobered.

'I grew up in a working-class family. My father died when I was young and my mother was an invalid. More often than not, the household chores fell to me. As I suspect they did to you, too, if your father was a scientist. I take it that it was his house that you kept.'

She'd always thought it was hers, too. Just for a moment their gazes caught and clung. Shaking herself, she poured coffee into two mugs. 'I believe it's called character building.'

He gave another of those rare chuckles that threatened to wrap around her like a warm blanket.

Don't think about warm blankets. Or rumpled sheets.

Straightening, she forced her mind back to their conversation. 'What I'm trying to say is that embroidery has always been my escape from the real world.' She handed him a mug. 'I've never been commissioned to make something for someone else. I mean, I've made gifts for family members and friends, but I've never had to make something to measure like you. Things have to change when art becomes your work.'

'It does not feel like work. To be able to make a living from my art has been a joy.'

It was hard to associate joy and Gabriel in the same sentence.

'Is that what has been worrying you? That you now have to share your art? Is that why you haven't been able to work this morning?' His eyes narrowed, and he shook his head. 'No, that is not it.' He shrugged when she sent him an exasperated glare. 'What? You have an expressive face.'

'Then I'm going to need lessons in how to look like a closed book.'

'That is something I can help you with, too.'

She might just take him up on it. 'Yesterday afternoon Marguerite called me into her private apartment for a chat.'

His mouth flattened. 'Come, let's get some fresh air.'

He led her outside to the wooden table and benches that rested on one side of the studio. With the sun warm on her face, she sank down to a bench to gobble up the expansive views of unruffled water in various shades of silver, deep blue and navy green that spread before her. Timeless mountains rising silent and majestic all around.

'What did Marguerite say that still has you chafing a day later?'

She snapped back with a bump. 'She warned me off you.'

His face became enviously unreadable, and she swallowed.

'Remember what we agreed. What's said in the studio stays in the studio.'

'Absolutely.'

She bit her lip. 'Are you offended?'

She'd love to somehow bridge the uncomfortable gap that existed between Marguerite and Gabriel. It'd be far more pleasant for Lili if her father and grandmother could be friends. And Lili *was* her niece. She'd do all she could to ensure the little girl was happy and content.

'Why should I be offended? As you know, she has already given me that same lecture.'

It wasn't an answer.

'Marguerite is always scheming, though. I do not trust her.'

Marguerite had likewise been far from flattering about Gabriel. She'd said that he wasn't to be trusted where women were concerned; that he'd become too angry and embittered after Serafina's death—as if he wanted revenge on the entire female population.

Revenge? Because no woman could ever live up to his memory of Serafina? The thought had made her stomach churn.

Marguerite had said she didn't want to see Audrey suffer at his hands. Audrey didn't want that, either.

'She made me promise to not fall in love with you.'

He shot to his feet. 'And you *agreed* to such an archaic directive?'

Those grey eyes glared at her, his large body bristling with outrage, but he didn't alarm her. Not anymore. She'd seen beneath the bluster. Whatever Gabriel wanted her and the rest of the world to think of him—and, again, she doubted he cared—she knew that beneath that bristling demeanour, he was a good man.

Wasn't he helping her with her art? And hadn't he rescued her on Saturday night when Alessio's hands had been straying? And the fact his daughter adored him spoke volumes.

Yes, Gabriel Dimarco, despite whatever Marguerite thought, was a good man.

She lifted her chin and glared back at him. 'Of course I did. I thought you'd be pleased.'

His mouth worked but not a single sound emerged.

'Why all this outrage? Didn't you demand the same promise from me? On this one issue, at least, you and Marguerite seem to be in complete agreement.'

And so was she. He might be a good man, but to fall in love with him…

She went cold all over. She hadn't been enough for her mother and she hadn't been enough for her father. She wasn't making the mistake of falling in love with Gabriel, because she'd never be enough for him, either—not enough for him to overcome his prejudices; not enough for him to be a part of a family he loathed; not enough for him to risk getting his heart burned again. No, she was nowhere near enough for him on any level.

All she was good for was as an aunt to his daughter. One he could trust to be sensible. And that was something. She knew that. But it was a line drawn in the sand…and he wasn't even totally convinced she could be that person yet, either. She suppressed a shudder, imagining what it would be like to give your heart to such a man. He'd shred it. Oh, he wouldn't mean to, but his coldness, his inflexibility, his indifference… It would be the chilliest, loneliest of prisons.

Not going to happen.

Nonna had taught her that comfort and strength came in the shape of family. Her parents might've let her down, but her sister, grandmother, aunt and her cousin had all been there for her. She'd find strength and solace in her new family. *That* was where she needed to focus her efforts.

Gabriel stared at Audrey and wanted to yell; wanted to slash dark, ugly colour across a canvas. It made no sense. He had extracted the same promise. Why should it infuriate him that Marguerite would request it, too?

Because it was none of Marguerite's business who he dated or slept with.

'On Saturday night, when she saw how ably you rescued me from Mr Wandering Hands, she wanted to make sure I didn't read too much into your gallantry.'

His hand had clenched on the table beside his mug. He forced it to unclench. 'Why, then, when she could have the finest and most celebrated teachers here with a click of her fingers, would she entrust me with your artistic instruction?'

She leaned towards him as if he was hard of hearing…or slow of understanding. 'She said you are one of the most important artists of your generation. She knows what a coup it is that you've taken an interest in my education.' She folded her hands in her lap like a prim schoolgirl. 'I've been ordered to learn all I can from you.' Lovely lips twitched. 'And to not make a nuisance of myself.'

His eyes practically started from his head. 'I do not believe you.'

An eyebrow rose, but laughter still remained in the depths of those spice-coloured eyes.

'Sorry, that was a figure of speech, of disbelief, not an accusation. I know you do not lie.'

Her eyes abruptly dropped and a burning started in his chest. What wasn't she telling him? Had Marguerite told her he was a beast where women were concerned—that he used and abused his paramours before discarding them with nary a thought?

As far as the Funaros were concerned, he had never been good enough for their darling Serafina. And now he clearly wasn't good enough for their darling Audrey, either.

A sigh escaped soft lips, and things inside him tightened as his gaze fixed on those lips. Dear God, he had to stop fixating on them—their shape and texture—and wondering what it would be like to kiss them. Wondering what kind of lover Audrey would be—would she be shy or bold? He thought she would be shy, but he suspected there was fire banked beneath that unflappable exterior and he'd—

Stop!

'What's the issue between you and Marguerite anyway?' Her brow pleated. 'Is it to do with Serafina?'

He stiffened at his wife's name.

She huffed out a laugh. 'Bingo. Nobody wants me to ask questions, but this is my family. I don't understand what happened or why this has made everyone the way they are.'

'And how do you think they are?'

She stared out at the lake, rubbed a hand across her chest. 'Broken,' she finally said.

The single word made him flinch. So did the sorrow in her gaze—all this concern for these people she barely yet knew.

'Nobody speaks of either Serafina or Danae. As soon as I mention either name, the conversation is deftly changed to some other channel or people excuse themselves, because there's something that they have to *see to immediately*. If a long-lost daughter turned up to meet my family in Australia, we'd regale her with all the stories we could about the mother she'd never known…and the sister.'

He silently swore.

'Obviously, the stories are far from pretty. Obviously, they're painful. But I don't see how keeping me in the dark is going to help.'

'I suspect Marguerite is wanting you to get used to everything else before subjecting you to the less salubrious side of the family history.'

Firm eyes met his. She might appear meek and quiet on first meeting, but there was a surprising strength to this woman, too. 'What's the deal between you and Marguerite?' she asked again.

Things inside him clenched and burned. 'Marguerite holds me responsible for Fina's death.'

Her face fell.

'While I hold *her* responsible.' She opened her mouth, but he held up a hand. 'No more for today.'

With a nod, she transferred her gaze to her coffee. 'Can I ask a side question, then? Why do you spend the summers here on Marguerite's estate?'

'Lili. It is an arrangement made between lawyers, to give her the opportunity to know her mother's family. Marguerite could insist that I drop Lili off and leave her here, but we both know Lili will be happier if I am here, too. So Marguerite tolerates me. In return, I allow her visits throughout the rest of the year.'

The smallest of smiles touched those lips.

Don't notice the lips.

'You've found a way to work together—for Lili's sake.'

'If I had my way, Lili would have no contact at all with the Funaro family.'

She frowned. 'You have to believe it's only right that she knows both sides of her family—'

'No, I don't!'

He couldn't help the savagery with which he spat out those words. He hated himself for them when Audrey flinched, but he couldn't take them back. They were the truth. 'The Funaro family are poison.' And with everything he had, he wished he could protect Lili from them.

Her eyes throbbed into his. 'You hate them.'

He normally kept a more civilised facade on these emotions, but Audrey had somehow prised that lid off and it was taking all of his strength to hold them in check.

'I'm a Funaro. Do you hate me, too?'

Exhaustion overtook him then. 'I do not hate you, Audrey. You are not a true Funaro. You are, I suspect, very much a Martinelli.' And his hate was not so illogical.

Are you sure?

Of course he was sure. He loathed the Funaros for not believing the rules applied to them, for thinking themselves above the laws that defined and governed normal behaviour—for their excesses and entitlement and selfishness.

'There's something I don't understand.'

He frowned. 'Just the one?'

'Why *have* you agreed to take my artistic education in hand if you hate the family so much?'

The way she said *hate* made him sound like a monster. And who knows? Maybe that was exactly what he'd become. If he'd managed to corral his anger and resentment towards Fina, she might still be here. And Lili might still have her mother.

'Lili.' The single word cracked from lips that didn't want to cooperate, but he suddenly and desperately didn't want this woman to let his daughter down the way her mother had. He would do everything in his power to prevent that, regardless of what he thought of the rest of the Funaro family.

'Lili?'

She said his daughter's name with such affection. Nodding, he rubbed a hand over his face. 'She adores you.'

'I adore her, too.'

'Do you know what she said to me the other night? She said that she loved you and that she was certain her mother would be just like you.'

Audrey gave a funny little hiccup, her eyes growing suspiciously bright.

'And then she asked me if you were going to die like her mother had died.'

The soft gasp speared to the very centre of him.

'The Funaro women sometimes self-destruct, Audrey. It is what they do. It is what your mother did and it is what your sister did. Nobody talks of it because it brought shame and scandal to the Funaro name—and that is something that Marguerite finds unforgivable.'

She stared at him for a long moment. 'The reason Marguerite doesn't talk of them is because their deaths hurt her too much. She loved them and it hurts her to remember how they died.'

'You are seeing what you want to see. You only see the best in people.'

'While you only see their worst.'

She didn't say it as an accusation. Just sadly, as if she felt bad for him. An itch settled between his shoulder blades. 'I did not see what was happening to Fina. I didn't realise how close she was skating to the edge. Marguerite did not see it, either.'

'And as a result, you blame each other.'

He ignored that. 'Fina had nothing to fall back on—no resources beyond partying ever harder and trying an ever-greater array of drugs.'

He watched her digest that.

And lovers. Fina had also taken lovers. Lots of them. He left that unsaid, though. Even now Fina's infidelity chafed at him. He'd have given her everything, but she hadn't wanted anything he'd had to offer.

All she'd wanted was to annoy her grandmother by marrying someone none of them considered suitable. He'd been nothing but Fina's act of rebellion, and the knowledge left a bitter taste in his mouth. He'd been too focused on getting a divorce, and custody of Lili, to see how far down Fina was spiralling.

He leaned towards Audrey now. If he had any say in the matter, this woman would not follow Fina's path. 'Your art will give you something to fall back on—somewhere to escape to when the pressures of life in the fast lane, the pressure of being a Funaro, become too much. I do not want you to let Lili down the way Fina let her down.'

'Oh, God, Gabriel…'

She stared at him, stricken. Reaching out, she gripped his forearm, her hand small and pale against his tanned skin. 'I am *not* a life-in-the-fast-lane person.'

'Not yet.'

'And I am *never* going to take drugs.'

'So you say now, but how can you be so certain?'

'Because I care about my health!'

She was a nurse's aide. She must've seen what drugs did to people.

'Do you take drugs? Or do you mean to in the future?'

He stiffened. 'Absolutely not!'

She glanced to where her hand rested on his arm, as if his muscles tensing beneath her fingertips was a fascinating sensation. He flexed his arm again. The action involuntary. Her fingers firmed against him as if to test the solidity of the flesh beneath… And then she snapped away as if he burned her. The way she swallowed and glanced out at the lake had his every primal instinct firing to life.

Audrey found him attractive. And he found satisfaction in that knowledge. A deep, burning satisfaction. If he turned her face towards him, would she let him kiss her? If he kissed her with the deep, thorough hunger pouring through him now, would she kiss him back with the same abandon? Would she wrap her arms around him and press herself against him in a silent plea for more?

His breath sawed in and out of his lungs. Would she let him peel the clothes from her body and lose himself in the—

What the hell…?

This woman was off-limits. No matter how much he might wonder what it would be like to bed her, it was not a fantasy in which he could indulge. For Lili's sake. For Audrey's sake, too.

And his own.

She turned with eyes that seemed to shine with some powerful inner light. 'You've agreed to take charge of my education because you want to protect me.'

'Do not look at me like that.' He pointed a shaking finger at her. He was not a knight in shining armour.

'Like what?'

'Like I am a hero.' The idea was laughable.

'You said I like to see the best in people.'

'You will be foolish to see what isn't there.'

'Or maybe you need to start seeing yourself through eyes like mine.'

This woman had no idea, and she would be hurt, and hurt badly, if this was the way she meant to deal with the Funaros.

'I fear for you, Audrey, but I will not be drawn back into that world—the one the Funaros inhabit.'

'That sounds like a warning.'

It was. 'Why is this family so important to you?'

She folded her arms. 'Why is Lili so important to you?'

He waved that off. A child was an altogether different thing. He thought back to the things that she'd told him. 'Your nonna recently died,' he started slowly, 'and your father has abandoned you for pastures greener.'

'He hasn't abandoned me!' But her gaze slid away.

'It was his house that you kept. This I know already. You told me as much. No doubt you cooked and cleaned for him.' Cared for him.

She shrugged, but a new tension threaded through her. 'It was my home, too. It was the family home.'

His heart started to thump. She'd said her father had taken a new job in America. 'Audrey, what happened to the family home?'

She moistened her lips, not meeting his eyes. 'It was sold.'

Dio! No wonder she felt so lost, so rootless. But to pin her hopes on the Funaros… 'You are lonely, feeling at a loose end. And are now hoping this new family you've discovered will fill the holes in your life and your heart.'

She turned to him fully, a frown in her eyes. 'I want to love them and I want them to love me.' She touched a hand to her chest. 'I want to belong. What's so wrong with that?'

'The Funaros are not that kind of family.'

'So says you, and you clearly don't want to belong to anyone. You'll have to excuse me if I take what you say on the subject with a grain of salt.'

'You want them to save you. When they cannot even save themselves. You will be disappointed and disillusioned and—'

'Let's agree to disagree on that one. Or we'll have an awful falling out and I'd prefer that we didn't.'

He'd prefer that, too.

'Do you ever sketch, Gabriel?'

The change in topic threw him. 'Yes, of course.' He made multiple sketches of his sculptures before starting them.

'Me, too. I want to sit on that rock over there and sketch out a design that's started to come to me. I want to somehow try and capture all this.' She gestured at the view.

'Very well. And once you are done you can explain your process to me.'

'Okay, but fair's fair. You need to sketch, too, and explain your process to me.'

He didn't have a process at the moment. He had nothing!

Which meant he didn't have anything to lose, either. 'Very well. I will remain here and try to capture the mountains.'

Fifteen minutes later he gave up with an exasperated sigh. Glancing across at Audrey, who sat on her rock at the other end of the small bay, he found her with head bent over her sketchpad. Picking up a charcoal, he drew a few lines to make the shape of her. Audrey was an interesting combination of frailty and strength. And as the clash between weakness and strength was what he often took as his subject...

Frowning, he drew a few more lines. And then some more. Before he knew it, his hand was flying across the page.

CHAPTER SEVEN

GABRIEL'S STICK OF CHARCOAL raced across the page of his sketchpad as if afraid that if it didn't keep moving, the image it was trying to capture would disappear and fade to black.

Audrey wanted to go peer over his shoulder, curious to see what had finally sparked his creativity, but didn't dare disturb him. Instead, she sat on the nearby rustic retaining wall with her sketchpad in her lap and remained silent.

A breath of warm air fanned the hair at her nape and a beetle negotiated the grass and pebbles at her feet. She watched its progress, but Gabriel's earlier words continued to go around and around in her mind.

You want them to save you when they cannot even save themselves.

Her heart pounded. She'd never felt so seen—so *judged*. Was that what she wanted—for them to save her?

Losing Nonna had made her realise that there were only Aunt Deidre, Frankie and herself left of her family. Oh, she'd still have her father, but while he'd been physically present, he'd been as absent as her mother in all the ways that had counted. But if anything were to happen to Aunt Deidre or Frankie…

Her mouth dried. Did she really hope the Funaros would fill that gap?

They cannot even save themselves.

She pulled her gaze from the beetle and stared out at the water. Maybe she could do something about that. She wasn't weak and she wasn't pathetic. Her heart was big enough and strong enough to take a few knocks if the prize at the end was a family that loved each other, that pulled together.

She'd had that with Nonna and Johanna, and Frankie and Aunt Deidre. There was absolutely no reason why she couldn't have it with Marguerite and Lili and the rest of the Funaro family as well. She had no intention of replacing one family with another, but she could widen her circle. And it wasn't a one-way street. She'd be gaining them, but they'd be gaining her, too.

Something trilled a pretty melody from a nearby tree. As she turned to try and spot the culprit, she realised the scratching of the charcoal had ceased and Gabriel now stared at her, brows lowering over his eyes.

'When did you move?' The frown deepened. 'In my mind's eye you've been on that little headland for the last hour.'

She shrugged. 'Time seems to move differently here. But probably twenty minutes ago.'

He shook himself, patted the table. 'Come. Let me see your sketches.'

She moved to the seat opposite. 'May I see yours?'

He hesitated, but with the smallest of shrugs, nodded. They exchanged sketchpads.

His was still open to the final sketch he'd done. Glancing down, her mouth dried. Turning the pages over, she followed them back to the first of his drawings before returning to the last one, her heart pounding. She knew he watched, and the weight of his stare did strange things to her insides. Moistening her lips, she tried to find something to say.

'What do you think?'

She didn't know if her opinion mattered to him or not. 'They're all of me,' she blurted out.

'Yes.'

He gave no explanation, his face giving nothing away. But…

What did it mean? Why would he draw her? Why would he find her so fascinating?

Just like the sculpture in Como that had enthralled her, one couldn't tell if the figure on the rock—*her*—would remain there strong and steadfast, or whether the water would rise up to engulf it.

'It is important for you to develop an artistic sensibility. What do you think of it objectively?'

She forced herself to focus on the overall impact of the sketch—the strong lines, the ambiguity… Its strange beauty. 'Because the subject is me, and I've never been the subject for a work of art before, it's hard to be objective. This is only a sketch, but it has a real impact. It feels…alive.'

He took the sketchpad from her and surveyed it with narrowed eyes. 'Yes.' He nodded. 'This is something I can work with.'

'Why?'

He glanced up.

'Why me?'

One broad shoulder lifted. 'I was sketching the mountains, but they bored me. And then I saw you and there was something about your posture that caught my attention. Before I knew it, I was trying to capture it in a sketch…and then sketching as if my life depended on it.'

A thrill shook her to her very core. Something about her fascinated him. To think that a man like Gabriel would find someone like her captivating… She hugged the knowledge close. Very slowly, however, the excitement drained away. The water in the drawing, so still, somehow evoked a quiet menace that threatened both woman and rock.

Some Funaros self-destruct.

That was the subject of the sketch. He feared she'd follow in the footsteps of her mother and sister. He had no faith that her strength would prevail over whatever innate weakness he thought resided in her blood. He was recording a downfall that may not happen.

A downfall that *wouldn't* happen!

Lifting her chin, she glared at him. His eyes flashed with brief amusement, before he closed his sketchpad and slapped hers on top of it. Flicking through the various sketches, his lips pursed, his gaze halting only briefly on the final drawing. Eventually, he handed it back to her. 'It will make a pretty piece.'

She blinked. 'That sounds dismissive.' What was wrong with pretty?

'Pretty has its place.'

That sounded even more dismissive. 'But?'

Leaning back, he folded his arms and it drew her attention to the rock-hard strength of his chest. She swallowed, a pulse at the centre of her starting to pound. He'd taken her as his subject, and now all she could think about was if she had the skill to commit all of that raw masculinity to an embroidery—capture it in linen, silk and wool. To wonder what it would be like to draw close enough to touch all of that raw power.

Her pulse pounded harder, making it difficult to draw breath. What would it be like to press herself against such a body? Watch as that body rippled with awareness of a feminine presence—a feminine presence that could fire it to life and exhort it to—

Dear God!

Dragging her gaze back to his face, she found those merciless eyes watching her with a narrowed chill. Had he read her thoughts? Recognised her desires? If he had, the chill in his expression told her it wasn't an attraction he reciprocated.

Heat flooded her face.

Channel Marguerite.

With an effort, she kept her chin high. Women must find Gabriel attractive all the time. It didn't have to mean anything.

She *had* to keep her guard up. For heaven's sake, he was

waiting for her downfall. He didn't want it to happen, and yet he expected it. *Daily.* She might fascinate him, but he had no faith in her.

'What's wrong with pretty?' she repeated, her voice little more than a croak.

'You need to start taking risks with your art, Audrey. You need to experiment and free yourself from the usual conventions that hold you back.'

He's talking about artistic conventions.

He flicked negligent fingers at her sketchpad. 'Where is the movement? Where is the interest? What is the point?'

She stared at her sketch. She'd been so happy with it. Her brow furrowed. Pulling the pad closer she *really* stared at it. Swallowed. He was right, darn it.

'What were you thinking when you sketched that?'

'Just…how beautiful the scenery was. The beauty here overwhelms me. It's so different from home.' She moistened her lips. 'My sketch is pretty, but it's…sterile.'

'Because the beauty does not touch you here.' He pressed a hand to his chest. 'You need to find the courage to create the things that make you feel deeply. That is what will touch other people and draw them to your work.'

Her hands gripped each other tightly in her lap. 'What were you feeling when you sketched me?'

He hesitated. 'Anger.'

She flinched.

He shrugged, but he didn't apologise. 'I didn't say I was angry *with* you.'

No, but—

'Artists channel their emotions into forms and works that have no relation at all to the source of their emotion.'

She thought of the things she'd made in the aftermath of Jo's death, and nodded slowly.

'Will you sit for me?'

The question had her stiffening, though she realised belatedly she should've expected it. Maybe she should even feel flattered. But she didn't. Instead, she prickled and itched and burned and had to fight a scowl. What would he title the piece? *Before the Fall?*

'Will you sit for me?' she shot back instead. She could call hers *Pig-headed Male*.

His head rocked back.

And she crashed back with a thump, rushed back into speech. 'The answer is yes, of course I'll sit for you, Gabriel. It's not dependent on you sitting for me.'

He was doing so much for her, and she'd oblige him in any way she could. If something in her had helped him overcome the block that had him in its grip for the past eight months, she'd be honoured to help him.

She gritted her teeth. *Honoured*, she repeated silently.

He leaned towards her. 'You would like me to sit for you?'

'I've never thought to take a person for my subject before.' She bit her lip. 'I've no idea if I could do it.'

'You have the skill.'

His quiet certainty had her straightening. 'You have a lot of faith in my abilities.'

'I do not understand why you don't have more faith in them yourself.'

Because, until now, she'd not had anyone recognise anything particularly wonderful about them. She'd never believed Nonna and Frankie when they'd told her how amazing her creations were. Oh, she knew they believed it, but they loved her. They were biased.

'How is it you've never pursued your art further? I do not understand. You tell me it is a passion of yours. Why, then, have you not attended art classes? And before you say you had neither the time nor opportunity to study art at university, there are night courses you could've taken. Hobby groups you could have joined. There your talent would've been recognised.'

His incredulity needled her. 'A person can have more than one passion.'

'What are these other passions of yours?'

'Family.'

He stared. With a muttered curse, he rubbed a hand over his face. 'I sometimes forget that not everyone is as caught up in their art as I am in mine. I apologise if I sounded uncompromising just then.'

She folded her arms. He was just like her father, caught up in his own world, uncaring and oblivious of anything—or anyone—else.

No, he's not.

Her heart started to thump. As soon as she'd been old enough, she'd looked after not just Johanna, but her father, too. Nonna had been getting on *and* was running a restaurant. And when Uncle Frank had died, Aunt Deidre had gone into such deep mourning, Audrey had refused to be an additional burden.

She hadn't minded looking after the house, though, and although her father had never said as much, she'd thought that he'd appreciated her efforts; she'd thought that she'd mattered to him. But she hadn't—at least, not as much as his own ambition. The way he'd just up and left for America, selling her childhood home from under her, proved that. Too late she'd realised she'd always given him more than he'd ever given her.

Was Gabriel like that? She moistened her lips. 'If you had to, would you give up your art for Lili?'

'Yes.' He watched her through hooded eyes. 'This is what you had to do for your family?' He let out a long breath. 'I'm sorry if you have been burdened with familial responsibilities and obligations that have prevented you from following your own dreams.'

She shot to her feet, her hands clenching so hard she started to shake. 'My family hasn't been *a burden*, Gabriel. Is that how you view Lili?'

His head rocked back. 'Of course not.'

'Then why would you say such a thing? I—'

Whirling away, she started to pace. She'd give up all of this—the chance to develop her art, Lake Como and all these riches—to have Johanna and Nonna back.

She swung around. 'You can't—'

Her words stuttered to a halt. He stood a hand's breadth away.

'I'm sorry.' Strong hands reached out to grip her shoulders, wrapping around them with a comforting warmth. It was the sincerity in his eyes that undid her, though. 'Audrey, I'm very sorry for upsetting you. I've blundered in with my blind judgements.' Those intriguing lips twisted. 'I'm always so sure I'm right. It is a failing of mine.'

The fight went out of her, just like that. She tried to smile and shrug at the same time but it emerged more like a hiccup. 'Forget about it.'

He led her back to the table, made her sit and then he went and made a pot of green tea and brought it out along with *chocolate biscuits*. She suddenly realised how ravenous she was.

'Please…' He gestured to the plate.

She needed no second bidding. Biting into a biscuit, she closed her eyes and let the sweetness coat her tongue. When she opened them again, she found him watching, but he quickly seized the teapot.

After pouring the tea, he pushed a cup towards her and then lifted his own and blew on it. 'I would like to hear about your family if you wish to talk of them. If Marguerite hasn't forbidden you from doing so.'

She felt a twang of sudden resentment at Marguerite. She had no right to ask her to keep Johanna a secret. Her gaze lowered to their sketchpads lying side by side. She recalled the threat that stretched through his sketch and hitched up her chin. Gabriel needed to know she had more strength than he'd given her credit for. She *wanted* him to know that.

'I had a twin.'

He froze.

'Her name was Johanna. Unfortunately, there were complications during the birth and she was starved of oxygen. She was diagnosed with cerebral palsy when she was fourteen months.'

He swore softly.

'It affected her movement and speech particularly. She could walk unassisted but it took a lot of effort so she mostly used a wheelchair. And while she could talk, it took her a long time to say what she wanted to. But she was whip smart and had a wicked sense of humour. She made you laugh at the most inopportune times.'

He smiled and she couldn't help but smile back. 'And,' she continued, 'took much delight in it, too, I might add. But she needed a lot of care.'

'And that care fell to you?'

'Nonna and Aunt Deidre helped out a lot. They basically raised us.'

'Where was your father all this time?'

'Playing the helpless male.' She rolled her eyes. 'I mean, we lived in the same house as him, which I can see now simply made more work for Nonna and my aunt. But they obviously thought it was the right thing to do—and it probably was—but single fatherhood was too much of a challenge for him, and he threw himself into his work instead.'

His lips thinned but he didn't say anything.

'We had part-time carers for Jo as well, but when I finished school I became her full-time carer. Not because anyone requested it of me, but because I wanted to. I loved her. She was my sister.'

Because of their father's preoccupation, she and Jo had become a team, had become each other's cheer squad. They'd shared everything—their hopes, dreams…secrets. She missed it more than she could say.

He nodded, no trace of judgement in his eyes. 'What happened to Johanna?'

'She died in a car accident four years ago. Just one of those freak things—a tyre blew out when they were on the freeway. The driver lost control and slammed into a truck.'

A strong tanned hand reached across and squeezed hers. 'I'm sorry.'

'Losing Johanna… That's when I realised how hard it is to love someone.'

'Because you sacrificed so much for her?'

'Because when I lost her, I felt I'd lost everything.'

That hand tightened about hers. 'Audrey, in some ways you did. You'd built your whole world around her.'

Of course he would think like that. She squeezed his hand back. 'I didn't lose everything, Gabriel. I still had Nonna and Aunt Deidre and Frankie, and Dad, even if he was rather detached. I still had the ability to work and earn a living. I had my embroideries.'

'And yet, even surrounded by all of those good things, a heart can break.'

And yet, broken hearts did mend.

She nodded at their joined hands, hers looking small and pale beside his. 'You're muscled and strong on the outside, Gabriel, while I look feeble in comparison. But don't let appearances fool you. I've had to be strong—for Johanna's sake and for my father's. And, yes, I know I'm out of my depth here in this brave new world I find myself in, but I will eventually find my feet. And I *will* be the director of my own destiny.'

Grey eyes met hers and he nodded. 'That's me put in my place, then.'

She bit her lip. 'I didn't mean it that way.'

'I know.'

To her relief he didn't look at all offended.

With one final squeeze, he reclaimed his hand and she tried to ignore the way her body protested the missing contact.

'Danae left when she discovered the issues Johanna would have to face in the future. I have no memory of her—Jo and I weren't even two years old yet.' She hitched up her chin. 'I'd never run away from the people I love. Especially when they needed me most.'

He remained silent.

'And I love Lili. I know I've only known her for a short time, but I love her. I plan to be there for her.' She shrugged, suddenly self-conscious. 'Just so you know.'

'I will sit for you, Audrey.'

She blinked at the sudden change of topic. His words and the pictures they evoked in her mind throwing her off balance. She leaned towards him. 'Really?'

'Would you like me to sit for you naked?' he said with a teasing glint in his eye.

Yes!

'No!' Heat flooded every atom of her being. Closing her eyes, she tried to shake the images from her mind. He chuckled and she knew she must be scarlet. Her eyes flew open and she pointed a finger at him. 'And I won't be posing for you naked, either.'

'What a shame.'

Her jaw dropped, but he merely threw his head back and laughed. 'Johanna would've enjoyed the joke, I'm sure.'

She snorted then, too. Seizing another chocolate biscuit, she held the plate out to him. 'Have a biscuit and stop teasing me.'

But he didn't. He'd stilled. *'That's* why you asked me about charities and how to become a patron. You want to set something up in Johanna's name.'

'Maybe.' She wished her voice didn't sound so suddenly small or defensive.

He stood and stalked to the edge of the clearing. When he turned back, he widened his stance. 'Marguerite has banned you from talking about Johanna, hasn't she?'

She didn't want to answer, but he clearly read the answer in her face. Giving a harsh laugh, he shook his head. 'I should've realised sooner. She wouldn't want the wider world knowing she'd had a granddaughter who was anything other than physically perfect. Heaven forbid anyone suspect something so shocking.'

'No,' she croaked. 'I'm sure you're wrong. I think she finds it painful she never met her.'

A sceptical look crossed his face and he folded his arms. 'How do you think you're going to get Marguerite's approval for a foundation in Johanna's name? How do you think you're going to reconcile her to you talking freely about Johanna *publicly*?'

That, of course, was the question. Because as things currently stood, Marguerite couldn't tolerate so much as the mention of Johanna's name. But it'd get better. She swallowed. It *would* get better.

If wishes were fishes...

She pushed that thought away. Marguerite *had* to reconcile herself to Audrey's talking about Johanna publicly because nobody, not even the Funaros, would have her turning her back on her sister. Even if it meant they'd disown her. 'She just needs time.'

He gave a disbelieving laugh.

Pain pounded behind her eyes. 'I'm going to talk to her about it...soon. And then you'll see.'

Those infuriating brows rose.

'You'll be eating your words before you know it.'

CHAPTER EIGHT

'IS CONVERSATION BANNED while I sit?'

Gabriel was midstretch when Audrey asked her question. If she'd asked him five minutes earlier, he'd have probably not even heard her. He hadn't been this intensely captured by a work in…

He couldn't remember.

Thankfully, his creative drought was at an end. He felt alive, invigorated, as if all of his body was breathing again.

Despite that, his instinct was to answer in the negative and demand silence as he was working. But she'd agreed to sit for him without a murmur of complaint. It'd be churlish of him to refuse.

'We can talk if you like…as long as you don't move too much.'

He had her sitting on a mound of cushions on the floor—a make-believe rock—with her face turned towards the wall of glass, side on to him. She held her sketchpad and a pencil.

She chuckled. 'You didn't complain a little while ago when I stretched out a cramp in my calf. You were clearly immersed in your drawing.'

He glanced at the clock and swore. '*Dio*, Audrey, it has been two hours! Why didn't you say something? You can get up and move if you wish.'

'I'm fine. You have me for another half an hour and then I'm done, so you might as well make the most of it.'

He picked up his pencil again. He would refine what he

could in the next thirty minutes. 'In light of your patience, I'll even start a conversation.'

Those mobile lips curved upwards and he wondered how he could capture their compelling combination of softness and strength. And what would be the better material to use to capture them—steel or wood?

Doing his best to ignore the heat prickling through his veins and the persistent ache of his groin, he dragged his mind to the promised conversation. 'Why, when I asked you to wear your oldest, most comfortable jeans when you were sitting for me, did you not just wear them for the whole day? Why did you bring them to get changed into?'

She started to shrug, but stopped as if remembering she was supposed to be still. 'Because I didn't want Marguerite to see me in them.'

He scowled. 'Why would it matter if she did?'

She huffed out a laugh. 'Are you scowling, Gabriel?'

He cleared his face. 'Absolutely not.'

'Because she doesn't like them, and I don't wish to upset her.'

'You don't have to live your whole life to please her. Why even consider doing such a thing?'

'You ask the wrong question.' She turned her head a couple of inches to meet his gaze and the expression in her spice-coloured eyes had his pulse picking up speed. 'Ask yourself *why* these jeans bother her so much.'

That was simple. 'Because they do not fit the sleek, sophisticated image she would wish for a granddaughter of the Funaro family.' As far as Marguerite was concerned, the image the Funaros presented had to be perfect.

'You're wrong.' She turned to stare back out at the window, but where before the lines of her body had been passive, they were now firm—that pointed chin squared and those eyes narrowed. 'These jeans remind her that I grew up in a world far removed from hers. They remind her of all the years we didn't know each other and can't get back. The sight of my old, shabby jeans makes her grieve, because she wasn't there to help out financially or to offer any kind of emotional support when I was growing up.'

Her words made something in his chest cramp. 'You imbue her with feelings she doesn't have.'

'While you seem determined to believe she has no feelings at all.'

He rolled his shoulders. That wasn't true. Was it?

'Tell me about Serafina.'

'No!' The word shot out of him with the violence of a summer storm, and he found himself breathing hard. The request had taken him by surprise, but it shouldn't have.

Audrey flinched, but a moment later resumed the pose. 'Why not?'

'I do not talk about Fina.'

Her entire body drooped as she let out a breath. 'Nobody does. You must all miss her very much.'

His fingers tightened about his pencil. She had no idea. And he had no intention of enlightening her.

'She was so young. And so beautiful.'

Oh, yes, Fina had been very beautiful. On the outside.

'Lili is going to want to know about her, you know. Eventually, she'll start asking more demanding questions, and she won't be put off with one-word answers. She'll expect more from you.'

He knew that. But it wouldn't be for several years yet. He had time to work out what he would say. And maybe time will have softened him, and he'd be able to utter the lies without giving himself away. He scowled. 'Why are you so interested in Fina anyway?'

She turned fully around to face him. 'She was my *sister*. How would you feel if you suddenly discovered a sibling you never knew you'd had? Wouldn't you want to know all about him or her?'

'Assume the pose, please.' She did, but it didn't ease the burning in his soul. Her words had found their mark, but they didn't make him any more eager to talk about Serafina. Yes, he understood her curiosity, but if she'd ever met Fina, she'd have been disappointed in the other woman.

Bitterly.

Just as he had been.

'Fine, then tell me about Vittoria, Livia and Adriana.'

Her cousins? 'Why?'

'Because I'm having lunch with them tomorrow.'

And so it begins...

This family would engulf her, take her over and re-create her into their own image. They'd destroy her. He threw his pencil down. 'We're done here for the moment.'

She glanced around, registered the expression on his face and nodded. But as she started to rise, she winced and grabbed her calf. He immediately moved to assist her, his hand reaching down to hers. Her fingers tightened in his and she gasped and hopped. 'Gah, cramp! I'm not used to sitting so still for so long.'

As a nurse's aide, she must spend long days on her feet. He should've taken that into account and ensured she had regular stretching breaks.

Kneeling down, he brushed her hands aside, working his fingers on the calf muscle that had tightened beneath the soft denim of her jeans. She gasped, groaned and half hopped. 'Lean against my shoulder,' he ordered.

A hand immediately landed on his shoulder, and the soft weight of her and the feel of her warm flesh beneath the thin, butter-soft denim made him aware of her in a way he'd been trying to avoid all morning. Her scent swamped him, invading his lungs and moving with a slow surety to his blood, his limbs growing languid. As the tightness in her calf gave way beneath his hand, his fingers, too, became more leisurely—exploring, caressing, wanting to learn the shape of her.

He suddenly found his hands empty.

'It's all good now, thanks,' she choked out.

Rising, he found her eyes wide and dark colour staining her cheeks.

'Where did you learn to massage like that? It's very effective. I'm dying for a coffee. You?'

She was babbling and he knew why—because she felt the pull between them, too. And because of Marguerite, she was determined to ignore it.

And because of you.

Dragging a hand down his face, he nodded. He'd told her not to fall in love with him or to think of him in any kind of romantic way. Just because Marguerite was of the same mind didn't mean he had to change his.

Dio! He knew he was bitter, but what kind of man would it make him if he seduced Audrey simply to disoblige Marguerite? He was not in the habit of breaking hearts and destroying people. He left that to the likes of the Funaros.

Audrey had moved to the kitchenette and he dragged in a breath and tried to steady himself. 'I used to play football when I was younger. Not professionally. I wasn't that good. But I played for years in a local league. Cramps were common.'

When she finally turned back, her colour was normal again. Handing him a coffee, she took a turn about the studio, studying the various pieces he'd started and abandoned. 'So, Vittoria, Livia and Adriana?'

His nose curled.

'It seems to me you don't like to talk about any of the Funaros.'

'Esattamente,' he muttered. *Exactly.*

'But nor do you want me letting Lili down. You want me to be a regular fixture in her life.' She turned and pinned him with those eyes. 'So help me fit in here, Gabriel. Explain the undercurrents and all the things I'm in ignorance of.'

A dark anger pierced him. This woman deserved so much

more. 'How can family mean so much to you when your own parents were the antithesis of what family stood for?' How could she still have so much faith in family?

'My parents got it wrong. For heaven's sake, why would I emulate them? Why would I make the same mistakes they did?' She pointed a finger at him. 'It was my nonna who got it right. *That's* who I want to emulate.'

With the Funaros? Was she mad?

Those dark eyes narrowed and sparks flashed in their depths as if she could read his thoughts in his face. 'Nonna gave me so much. She taught me that there's strength in a family, not to mention a sense of belonging and love. She *proved* that to me. And I'm going to do everything in my power to create that with my family here in Italy. I'll continue the legacy she gave me.'

He opened his mouth.

'And just because I wasn't enough for my father or my mother, doesn't mean I won't be enough for Marguerite or the rest of the Funaros.'

He wanted to swear.

'And just because *you* don't value family, doesn't mean the rest of us feel the same way!'

He valued family!

'And just because the Funaros aren't enough for you, doesn't mean they're not enough for me!'

He gaped at her.

'Family matters *so much*. I'd hate to think what would've happened to Jo if it weren't for Nonna and Aunt Deidre.'

Or Audrey, he added silently.

'If she'd been alone in the world...' She shuddered. 'It doesn't bear thinking about. And *I* don't want to be alone in the world, either. What if something happened to me? Who could I turn to?'

His hands clenched at the thought.

'I know you're besotted with this whole "I'm a lone wolf and untouchable" thing you've got going on.'

'My…*what*?'

'But there's a reason solitary confinement is a punishment. People weren't meant to be isolated and alone. And just because family politics are tiresome and some family members can be annoying, doesn't mean one shouldn't make the best of what they've got.'

'Have you not heard the proverb that you can't make a silk purse from a sow's ear?' he ground out.

She clenched her hands so hard she shook. 'Vittoria, Livia and Adriana?'

After dragging in a breath, he let it out slowly. He couldn't force Audrey to see what she didn't want to see. Eventually, he nodded. 'Vittoria went into business with a friend—fashion, I think… Something to do with earrings if I'm not mistaken. Anyway, she plugged a great deal of money into it, but it was a failure. Marguerite refused to bankroll her any further.'

She bit her lip. He did his best to not notice how it deepened the colour and plumped it—as if she'd just been kissed. Her colour was still high from their somewhat heated exchange and… He swallowed. Audrey would look sublime mussed up after a bout of vigorous lovemaking.

Dio! Stop imagining such things.

'Livia was at the centre of a sex scandal. An ex-boyfriend leaked a piece of naked footage he'd taken of her on his phone.'

Her eyes widened. 'That's appalling.'

'Welcome to the world of the Funaros.'

She rolled her eyes. 'And Adriana?'

'Has recently returned from drug rehab.'

Her shoulders slumped. 'Okay, so that's…a lot.'

'They each have a big black mark against their name as far as Marguerite is concerned.'

'And are all desperate to make amends.'

It was true that all of them would like to be in Marguerite's good books.

'And what about some of the older family members—my

mother's contemporaries—like Caterina, Anna, Nicolo and Davide? There's going to be a dinner later in the week.'

They were the children of Marguerite's siblings. He filled her in on some of the family politics.

She listened in silence. When he was done, she pointed to one of his sculptures. 'Next time I sit for you, would I be able to look at that?'

He frowned. 'Why?'

'I don't know, but there's something about it…' She fixed him with a frown. 'Surely, it's an easy enough question—yes or no?'

'*Si*, if you wish it.'

Her shoulders and jaw relaxed. 'Thank you.'

Something inside him unhitched then, too, but for the life of him he couldn't explain what it was.

'How did your lunch with Vittoria, Livia and Adriana go?' Gabriel asked the following Monday when she was once again sitting for him.

He'd arranged the sculpture on a low table in front of her. Her attention had been fixed on it for the past hour, and it was her attitude of concentration that had caught his fancy today. He glanced down at his sketch and nodded, satisfied.

'Okay, I think. I liked them.'

That surprised him.

'And the dinner with Caterina, Anna, Nicolo and Davide?'

'Okay, too, I think.'

The brevity of her answers needled him. 'Was Marguerite at the dinner?'

Her dark hair fanned about her face when she shook her head. 'She had other plans.'

He froze. 'Marguerite left you to face the slathering horde alone?'

'I told her I was more than capable of going alone. And they're not a slathering horde.' She bit her lip. 'Though they're all a bit reserved.'

By reserved, he bet she meant rude, impenetrable and unwelcoming.

She gestured at his sketchpad. 'Are we done?' At his nod, she rose and shook out her arms and legs. 'They're not exactly a happy bunch, are they?'

'You know you could just walk away from them.' He hated the thought of her expending time and energy on people who didn't have her best interests at heart. 'You don't owe these people anything.'

She turned her back on him. 'We've had this conversation before. That's *not* what family does. And as I already know you don't want me walking away from Lili, why should I walk away from anyone else?'

She had a point even if he didn't want to admit it.

She turned. 'I'm also including you in my *not a happy bunch* comment.'

He stiffened. 'Not happy? *Me?* I'm happy!'

'Shout a little louder. I'm sure that'll convince me.'

He scowled. When he wasn't stuck at Lake Como on the Funaro estate, he was happy.

And when he didn't have a creative block.

And when he didn't have to think about Fina or the legacy she'd left their daughter.

'Gabriel, when was the last time you played football?'

He blinked to find her staring at him with her head cocked to one side. 'I… A long time.'

'Maybe you ought to take it back up again.'

'Why?'

One shoulder lifted in an elegantly eloquent shrug. 'Why not? Exercise is good for the soul as well as the body. Maybe you've got into a rut and that's why you've been having trouble with your sculptures. Maybe you need to try new things, do different things… Have some fun.'

She might have a point, and if he could've focused on it, he might have pursued it further, but… He pointed a shaking finger at her shoulder. 'Have you been having *deportment* lessons?'

She jumped up and down on the spot, clapping her hands. 'You can tell?'

It was *awful*!

'You've no idea how wonderful it is to have your body say exactly what you want it to, to *behave* exactly as you want it to.'

She… It—

'No, scrap that.' Her soft laugh slammed into him. 'You're a master at silent communication. You know *exactly* how empowering it is.'

He had absolutely no comeback for that.

CHAPTER NINE

AUDREY CLOSED THE villa's front door as quietly as she could. Leaning against the door to catch her breath, she slipped off her high heels. What a night.

She was too keyed up for bed, even though it was the wee small hours of the morning. And she was starving. An image of the cake she'd made earlier in the day rose in her mind but before she could turn in the direction of the kitchen, footsteps sounded on the stairs.

She immediately straightened—slouching was bad, or so her deportment teacher informed her—but relaxed again when her gaze collided with the piercing grey of Gabriel's. Somewhere deep inside a tic started up.

'Do you know what time it is?' he hissed when he reached the bottom stair.

She gurgled back a laugh, pitying future teenage Lili. 'Yes, I do.' She folded her arms. 'What do you mean by staying out so late, Gabriel?'

His mouth opened but no words came out.

She took pity on him. 'Hungry?'

Not waiting for an answer, she made for the kitchen, going to the hidden spot on the other side of the island where Anna the cook had secreted the cake. Lifting it up, she raised an eyebrow in question.

'You're having a midnight feast?'

She giggled. 'Technically, I think you'll find it's a 2 a.m. feast.'

Dark brows lowered. 'Are you drunk?'

She set the cake on the bench between them. 'A little tipsy, perhaps, but not rolling drunk. You get the milk while I cut the cake.'

His eyes practically started from their sockets. 'Milk?'

'Yes, it comes in cartons and is usually kept on the top shelf of the refrigerator, which is that huge stainless-steel monolith over there and—'

'Yes, yes, thank you.' Without another word he grabbed two glasses and the carton of milk and then hesitated. 'Do you want it heated?'

She shuddered. 'Hot milk is disgusting. Cold milk is perfection.'

With lips twitching, he set a glass in front of her and filled it to the brim. 'Do you know how many calories are in this?' He gestured at their feast.

'If that's the stance you mean to take with Lili as she's growing up, I'm afraid we're going to butt heads.'

'I...no. But Marguerite would have a fit if she could see you now.'

That made her laugh. 'Marguerite told me slim women held all the power, but I pooh-poohed that idea. I told her *healthy* women held all the power. I said, *It's the twenty-twenties, Grandmother, not the nineteen-sixties, when Twiggy was all the rage.* She found the idea...not without merit.'

He stared.

Pulling one of the plates towards her, she forked a generous mouthful of sponge into her mouth, relishing the sweet softness of cake, the hint of raspberry jam and fresh cream. 'Try it,' she ordered when he remained rooted to the spot. 'It's my signature cake.'

'*You* made this?'

'Why so surprised?'

'Everything you do surprises me,' he muttered. 'You're nothing like any of us expected.'

She was starting to think that could be a good thing.

Ignoring his fork, he lifted the cake in his fingers. A firm mouth and strong white teeth bit into it. She held her breath as he blinked, his eyes widening…and then he took another gigantic bite and swore softly in a way that sounded like a caress. 'You are a witch.'

'Why are your eyes grey? I like them, but the colour is unusual.'

'Are you sure you're not drunk?'

'Pretty sure. It's a 2 a.m. thing, I think.' She ate more cake and sipped her milk. 'People have a tendency to say things they wouldn't normally say in the wee small hours.'

'Where were you tonight?'

'Where were you?'

'Having dinner with a prospective client.'

And he'd checked on Lili before going back to his cottage. Because of course he had.

'I was out dancing with the girls.'

'The girls?'

'Tori, Livy and Ana.'

He leaned towards her. 'Who?'

'Vittoria, Livia and Adriana.'

'You've given them pet names?'

'Nicknames are a big thing in Australia—a sign of affection.' When he didn't say anything, she added, 'If you lived in Australia, you'd be called Gabe. But I prefer Gabriel. It suits you.'

'And what is your name shortened to?'

'Aud, sometimes, but that's not very pretty.'

'No, I prefer Audrey.'

They finished their cake and milk.

'Did you enjoy the dancing?'

She suppressed a yawn as she rinsed their plates and glasses before popping them in the dishwasher. 'Very much. Due to various things over the years, there hasn't been too much dancing in my life. Not that I'm complaining. But tonight was a real treat. I danced so hard I earned my cake.'

'And is that all you did?'

'Of course not. We chatted—girl talk, you know—and drank French champagne, which is *truly* delicious.' She winced. 'Though, it's wickedly expensive.' Apparently, she had the money to indulge such treats these days, but it was still hard not to count pennies when she'd been doing so all her life.

'Anything else?'

He'd gone all stiff and disapproving, and she suddenly realised what he was asking. He wanted to know if she'd indulged in any flirtations. 'That's really none of your business, Gabriel.' Normally, she was conciliatory, but he made her want to throw things with his casually negative judgements. 'Just because I go out dancing and enjoy a couple of drinks with the girls doesn't make me a bad person. It doesn't mean I'm about to self-destruct. And neither does meeting a man who might take my fancy and exploring that further. So you can take your nasty mind and its vile conclusions and shove them where the sun doesn't shine.'

His head rocked back. He opened his mouth, but she shook her head. 'You're acting like a dog in the manger. And I don't get it.' She leaned in close and his swift intake of breath speared into the centre of her, the chill in his eyes replaced with a heart-stopping heat...and that heat started to inch through her, too. She snapped back before she fell into them and did something totally *stupid*.

'It wouldn't matter if I were the most perfect woman in the world.' She said it for her own benefit as much as his. 'The fact that I'm a member of the Funaro family is a black mark I can never overcome.' He wouldn't fall in love with her on principle—because it would mean having to forgive the Funaros and he had no intention of doing that. 'In your eyes I will always be tainted by association.'

He stiffened. 'I...'

She huffed out a laugh. 'You can't even offer me friendship. I mean, if you were even so much as friends with me the world would come tumbling down, right?'

He blinked.

'So here's the thing, Gabriel. You don't get to tell me who I can and cannot date, any more than Marguerite can.'

He started to say something but she cut him off.

'Don't say a word. I repeat… It's. None. Of. Your. Business.'

With that she turned and walked away.

Audrey eased back to stare at her handiwork, the light outside that enormous window flooding the studio and haloing the piece she'd been working on. She'd created a glittering web of golds and blue, but threaded beneath it here and there were strands of black and grey—the exact same grey as Gabriel's eyes.

She glanced around, but he was working on something and had his back to her—as if deliberately ignoring her. It had been a week since that incident in the kitchen, and while he'd apologised to her the next day, the memory of it still somehow throbbed between them.

It was there when she sat for him.

It was there when he explained some detail of his methodology.

It was there when they explored the work of other fibre artists.

And it was there in his eyes whenever she spent time with Lili.

Shaking the thought off, she focused on the web and backdrop she'd created and then glanced across at the sculpture she'd studied so thoroughly while sitting for him. It was a clay model of something he'd probably hoped to eventually make on a far greater scale from recycled metal and timber. At the moment it wasn't much more than a fluid shape half a metre tall, but nevertheless, the outline suggested to her a figure wrestling with…well, itself, she supposed.

The web she'd made was supported on seven sticks she'd sourced from fallen branches outside, and she wanted to place it over the sculpture, engulfing it. She'd taken measurements, had envisaged it in place…

She now needed to see it all as one piece before she decided how she ought to continue with the backdrop, which was the piece of linen from which all the threads emanated. Glancing across at Gabriel, she bit her lip. If she was quiet, she could tiptoe over to the sculpture, set the frame in place, assess the effect and then tiptoe the frame back to her workbench. If she was quick and careful, Gabriel would be none the wiser.

She couldn't explain why she didn't want to share this with him yet. It's just…she wanted it perfect before he gave her feedback. And she didn't want to risk either his scorn or indignation that she'd improvised from a work of his. Maybe he'd think she was taking advantage of him.

She grimaced. Maybe he'd be right.

In the next moment she thrust out her chin. He'd told her to experiment. That was what she was doing.

Glancing across again and assuring herself that Gabriel was utterly immersed in whatever he was working on, she picked up her intricate web and moved silently across to the sculpture on its low table and set her frame in place.

After easing back a couple of steps, she crouched down to view it. Her pulse suddenly quickened. She'd never created anything like this before—but the moment she'd conceived it, it had consumed her.

Rubbing her nape, she nodded. She was definitely on the right track. Straightening, she went to remove the frame, when a commanding voice behind her bellowed, 'Do not touch it!'

She froze. *Damn.* She should've waited until he'd gone outside for a walk or a coffee.

Though his footsteps were silent, she could feel him moving closer. He stopped just behind her. She could feel the heat that flowed from him and the invigorating sting of his scent. Combined, they made her feel both confused and alive. Like so much about this man, her reaction made no sense.

She did what she could to channel Marguerite's unflappable calm—but inside butterflies the size of seagulls squawked and divebombed. Pressing her hands to her waist, she kept her gaze firmly fixed on the piece before them. She would *not* be the first to speak.

In fact, she shifted her weight and continued what she'd been doing in the first place—assessing the piece and deciding what else she could do to improve it. She'd take her time. Gabriel kept telling her she was an artist. Fine! She'd act like one, then.

Making a circuit around the piece, she halted at the backdrop that she was still in the process of embroidering. From the statue side the threads shot out to the rest of the frame, but on this side she was trying to create an abstract pattern.

'What are you thinking?'

He spoke from beside her, and she pointed. 'I need to remove the black.'

'And replace it with...?'

'Pink.' She frowned. Pink hadn't been part of the colour palette she'd used, but she instinctively knew it would work. It would create a contrast—not lightening the piece like gold or blue would, but softening it. 'And, actually, I'll keep a thread of black here and here.'

'Why?'

'Because it's what's true to the piece. It will make it more... human.'

They continued their circuit until they stood in front of it once again.

'What are you titling it?' When she didn't immediately answer he offered, *'Tangled Web?'*

She shook her head. There was nothing tangled about her web. It was quite deliberate. *'Ties That Bind,'* she decided.

'Audrey.'

She finally turned and met his gaze. Grey eyes raked hers and firm lips lifted. 'Excellent.'

'What?' She frowned. The piece? Her experimentation? Or...?

'You do not care what I think of this piece. It is something of which you are happy to take complete ownership. It is something of which you are proud.'

His words made her blink. 'I am proud of it,' she agreed. 'But it's not entirely true that I don't care what you think.'

'But if I told you this was rubbish?'

She shrugged. 'I'd continue to work on it.' *She'd* still like it.

'*Si*, this is what I mean.' He considered the piece again. 'But in this instance, we're in agreement. What you have done here, it is extraordinary.'

He really thought so?

'I can see how beautifully you've incorporated what you learned from our studies of both Marley and Sinestra.'

She couldn't prevent her hands from going to her hips. 'Then why haven't you called it derivative?' Which is what he'd called a piece she'd been working on earlier in the week.

'Because here you have employed the techniques in your own unique fashion.' That gaze settled on her, a crease deepening his brow. 'If my derivative comment stung, you perhaps need to grow a thicker skin.'

'And maybe you need to recognise that I work differently than you. You see something new and immediately want to experiment with it. I see something new and want to practise the technique to know that I can master it before I begin experimenting.'

He eased away a fraction farther to survey her more critically. Eventually, he nodded. 'There is a reason I am an artist and not a teacher.'

His words immediately had guilt crashing down on her. 'You're an excellent teacher, Gabriel. I shouldn't have inferred otherwise. I've learned an enormous amount from you and I'm very grateful.'

He merely shrugged. 'You are a consummate recycler, too, because I had every intention of throwing that sculpture away. Now instead, I can gift it to you.'

She gaped at him. 'You can't do that!'

He thrust out his chin at a haughty angle. 'I can do what I wish with my own work. Would you prefer that I throw it in the bin for you to retrieve later?'

'Of course not. I—'

'Then accept this gift in the spirit it was given—a gift from one artist to another. You had a vision for the sculpture where I did not. You've *earned* the sculpture.'

She stared at him, blinking.

'Simply say thank you and accept the gift.'

Drawing in a breath, she nodded. 'Thank you.' She knew precisely how extraordinary such a gift was.

Gabriel could sense how much Audrey wanted to get back to work, but he couldn't let the piece go just yet. Even unfinished, it captured the attention and held it hostage. 'This needs to be shown.'

'I beg your pardon.'

Her incredulity had him smiling. Maybe once she saw other people's reactions to her work, she would finally start to believe in herself. Before the summer was over, they might have enough of her work assembled to hold an exhibition.

'How many exhibitions have you been to since arriving in Italy?'

'Only a couple. I saw one in Rome before coming to Lake Como, and then another in Como. Though I have spent a lot of time at the art gallery.'

'Would you like to attend the new exhibition at the Galleria Pensiero with me in a fortnight?'

She started to dance on the spot. 'Are you serious? I'd give my eyeteeth to go to an opening night like that one.'

He shook his head, but he suspected his eyes might be dancing, too. 'Then you need to tell Marguerite's secretary and she will ensure you get all such future invitations.'

Her mouth dropped open. 'Just like that?'

He couldn't explain why, but she made him want to laugh; she made him feel young again. Even now she had no idea what doors her name and fortune could open for her. 'Just like that.'

'Wow.'

'But in this instance, you can come as my guest, yes? There are several people from the art world I would like you to meet.'

'Are you sure it's no bother?'

'Of course it isn't. It will be an interesting night and should be fun to compare opinions on the different pieces. Consider it part of your ongoing education.'

'Then thank you. I'd like that very much.'

'It's finally finished.'

Audrey had continued working on *Ties That Bind* for the rest of the week and Gabriel set down his tools now and moved across to where she stood.

Every time she'd left the room during the past week, he'd found himself drawn across to it. Something in it ruffled his soul, made him feel too much. He could count on the fingers of one hand the artworks that had such an impact on him.

The finished piece was shocking. And beautiful. The longer he stared at it, the more his heart ached.

'What's wrong?'

The quiet question throbbed between them.

'Gabriel?'

His name on her lips broke the spell and had him slamming back. He swallowed and gestured. 'It is powerful.'

She sucked her bottom lip into her mouth; her forehead creased. 'I can hardly believe I created such a thing.'

He knew what she meant. He sometimes felt like that when he finished an installation. Somewhere between vision and execution, a work could take on a life of its own.

'Is that how you see yourself?' he suddenly burst out. 'Trapped behind a beautiful web and unable to break free?' Because while there was no denying the beauty of the web, it still held the figure fast inside.

Her brow pleated.

'I mean, you have made the figure strong. Or at least you have given the sculpture an appearance of strength.' But that didn't change the fact that the figure was trapped.

She stared at the piece. 'Is that how you see it?'

Did she not?

Shaking her head, she met his gaze. 'That's not me, Gabriel.'

Her face confirmed the truth of her words. He couldn't explain why, but something inside him unclenched and he was able to breathe again. He did not want her feeling trapped like that. This woman deserved to be free.

Gabriel was aware of the glances he and Audrey drew as they entered the Galleria Pensiero, but he ignored them. The gallery was built on classic lines, and the inside foyer was a soaring auditorium of Italian marble and sparkling chandeliers, the light glinting off crystal glasses balanced on elegant trays circulated about the room by stylish waitstaff.

At his side Audrey gave a dreamy sigh, and for once he agreed with her. With practised ease, he seized two champagne flutes from a passing tray and handed her one. Smiling her thanks, she touched her glass to his before taking a sip, her lids fluttering in appreciation.

In that moment he knew she would never take French champagne for granted; that she would always acknowledge the wonder of it with every sip. The knowledge lifted something inside him. Fina had knocked the stuff back like there was no tomorrow. She hadn't cared whether it was French champagne, vodka, or a nice Brunello. It had all been one and the same to her.

Maybe, just maybe, Audrey would be able to avoid the same fate as her mother and sister. For a moment he allowed himself to hope. He would do whatever he could to make sure she had all the props and supports she needed; that she had something to fall back on. Something other than drugs, alcohol and sex. And then Lili would have at least one female relative she could take as a role model.

'Thank you so much for bringing me tonight, Gabriel.'

'You have already thanked me three times. This thanks is not necessary.' He gestured for them to move towards the works on display. 'It is my responsibility as your mentor to ensure you receive ample opportunities for development, yes?'

She glanced across, a frown in her eyes. 'And what about when we are no longer mentor and mentee?'

'We will still be colleagues.' They could continue to discuss art and the projects they were working on. She would still be Lili's aunt.

'Not friends?'

When he didn't answer immediately, the light in her eyes dimmed and it left him feeling like a heel. He hated having put that expression in her eyes. But could he and this woman ever be friends?

She sipped her champagne. 'That's clearly a *no*, then.'

What if they became friends and then she followed in Danae and Fina's footsteps, after all? Where would that leave him and Lili? He swallowed, his collar drawing tight about his throat. 'I do not give my friendship quickly,' he finally said. 'I am not one of these people who needs a lot of friends. But the ones I have I take very good care of.'

'That's good to know.' But the happy sparkle in her eyes didn't return.

'I am not saying we will not be friends.'

She nodded, but didn't look at him, pointed instead at the painting they surveyed. 'That's an interesting colour combination.'

They were both silent as they assessed the painting before moving along to the next one.

'In the meantime—' she swung back, her attempt at restraint clearly failing '—you'll just keep fatalistically waiting for the worst to happen and miss out on all the good things friendships—and family—can give you?'

He choked on his wine. Was she inferring…? 'The Funaros are *not* my family.' He kept his voice low but the words shot from him like paint splatter.

'Of course they are. You married into them, didn't you? They're Lili's family.'

'But—'

'Sure, you can keep your distance and be all grumpy and broody and disapproving. But it doesn't change the facts.'

You bet your life he'd keep his distance, but he couldn't prevent a thread of curiosity from rising through him then, too. 'How, I would like to know, do you think I could—' he searched for an appropriate word '—*integrate* myself into the family?'

'By getting to know them better… Socialising and mixing with them. Like, for example, attending the surprise seventy-fifth birthday party I'm throwing for Marguerite.'

She was doing *what*? Marguerite would *hate* a surprise party.

'I don't like this piece.' She scrunched up her face at the canvas in front of them. 'Odd, as I can see the expertise, the superiority of the artist's technique.'

He found himself in accord, but he didn't say that out loud. It was strange how attuned they could be about art, and yet how out of step they were when it came to family.

'It would mean a lot to Lili.'

He knew that, but… Huffing out an exasperated breath, he glared at her. 'You are not easy company.'

'Not true! I'm very easy company when I sit for you.'

Then she thankfully seemed content with her own thoughts and kept them to herself, instead of giving voice to them and ruffling his mood.

'Ah.' He looked up. 'I just spotted Marco. I would like to introduce you to him. He is an agent and I suspect he would be very interested in what you are doing with your fibre art.'

She stared up at him with deer-in-the-headlights eyes, her throat bobbing as she swallowed.

'No.' He pointed a commanding finger at her. 'You are not going to be nervous or self-effacing. You are going to own the fact that you are an artist and that the work you are doing is unique and powerful and needs to find a greater audience.'

'Oh, but—'

'No buts! You have talent. You will project confidence and conviction in your work.'

The glass in her hand wobbled.

'Close your eyes.'

She did as he said. Staring into that beautiful face with the hair gathered up high on her head and dark ringlets falling down around her neck, a deep hunger surged through him. He ground his teeth against it. 'Picture in your mind your *Ties That Bind* piece. Recall how you feel about it—the pride you have in it and the wonder—revel in the knowledge that you created it.'

She swallowed. The glass in her hand steadied and she opened her eyes. 'Okay, you're right. I have work I'm proud of. I'll do my best not to embarrass you.'

Her words softened something at the centre of him. 'I know you won't. Even if you did, I wouldn't care. But I do not wish you to do yourself a disservice. This is all.'

Taking her arm, he manoeuvred her towards Marco. 'You once asked me about the colour of my eyes.'

She swung to him. 'I did! You never did tell me where they came from.'

'From my mother. She was half Irish.'

She stared. 'Have you been to Ireland?'

'*Si.*'

'Do you have family there?'

What was it about this woman and family? 'A couple of distant cousins.'

'How lovely. Tell me. Is Ireland as green as everyone says?'

He nodded. 'I'm sure you would find it most inspiring. Marco!' He hailed the agent. 'It is good to see you.'

He made the introductions, and with a few choice words didn't just pique the agent's interest in Audrey's work, but had him covetous to be the first agent to see it.

'Is this piece really as extraordinary as you say?' Marco demanded, handing Audrey his card.

'It's one of the most powerful artworks I have ever seen.'

Marco took Audrey's hand. 'You must contact me soon, yes? I will come view your work and then—'

'Excuse us. I just spotted someone I'd like Audrey to meet.' Gabriel smoothly detached Audrey from the other man's grip and whisked her off to introduce her to a rival agent. Marco would be the perfect agent for Audrey, but he'd appreciate her all the more if he had to fight for her.

'Oh, my God! Oh, my God!' Audrey chanted under her breath for his ears only.

'Smile. Chin up. Confident, remember?'

She gurgled back a laugh. 'Would it appal you to realise how much like Marguerite you just sounded then?'

He tried to feel affronted, but couldn't manage it. He satisfied himself with a flippant, 'Do not spoil the evening.'

Her laugh made him grin.

CHAPTER TEN

'AT BREAKFAST THIS MORNING Lili was talking about this party you're planning for Marguerite.'

Audrey halted midstretch, glancing up from the piece she was currently working on—a traditional embroidery on a piece of square linen the colour of midnight—and realised Gabriel's hammering and welding had been nonexistent for the past twenty minutes. Had he been waiting for her, not wanting to break her concentration?

Shaking herself, she completed her stretch. 'She's very excited about it. Coffee?' She started towards the kitchenette. 'Of course, when you're four, parties *are* very exciting.'

'I will make the coffee if you will cut whatever sweet wickedness you brought with you today.'

She'd cut the chocolate brownies before they'd left the villa—leaving instructions with Maria that both Lili and Marguerite had one for their morning coffee as well—but she dished them out now onto the plain white plates he kept in the cupboard.

As had become their habit, they took their midmorning coffee outside to the wooden table, sitting on the same bench so as to face the lake and drink in the view. Not so closely, though, that shoulders or thighs brushed. She could feel the heat that emanated from him, though, as warm against her left side as the sun overhead.

'Audrey, do you have much experience with children?'

'A couple of my girlfriends have children, and I enjoy their company on the odd occasion I get the chance. Why?'

A frown creased his brow and her heart plummeted. 'Have I done something wrong with Lili?' Her hands clenched. She'd never knowingly do anything to hurt her delightful little niece.

'That is not what I meant. It is just…'

He turned to face her more fully, his knee bumping hers, sending a rush of awareness streaking through her. She tried to look unmoved, but heat crept into her cheeks, no doubt turning them pink. She hoped he misread it as her horror of doing something that would harm Lili.

He shuffled away until their knees no longer touched, and it occurred to her that this awareness might not be one-sided. A pulse in her throat fluttered to life, and so did one low in her abdomen—a deep and insistent *throb-throb* that the rest of her body took up.

Dragging a breath into cramped lungs, she ordered herself to ignore it. They'd both made their positions clear. What was the point getting all hot and bothered when she couldn't do anything about it?

'Have I done anything wrong?' she asked, staring doggedly at the infuriatingly placid lake.

'Not wrong so much, as… It's just that a four-year-old doesn't fully understand yet the concept of keeping a secret.'

Blowing out a breath, she relaxed again.

'If Lili in her excitement should blurt out the secret to Marguerite, I would hate for you to be vexed with her.'

She reached out to touch his arm. 'Of course I won't be vexed.' She'd meant her touch to be a sign of reassurance. Instead, the power and heat of the man filtrated into her blood, making her want him with such an elemental fierceness she sucked in a breath. Snatching her hand back, she rubbed it against the linen of her trousers.

'Actually, Gabriel, I'm very much hoping she will let the cat out of the bag.'

That clenched hand on the table in front of him immediately loosened. He swung to her. 'You *want* Marguerite to find out?'

'Absolutely. She'd hate a surprise party, don't you think?'

'*Si.*'

'But a surprise party she knows about and can plan for...'

'You—'

He broke off, his face darkening, but she couldn't tell if it was in outrage or surprise.

'Think about it.' This time it was she who turned to him, though she was super careful not to bump him. 'This way Marguerite gets all the advantages of a surprise party, but with none of the drawbacks. Try your brownie.' It might help sweeten his mood.

With a disgruntled huff he bit into it, and as he slowly chewed, his eyelids lowered to half-mast with drowsy appreciation. Her breath caught. If she tasted him with the same lazy appreciation, would he—

Don't!

He sent her a sidelong glance from those grey eyes. 'You are a crafty harpy.'

'I'm not a *harpy*!' She feigned affront.

'A manoeuvrer then, a puller of strings.'

'But in a nice way.' She bit into her brownie, too, and groaned a little.

He gestured. 'Did you make these?'

She nodded. 'Nonna owned a restaurant and let me and my cousin Frankie help out in the school holidays. We loved it. Frankie adored being in the dining room with the customers—chatting and laughing and taking orders. But I loved to sneak into the kitchen and help out there.' It had been another haven.

He stared at her for a long moment. 'And Johanna? Did she love the restaurant, too?'

She loved that he asked, as if it'd be the most natural thing in the world that her sister would also be involved. 'Jo said nobody was tying her to a kitchen. She usually went away to camp during the school holidays—did far more exciting things like horse riding and kayaking.'

He laughed, and the sound of it made her feel happy and light, like she did when listening to her favourite pop music.

'Maria doesn't mind having you in her kitchen?'

'Not in the slightest. She understands that cooking can be a comfort. That it can help quieten the mind and soothe the soul.'

Intriguing lips pursed. She forced herself to look away.

'It has been a tempestuous time for you, yes? I had hoped the art would help, but—'

'Of course it's helped! Working here with you invigorates me. It fires me up—it's frustrating and satisfying in equal measure. But it's not *relaxing*. Do you find it relaxing?'

He opened his mouth, but closed it again with a frown. 'I find myself lost to it sometimes,' he finally said, 'and when I come back to myself, I am exhausted. But you are right. It is not relaxing. It is good that you have an outlet that is soothing and relaxing, too. Very good.'

'It's not the only one. Spending time with Lili is a delight.'

Something in his eyes lifted. 'Yes.'

'And with other members of the family, too.'

'With *the girls* as you call them?'

She nodded. 'And Marguerite.' Though she knew he wouldn't believe her. 'And I have hopes that the older members of the family will thaw as they get to know me better.'

He dragged a hand down his face, looking suddenly tired and grey. 'Have you approached Marguerite yet about setting up a foundation in Johanna's honour?'

Her chest clenched. 'I've mentioned it. She's thinking about it.' Forcing a smile, she lifted her chin. 'She'll come around, you'll see.' It would all work out.

'Audrey, you will be disappointed—'

'It's a risk I'm prepared to take.' She nodded at his abandoned brownie. 'Eat up. You call me a puller of strings, but you're wrong. I'm not pulling strings. I'm building bridges. I'm hoping that Marguerite knows by now that there's a surprise party in store for her—and that while I'm the brains behind it, the rest of the family is helping me in every way they can.'

'And what do you hope that will achieve?'

'Goodwill.'

'Audrey...'

She rushed on before he could pour cold water on her plans. 'And in the evenings that Marguerite and I spend together, I'm asking her advice about various family members.'

She watched him wrestle with his curiosity and saw the exact moment he surrendered to it, and it gave her a silly thrill of triumph. 'What kind of advice?'

'I asked her who I should set Livia up with. Do you know Livy hasn't dated since that awful sex scandal? No? Neither did Marguerite. I told her I thought it was dreadful what had happened, but that I didn't think it should put Livy off a relationship forever. Not all men are selfish jerks.'

'Did she suggest anyone?'

'Well, we discussed it long and hard because Livy needs someone kind-hearted and patient. We made a short list. I told her I'd get Tori and Ana's feedback, too, as they no doubt know these short-listed guys. I've told her I trust their judgement.'

His jaw dropped. 'You...'

'Bridge builder,' she provided for him. 'Also, Tori is thinking of starting up another business—she wants to help a community of women affected by domestic violence who've pooled their talents to make a range of funky T-shirts and earrings. Part of the proceeds go back into helping fund women's shelters. Tori's going to use her connections to create a more global platform for them.'

The pulse at the base of his throat throbbed. 'And Ana?'

She beamed at him. 'I'm glad you asked. Prior to her stint in rehab, she'd been working in her father's firm.'

He raked both hands back through his hair. 'You say *father's firm* like it's some kind of small holding. Audrey, it is one of the most prestigious real estate firms in all of Italy.'

'Whatever. The fact is she loved her job but her parents are so embarrassed at her downfall they'll barely speak to her, let alone give her old job back to her.'

'Yes, but—'

'She didn't steal from them, Gabriel. We all make mistakes. And we all deserve a second chance.'

'And this is the argument you presented to Marguerite?'

She bit into her brownie. 'I asked her advice for how we can best convince Ana's parents to give her her old job back.'

Autocratic lips twisted. 'I can already tell you how that went.'

'Go on, then.' She continued eating her brownie.

'If she didn't simply dismiss the idea and say it served Ana right.'

'Which she didn't.'

She licked her fingers clean of crumbs and Gabriel watched her as if mesmerised. Things inside her clenched up tight. He looked as if he'd like nothing more than to gobble her up. Shaking himself, he glared out at the water. Sagging, she seized her mug and buried her nose in it.

'Then she'd have said she would simply order Reggio and Claudia to give Adriana her job back.'

She nodded. That was exactly what Marguerite had said.

'What did you do?'

His voice was laden with doom and she couldn't help bristling a little. Why was he so sure she'd mess up and fall out of Marguerite's good graces?

'I didn't *do* anything. I simply laughed and told her I was starting to see why everyone was so terrified of her.'

His eyes widened and for a moment she could've sworn his lips twitched. 'What did she say?'

'She said that was *utter nonsense*. But I told her Nonna's motto had always been "You win more flies with honey than with vinegar."'

He choked on his coffee. 'You invoked your paternal grandmother?'

Admittedly, it had been a risk. But it had paid off. 'I suggested it might be better for domestic harmony—for Ana's relationship with her parents—if Marguerite made some throwaway comment about how well Ana seemed to be doing and suggested it might be time for her to get back to work, or something along those lines.'

'*Is* Adriana doing well?'

His face had closed up and it took a force of will not to seize what was left of her brownie and mash it against the front of his shirt. 'Of course she is! I don't lie, Gabriel. How many more times do we have to have this conversation?'

But the exhaustion that crossed his face tugged at her heart. Ana's drug addiction must remind him of Fina's. And anyone could see how badly Fina's death had marked him. How it still marked him.

'Sorry,' she murmured. 'I didn't mean to snap.'

'While I shouldn't have been so sceptical. I barely know Ana.'

She glared into her coffee. 'You hardly know any of them and yet you're happy to dismiss them wholesale as a bunch of hedonistic partygoers without a care for anyone but themselves and their own pleasure. Or in Marguerite's case that she'd sacrifice all for the family name. But you're wrong. The Funaros are like any other family—a complicated mix of good and bad. People aren't perfect, Gabriel, and it's unreasonable to expect them to not make mistakes.'

She wanted to add that what had happened to Fina wasn't anyone's fault—not his and not Marguerite's—but snapped her mouth shut. She'd already said more than she'd meant to.

'And this is what you are also trying to do between me and Marguerite—and the rest of the family—build a bridge?' Dark eyebrows rose over flinty eyes. 'You are trying to get me to see them in a different light.'

'I *would* like you to see them in a different light,' she admitted. 'A truer light.'

'Truer for whom?'

'I'm not being dishonest.' She crumpled her paper napkin. 'I'm not lying or making things up. Everything I tell you about Marguerite is the truth.'

'As *you* see it.'

'As I see it,' she agreed. 'In a way that isn't twisted by bitterness or hate.'

'If you should continue to attempt this thing, you will be making a mistake.'

He didn't speak with anger, but his quietness was ten times worse. She pressed fingers to her forehead. She would love for him and Marguerite to loosen their grip on the prejudices they held about each other.

'And then we will not be friends. I will not allow you to be my puppet master, Audrey.'

Her chin lifted. 'And are we friends?'

For the briefest of moments, stern lips relaxed into a smile. 'I am friendlier with you than I have ever before been with a Funaro.'

Not counting Fina, of course. Though that remained unspoken.

'I'm not manipulating anyone. I'm simply providing a vision of the truth that you are uncomfortable with, and I suspect Marguerite is, too, though she does a better job of hiding it. I believe you're a lot of things, Gabriel. I suspect you can be every bit as ruthless as Marguerite claims. But I also know you can be patient and kind. The one thing I didn't expect you to be was closed-minded.'

His jaw dropped.

'And from all you've lectured me on artistic practise, closed-mindedness is the death of art.'

If possible, his jaw dropped even farther.

She stood and planted her hands on her hips. 'Do you think I'm doing harm with this so-called string-pulling? Do you think I'm doing a bad thing? Do you think I am making a mess, making things worse?'

With a visible effort, he hauled his jaw into place. He neither glared nor yelled. Behind the grey of his eyes, she sensed his mind racing. Finally, he shook his head. 'You are trying to create harmony, and I think that in these instances—with *the girls*—you will succeed. You are looking after your friends. It is admirable. But I still think you are going to be disappointed.'

She sat again, tracked an eagle high above, circling on air currents. She kept her gaze trained on it. 'Why?'

'Because you are trying to create one big happy family here in Lake Como and that will never happen. You yearn so much for the love and security of family and are prepared to give your all for it, but you do not see how others can, and probably will, take advantage of that to promote their own agendas.'

She had to swallow. His perception—his recognition of her feelings about family—left her feeling raw and vulnerable. And yet, she wouldn't be as cynical as he was for all the world, even if the Funaros should end up breaking her heart.

'Or maybe they just need to experience someone loving them without an agenda, to understand what it's like to be loved unconditionally, to discover what it's worth. Maybe they need to be loved like that first, before they can see how they, too, can love like that.'

He swore under his breath. 'You need to develop some armour against the world, Audrey. You need—'

'I don't see your armour bringing you any joy, Gabriel, so excuse me if I don't jump on board your armour train. You are dismissing vulnerability as something to be afraid of. You don't understand what a gift it can be. Armour?' She snorted. 'Armour simply weighs one down.'

Gabriel watched Audrey return to the studio with her plate and mug, her shoulders back and her head held high, and an icy fist reached inside his chest and squeezed.

She had such faith in people. What would happen when this family took all she had to give then stomped all over her? Who and what would she turn to for solace when they refused to live up to her expectations and behaved their worst—when she felt discarded and unloved and betrayed?

She enjoyed the finest French champagne now, but would she start chugging back bottles of the stuff to take the edge off the pain? Would she lose herself to a string of love affairs and one-night stands in an effort to find a physical release from her sadness and sense of failure? Would she turn to drugs...?

Breathing hard, he ran a hand over his face. He and Lili would be there for her, and so would her art, but would it be enough? What else could he give her that would provide some comfort if this came tumbling down around her ears?

If? Don't you mean when?

Tapping fingers against the table, he realized that if things truly did go badly, he wasn't sure she'd know how to get away from the villa. Marguerite could stymie a cab driver, refuse them entrance. His lips pressed into a tight line. That at least was something he could help with.

Seizing his mug and plate, he, too, returned to the studio. 'Audrey, do you know how to drive?'

She glanced around from *Ties That Bind*. He thought she'd finished it.

'I have an Australian driver's licence, but I've not driven in Italy yet.' She shuddered. 'You guys drive on the wrong side of the road.'

He ignored the shudder. 'Would you like to learn to drive here?'

She turned around fully. 'Are you offering to teach me?'

'*Si.*'

'Why?'

'I think it is wise for every person to have as much independence as possible.' He would do for her what he'd never thought to do for Fina.

'You think there might be a situation in the future where I'll need to make a quick getaway?'

Her lips twitched as if she found him amusing. He didn't care. She could be amused all she liked as long as she was also prepared. 'It is better to be safe than sorry.'

She stared at him for several long moments, but to his relief, finally nodded. 'I'd very much like to practise my driving with someone capable. As you say, you never know when such a skill might come in handy. Thank you for the offer.'

Excellent. He gestured at *Ties That Bind*. 'I thought you had finished.'

'I did, too, but something in me refused to rest. And it just occurred to me that one can lift off my frame and the figure beneath is suddenly freed, but…that's not the truth of the piece. It's not the way things work in the real world. So now I want to send threads from here to here—' she pointed '—and here to here. So that it is all fully integrated. I know it will make the piece harder to transport. That two pieces now become one, but…' She shrugged.

He stared at the piece, and as always, things inside him clenched.

'Are you sure the figure there trapped behind that beautiful web is not you?' He wasn't sure he could stand it if that was how she felt.

'I don't feel trapped, Gabriel.'

He tried to feel relief, but it wouldn't come. 'Who *is* the figure, then?'

She frowned. 'Why does it have to be anyone?'

Because every instinct he had told him she'd created that piece with someone particular in mind. Johanna? Marguerite?

Before he could ask, her frown deepened. 'Who was the figure in *Maybe*? Who was your muse for that piece?'

'Fina.'

She flinched and it had him refocusing fully on her rather than her artwork. She stared at him with wide eyes, the colour draining from her face. How was it possible for her to grieve so hard for the dead sister she'd never known? Exhaustion swamped him and he dropped into the nearest chair. 'It was when I didn't know if she was going to overcome her addiction or give in to it completely.'

It had been during her second stint in rehab. He'd had such high hopes. They hadn't been realised, and even now the acrid taste of disappointment burned his throat.

Audrey gave a low laugh, but it held no humour. His every sense was on high alert.

'*That's* what me sitting for you has been about?'

Her mouth twisted in self-derision, as if she'd been a fool. He found himself on his feet. 'What do you mean?'

She paced the long length of the bench running the width of the room. 'You haven't wanted me to sit for you because of who I am, because there's something about *me* that speaks to you.' She thumped a hand to her chest.

What the hell...?

She swung around, eyes flashing. 'I've just been a substitute for your real muse—*Fina!*'

She had this wrong. *So* wrong.

'I thought your creative block was because you'd been trapped in your grief for so long that you'd forgotten how to have fun and enjoy yourself. I thought I'd somehow helped to pull you out of that funk—that in agreeing to be your student, I'd given you a different focus.' She flung an arm in the air. 'I thought having a female role model for Lili—a woman who would love her—had helped quieten some of your fears. I thought those things combined—'

She broke off, breathing hard. 'God, I must have an ego the size—' she gestured out the window '—of a lake!'

The magnitude of her misapprehension left him speechless. He tried to make his brain work; tried to formulate words to tell her how mistaken she was.

'Instead, all of this time I've been a substitute, a very sad second best, but a chance nonetheless for you to relive your glory days with Fina.'

The expression in her eyes pierced him to the very core.

'No wonder you didn't want to be friends. Were so intent on keeping me at a distance. You didn't want to bring the temporary fantasy that Fina still lived crashing down.'

'You are so wrong!'

The shouted words reverberated around the studio, reaching into the farthest, darkest corners.

'Incredibly, stupendously and momentously *wrong*!' he roared.

Her head rocked back.

He stabbed a finger at her. 'I hadn't been married to Fina a full year before I realised what a mistake our marriage was.'

The shock in her eyes was far more welcome than the previous self-loathing.

'I wanted a divorce.'

Her hand flew to her mouth.

'But then Fina became pregnant and…' He raised his arms, let them drop back to his sides. 'I hoped things would change. We had made vows. It is wrong to give up on a marriage without a fight. I wanted to be there for Fina and I wanted to be there for our child.'

Neither of them said anything for several long moments.

'My relationship with Fina was not the great romance you seem to think it.'

She took several steps towards him. 'You must've loved her once.'

'She didn't marry me because she loved me. She married me as an act of rebellion…because she knew Marguerite would not approve.'

She moved another step closer. 'But *you* must've loved *her*.'

'I must've done,' he agreed. 'But I cannot remember feeling that way now. All I remember is her destructiveness and her selfishness, and how I wished to break free of her. You are wrong, Audrey. I am not mired in grief.' He was mired in guilt. He did what he could to get his raging emotions back under control. 'However, Lili has lost her mother, and that is a great tragedy.'

'I'm sorry,' she offered quietly.

He moved across until they stood toe to toe. 'You have not been a sad substitute. You do not, thankfully, remind me of Fina in any fashion. You are ten times the woman she was.'

Her lips parted and she blinked.

He leaned down until they were eye to eye, the cleanness of her scent welling up all around him. 'I keep my distance because I am the one who demanded there be no romantic entanglement between us. And yet, when you are near, all I can think about is kissing you.'

Her throat bobbed and her gaze lowered to his lips, clove-coloured eyes darkening to walnut. 'So…' That gaze returned to his and she swallowed again. 'I haven't imagined that?'

His hands clenched to fists to stop from reaching for her. 'You haven't imagined it.' He would not undermine her confidence or sense of self the way Fina had his, no matter what the admission might cost him.

'And you know I feel the same way. That sometimes I look at you and—'

'Yes!' He cut her off before her words could inflame him further.

'So…it's safer to keep our distance.'

He tried to push another yes from his throat, but it wouldn't come.

She moistened her lips. 'What would happen if we broke those rules?' She said the words as if to herself. 'Would the sky fall in?' The pulse in her throat fluttered. It took all his strength not to lower his head and touch his lips to the spot. 'Should we amend the rules?'

This was madness, but as he stared at the line of her throat, took in the oversized man's button-down shirt she wore when she worked, the vee of the neckline hinting at shadowed cleavage, hunger roared through him. 'Amend the rules how?' The words rasped out of him.

'I still don't want a boyfriend. But I've never wanted a man the way I want you. What I feel for you is...*greedy*. I've been careful my whole life not to be greedy, but I see you and I want...'

She reached out and placed her hand on his chest. The warmth of her hand penetrated the thin cotton of his T-shirt and he sucked in a breath. 'And you want what?' he demanded.

She met his gaze and her eyes widened—at whatever she saw in his face or her own audacity, he had no idea.

'I want to claw off your clothes and feast on you, and have you feast on me. I want to be greedy.'

She spoke clearly, as if she wanted her every word to hit him with the force of a mini tornado. He couldn't move. If he did, he'd kiss her, and there'd be no going back.

'Can I kiss you, Gabriel?'

His body shook from the force of holding back. 'If we kiss, Audrey, we will not stop.' He reached out and pulled the clip from her hair. Her hair fell past her shoulders and he wrapped his hand around it, pulled her head back until her throat was exposed to him. He pressed a kiss there, grazed the sensitive skin with his teeth and she whimpered. The sound arrowed to his groin.

'Release my hair, Gabriel.'

He didn't want to, but he did as she asked. Rather than move away, though, she hooked a hand behind his head and drew his face down to hers, her eyes glittering and her breath shallow. 'We keep it here, at the studio. We don't take it back to the villa or anywhere else. Agreed?'

His heart beat so hard he thought she must hear it. 'Agreed.'

Bunching her fingers in his shirt, she dragged it over his head and then simply stared at him. 'Can I change my mind? Can I ask you to sit for me naked?'

'You can have me however you want.'

And then they were tearing at each other's clothes. It was raw and physical and primal. He wanted to slow it down, but she wouldn't let him. She seemed to know exactly how to touch him to inflame him and make him forget himself.

'Now,' she demanded, sobbing when he touched her in that most intimate of places. She was soft and wet and ready. Wrapping a hand around him, she squeezed gently and he bucked into her hand. 'Now, Gabriel, now!' she demanded. 'I want you inside me *now.*'

He went to sweep the bench clear, but it would mean disturbing her current embroidery.

He swung away to the other bench. 'We'll hurt your work,' she groaned.

Stumbling together, they hit the back wall. He took the force before swinging them around and lifting her up, her back braced against the wall as he fumbled with a condom from his wallet on the bench. Her legs wrapped around his waist and he lowered her down. They both shook as she closed around him.

They stilled, staring at each other. It felt as if not just time but the world itself stopped, and then they were moving with a greedy fervour that shook him to his core. They moved with a mutual rhythm, not once breaking stride, not once falling out of step.

Her breaths, her moans and whimpers filled his ears. Her cries as her muscles tightened and she broke around him. His name on her lips.

From somewhere far off a guttural cry sounded—him?— and then he was sucked into a swirling vortex of pleasure that shook every atom of his body with its force—breaking and then rearranging it in a different pattern.

And leaving him feeling like a new man.

CHAPTER ELEVEN

AS GABRIEL LOWERED her feet to the floor, Audrey wondered if her legs would hold her upright. *Good legs.* She praised them when they did. *Very good legs.*

Not that he let her go. They were both breathing hard. She had one arm flung around his neck; the other drifted down to rest against his ample chest. He'd wrapped one strong arm around her waist and his forehead rested beside her on the wall.

Closing her eyes, she did what she could to catch her breath. That had been...*intense.*

Eventually, Gabriel roused himself and swore softly. 'Did I hurt you?'

Her eyes flew open and she reached up to touch his face. 'You took me to heaven.'

Grey eyes met hers. He traced a finger down her cheek. 'I lost all control. You probably have bruises on your back.'

'And you probably have scratch marks on yours.' She bit her lip. 'I might've even drawn blood.'

He smiled. And it was sweet and warm and every good thing. Things inside her melted and begged and did all manner of things she couldn't begin to decipher when her mind was still so full of him, and while he remained so close.

She needed him to stay close. She didn't want him moving just yet.

'I loved your enthusiasm,' he murmured, pushing her hair from her face. 'I loved how much you wanted me.' His gaze darkened. 'You made me feel alive again.'

He'd made her feel like a wild woman. 'I didn't know it could be that good,' she whispered.

His gaze roved her face and he nodded as if in approval. 'I have dreamed of seeing you mussed like this, and it is every bit as beguiling as I knew it would be. You are an extraordinary woman, Audrey.'

She melted some more, cupped his face and kissed him. A warm kiss that he returned with the same goodwill that threaded through her.

'I meant to savour you, though.'

She bit her lip and drew back a fraction, curiosity rippling through her. What did he mean by that?

'I meant to take it slow, meant to explore every inch of your body, learning what gave you pleasure, taking my time until you were begging for release.'

Warmth flushed through her cheeks. And other places. 'What? *Now, Gabriel, now. Please!* wasn't enough begging for you?'

His chuckle warmed her all the way through. 'Next time,' he promised. 'I am afraid I will not want to do any work if we are keeping this thing here and only here.'

'It has to stay here.' They both knew it.

It had to stay here, because if they took this thing into the real world, she was afraid she'd fall in love with him. As long as they kept it within these four walls it would continue to feel like nothing more than an escapist dream, a flight of fancy—something not quite real.

Gabriel didn't want her falling in love with him. Marguerite didn't want her falling in love with him, either. An icy drip slid down her spine, and she wasn't masochistic enough to set herself up for that kind of heartache.

Gabriel would never fall in love with her. She was a Funaro, and that was something he'd never be able to overlook. He might make her body sing, but she'd be a fool to expect more. If he thought her feelings were getting involved, he'd walk away without a backwards glance—perhaps tossing her one of those blisteringly sardonic smiles over his shoulder first.

She shivered, and he rubbed his hands up and down her arms. 'Are you cold?'

Pulling in a breath, she smiled. 'No, I'm fine.'

Nobody would fall in love with anybody. They'd keep things light, they'd keep them fun…and they'd keep them separate. They'd enjoy each other, be kind to each other and remain friends when this eventually ended. Because regardless of anything else, she did feel that finally they were friends.

Over the next week Gabriel introduced Audrey to a brand-new world of sensuality. He showed her exactly what he intended when he'd said he'd meant to savour her. He made her beg as he promised he would. He made her soar. He made her feel replete. He made her feel *complete*.

In turn, she savoured him with the same slow relish; learned all she could about his body and what gave him pleasure. It made her want to pinch herself to know she had the power to affect him so greatly. To see that masculine body trembling at her touch. She made him beg, too; made him lose control… made him soar.

'How long before it burns itself out?' she asked after a particularly earth-shattering session of lovemaking. Her hand trailed a path across his naked chest as they lay on the bed in the mezzanine level he'd revealed to her the afternoon of the first day they'd become lovers. The view outside that enormous wall of glass was as spectacular as ever, but it was the man who captured her attention and held it.

'I do not know.' His fingers traced delicate patterns across her back. She wondered if she could capture those patterns and this feeling in an embroidery. 'You wish to be tired of me already?'

'Absolutely not!' But in a far-off corner of her mind, she hoped the need and intensity would soon lessen. At the villa they tried to avoid each other. Oh, she spent time with Lili, but he no longer accompanied her. They might have rules about where and when and how they could indulge their explosive chemistry, but their bodies had minds of their own.

And refused to be ruled.

The driving lessons he insisted on giving her were a special form of torture. But neither of them broke the promise they'd made. Even though she could see in the set of his jaw, the pulse in his throat and the fire in his eyes that he wanted her every bit as much as she wanted him.

'We are friends now, Gabriel, yes?'

He lifted up on one elbow, a frown in his eyes. 'Of course. I like you. I care about you.' He blinked as if the admission surprised him. 'Do you doubt it?'

She shook her head. 'I feel it in here.' She touched her chest. A hungry light came into his eyes as he glanced at her chest, making her swallow. 'I just wanted to make sure you felt it, too. Gabriel...' She hesitated. 'You know I've no desire to hurt or vex you?'

His frown deepened. 'I trust you, if that is what you ask. Why?'

'Because I want you to tell me more about Fina. What happened? How did she die?'

He sat up, a mix of emotions racing across his face as he settled back against the headboard.

She sat up, too, but rather than rest beside him, she curled against his chest, her head nestled beneath his chin, and she let out a sigh of relief when, after a moment's hesitation, his arm went around her.

'I know this sounds silly. I mean, I didn't even know I had a sister until a few weeks ago. But now that I do—not having had a chance to meet her, know her, makes me feel as if a part of me is missing.'

'Audrey.' Her name was nothing more than a murmured sigh, and when she glanced up, the tired expression in his face pricked her heart. 'Do you have this image in your mind of a lovely, warm woman with whom you could've been best friends?'

She let out a breath. 'Not anymore.'

'The things I tell you won't make you like her very much.'

'And yet they'll be the truth. And that's what I want—the truth.'

She watched him war with himself. She settled back against his chest. 'Please?' she whispered.

'Where to even start,' he murmured.

'At the beginning.' She kept her voice soft, though she wasn't sure why. 'How did you meet?'

'We were both living in Rome at the time. We met at one of my exhibitions. When I saw her—it was as if someone had punched the breath from my body. I had never met anyone more vibrant. She was very beautiful, very charismatic…and so confident.'

'She bowled you over.'

'Completely. Ours was a whirlwind romance. We were married within six months of meeting. I have never been a rash man, and yet I rushed into that marriage without thinking twice. I didn't notice—or didn't want to notice—that she was also headstrong and reckless. I thought they were simply factors of being a Funaro and that once she married, she would settle down.'

'That's not what happened?'

She glanced up to see him shake his head. 'At first, I was happy to attend the parties and society functions that she so loved, but the novelty eventually wore off. I had commissions to fill and wanted to get back to work. She kept promising we'd move to Milan, near to her family, and start living a quieter life. But that day never seemed to come. That's when I realised we barely knew one another.'

'What did you do?'

'I hired studio space in Rome so I could at least work, and then set out to woo my wife—to make her truly fall in love with me. I didn't care where we lived, but I wanted to spend time with her. And I wanted her to spend time with me.'

'That didn't turn out the way you wanted?'

Doh! Clearly, it hadn't.

He gave a mirthless laugh. 'Oh, she was more than happy to have me in her bed, but it didn't stop her partying. It didn't stop the excessive drinking or the recreational drugs.'

She winced.

'And then she became pregnant. I hoped rather than believed things would change. I seized on the opportunity to settle us into a different routine—away from the drinking and drugs. We bought a villa on the outskirts of Milan, which she spent a fortune redecorating and furnishing.'

'And were you happy?' She wanted them to have had at least a taste of happiness before it all went so terribly wrong.

He was silent for several long minutes. 'We'd moved to Milan to be closer to her family. It was where she'd grown up. I foolishly thought she would appreciate having them near, to have their support during her pregnancy, but she missed her social life in Rome. She started throwing lavish parties, which I attended to make sure she didn't drink or take drugs while pregnant. Funnily enough, she didn't seem to mind that, and the parties kept her entertained for a while. But then she became...'

'What?'

'Resentful of the changes in her body.'

She couldn't hide her dismay.

One powerful shoulder lifted. 'I did what I could to reassure her...'

The set of his jaw and the expression in his eyes told her how that had played out.

'She went into self-imposed seclusion until Lili was born. Shut herself away, refused to see anyone, including Marguerite. She'd barely talk to me—blaming me for the state she found herself in. I hired a team of doctors and nurses and they did everything they could.'

Fina had taken no joy in her pregnancy? Audrey sagged against him. It should've been one of the most joyful and exciting times of her life.

'I had heard of postpartum depression, of course. What I hadn't known is that seven percent of pregnant women also suffer from depression.'

'And Fina was one of them.'

He shrugged. 'Or maybe she was simply a selfish brat who hated anyone or anything curtailing her freedom.'

Whoa!

'Why do you say that?' she asked carefully.

'Because as soon as Lili was born, and she'd lost the pregnancy weight, she immediately started partying again. She had absolutely no interest in the baby, and when I confronted her about it, she told me that in birthing a new Funaro heiress, she'd performed her duty. And that if I didn't want the bother of a child then to hire a nanny.'

Her hand flew to her mouth.

'That was the moment I realised what a spoiled young woman Fina was. It was the moment I realised that she cared nothing for either Lili or me.'

She wrapped an arm around his waist, hugged him tight. 'I'm sorry, Gabriel.'

'She moved back to Rome, started drinking again, taking drugs…and lovers. While I started getting legal advice about a divorce and getting custody of Lili. I wanted nothing more to do with Fina. I hated her for disregarding Lili like she had, for dismissing her as if she was worth nothing. Marguerite, of course, caught wind of what I was planning and we had an awful row. She blamed me for Fina's fecklessness and I blamed her.'

Audrey winced.

'But she convinced me to come to Rome with her to confront Fina together. And then there was another row. That was when I discovered Fina had married me to spite Marguerite. I hadn't known until then that Marguerite had been against the match. I left without a backwards glance. Headed back to the lawyers in Milan. But before I could start divorce proceedings, Fina died. She'd been partying on a yacht off the coast of Portofino, had taken a cocktail of party drugs and slipped overboard. A couple of people saw her fall and raised the alarm, but they were terribly inebriated and by the time Fina was found, it was too late. She'd drowned.'

Audrey closed her eyes. Just as Gabriel had said, Fina had self-destructed.

He'd fallen headlong in love with Fina and he'd never be that unguarded again…that *wholehearted* in his emotions. The thought had her aching for him, even as a chill crept over her.

Would there be a price to pay for these stolen moments?

Don't be foolish.

This thing they shared wasn't love. It was…pleasure, respite, fun.

Actually, it felt a lot like family—the sense of belonging, the no need to be on one's guard, to be with someone with honesty and trust. It was what she'd had with Jo, Nonna, Aunt Deidre and Frankie. When this thing between them had run its course, she and Gabriel would still have that.

'The coroner said there were so many drugs in her system that she'd probably lost consciousness before she hit the water.'

And just like that, a young woman had lost her life. She shivered.

'I'm sorry, Audrey.' He rubbed her arm as if to warm her. 'It's a far from edifying story.'

'But I wanted to know. And I'm glad to know. Thank you for telling me.' She rubbed her cheek against his chest, welcoming his warmth. 'I don't think Fina and I would've become friends.'

'No.'

'I think she must've been a terribly unhappy person to act the way she did.'

'I agree.'

'But her unhappiness stemmed from a time before she met you.' She struggled into a sitting position. 'You do know that, don't you?'

He nodded.

Subsiding back against the headboard, they both stared out at the view, but things inside her continued to throb. 'Gabriel, all of that is in the past now. It happened two years ago, but as you just said, you and Fina were over long before then. Why haven't you met someone else? You're young and virile.'

And so alone.

She hated the thought of him with someone else. But she hated the thought of him being alone more.

'You listen to my ugly story and you don't judge any of us, but perhaps you should. None of us are nice people.'

'That's not true!' He'd been kind to her—gruff at times, stern, even unfriendly, but still kind. He was a generous lover. And he adored his daughter. He was a good man.

'If I had tried harder, if I might've seen beneath Fina's recklessness to the unhappy young woman she really was, I could've helped her. Instead, I let pride and hurt feelings override what I knew in my gut—that if she continued on her path, she would die an early death.'

Even though he spoke the truth, his words cut him like knives. Shoving the sheet back, he pulled on a pair of shorts and strode to the railing, not really seeing the view spread in front of him.

'It was your mother, Danae, who got her onto drugs. Did you know that? She abandoned Fina when she was two years old and didn't return until Fina was sixteen.'

'I thought Danae returned to her family here after she left Australia.'

Danae, another troubled Funaro heiress, had taken recklessness to new heights. He turned to meet Audrey's gaze. She reclined against the headboard, those walnut eyes watching him, and his body tightened and hardened at the sight. 'According to the rest of the family, she would never say where she'd been or what she'd been up to. She was missing for thirteen years, and when she came home she refused to act the mother to sixteen-year-old Fina, taking instead the role of the rebellious older sister.'

She leaned towards him. 'But to introduce your own daughter to drugs? What kind of person does that?'

'She left less than a year after she'd returned. I can see now how much that marked Fina.'

'To have your mother come back into your life simply to leave again. Poor Fina. She must've felt doubly abandoned. As if she were somehow not enough.'

It took all his strength not to flinch at her words. She hadn't uttered them as an accusation, but it was what he deserved—to be held accountable.

'I never met Danae. I found out only after Fina died what had happened to her.'

'What did happen to her?'

He didn't want to answer, but if anyone deserved the truth, it was Audrey. 'She took some mind-altering drug while she was away travelling...it addled her brain.'

'She died of a drug overdose?'

He rubbed a hand over his face. 'She's not dead, Audrey. But her mind is lost. She's in a private clinic north of here on the Swiss border.'

She shot out of bed to stand in front of him. '*Not* dead?'

He forced himself to look at her. 'It's the Funaro family's greatest secret, and most of them don't know it.'

'But Marguerite told me she was dead.'

'She might as well be. Her body lives on, but... If you were to visit her, she'd not know you.'

'I don't want to visit her.' She dropped to the bed as if her legs would no longer hold her up. 'Did Fina know the truth?'

'No.'

She buried her face in her hands. Long moments passed, but she eventually pulled them away, her eyes murky with sorrow. 'And as a result, Marguerite bears the same burden of guilt that you do.'

He stabbed a finger at her. 'Fina should've been told the truth!'

'Because maybe then she'd have avoided taking drugs to ensure the same thing didn't happen to her?'

Yes! 'I should've known the truth!' If he'd known the truth, maybe he'd—

What? mocked an ugly voice. *Tried harder?*

He hadn't been able to get away from Fina fast enough. *That* was the truth. He hadn't *wanted* to try harder.

Wheeling around, he gripped the railing with all his strength. Feeling the weight of his own culpability. 'It is true that I blame Marguerite. But I married Fina. I was supposed to look after her. I failed her, and because of that Lili no longer has a mother and—'

'Stop it.' Warm arms slid around his waist. 'You aren't to blame for the choices Fina made. Neither is Marguerite. And if we want to be brutally honest, neither is Danae.'

Outrage made him turn, but one look at her face and he didn't have the heart to break away.

'Fina was an adult, Gabriel. A grown woman in charge of her own destiny. She had other options available to her to deal with her problems. She didn't have to turn to drugs. She made bad choices.' Her grip tightened, urging him to meet her gaze. 'Did you suggest counselling? Drug rehabilitation?'

'Of course I did. I—'

'You couldn't drag her there against her will, though. She needed to make that decision of her own free will. You couldn't impose it on her—no matter how much you wanted to save her.'

He hated her words at the same time as he hungered to believe them.

She cupped his face in both her hands, her eyes swimming with unshed tears. 'If Fina's daughter couldn't save her, Gabriel, you and Marguerite didn't stand a chance. And all of this guilt and regret, it's eating you alive. You need to let it go.'

She stood there offering him a vision of a future he didn't dare believe in. Reaching up on tiptoe, she kissed him, and he kissed her back with a need he could barely temper, wanting to lose himself in her warmth and softness and belief. She opened up to him without reservation and he took everything she gave, searching for peace and release…and absolution.

'Tomorrow is Thursday.' Thursday was one of the days Audrey didn't work at the studio.

She glanced around from pulling on the cotton sundress over her head, and Gabriel wanted to pull it back over her head, drag her back to bed and make love with her all over again. But the afternoon shadows were starting to lengthen and he would need to take her back to the villa soon.

'We've barely worked these last two weeks.'

They'd both tried to settle to their respective works in progress, and Audrey had even started a new piece, but their hunger for each other had yet to subside, and their concentration for anything work related never lasted long. 'If you wanted to come here with me tomorrow…' he offered now.

Her eyes danced. 'But would we work?'

Righting her dress, she surveyed him reclining on the bed completely naked and swallowed. A smile built inside him. He revelled in the way just the sight of him could undo her. He stretched and sent her a lazy grin.

Her breath hitched and she gave a shaky laugh. 'You stop that right now, Gabriel Matteo Dimarco!'

He loved it that she called him by his full name when she was trying to be stern with him.

'Up!' She made shooing gestures with her hands before throwing his jeans at him. 'Get dressed.'

'Why the hurry?'

'It's Wednesday night.'

Some of the brightness bled from the day. Wednesday night was the one night of the week Marguerite demanded Lili spend at the villa rather than in the cottage with him. Though if Lili was otherwise occupied…

'Would you like to come to the cottage tonight?'

She froze.

'I could cook for you.' He would like to do that. 'And—'

'I can't.'

Her voice sounded strangled and he frowned, but then she smiled and he thought he must've imagined it. But something chafed at him; something he couldn't explain. After rolling out of bed, he dragged on his jeans.

'It's date night with Lili and Marguerite.'

Standing on opposite sides of the bed, they made it, smoothing out the creases and fluffing up the pillows and the duvet until it looked smooth and fresh, as if they'd never been there. He immediately wanted to mess it up again. Mess her up and convince her to change her plans for him tonight.

Audrey stared at him across the divide of the bed. 'We agreed to keep things here, at the studio.'

'Would it matter if we stole a few extra moments elsewhere?'

'Yes.'

'Why?'

She hesitated.

'Audrey?'

'I don't want Marguerite knowing about us.'

Ice crept across his scalp. He recalled that fight between Fina and Marguerite.

'I loved how much it irked you when I married a lowbred, impoverished artist. The expression on your face when you discovered I was pregnant by him. It was worth the price I had to pay.'

His nostrils flared. His hands clenched. 'I'm fine to sleep with just as long as nobody knows. Is that it? I lack the polish the Funaros are renowned for and you don't want to be sullied by association. You'd—'

'If that's what you think, then you don't know me at all!'

Her eyes flashed, and shame, hot and hard, hit him in the gut. Audrey wasn't Fina.

'We agreed to keep this thing between us here where it's contained and...not real. Once we take it into the everyday world, it becomes *real*. And if it becomes real it'll lead to complications.' She strode around the bed to poke him in the chest with a hard finger. 'Do you want complications, Gabriel? Because I was under the impression you didn't.'

He didn't want complications. He'd do anything to avoid those. Reaching out, he cupped her face, lowered his brow to hers. 'I am sorry. I know you are not like that. It was an appalling thing to say. Please forgive me.'

She gave a funny little hiccup. 'Why did you say it, then?'

'Frustration.' He couldn't seem to get enough of her. 'Jealousy that you're spending tonight with someone else rather than with me in my bed.' He released her with a frown. 'What happens on Wednesday nights anyway?' The words growled out of him but he couldn't help it. 'It seems as if it's some top-secret thing. It makes me suspicious. Whenever I ask Lili she says it's a girls' night.'

'Because that's what it is—a girls' night.'

Was Audrey in on this, too? Were she and Marguerite in cahoots...?

To what? He was being paranoid.

He frowned again. He had every right to be paranoid where Marguerite was concerned. She—

'If we're really friends, Gabriel, then you shouldn't mind spending time with me outside of the bedroom.'

Her words had him stiffening. 'Of course I enjoy spending time with you doing other things!' He looked forward to their driving expeditions, even though his body hungered for her the entire time. He enjoyed the conversations they had after their lovemaking, or over coffee during their breaks. He enjoyed working side by side with her. 'I value you for more than just the sex, Audrey. You must not doubt that.' He wanted her to understand that she was valuable to him on many levels.

She stuck out her hip. 'Then join us for our girls' night tonight. But if you agree, you have to understand that for the evening, you are an honorary girl. And you are not allowed to criticise proceedings or to have an opinion on what happens.'

His eyes narrowed, his suspicion radar pinging madly. 'How is it possible to not have an opinion?'

She pursed her lips. 'Okay, that's true. Then you need to agree to keep your opinions to yourself.'

Could he do that? If he didn't, it would earn her a big black mark in Marguerite's books. He might not like Marguerite, but he knew what family meant to Audrey and he wouldn't do anything to damage that.

He gave one hard nod. 'You have a deal.' He would take this chance to enter the inner sanctum and judge for himself if Marguerite was leading his daughter astray, putting pressure on her to conform to a certain image and behaviour, and grooming her for a life of a socialite when he wanted so much more for her.

As directed, Gabriel turned up at the villa at 6 p.m. on the dot. Audrey met him with a smile and led him upstairs and down several corridors he'd never ventured along before. Opening a door, she led him into…

A media room.

He couldn't have said why, but it was the last thing he'd expected. An enormous TV took up most of one wall, and four sets of three-seater sofas rested in front of it—the second row slightly raised like in a theatre. Each seat had cupholders, a table in the arm that pulled out, and each seat reclined.

'Here's our mystery guest,' Audrey announced.

Marguerite glanced up, partially hidden by a drinks cabinet, and rolled her eyes, but remained mercifully silent. Lili bounced up and down. 'Papa! You're a girl tonight.'

'I am,' he agreed gravely.

'I get to decide where everyone sits—that's my job—because I'm Princess Lili.'

His lips twitched. 'And where would Princess Lili like me to sit?'

She cocked her head to one side. 'Tonight I'm sitting here.' She pointed to the middle seat of one of the front sofas. 'Princess Nonna is sitting here.' She pointed to the seat on the right of hers and Marguerite immediately took it. 'Princess Audrey's seat is here.' Audrey sat in the seat Lili pointed to on her other side. 'And Princess Papa,' she giggled. 'You get a whole sofa to yourself.' She pointed to the sofa directly behind her. He immediately moved to it because the others had taken their seats so quickly and he didn't want to get the etiquette wrong and spoil Lili's fun.

A knock sounded on the door. Lili knelt on her seat to face him. 'That'll be the pizza.'

Pizza? Marguerite was eating pizza?

'It's Audrey's job to order the pizza and Nonna's job to serve the drinks.'

Had he entered an alternate universe? He watched Audrey race to the door to take the pizza boxes from one of the maids and realised she wore her oldest jeans.

In front of Marguerite!

Marguerite moved to the drinks cabinet again. And he realised she wore a… Good God, the woman was wearing a tracksuit. While Lili was in her pyjamas.

'What would Princess Lili and Princess Audrey like to drink?' Marguerite enquired in her beautifully modulated voice. He felt as if he'd stepped into an alternate reality.

'Lemonade, please,' Audrey said.

'Orange juice, please,' Lili said.

'Princess Papa…' He could've sworn Marguerite uttered that with relish. 'What would you like to drink? We have sodas as well as orange, apple or pineapple juice.'

He'd kill for a beer, but that clearly wasn't on offer. 'A cola please… Princess Marguerite,' he couldn't help adding, and could've sworn the older woman's lips twitched.

Audrey handed around paper napkins and plates loaded with pizza. 'Tonight I chose a vegetarian pizza and a pepperoni pizza.'

'Lovely.' Marguerite passed around the drinks in cups with straws in them. Had he ever seen her drink out of anything but crystal or fine bone china?

With a wink in his direction, Audrey settled into her seat. 'What movie are we watching tonight, Princess Lili?'

'Ready?' Lili lifted the remote and pressed Play.

'Ooh, *Ever After*.' Marguerite rubbed her hands together as the opening credits rolled.

'I love this movie.' Audrey grinned at Lili. 'I love me a feisty Cinderella.'

'Me, too.' Lili nodded twice, even though he doubted she knew what the word meant. 'Can I be Feisty Princess Lili next week?'

'I think we should all be Feisty Princesses next Wednesday night,' Marguerite said.

Audrey nodded. 'Yes, let's.'

He watched in amazement as the three women—*princesses*—ate pizza, drank their juices and watched a fairy-tale movie with pure and easy enjoyment. Watched as Lili curled up first against her grandmother, and then eventually fell asleep in Audrey's lap.

He felt like Alice when she tumbled down the rabbit hole.

CHAPTER TWELVE

'I THINK THIS is where I say I told you so,' Audrey said as she passed a plate of thinly sliced ham to her grandmother the next morning at breakfast.

'I take it you're referring to our special guest last night?' Marguerite took a slice of wafer-thin ham and set it neatly on her plate.

That was one of the things she most loved about her grandmother—she didn't feign ignorance; wasn't the slightest bit coy. 'It wasn't dreadful or awkward or any of the things you were concerned about, was it?' She hadn't misread her grandmother's serenity of the night before, had she? Marguerite had still enjoyed their girls' night.

'You were right, Audrey, and I'm glad of it. Gabriel wasn't all bristling resentment as I expected.' She cut a small portion of ham and chewed it thoughtfully. 'He's a good father. It's something I never doubted. I'm glad he can put aside his own feelings to present a good face for Lili's benefit. It will be much easier for her, if her father and I can appear friendly when we're around each other.'

'It'd be best for Lili if the two of you actually stopped being so stubborn and got to know each other properly. I'm convinced that if you did, you'd become the best of friends.'

'My dear Audrey, it's best not to wish for the moon.' Marguerite eyed her from the head of the table. 'You aren't getting too attached to Gabriel, are you?'

Something weird and hot squirmed through her, but she

ignored it. 'He's become a friend—a good friend. I appreciate all he's done for me. I appreciate the fact he's promoted
my relationship with Lili. And—' She broke off with a frown.

'And?' Marguerite raised an eyebrow.

She blew out a breath. 'Well, he's blisteringly honest at
times, which can be confronting.'

Marguerite set her cutlery down. 'Has he hurt you?'

She sent her grandmother a swift smile. 'He hurt my feelings *dreadfully* when he called a particular piece I was working
on *derivative*. I had to take a little walk along the waterfront
to calm down.'

Marguerite's lips twitched.

'To make matters worse, he was right.' She pulled in a
breath. 'There's an awful lot of stuff we don't agree on, but
his honesty means I can trust him.'

'I can see how that could be a comfort.'

'He has a real chip on his shoulder about the Funaros—not
that that'll be news to you. But he told me about Fina.'

Marguerite stilled.

Audrey soldiered on. 'And Danae.'

Marguerite didn't outwardly flinch, but she sensed her
grandmother's tension. 'He had no right to speak about such
matters.'

'As I said, we're friends. And friends are honest with one
another.'

Marguerite's head rocked back. 'Are you saying that you
and I are not friends, Audrey?'

'Absolutely not. But I know how much you want to protect me.' She reached across and covered Marguerite's hand.
'And I can't begin to tell you what that means to me.' With a
squeeze, she straightened again, returned to her breakfast. 'I
know you all think me naive and soft and vulnerable. And I
guess I am naive in many ways, but it doesn't mean I'm weak.
I'm far stronger than you all give me credit for.'

'I'm sorry, *mi cara*. It is not that I thought you couldn't deal with the truth. But it is so ugly and I wanted to spare you. I would have told you eventually.'

'I know. But I'm glad to know the truth.'

They ate in silence for a bit. 'Grandmother, I'm really sorry you've suffered so much loss—first your daughter and then your granddaughter. It makes me understand why you've ruled the rest of the family with such an iron fist.'

Marguerite stared at her, opened her mouth, but no sound came out.

'I mean, every time someone else in the family makes a mistake—when there's a divorce, a failed business venture, or some kind of tabloid scandal—it must feel as if another person is going to follow the same path Danae and Fina did.'

'I gave the two of them far too much freedom.' The older woman sighed. 'I do not wish to make the same mistake with anyone else.'

'Their choices weren't your fault, Grandmama. They both had the world at their feet. They should've valued what they had. It's on them, not on anyone else.'

She pretended not to notice when Marguerite dabbed surreptitiously at her eyes. This woman took far too much blame for what had happened when all she'd been trying to do was keep her family safe.

'I have this same argument with Gabriel. He seems to think just because Danae and Fina went off the rails, the rest of the Funaros will go off the rails, too. He takes as his proof various family members' missteps, shortcomings and scandals and says, *"See? They're going the same way."* But that's absurd. All families are complicated, and every person makes mistakes regardless of how rich or poor, famous or obscure they are, and the Funaro family is no different.'

'My word, Audrey.' Marguerite's voice was faint.

She winced in her grandmother's direction. 'Some days we're so immersed in our different projects we barely speak.

But other days we seem to—' she shrugged '—cover a lot. And as I told him, he's a member of this family, too, so...'

She trailed off before reaching out to grip her grandmother's hand. 'I just wanted you to know that I know...about Fina and Danae.' She sent her a smile. 'I don't want you to worry so much about me.'

Marguerite squeezed her hand in reply.

'And to tell you that I trust Gabriel, and that I think you should, too.'

'But he doesn't trust me.'

'If the two of you would just give the other a chance, you'd see each other the way I see the both of you.'

'Well, I'll think upon what you've said. Now, speaking of letting each other into secrets...about this party you're throwing for me...'

She did her best to feign shock. 'Who spilled the beans?'

Marguerite laughed. 'I know exactly what you're up to so don't be coy with me, young lady.'

Audrey had to laugh then, too. 'Okay, so I figured you wouldn't really want to be surprised. But the rest of the family are so enamoured of the idea.'

'Yes, I'm sure they'd love to see me at a disadvantage.'

'You're wrong, you know? This is just giving people a chance to do it the way they want to do it—and in a way they hope will make you happy.'

One imperious eyebrow lifted.

'Okay, well, maybe there's one or two people who are mean-spirited enough to enjoy seeing you at a disadvantage, but families...what are you going to do, huh? We won't give them the satisfaction.'

'May I see the guest list?'

'Absolutely, though I was keeping it small and intimate—no more than fifty people—but I'd love to know if there's anyone else I should include.'

'I'd like to make sure a couple of old school friends are on the list.'

'Also, Lili is in charge of choosing your birthday cake. Now, I can easily sway her away from the ice cream cake she has her heart set on, so if you'd rather a black forest cake or lemon gateaux, now is the time to speak up.'

'My dear granddaughter, I'm sure you'll ensure there's a variety of desserts to cater to every taste. I'm more than happy with whatever Lili chooses.'

'Excellent.' She could tick that off her to-do list. Pulling her hands into her lap, she gripped them tightly. 'Now, on a completely different topic, have you given any more thought to the foundation I'd like to set up in Johanna's name?'

'I'm sorry, Audrey.' Marguerite rose. 'I have a rather important meeting with one of my brokers. We will talk about it later.'

Marguerite swept from the room and Audrey frowned at the pastry on her plate. But later *when*?

'Are Wednesday nights the hotbed of vice you were expecting?'

Audrey trailed her fingers across Gabriel's chest. She loved the feel of him—the firm smoothness of his skin. She loved touching him after they'd made love. She couldn't explain the sense of peace that stole over her; the warm afterglow and sense of wellbeing.

She'd meant to raise the topic of Wednesday night once they'd boarded the boat. But the moment she'd slipped into the car, he'd sent her such a heated glance that speaking had become impossible, and need and desire took possession of her. The moment they'd closed the studio door behind them, they'd started tearing off each other's clothes, greedy for one another.

He pressed a kiss to the top of her head now. 'Would you like me to apologise?'

'Of course not.' Reaching across, she hugged him hard. 'You should never apologise for having Lili's best interests at heart.'

'But?'

'No buts.' She rested her chin on his chest and glanced up at him. 'Did you enjoy yourself?'

Those stern lips broke into a rare smile. 'I did. As a one-time thing. I prefer sports to romantic comedies and Disney films.'

'And beer to lemonade.'

A laugh rumbled through him. *'Si.'*

'Also, I told Marguerite at breakfast yesterday that I know about Fina and Danae.'

He stiffened.

'I just thought you should know.'

His brow darkened. 'I suppose I should now expect to be called into the headmistress's office for a dressing down.'

'I don't think so. I told Marguerite that I was glad to know the truth and that everyone needed to stop treating me like I might break—that I'm stronger than you all give me credit for. And I told her I trust you and that she should, too.'

His eyes looked like they were going to start from his head.

'She said she'd think about it.' She pressed a kiss to his chest. 'So you need to stop being an idiot and give her a chance.'

'Such lover-like words,' he growled.

She laughed and pressed another kiss to his chest. 'Tell me you'll come to her party.' She kissed her way down his stomach. 'Please?'

'Are you trying to extort an agreement from me?'

She grinned up at him. 'Will that work?'

A laugh rumbled through that powerful frame again, those grey eyes dancing. 'I think it just might.'

'Well, let's see, then, shall we…?'

The day of the party arrived. Livia's car pulled up in the villa's circular drive, and as soon as Audrey saw it, she rushed through to the ballroom where everyone was gathered. Livia and her mother, Caterina, had taken Marguerite to have her hair done—the excuse they'd used to get Marguerite out of the villa so that everyone else could secretly arrive. 'Quiet, everyone, quiet. They're here,' she said, slipping into the room and closing the door behind her.

She took her place at the head of the crowd with Lili, who slipped her hand inside hers. Glancing back behind her, she caught Gabriel's eye. He'd secreted himself at the rear of the crowd. Then Nicolo turned off the lights and smothered them in darkness.

The outside conversation reached them clearly. 'Really, my dear Livia, your birthday is in winter. Surely, you'd prefer a party at the Milan estate.'

'Como is only forty-five minutes from Milan, and the ballroom has such beautiful views over the lake.'

Caterina's voice sounded outside. 'Why don't we just take a look?'

The door opened.

Nicolo snapped on the light.

'Surprise!' Audrey shouted, jumping up and down, grinning madly.

Taking their lead from her, everyone else also started shouting 'Surprise!' and 'Happy birthday!' in Italian and English, and then an unrehearsed but rousing chorus of *'Tanti Auguri a Te,'* the Italian version of 'Happy Birthday,' started up.

To Marguerite's credit, she looked utterly stunned. Though Audrey suspected it wasn't all feigned. Everyone did look ridiculously chuffed and excited. And the ballroom looked fabulously festive with balloons and streamers and tables laden with party food and drinks.

'A birthday party? For me?' Marguerite glanced around with wide eyes, one hand pressed to her chest.

Audrey and Lili danced up to her. 'Tell me you love it,' Audrey said, grinning at her.

'I adore it,' she said, kissing Audrey's cheek. 'Thank you, my dear.'

She said it with such tenderness, Audrey's throat thickened.

Lili hopped from one foot to the other. 'Were you surprised, Nonna? Were you?'

'Absolutely, Lili.' Her cheek was kissed, too. 'I'd have never guessed, not in a million years.'

Marguerite circulated about the room, thanking everyone and clearly enjoying herself. Which, in its turn, made everyone relax and begin to enjoy themselves as well, letting their hair down in a way Audrey hadn't yet seen them do en masse.

Before long, the French doors were opened to the terrace that had been set with an array of cast-iron tables. A game of croquet started up, and the '60s cover band Audrey had hired when she'd discovered Marguerite loved '60s music, started playing at one end of the ballroom.

People ate, chatted, danced. Marguerite exclaimed over her ice cream cake, blew out her candles and then beamed as everyone sang 'Happy Birthday.' It was the perfect party.

'You've danced with just about everyone except me.'

Gabriel's voice had all the fine hairs on Audrey's arms lifting in the most delicious manner. She turned to find him standing behind her, so close she could reach out and trace a finger down his chest.

Don't think of his chest.

'Would you do me the honour?'

Did she dare? They'd avoided each other so far—it had seemed wise. She was afraid that once she was in his arms, they'd give themselves away.

'It occurs to me that if we don't dance, it might look strange…raise questions.'

'Good point.' They didn't want to do that.

What harm can it do?

She allowed him to lead her to the dance floor. The band was currently belting out a Chubby Checker number. They wouldn't be dancing cheek to cheek, thigh to thigh.

Gabriel moved well, which shouldn't surprise her, but it had awareness creeping across the surface of her skin, and her lungs contracting. As if aware of the direction of her thoughts and wanting to break the spell, Gabriel took her hand and spun her around. She couldn't help laughing, and was breathless when the song came to an end. With a pounding heart, she waited for the next song. She'd allow herself the luxury—and exhilaration—of one more dance and then she'd continue with her hostessing duties.

The first notes of the Beatles' classic 'Hey Jude' sounded through the ballroom and she swallowed. Who didn't love this song? But it was a slower number and…

Glancing up from beneath her lashes, her pulse picked up speed as Gabriel's gaze darkened, but without a moment's hesitation, he pulled her into his arms. Everything inside her quickened. He held her closer to him and she allowed her eyelids to droop for just a moment, to relish it and breathe him in. They didn't talk. They just swayed to the music and lived in the moment.

All too soon, the song came to an end.

'Don't look around or get tense, but Marguerite's watching us,' he murmured in her ear. 'I'm going to cut in on Sergei and Paulette and we'll swap partners.'

'Excellent plan.'

They successfully avoided each other for the rest of the party. But the memory of being in his arms had burned itself into her mind. She couldn't wait for Monday to come when the two of them would be alone in his studio once more.

'Gabriel, Audrey…a word, if you don't mind?'

Everything inside Gabriel clenched at the imperious voice located somewhere behind him, but he kept his face bland and disinterested. His usual hostility where Marguerite was concerned was…well, not entirely absent, but certainly diluted.

Audrey's doing. She *had* made him see Marguerite in a different light. He just didn't know if he trusted in it yet or not.

He watched as Lili raced across to hug her great-grandmother before heading to the kitchen with the nanny. In movies and books, children were often used as a kind of barometer to indicate whether someone was good or bad beneath their crusty exterior. He reminded himself that was fiction, and how easily children could be manipulated. But even as he did, he couldn't deny the strength of the bond between his daughter and the older woman.

'Come.' Marguerite led them through several rooms on the ground floor to the library that acted as her unofficial study. She took a seat behind a large oak desk and waved them to the seats on the other side. His every sense went on high alert.

'This feels remarkably formal.'

Audrey voiced his own thoughts as they sat. It was an effort not to reach out and take her hand, to help support her through whatever ordeal was about to come. Because he was in no doubt that some confrontation was about to take place.

Marguerite laid both her hands flat on the desk and drew in a long breath. 'So…the two of you didn't heed the advice I gave to you when Audrey first arrived here.'

Audrey leaned forward. 'You're going to have to be more specific, Grandmother.'

'About the two of you not becoming romantically entangled.'

After one frozen second Audrey sat back again, lips pursed. She glanced at Gabriel. 'You don't lie.'

'No.' Though in this instance he would. If she wanted him to. And *that* realisation sent a strange kind of panic racing through him. He'd sworn to never change for another woman. It only led to heartache and—

'And I don't want to.'

The panic hurtled to a halt. He stared at her as she turned back to Marguerite. 'What gave us away?'

'You're not going to deny it?'

'Absolutely not. I've no desire to lie to you. I know you warned me off him, Grandmama, but...'

He wondered if Audrey was aware of the way her casual *Grandmama* affected Marguerite—the easy affection it indicated. The older woman hid it well, but the word sent a ripple through her every time it was uttered—like a light breeze through the fronds of a massive weeping willow.

He suddenly yearned to capture that image in wood and steel and glass.

He glanced at Audrey. This extraordinary woman waltzed into his life, and after an eight-month drought he was now brimming with inspiration. It made no sense.

'But?' Marguerite prompted.

'The thing is—' Audrey pressed her hands together '—I think you've misjudged Gabriel. And,' she continued, lifting her chin, 'I decided to follow my own instincts where he was concerned.'

Marguerite nodded, though it wasn't in agreement.

'He's not heartless or callous.'

Marguerite had told Audrey he was heartless and callous? He wanted to rail against such an assessment, but he couldn't. In their interactions since Fina had died, his ferocity had been on a tight leash, but at different times he'd allowed the older woman to see it—hoping it would keep her at a distance.

'It was our dance at the party, wasn't it?' Audrey said. 'It gave us away.'

'Does it matter?'

'No, I don't suppose so,' Audrey conceded.

Marguerite sighed. 'It was the way you so assiduously avoided each other at the party. You tell me that you and Gabriel are such good friends, and yet you do your best to not spend any time together when other people are around. It is a realisation that has been playing on my mind since our girls' night. Saturday's party confirmed it.'

'Grandmama…'

That ripple again—tree fronds moving gently in the air.

'Please don't take this the wrong way, but my relationship with Gabriel is nobody's business except his and mine.'

'I'm afraid, my dear, that's where you're wrong. What happens between the two of you has the potential to have a direct bearing on current custody arrangements pertaining to Lili.'

Audrey's jaw dropped.

'For the last two years, Gabriel and I have been walking on eggshells to avoid further unpleasantness. He would rather walk away from this family and would be delighted for Lili to not know any of us. He knows, however, that I would fight that with all the resources at my not inconsiderable disposal. We both know, as well, that such a battle would upset Lili. And we should like to spare her that.'

Audrey glanced from him to her grandmother. The distress in her eyes tore at him. 'We are all adults here,' he found himself saying.

'Fina was an adult, too,' Marguerite shot back. 'And we all know how well that turned out.'

'Fina was a fool,' Audrey said, making both him and Marguerite blink. 'From the little I know, I doubt any of us could consider her a fully functioning adult.'

Marguerite eventually shook herself, shooting a glare at Gabriel. 'I can't believe you would risk the hard-won equilibrium we have arrived at.'

Audrey gave a soft laugh. 'I'm not sure he had much choice.' Marguerite stared at her. 'Grandmama, you're a woman of the world. Have you never taken…*matters* into your own hands?'

For a moment he thought Marguerite might laugh, but the brief twinkle in her eye darkened again. 'Audrey, it would grieve me greatly to see you hurt.'

'But—'

'You tell me there is a great honesty between you and Gabriel. Does he know, then, that you have fallen in love with him?'

His every muscle stiffened in painful protest. Audrey didn't love him! Love had never been in the cards.

Audrey gaped at her grandmother.

Deny it, he ordered her silently. *Deny it!*

One of Marguerite's hands briefly fluttered to her throat, before it was once again clasped in front of her. 'You do not answer me.'

'I, um…' Audrey moistened her lips, and even through the panic and denial, a shot of desire, hard and dark, speared through him. He still wanted her.

But he didn't want her heart.

'Audrey?' Did that voice belong to him? 'We said…' He swallowed. 'Does Marguerite speak the truth?'

'I…' Her brow furrowed. 'I don't know.'

She didn't know? How…?

He watched her mind race behind those dark eyes, saw the awful realisation filter across her face in a slow, sickening wave. His hands clenched. He wanted to throw his head back and howl.

'Yes.' She swallowed. 'I just didn't realise it until this moment.'

He believed her. With any other woman he'd suspect some hidden agenda—a hope that she could trap him into a permanent arrangement. But not Audrey.

She gave a funny little laugh. *A laugh.* How could she laugh at a time like this?

'I told myself I could control my emotions. I kept telling myself I wouldn't fall in love with you, thinking that would make it true, but—' She broke off, her eyes dark in a pale face. 'Apparently, that's not the way emotions work.'

An ache gripped his chest.

She winced and sent him an apologetic grimace. 'If it's any consolation, I didn't mean to.'

It wasn't any consolation whatsoever!

'You make me feel alive. You make me feel as if I could

achieve anything. You're kind and smart and protective of those you care about. You're also demanding, and sometimes moody.'

He blinked.

'You're a generous lover, a fabulous father and...' She shrugged. 'Of course I fell in love with you. How could I not?' She stared down at her hands. 'I guess I didn't want to face the truth because I didn't want what we had to end.'

He rubbed a hand over his face. Of course it had to end, but things inside raised a ruckus at the thought. And the knowledge that he'd hurt her twisted through him in a torturous knot of self-condemnation.

'You want to know what my real mistake was? Thinking that we were like family. That just because I felt at ease with you and because we were honest with one another and because you saw something in my art and seemed to see something in me, that meant you'd stick.'

That he'd...what?

'In the same way that me and Jo and Nonna and Frankie stuck together—there for each other through thick and thin.' She didn't raise her voice, didn't shout and rail at him. 'But that was just wishful thinking.' She shook her head, her eyes narrowed as if the glare of the truth was hard to take. 'I was never special to you.'

'That's not true. You—'

She raised an eyebrow and he bit the rest of his words back. The fact remained that he didn't love her, and to give her false hope would be unkind.

'Gabriel, if you don't want to hurt my granddaughter more than you already have...'

He lifted his head to meet Marguerite's gaze.

'You have to discontinue this affair and walk away.'

She was right. He hated it. But she was right.

Marguerite pulled in a breath. 'Unless you, too, want more?'

'My heart was never on the table.' The words fell from his lips, strangely impassive. Beside him, Audrey flinched. 'We

agreed love was not part of the equation.' They'd *promised*!
'You're right, Marguerite. This needs to stop. I have no desire
whatsoever to cause pain to Audrey.'

He turned to her. 'Audrey—'

'Oh, God, please don't, Gabriel. I don't want platitudes or
sympathy. I already feel foolish enough.'

'You are not a fool!' Hearts had minds of their own. He
was the fool for thinking they could keep emotions out of it.

Audrey rose. 'I want to assure you both that I harbour no
resentment or ill feeling towards Gabriel. Nothing that has happened between us needs to affect the custody arrangements
you have in place for Lili.'

She turned with eyes that were strangely flat—as if the
sunshine had been bled from them. Her lips struggled into a
smile. His heart burned that it should now be such an effort
for her to smile at him.

'I hope you will still allow me to spend time with Lili.'

He rose, too; took her hand. 'Lili loves you. She will look
to you in the future. She needs you in her life. I will do everything in my power to safeguard your relationship.'

'Thank you.' She reclaimed her hand and her graveness had
a different kind of panic racing through him. Would they no
longer be able to share their ideas and challenge each other cre-
atively? Would she no longer chivvy him out of a dark mood
or make him see the beauty encased in *everything*? Would
they now be so distant from one another that—?

'If you'll both excuse me, I think I'd like a bit of time on
my own.'

But it was Monday, and they were supposed to be working
at the studio—

With a smothered oath, he crushed that thought. All of it
was now at an end, but he couldn't help grieving for what
they'd lost.

Audrey stiffened and then whirled on him. 'What do *you*

have to swear and be grumpy about? *Your* precious heart's still safe and sound.'

He swallowed. He understood her anger. 'I'm just sorry that—'

'No, you're not. Your world is still the safe little prison it's always been.'

His anger leapt then, too. 'We had a deal!'

'And I broke it.' Her hands slammed to her hips. 'So what? *Deal* with it.'

He gaped.

'Except you won't, will you?' She poked him in the chest. 'You won't do anything, because you're a coward. You'll run away every bit as fast as my mother and father did when things got too hard.'

He clenched his hands so hard, he shook.

'You think loving someone is a prison, but it's not. It can be wonderful and—' She broke off, breathing hard. 'You refuse to try again because it didn't work out with Fina. What kind of attitude is that? Art doesn't work like that, and neither does love or life.'

He opened his mouth, but nothing came out.

'You accuse the Funaros of being profligate, but it's better than being what you are—*a big, fat, emotional miser!* You set your heart against me before you even met me, and nothing that came after was ever going to change that. You said we were friends. You said I was special to you. You told me I was an extraordinary woman, but none of that was enough for you, was it? *Why?* Because biologically I'm a Funaro!'

She was breathing hard, but straightened and looked him dead in the eye. 'As long as your heart remains safe, you don't care how much you hurt anyone else.'

With that, she turned and left.

Everything inside him throbbed. He wanted to yell, chop wood, kick a ball as hard as he could...swim laps until he was exhausted. Anything to rid his body of this awful tension. Instead, he thumped back down to his chair.

Marguerite sighed. 'You're a fool, Gabriel.'

'I deserve something far harsher than *fool*.' Why hadn't he taken more care? Why hadn't he—?

'A fool for letting her go.'

It took a moment for her words to sink in. 'Don't pretend you're not relieved. You warned Audrey off just as you warned Fina off. You've never considered me good enough for this family.'

The older woman rested back, her fingers steepled. 'You have it wrong, my dear.'

He gritted his teeth. He was not her *dear*.

'It was the other way around. I warned Fina off because I knew she was using you as a weapon to make a childish and selfish statement. You were young and idealistic and I knew she would hurt you...lay waste to your dreams.'

His jaw dropped.

'She was such a troubled young woman and I did not know how to help her. Or you. I failed her. Just as I failed her mother. And as I've failed you, too.'

He hauled his jaw back into place, his heart thundering. He recalled all that Audrey had said to him about Fina and straightened. 'You didn't let either one of them down, Marguerite. You gave them both every advantage life had to offer.' Rubbing a hand across his chest, he nodded. 'Audrey is right. They failed themselves, and yet, we continue to bear the brunt of the guilt and regret.' It was time to let it go.

'Audrey is not like Fina.'

No, she was unlike anyone he'd ever met.

'She would not walk all over your heart and treat you as if you were worth nothing.'

'She is kindness personified.'

'And yet, you tell me you do not love her. *That*, my dear Gabriel, is what makes you a fool.'

He gaped at her.

'Go!' She waved an imperious hand at the door. 'I have better things to do than talk with stupid men. I need to ring the girls—'

'The girls,' he parroted.

'Livy, Tori and Ana. We shall rally around Audrey, drink champagne cocktails, eat chocolate and watch some dreadful movie.'

Without him. He was being forced out and the injustice burned through him.

Marguerite glared down her nose at him. 'Broken hearts mend, and we will help Audrey's mend as quickly as possible.' She nodded once, hard. 'We will find her a new prince, and soon you shall be forgotten, and all of this will feel as if it had never happened.'

Everything inside him rebelled at the thought. He shot to his feet, but the words he wanted to shout refused to push past the lump in his throat. Without another word, he strode to the door, but before he slammed through it, he swung back.

'You call me a fool, but you'll be the bigger fool if you don't support Audrey's plan to create a foundation in her sister Johanna's name.' If he could do nothing else, he could at least make Marguerite see sense on this one issue. 'Family means everything to Audrey, but she will not betray her past family to achieve one in the present. If you make her choose, she'll walk away.'

With a heart more broken than he'd left her with. He wanted to throw his head back and howl. Who would she then turn to?

Without another word, he left.

CHAPTER THIRTEEN

AUDREY FLED TO her room, craving sanctuary and quiet, but all too soon the enforced inactivity began to grate. After dragging on her old jeans, she headed outside to the gardens. The estate was large and, if she wished it, she'd be able to avoid bumping into anyone.

She set off for the gardens farthest away from the villa, where no one would be able to spot her from the windows. She walked briefly beside the water, but that didn't help. It simply reminded her of Gabriel's studio.

If Marguerite hadn't called them into the library, she'd be at the studio now. She'd have had a chance to make one more memory to help shore her up on the lonely nights ahead. Because she didn't doubt there'd be long, sleepless nights where the longing for Gabriel would wring her dry and leave her feeling torn and empty.

Turning her back on the extraordinary view, she started down the most beautiful of avenues—tall trees and shrubs towered on either side, making her feel as if she were the only person in the world. But even that brought no comfort.

Finally, she flung herself down in a shady clearing, the scent of wisteria and pine thick in the air. What on earth had she been thinking? Love hadn't been part of the plan.

Falling to her back, she stared up at an impossibly blue sky. She hadn't *wanted* to fall in love. It had been the furthest thing from her mind. For heaven's sake, Gabriel had been more than adamant about his feelings on the subject. It's not like she hadn't been warned.

How could she have been so stupid? So *blindly* stupid?

Pressing palms to hot eyes, she swallowed hard. She'd been so ready to believe they were friends. That what they had meant something to him. *Why?*

Because they'd been honest with each other, had shared a few secrets, had found common ground in their art? None of that had meant he cared for her. Nor did the fact that she'd helped him through his creative block, or that he saw something of value in her fibre art. She was the one who'd thought that'd meant something. Not him.

A growl left her throat. Why had she allowed herself to think it had signified something deep and lasting? Would she never learn?

She'd made that same stupid mistake with Gabriel as she had with her father—seeing something that wasn't there. Gabriel might not have meant to hurt her, but he didn't care for her any more than her father did, in a kind but careless way. As soon as something more was demanded of him, he'd turned tail and fled.

What she hadn't realised was how much loving a man like that would tear her apart.

I'm sorry, but...

A humourless laugh left her lips.

But. It was the story of her life. Gabriel had proved what she'd already known—that she'd never be enough for him. His prejudices, his bitterness, his resentments, were all so much bigger than any feelings he might have for her. And he'd cut off all such feelings at the knees rather than dare feel anything like that for her—*a Funaro.*

But she'd finally learned her lesson. Never again would she waste that much time, energy and effort on a man who'd closed his heart. Her hands clenched. She was tired of not being enough, of being made to feel less than, being made to feel like a fool.

A hard lump stretched her throat into a painful ache. And yet, even now she ached to see him with every breath she took. Even though she knew seeing him would be like torture.

She sat up. Should she leave Lake Como?

Her heart pounded, but her mind grew suddenly clear. To leave would hurt Marguerite and she wouldn't do anything to hurt the older woman. Marguerite had become dear to her. She might not be able to have the man she wanted in her life, but she did have her family. She loved this odd assortment of people who'd come into her life. And there was strength in love, even if Gabriel couldn't see it.

And why on earth should she let him chase her away when she'd found a place to belong? If he chose to remain an outsider, that was his problem not hers.

'Fine.' She hitched her chin at a particularly spectacular pine tree. 'I need to make a new plan.'

Actually, she had the plan Gabriel had created for her for when, as he'd put it, all her hopes and wishes surrounding the family came tumbling down. Except the family *was* everything she'd wished for—that wasn't the part of her life that was tumbling down.

A lump lodged in her throat. Neither she nor Gabriel could have envisaged then that it would be *he* who'd bring her world tumbling down. Because he lacked the courage to love.

Gritting her teeth, she ordered herself to focus on a new plan. First, she'd keep working on her art. She'd ask Marguerite for studio space somewhere on the estate. There must be a garden shed that wasn't in use that she'd be able to co-opt. And she'd take classes somewhere when this summer was over and the family returned to Milan. And she'd contact that agent, too; invite him to take a look at her work. She didn't need Gabriel for any of that.

Oh, but—

She cut that thought dead, pulled out her phone and sent Gabriel an email. She needed to draw a line under all that had gone before.

Gritting her teeth, she thanked him for mentoring her—she was grateful—added a line mumbling some nonsense about remaining friends, and ended with a request for him to let her know when it would be convenient for her to collect her materials.

And just like that, it was over. She swallowed a sob, dusted off her hands, she set her phone to the ground. One: her family. Two: her art. She'd throw herself with vigour into both.

On cue, her phone pinged. Turning it over, she found a text from Marguerite.

The girls are on their way. Champagne cocktails. Chocolate. Assorted movies at the ready. Anything else?

She had to blink hard as she read the message; acknowledged the love behind it. Gabriel might not love her. Her heart might be broken. But she had a family who cared, and that was something to be grateful for.

She texted back:

Face packs and pizza.

Then she hauled herself to her feet. She refused to wear her oldest, daggiest jeans to this impromptu pity party. She could do better than that.

The moment Gabriel strode into his studio, he knew it had been a mistake to come here. He should've done something else, gone somewhere else. Audrey permeated every inch. From her coffee cup left to drain on the sink, to the container of biscuits she'd baked, to the pile of yarn on one of the workbenches. Lavender scented the air, and the current silence mocked the remembered laughter, the arguments, the earnest discussions about art.

He glanced at the mezzanine and rubbed his hands over his face, his eyes burning. Everything *ached*.

Why the hell couldn't Marguerite have left well enough alone?

Because she didn't want to see Audrey hurt.

He stilled. He didn't want that, either. The knowledge he'd hurt Audrey, even unwittingly, rubbed his soul raw.

He should never have let a Funaro into his studio. He should've realised it'd cause nothing but trouble.

Except Audrey wasn't like the other Funaros. She was warm and friendly and open-minded—

His head lifted. Marguerite hadn't been cold and unfriendly this morning. She'd been concerned. Oh, she'd torn a strip off him for hurting her granddaughter, but that was nothing more than he'd deserved.

The party on Saturday hadn't been cold and unfriendly, either. It'd been fun, a true celebration.

Walking across to *Ties That Bind* and whipping off the dustcover, he stared at it once more. Audrey was a fine artist and the world would soon discover her. But she was a sculptor, too—of people. She dug until she found the good in them and she somehow brought that to the fore so everyone else could see it, too.

Marguerite and her kin hadn't been cold and unfriendly. At least, not in recent times. Maybe the cold and unfriendly one had been him?

The thought made him swallow. Audrey was right. He'd been so determined to ensure another Funaro couldn't take advantage of him that he'd built a wall around himself with huge no-trespassing signs tacked all over it to keep the rest of the family at bay. His hands clenched and unclenched. It wasn't an edifying revelation.

It might've been better for his peace of mind now, but he

didn't regret allowing Audrey entry into his sanctuary here. The only thing he regretted was hurting her. He'd move heaven and earth to make that otherwise.

You can.

His temples throbbed and his heart pounded. Wheeling away, he shook his head, but Marguerite's words sounded through his mind.

She's not Fina.

He knew she wasn't Fina! She was ten times the woman Fina was. But there was too much at stake. It wasn't just his heart he'd be risking but Lili's.

You're a fool.

Marguerite's words again, but what did she know? And—

His mouth dried. His heart thundered in his ears. Audrey *wasn't* Fina. If the worst did happen, if a romance between him and Audrey soured, Audrey wouldn't abandon Lili. He felt the truth of that in his bones. In that moment everything inside him yearned towards a future he'd never dared let himself dream about again.

Swinging back to stare at Audrey's artwork, he finally saw it in a new light—her light. The various threads crisscrossing the figure at the centre weren't shackles or restraints. Those threads were in shades of shimmering gold, peacock blue and pale pink. They *weren't* symbolic of the Funaro fortune as he'd previously thought. They were symbolic of family—of attachment, compassion…love.

These weren't ties that bound one against their will. They were the kinds of connections that anchored a person, helped them find their place in the world. These ties created a sanctuary, a safe place…a haven where a person could be themselves.

He glanced around his studio. Audrey's was the real sanctuary, not this place where he'd tried to keep the rest of the world at bay. His studio wasn't a sanctuary; it was a hideaway.

In that moment he agreed with Marguerite—he was a fool.

He loved Audrey with every atom of his being; he'd just been too much of a coward to admit it.

His phone vibrated, alerting him to an incoming email. His heart leaped when Audrey's name flashed across the screen. With fingers that shook, he opened the message.

Dear Gabriel,

I'm very grateful for all you've done. Under your expert eye, my technique and artistry have improved a hundredfold. Clearly it is not going to be viable for me to continue to study under you, given today's revelations, but I very much hope we can remain friends.

Friends? He didn't want to be friends. He wanted them to be lovers. For the rest of time.

If it's not too much trouble, I would appreciate it if you could arrange for my supplies and the pieces I've been working on to be packed up and sent to the villa. Or, if it's more convenient, please let me know a time when I can organise to do so myself.

She was already moving forward with her life—sensible, straightforward, classy. It hit him then how strong Audrey really was. She'd never needed a protector. All of this time, she'd been the warrior fighting for the family she could see beneath all the hurt and bluster and pride.

He lifted his head. It was time to stop hiding. It was time he started fighting for the life he wanted, too. And he wanted Audrey—heart, body and soul. And if he was going to convince her that he truly did love her, that he would do everything in his power to look after her and make her happy, he was going to have to prove it to her.

He stared at her artwork and knew exactly what he had to do.

CHAPTER FOURTEEN

THE BOAT POWERED across the lake with a no-nonsense speed that set Audrey's teeth on edge. She didn't sit in her usual seat. She didn't face forward as she normally would. There was nothing normal about any of this.

It made no sense, but she wanted to rail against the fact that it wasn't Gabriel driving the boat. He'd hired someone to take her across to the studio so she could oversee the packing up of her equipment.

Folding her arms, she glared at the whitewash they left in their wake. He couldn't make his stance any clearer if he'd bellowed it at the top of his lungs from a megaphone. He *didn't* want to see her. He *didn't* want to remain friends.

Jerk!

In a dim part of her mind, she knew he was only trying to save her further pain. A low growl sounded in the back of her throat. Why did everyone think she was going to fall in a heap just because she'd had her heart broken? She wasn't that pitiful.

And not seeing him—having him avoid her as if she'd *betrayed him*—

Closing her eyes, she concentrated on her breathing. The one good thing about today was not being the object of the loving but watchful gazes of Marguerite and the rest of the family. She knew they only wanted to help, but… Yesterday she'd only just managed to stop herself from yelling at everyone to stop watching her.

It will get better. It will get better.

She crossed her fingers.

The boat slowed and bumped to a rest at the tiny dock. She pulled in a breath, girded her loins before disembarking with an ease that had been alien to her two months ago. She glanced at the driver, who cleared his throat and shrugged. 'My instructions were to remain here.'

With a nod, she set off along the path that wound through the trees. The men hired to help her pack were probably already at the studio. As she rounded the curve and topped the rise, though, and the studio came into view, she stuttered to a halt.

Everything that had happened there played through her mind. The disagreements between her and Gabriel, the challenges they'd thrown at each other, the moments when they'd worked together in complete harmony. He'd called her an artist; had given her the permission to explore and experiment; had urged her to dig deeper and discover the heart of the things that moved and interested her. Here her knowledge had deepened and her skills had developed and...

He'd opened up a new world to her.

She refused to think of the other new world he'd opened up to her—a world of sensuality and pleasure and intimacy. Today she'd focus on the future. Not what had been. He'd given her the tools and the contacts to continue to develop her art. *That* was what she'd think about.

That and setting up The Johanna Foundation. This morning Marguerite had called her into the library and had agreed to support Audrey's desire to set up a foundation in Johanna's honour. She'd apologised for her tardiness and had confided her grief at never having had the chance to meet her late granddaughter. 'Whenever I began thinking about how we would set the foundation up and how to make it work, it was... I found it so painful to think about. I so wish I'd had a chance to meet Johanna the way I've had the chance to meet you. I know that I would have loved her, too. So I kept putting it off, kept trying to avoid the grief and regret. I can see now that wasn't fair to you.'

She'd also confided that it was Gabriel who'd convinced her to move forward with Audrey's plan. Apparently, that was something else she ought to feel grateful to him for.

Shaking herself, she continued along the path. Not giving herself a moment to think, she reached for the door, sighing in relief when it opened. That could've been awkward. Gabriel had never given her a key.

'Oh, like that's a surprise,' she muttered under her breath. He'd only ever given her the parts of himself he'd been comfortable sharing.

Her fleeting resentment, though, was no match for the memories that immediately assailed her—none of them to do with embroidery or art of any kind. She stared at the back wall, recalling their first time and how they'd not even fully undressed—too hungry and greedy and wild for each other.

She should have known then. Should have known that to feel so much so soon meant she was already too invested. That it would end in tears.

Shaking the thought off, she faced the room. Nothing stirred. Nobody stood to greet her or awaited instructions.

'Hello?' She moved farther inside, resolutely averting her gaze from the mezzanine level. Now wasn't the time to wallow. She could do that tonight in the privacy of her own room where no one could see.

Her voice echoed in the space, but nothing else moved. Had she misunderstood the message? Maybe she was supposed to pack her things up and leave them for someone to bring back to the villa later. Had Gabriel left a note?

She strode across to the bench where she'd worked, but there was no note there, and then across to the kettle. Nothing. Opening the side door, she glanced out, but nobody sat outside enjoying the view or the sunshine.

It wasn't until she turned back that she saw it—the easel sitting directly in front of the huge wall of glass. A cloth draped over the easel hid the picture, painting, or whatever the artwork was, from view. Was this Gabriel's current project?

Biting her lip, she glanced around. There was nobody to see if she had a peek. Gabriel had never minded sharing his work with her—unfinished or not.

Lifting one corner of the cloth, she glanced beneath... Reefing her hand away, the cloth fell back into place. Her heart pounded.

Was that...*her*?

After glancing around again, she reached out and pulled the cloth completely away to stare at the charcoal drawing encased in a simple wooden frame.

The piece had the same compelling power as his *Maybe* sculpture.

Except this time *she* was the subject. And unlike *Maybe* there was no ambiguity here—no *will she...? won't she...?* questions threaded beneath.

The sketch was of her on the rocks that jutted out into the lake. Where he'd sketched her sitting with her sketchpad all those weeks ago, she now stood, facing the water. Above her, rather than a sun hung a moon, radiating light...somehow bathing everything in the sketch in light.

She took a step closer, trying to work out how he'd done that. The man really was the most extraordinary artist.

The water in this sketch wasn't threatening. All around her it was millpond smooth, though farther out where the light of the moon couldn't quite reach, waves loomed. She took a step back again, her frown deepening. It was as if, because the water farther out wasn't under her influence, it was storm-tossed and restless. Unhappy.

What on earth did it mean?

She pressed a hand to her brow.

If—

She swallowed.

If she saw this picture in an art gallery, and if the woman wasn't her, and if the artist wasn't Gabriel, she'd think the artist had drawn the woman he loved.

But she *was* the woman. And the artist *was* Gabriel.

A footfall sounded behind her and she swung around. *Gabriel.*

Eyes as storm-tossed as the distant waters in his sketch stared at her from a ragged face in dire need of a shave; his hair a thick, tousled mess. He looked how she felt.

For a long moment neither of them moved. He opened his mouth, but she held up a hand and he closed it again. Her heart beat so hard she was sure he must hear it.

Turning to stare at the sketch once more, she forced her spine into straight lines. 'You don't lie?'

'I don't.'

'Then what does that mean?' She gestured at the sketch.

'Many things.'

Exhaustion hit her then. She didn't want to play games. If he didn't want to tell her, fine. Turning away, she made for her bench.

'It means I was wrong about you.'

She stuttered to a halt, but she didn't turn back.

'All of this time you've been telling me that you're strong enough to deal with whatever life throws at you, but I didn't believe you.'

His laugh, full of self-mockery, had her turning.

'I wanted to save you from the same fate as Fina. I couldn't save her, but by God, I'd do my utmost to save you.'

She couldn't move; stood rooted to the spot.

He took a step towards her. 'But it was the rest of us who needed saving. You were right—you are strong, stronger than the rest of us put together. I'm in awe of you, Audrey. You did the impossible—you created a family from practically nothing.'

'Not nothing.' Her voice was low. She tried to strengthen it. 'The framework was there. It just needed…fortifying here and there—the odd wall knocked down and bigger windows to let in the light.'

'You've saved this family.'

The way he said that… Her eyes narrowed. 'Are you now saying *you* feel a part of this family?'

'Yes.'

That was something at least. 'I'm glad.'

'I wanted you to know that I now see how strong you are.' He gestured at the picture. 'That was one of the reasons for the sketch.'

'Okay.' But while it was a definite compliment, it wasn't a declaration of love. She still wasn't enough for him, and the knowledge burned like acid through her. 'Thank you.' Turning away, she seized a box and started tossing in sketchpads, pencils and yarn.

'I'm out here.'

Holding on to the threads of her temper, she glanced around again. It wasn't his fault he didn't love her. But he had to know that seeing him like this was torture.

He met her gaze—and even with at least twelve feet between them, the intensity of it hit her with the force of a cyclone. His finger pointed to the edges of the sketch where all was dark and storm-tossed. 'I'm here,' he repeated. 'But I want to be here.'

He moved his finger until it was right beside her in the sketch.

'I want to be the innermost person in your circle, Audrey.'

Her heart thundered. 'But you said…' He'd said his heart wasn't on offer. That it had never been on offer.

He moved towards her, those long legs closing the distance between them, his face unreadable.

If he wasn't offering her his heart…? She slammed her hands to her hips. 'So now you're telling me that you want to be friends?'

He halted in front of her. 'I *don't* want to be your friend.'

She rolled her eyes, knowing she was being contrary but unable to help it. 'Charming.'

'I want to be your lover.'

Her body leapt in instant excitement, but she held it in check. She couldn't do this. Not anymore. 'I want more, Gabriel.'

He shook his head. 'I do not mean in a physical sense.'

She blinked.

'I mean, I do want you in a physical sense—of course I do.' He reached out and took her unresisting hands in his. 'No woman has ever fired my blood the way you do. But I want to be your lover, your *amore*, in every sense of the word.'

She gaped at him, too afraid to hope. She pulled her hands free. 'On Monday you said your heart wasn't on offer and you don't lie and—'

He touched gentle fingers to her lips. 'Clearly, I do lie because I do love you and my heart is yours whether you want it or not.'

The world tilted.

'I lied to you and Marguerite, but only because I was lying to myself. I never wanted to find love again. You were right. It frightened me too much. I told myself one day in the future I would take the plunge again, but—'

He shrugged, his lips twisting as if in disgust. 'I told myself that my affair with you was controllable—pleasurable, but ultimately short-lived—and that it would burn itself out. The thing is, Audrey, it didn't burn itself out. It grew bigger and you became more and more dear to me.'

He was saying... Was he really uttering these beautiful words?

'Marguerite called me a fool when I let you go. Did she tell you that?'

She shook her head.

'It wasn't until you were gone that I realised that she was right.'

'I didn't go anywhere,' she whispered. She'd been mooching about the villa, pining for him.

'But you weren't here!' He gestured around the studio. 'There was no *us*. And I found myself cast adrift.'

She couldn't utter a single word.

'I do not lie, Audrey. I love you.'

Did she dare believe him?

He gestured at the picture. 'I drew that so you could see yourself the way I see you—strong and beautiful and the very heart of your family. I wanted you to know that you *are* enough, Audrey. That anyone lucky enough to have you in their lives is blessed.'

Tears blurred her eyes. The artist *had* drawn the woman he loved. Gabriel *did* love her.

Suddenly, she was in his arms and his hands were cradling her face and they were kissing each other with a desperate need that had their hips and bodies careening off the furniture.

Seizing her by her upper arms, he dragged her away, his breathing ragged. '*Dio*, I become a beast!'

'I like it when you become a beast,' she panted.

'You undo me.' He tried to frown, but there was a new lightness in his eyes that had her heart lifting. 'At the moment, though, I do not wish to lose control.'

'What a shame.'

He laughed, but sobered again a moment later. 'I love you, Audrey. I love you with all of myself. I know I let you down badly—like your father did, and your mother. I know I hurt you and made you feel less, but I will make it up to you. I swear, if you give me a chance, I will show you how splendidly and perfectly enough you are. I will do all I can to make you love me again. Please tell me I haven't ruined my chance to make amends.'

The lines in his face deepened and he turned grey as if the thought made him physically sick.

Reaching up, she cupped his face. 'I love you with all of myself, too, Gabriel, and I will never let you go. I will always love you and I will always look after you.' She would prove to him that love could be a joy and a wonder and a sanctuary.

As she spoke, the lines in his face eased and the light in his eyes made her heart soar. Holding her gaze with his, he went down on one knee. Her heart crashed about in her chest and her lungs refused to work. 'Gabriel?'

Reaching into his pocket, he pulled out a velvet box. After snapping it open, he held up a ring—a beautifully cut pink diamond that sparkled as the light pouring in at the window caught it. A lump lodged in her throat.

'Now that I know the truth, *carissima*—that I love you—I do not want to leave you in any doubt of my intentions, or what I want for our future. I want you to marry me and be my wife. I want you to be a mother to my daughter. I hope that in time, if you desire it, we can have more children. I want to build a long and happy life with you. I want to dedicate my life to making you happy.'

His outline blurred as tears filled her eyes.

'And just so you know, I sought Marguerite's blessing, too. I did not want to cause any disharmony between you and your grandmother.'

Of course, Marguerite had known what would take place today. She gulped back a happy sob. 'This morning she told me you'd convinced her to pursue the setting up of the foundation in Johanna's honour.'

He rolled his shoulders. 'It was nothing. I simply did not want her making the same mistakes that I had. And I wanted you to have the family you deserve.'

Another sob lodged in her throat, making speech impossible.

He rose, snapping the velvet box closed. 'You do not need to give me your answer now. You can take as much time as you need. I just did not want there to be any misunderstandings or misconceptions. I have been a fool for long enough. I wish to be an open book now and—'

She reached up and pressed her fingers against his lips. 'Gabriel, are you babbling?'

'*Si*. I am very nervous. I love you. This matters a lot to me.'

She pinched herself. This strong, beautiful man really had

just gone down on his knee before her. He'd offered her everything he was. Couldn't he see it made her the luckiest woman in the world? 'I would love to marry you. I can't think of anything that would make me happier than to build a life with you and Lili.'

Her words electrified him. 'You mean this?'

'With all my heart.' Reaching up on tiptoe she wrapped her arms around his neck. 'Gabriel, you have the kindest heart and the most honest soul of any person I've ever met. You make me feel seen and known…and loved. I've never felt more alive in my life than I have here in the studio with you. I know how badly your experience with Fina hurt you, but you've found the courage to love again. You're the most wonderful man I've ever met.'

He kissed her then. Warm, firm lips moved over hers, telling her how much he loved and desired her, how she, too, had brought him alive, opening up a world he'd never imagined. He kissed her until she became boneless with need and drunk on the taste of him. He kissed her with the wildness that she loved.

Lifting her head, she stared into his eyes. 'Is it okay if we lose control now?'

She gasped when he lifted her into his arms and strode towards the staircase. 'Your wish is my command,' he said, grinning down at her.

'Hmm…' She cocked her head to one side and pretended to consider his words as he carried her up the stairs. 'Aren't you being just a teensy bit derivative with that line?'

But then he did something wholly original with his tongue and his hands, and her pulse skyrocketed. 'Okay, scrap that. My mistake.'

Laughing, they fell down to the bed together into a future filled with love and laughter and family.

EPILOGUE

The following summer

DRAGGING A DEEP BREATH into her lungs, Audrey cast one last glance in the mirror before exiting the bedroom she'd been allocated. The excited voices coming from the direction of the living room told her the bridesmaids were ready. Instead of turning towards them, though, she moved down the hall to knock on the door of the master suite. 'Frankie? It's me.'

Frankie threw the door open and they stared at each other in open-mouthed amazement, before Frankie grabbed her hand and hauled her into her bedroom and closed the door.

'You look—' They both started at the same time and then laughed.

Neither she nor Frankie had ever dreamed of a big white church wedding where they wore dresses that weighed almost as much as they did. Their dream wedding had always been much simpler—a garden wedding surrounded only by the people they loved.

'Frankie, you look perfect.' And her cousin did. She'd chosen a boho-inspired ankle-length wedding dress with peekaboo lace and intricate embroidery. The V-neckline was playful and sexy and the pink toenails peeping from their pretty sandals made her smile. 'The most beautiful bride that ever was.'

Frankie laughed. 'I love my dress, Audrey, but I think you might win the honours for most beautiful bride.'

Wrapping an arm around each other's waists, they turned to

stare into Frankie's full-length mirror. 'I love my dress, too,' she confessed. The sweetheart neckline, lace bodice and A-line skirt in a soft tulle that floated about her calves were more traditional, and they made her feel like a fairy-tale princess. 'I feel like Cinderella.' She swung to Frankie. 'I'm so glad we're having a double wedding.'

Frankie's eyes sparkled. 'We embarked on this adventure together, Audrey. It's only fitting we now walk down the aisle together as brides. I can't believe it's ended so *wonderfully*. Who knew that one summer could change everything? And this—' she gestured at the two of them '—is the best happy-ever-after possible.'

Audrey's grin widened. Marguerite would probably sigh and shake her head at her granddaughter's inability to contain her happiness, but secretly she knew her grandmother loved that about her. 'I wonder if Nonna knew we'd find our destinies here.'

Frankie shook her head. 'I think she wanted to give us the opportunity to take stock of our lives and decide what was important to us...to help us choose the path that would make us happiest. But not even she could foresee how momentous this summer would prove to be.'

It had been the best gift she'd ever received. 'And are you truly happy with the path you've chosen, Frankie?'

Frankie had recently finished her medical specialty, and when she returned from her honeymoon in Venice, she'd start practising as a family doctor in the nearby village. It was a far cry from her old dream of becoming a neurosurgeon.

Frankie squeezed both of Audrey's hands. 'Totally happy, Audrey, I promise. I know it seems like an abrupt about-face, but this is the right fit for me. And I love Dante with all of my heart. Marrying him... It makes my heart sing.'

Audrey could relate to that 100 percent.

'And I don't have to ask if you're happy. I can see it shining from every pore. Gabriel is a lucky man.'

And she was the luckiest woman alive. Gabriel was everything she could hope for in a husband.

Frankie gave an excited shimmer. 'Are you ready to marry the man of your dreams?'

'I've never been readier for anything in my entire life.'

Not a single cloud marred the blue of the sky on the short drive to the vineyard where their guests—*and grooms*—waited for them. The terrace of Dante's restaurant Lorenzo's had been transformed into a fairyland with flowers and fairy lights, and Audrey and Frankie stood beneath an arbour of flowers at one end of the aisle, smiling guests seated in front of them. At the other end of the aisle against a glorious backdrop of golden hills, green grapevines and a stunning sunset, their grooms waited for them.

Lili looked enchanting as their flower girl, and Dante's sisters looked gorgeous as the bridesmaids in their identical dresses, each in a different pastel shade—Maria in rose, Sofia in peach, and Giorgia in mauve. The small crowd oohed and ahhed as the attendants moved down the aisle, and both Aunt Deidre and Dante's mother, Ginevra, began dabbing at their eyes with handkerchiefs. Even her father looked suddenly emotional and proud. Marguerite might not have a tear in her eyes, but her smile was so large it made Audrey want to sing.

Frankie held out her hand, Audrey took it and they walked each other down the aisle. They'd been each other's main support for as long as they could remember, and it only seemed fitting they should support each other now and walk boldly into their new futures together.

Despite the beauty of the setting, despite being surrounded by all the people she loved, Audrey only had eyes for one person—Gabriel. Those grey eyes never left hers as she moved towards him. Her pulse fluttered with appreciation at the way he filled out his tuxedo—but it was the expression in his eyes that held her spellbound. The desire, the possessiveness, made her skin tighten, but it was the love in his eyes that made her heart pound. For this man she was *enough*. For this man she would *always* be enough.

As they made their vows, their voices rang out sure and true.

When the celebrant pronounced them husband and wife, and told the grooms they could kiss their brides, Gabriel kissed her with such fierce conviction it stole her breath. 'I love you,' he murmured.

'I love you,' she murmured back.

He pressed a warm kiss into the palm of her hand. 'You are beautiful.'

He made her feel beautiful.

Much later, after a glorious dinner, and the cakes had been cut and the bridal waltzes had been waltzed, Gabriel whisked her off to a far corner of the terrace where a huge urn filled with roses hid them from view and pulled her into his arms to kiss her. 'I have been dying to get you to myself.'

Breathless, she reached up to touch his face. 'Happy, Gabriel?'

'*Si.* More than I ever thought possible. Loving you, Audrey, has done what I never thought possible.' He took her hand and placed it over his heart. 'You have healed my heart. I mean to cherish you every single day of our lives together. And you, *cara*? Are you happy?'

'I'm so happy there aren't words—in either English or Italian—to describe it.'

His grin made her heart soar. 'And are you still happy with our honeymoon plans?'

'Yes!'

They'd bought a beautiful old villa on the outskirts of Bellagio that had a gorgeous view of Lake Como and the surrounding mountains. The sale had only gone through last week, and on the spur of the moment they'd cancelled their honeymoon plans to spend it there. Alone. Everyone else still thought they were going to Paris.

The villa was in need of some updating, but that gave them

the opportunity to make it truly their own. What's more it had a huge barn they had plans to convert into a joint studio, which might have to take precedence if they were to be ready for their joint exhibition in the autumn. Audrey still couldn't believe the acclaim her work was starting to garner.

'You will not miss the romance of Paris?'

She wound her arms around his neck. 'I can't think of anything more romantic than spending the first week of married life in our new home and truly making it our own. Besides, you have never been away from Lili for a whole week before, and while I know Marguerite has lots of exciting plans to keep her busy, we want to be near at hand in case she should need us.'

Lili's excitement that Audrey was her new mother knew no bounds, but that didn't mean there wouldn't be teething problems. Audrey wanted to make the transition as smooth for her as possible. It was the reason they'd waited a whole year to marry.

'Maybe we can spend our first anniversary in Paris,' she said.

'You are a remarkable woman, Audrey. Do you know that?' He kissed her long and deep, and when he lifted his head, she had to cling to him to remain upright. 'What do you say to leaving for our honeymoon right now?'

Reaching up, she kissed him. 'I think that's an excellent plan.'

* * * * *

COMING SOON!

MILLS & BOON®

Coming next month

PREGNANT PRINCESS AT THE ALTAR
Karin Baine

"Your Majesty." He nodded to each in turn. "I know the circumstances are less than ideal and this morning's headlines haven't helped, but I don't think berating Gaia is going to fix things either. She needs our support."

"Do you comprehend the seriousness of impregnating my granddaughter out of wedlock, Mr Pernici?"

Neither of them had dared contradict the King's misunderstanding of the baby's parentage and Niccolo didn't think telling him there was another man involved would placate him in any way. If anything, it would further enrage him and Gaia didn't deserve any more of a pile-on.

"I understand that this is a very delicate matter—"

"Are you going to step up to your responsibilities and marry my granddaughter?"

"Pardon me?"

"Grandfather, no, Niccolo isn't—"

In that second Niccolo believed there was only one option available to both of them. A single deed which could save both of their reputations and save them from any more of the King's ire. It didn't matter what he did to try and distance himself from the whole scandal, as far as everyone was concerned he was involved.

"Yes, we're getting married," he announced, surprising himself as much as everyone else in the room. He put an arm around Gaia's shoulders and she leaned into him as if he were the only thing keeping her upright.

The only way he could see to salvage his reputation and his livelihood before they were ground into the dirt again was to act as though he *was* this baby's father. It wasn't a role he'd ever wanted, and he didn't know how he was going to fake his way through it. He would have to embrace the part completely. Having an emotionally distant parent was as damaging as losing one. Gaia's baby didn't deserve to feel as though it was a burden, so he would have to come to terms with accepting complete responsibility for this child and not simply be a token father figure. He had no intention of imitating his dad but it wasn't going to be easy raising someone else's child. Especially in these circumstances, where he'd been forced into a corner if he wanted to keep his career and the life he'd just got back.

Continue reading
PREGNANT PRINCESS AT THE ALTAR
Karin Baine

Available next month
www.millsandboon.co.uk

MILLS & BOON

THE HEART OF ROMANCE

A ROMANCE FOR EVERY READER

MODERN

Prepare to be swept off your feet by sophisticated, sexy and seductive heroes, in some of the world's most glamourous and romantic locations, where power and passion collide.

HISTORICAL

Escape with historical heroes from time gone by. Whether your passion is for wicked Regency Rakes, muscled Vikings or rugged Highlanders, awaken the romance of the past.

MEDICAL

Set your pulse racing with dedicated, delectable doctors in the high-pressure world of medicine, where emotions run high and passion, comfort and love are the best medicine.

True Love

Celebrate true love with tender stories of heartfelt romance, from the rush of falling in love to the joy a new baby can bring, and a focus on the emotional heart of a relationship.

Desire

Indulge in secrets and scandal, intense drama and sizzling hot action with heroes who have it all: wealth, status, good looks…everything but the right woman.

HEROES

The excitement of a gripping thriller, with intense romance at its heart. Resourceful, true-to-life women and strong, fearless men face danger and desire - a killer combination!

To see which titles are coming soon, please visit

millsandboon.co.uk/nextmonth

JOIN US ON SOCIAL MEDIA!

Stay up to date with our latest releases, author news and gossip, special offers and discounts, and all the behind-the-scenes action from Mills & Boon...

 @millsandboon

 @millsandboonuk

 facebook.com/millsandboon

 @millsandboonuk

It might just be true love...

MILLS & BOON

MODERN

Power and Passion

Prepare to be swept off your feet by sophisticated, sexy and seductive heroes, in some of the world's most glamourous and romantic locations, where power and passion collide.